The Mountain of Gold

The Mountain of Gold

J. D. DAVIES

HOUGHTON MIFFLIN HARCOURT
BOSTON   NEW YORK
2012

First U. S. Edition
Copyright © 2012 by J. D. Davies

www.hmhbooks.com

First published in Great Britain by Old Street Publishing, 2011.

Library of Congress Cataloging-in-Publication Data
Davies, J. D.
The mountain of gold / J. D. Davies. — 1st U.S. ed.
p. cm.
Sequel to: Gentleman Captain.
ISBN 978-0-547-58099-9 (hardback)
1. Ship captains — Great Britain — Fiction. 2. Pirates — Fiction.
3. Treasure troves — Fiction. 4. Great Britain. Royal Navy — Officers — Fiction.
5. Great Britain — History — Charles II, 1660–1685 — Fiction.
6. Great Britain — History, Naval — 17th century — Fiction.
7. Africa, North — Fiction. I. Title.
PR6104.A863M68 2012
823'.92 — dc23   2011028559

Printed in the United States of America
DOC 10 9 8 7 6 5 4 3 2 1

Good God, what an age is this and what a world is this, that a man cannot live without playing the knave and dissimulation.

The Diary of Samuel Pepys, 1 September 1661

It is by my order and for the good of the state that the bearer has done what has been done.

Cardinal Richelieu in *The Three Musketeers* by Alexandre Dumas

PART ONE

❦

His Majesty's Ship, The Wessex

The Western Mediterranean and Tangier
June 1663

One

The Last Trump sounded, summoning all the dead to rise again.

This inconveniently interrupted my stimulating nocturnal activities with both the Queen of Spain and my wife in the perfumed opulence of the Khan of Samarkand's state bedroom. A state bedroom with walls of rough oak. Walls that vanished, one by one, as a scrofulous carpenter's crew tore them down. Perfumed fragrances that gave way in an instant to the all-pervasive stench of tar, tobacco, piss and sweat. A provocatively naked Queen of Spain replaced in the blink of a waking eye by the ugly bald pate and eternally pained face of my clerk Phineas Musk. He held a breastplate in one hand and my sword in the other.

My thoughts and ears finally caught up with my eyes. On the deck above my head, men were running to our ship's guns, our drummer was beating to quarters, and our trumpeters were sounding a chorus of defiance that their somnolent captain had mistaken for the harbingers of the *Dies Irae*. I was aware again of the heat, the ceaseless, unforgiving heat that had kept me awake until moments before my dream-time wife and the Queen of Spain began to …

'Fog's lifted,' said Musk in his gruff Thamesman's voice. 'We're right on top of a corsair galley. Another one in sight, too. Both crippled and sinking, by the looks of things, after fighting each other nigh to Hell and back. Probably fallen out with each other over some fat argosy. Mister Castle's talking about it as the easiest prize we'll see in all our days, if not two of 'em at once. Looks like the good Lord smiles on you once again, Captain Quinton.'

I buckled on the sword but declined the breastplate, ignored the unceremonious disregard with which my men were throwing my worldly belongings into the hold, and made my way up onto the quarterdeck, where the full force of the morning sun struck me at once. My shirt was open to the waist. My chest, the palest dove-white at the beginning of our voyage, was now as red-brown as that of the longest serving foremast-man.

The guns were already run out, and the ships' boys were bringing up extra powder and shot. The trumpeter kept up his cacophony, and the drummer added a persistent rhythm to our preparation for war. Everywhere, men wore the grim smiles that anticipated bloodshed and prize money, with little heed of the possibility that they might be on the cusp of their own mortalities.

The *Wessex* was ready for battle, and only her captain remained ignorant of her enemy.

William Castle, my veteran lieutenant, raised his plumed hat in salute. He was even more jovial than was his wont, this round, red-faced man of forty or so whose left hand had been carried away by a Spanish shot when Myngs took Santiago da Cuba a few years before. He said, 'A good day to you, Captain. A very good day indeed, by all the heavens. We come out of that dismal fog, and straight away there she lies, right in our path. If ever a man needed proof of God's divine providence, there it is, sir.'

I turned and looked out no more than half a mile. There, off our starboard bow, was the galley. Not a large one – perhaps thirty oars on each side – but she was in a dire state. Her masts were all gone, and much of her larboard quarter with them. Perhaps half the oars on that side were shattered or missing altogether. Dark stains, some still discernibly red, marked her hull: the blood of the godly slaves who had manned her oars, and equally of the heathens who had whipped them into battle. Blood mixed once and for all in the indiscriminate ooze of death. A torn black flag still flew defiantly at her staff, and I could hear the howls of a few of her crew, still determined to give a feeble imitation of the terrifying noise that brought not a few of our merchants' ships to surrender before they had even engaged. Plainly, these men had fought long and hard, and they might have won their passage back to Algier or Tunis, but for the leaks that would surely sink them long before they got there – that, and coming out of a fog to find themselves directly in the path of the *Wessex*, a good stout English frigate of forty-six guns commanded by Captain Matthew Quinton, who despite his tender twenty-three years was already in his third command, a veteran of battle, wounding and shipwreck, and an increasingly consummate seaman. Or so he liked to believe.

I took my telescope from Musk and levelled it on the second galley, perhaps a mile and a half or two miles away. This one, much larger, was almost as dreadfully shattered, but still had a jury mast for her lateen rig – terms I had learned barely a month earlier – and rode a little higher in the water. Her flag, too, still flew from her staff, but it was of a very different nature to the black banner of the corsair in our path. On a red field, riddled with musket holes, was emblazoned a white or silver cross, its ends pointed.

I lowered the telescope and said, 'A galley of Malta, gentlemen. She flies the flag of the Order.'

There was a hum of disappointment about the deck (some of it emanating from Phineas Musk) as men realised that a Maltese galley would be no prize for a Christian ship of war; quite the reverse, in fact. The galleys and knights of the Order of Saint John of Malta were legend. A hundred years before, the tiny, barren island fortress of the Knights had beaten off the greatest siege the world had known, and with it the vast and previously invincible armies of Sultan Suleiman the Magnificent. The Order waged an unending war against the heathens who fought under the Crescent. So I knew the legend of the Knights of Malta, and I respected those who maintained its ideal; indeed, but a week earlier we had fulsomely saluted two of the Order's galleys that we encountered off Sicily. But the Maltese galley was much further away than the *Wessex* from the enemy that she had evidently fought almost to destruction. Her own damage meant that it would be an hour or more before she could come up with the corsair, if she ever did – for the corsair could sink, or make good its repairs and escape, or blow itself up rather than fall into the hands of the infidel. I had heard of such things.

One thing for it, then.

The gazes of Lieutenant Castle, Phineas Musk, the half-dozen other men on the quarterdeck, and not a few of the men at the guns on the upper deck, were focused intently on me. There was Martin Lanherne, ship's coxswain, and behind him his fellow Cornishmen, the likes of the simian John Treninnick, the mountainous George Polzeath and the minute but formidable John Tremar. Then there was the black Virginian Julian Carvell and the young Scot Macferran. All of their faces were lined with undisguised, brazen avarice. These men had served in my previous command, the frigate *Jupiter*, and had volunteered to sail with me again, even though that last commission had come perilously close to despatching us all to the seat of judgment. Only my young friend and mentor Kit Farrell was missing, for he was bound to the Barbados as master's mate on a large London vessel with a sure cargo of tobacco waiting to be brought home, and was thus guaranteed rather more substantial pay than he could expect in the same rank aboard the *Wessex*.

At last, I smiled and said, 'Our prize, I think, Mister Castle. A shot across her bows, if you please, followed by a summons to surrender.'

Rarely in the history of the navy can an order have been carried out with such rapidity and ill-concealed delight.

* * *

The corsairs of the Barbary Coast were the most feared spectacle on all the seas, particularly in their own, the Middle Sea that stretches from the Pillars of Hercules to the Holy Land. They preyed upon the shipping of Christian countries, and even roamed as far afield as the shores of England and beyond. Thousands of poor innocents were held as slaves in their hell-hole cities, above all in Algier, with which my master King Charles was formally at war. After all, this was why we were where we were; the *Wessex* was convoying six valuable cargoes back from Smyrna in the Levant, for the merchants of London demanded – and were duly given – naval protection against the ever-present threat of the corsairs. We were cruising independently only because Sir John Lawson, the admiral commanding our fleet in those seas, had temporarily entrusted our charges to the lumbering *Paragon*, freeing my *Wessex* (a better sailer, clean and fast) to hunt down the Barbary scourge.

We had pursued a corsair ship off the coast of Minorca only a few days before, trading round shot with him before the wind died away and he put out his oars. On that occasion the captain had laughed heartily as, stroke by stroke, his craft pulled away from us, free to fall on other benighted mariners.

But even a corsair sometimes has to acknowledge the harsh reality of defeat, particularly when half his crew is dead and his craft is sinking, and even more so when a broadside of over twenty iron guns on each side can send him to Allah in a matter of minutes. The stricken galley's captain, a swarthy, turbaned man of forty or fifty, even raised his curved scimitar in salute to me as his men hauled down their black flag.

Lieutenant Castle organised a prize crew to take possession, its chief task being to liberate the poor souls who had spent many long years chained to oars on behalf of their heathen masters. I could see and hear them as they were brought up from below, pale creatures, some stark naked, others clad only in a cloth about their privates, all with wrists and ankles red and bleeding from their newly-broken shackles. A few looked around uncomprehendingly, but others cried out in joy, not a few wept uncontrollably, and some pointed to the *Wessex* and her captain, bowing and waving in relief and gratitude.

I remember that sight, I hear the sounds, and I smell the stench, as though it was all but this morning. In all my long years on this earth, I have seen many sights to turn a stomach or elevate a heart, but only once have I witnessed a scene that brought on those two sensations together. All these years later – past sixty of them – I can still see the tears on the face of one thin grey-bearded old man, his hands clasped in prayer as he offered up thanks for his deliverance. In that moment, he fell down to the deck. Even though I was standing on another ship a few hundred yards away, I did not need the shake of the head from my crewman who attended him to tell me that the old man was dead. True, he had died a free man, but ever since that day, I have debated in my mind whether the sudden realisation of that very freedom killed him.

In their turn, the captain of the galley and his surviving officers were brought over for questioning. I watched them brought aboard, these three dark-skinned men in their long white robes. They looked about our deck with disdain, as though only a trick of the unkindest fate had put them into my power; as, indeed, it had. Coxswain Lanherne led the captain down to my cabin. He was tall and defiant, this Moor, his bearing that of a nobleman. He was clean shaven, a thing unusual for that race. He saluted me with an elaborate wave of his hand, after the fashion of his kind, and muttered some imprecations that might or might not have been calling down the blessings of Allah upon my head. I began by asking him the name of his home port, for I assumed that like so many of the men of the African shore, he would have acquired at least a smattering of the tongues of those whose ships he preyed upon relentlessly.

He stared at me, uncomprehending.

I tried again in French, in which I was fluent, and Dutch, with which I was reasonably conversant (having lived in that country for some time before the happy restoration of King Charles, and having acquired a vivacious Dutch wife and tedious Dutch brother-in-law as a consequence).

The brown-red face remained a mask, even when Lieutenant Castle tried his competent Spanish and Phineas Musk attempted the rudimentary Greek that he had acquired a few weeks earlier from an intriguingly immoral nun on Rhodes.

I spoke to Musk, who returned after a short while with a man as dark-skinned as my captive, albeit shorter by a head. This was Ali Reis, an Algerine renegade who had served with me on the *Jupiter*. I asked my questions again through my interpreter, and at last the corsair captain launched into a babble of incomprehensible speech, rolling his eyes to the heavens (or at least, to the deck a few inches above his head) and gesticulating wildly. Finally he drew breath, and Ali Reis said, 'He claims to be of Oran, Captain, and says his name is Omar Ibrahim. His galley was twenty days out of Algier when it encountered the Maltese. But there is one thing more, Captain.'

Ali Reis stepped across to me and whispered in my ear. I frowned and asked, 'Are you certain?'

The Moor nodded determinedly, placing his hands on his chest and head. I looked hard at the corsair captain and said, 'Omar Ibrahim of Oran, indeed. A shame for you, Omar Ibrahim, that Ali Reis, here, has a better ear for languages than all the diplomats of the Pope, the King of France and the Sultan combined, even if you locked them all away together in the Tower of Babel for a hundred years. He tells me that as an Algerine himself, he has encountered many men from Oran, but never one who speaks Arabic with the brogue of County Cork.'

At that, Musk reached out and pulled off the man's turban, revealing a shock of sun-curled red hair. The corsair captain nodded slowly, as though ending some secret inner game, looked me in the eye, and said in rolling Gael-English, 'Ah well, Captain. God bless all here.'

Lieutenant Castle raised his eyebrows and nodded vigorously. 'A renegade, then, and what's worse, a damned Irish renegade! A king's subject turned Turk, by God. There's only one outcome for that, Captain. Hang the bastard. Send him up to meet Saint Peter and then down to meet Lucifer, fast as you like.'

Castle pronounced the sentence with his usual good humour, making a public execution sound like a forfeit in some hilarious tavern game, and Musk (who had found the perfect carousing partner in my veteran lieutenant) nodded heartily in agreement. Now, I am no milksop in such matters – as I get older, my list of those who should be summarily hanged lengthens almost daily, the most recent additions being my cook and most of the inhabitants of Winchester. But as it was, my more tolerant younger self sensed that more might be gained by questioning this Irish Turk than by at once placing a noose around his neck and throwing him off the main yard.

I attempted to make myself as grand and terrifying as possible, saying, 'Well, my renegade friend, Lieutenant Castle has spoken justly. The King himself instructed me to execute any of your kind that we encounter.' (This was strictly correct, as my orders contained such an injunction; but my attempt to convey the impression that Charles the Second and I spoke intimately about such matters was the merest bluster.) 'But we Quintons don't despatch men to their maker without giving them the chance to tell their tale.'

Castle shook his head, clearly believing this to be an unnecessary diversion which delayed a good hanging. He excused himself, returning to the quarterdeck to monitor the slow approach of the Maltese galley. Ali Reis went with him, for evidently I now had no need of an interpreter, and both Musk and John Treninnick, who guarded the door, carried enough weapons to deter a small regiment, let alone one unarmed Irishman-turned-Turk.

The corsair captain grinned and said, 'Ah, but you're a fair man, Captain Quinton. Now that's a name of some honour, I think, that I knew from my old life. Is it not so? I was in Kinsale town, a lad of seven or eight, when Lord Buckingham's fleet came back from Cadiz. There was one ship especially, with an old captain on her quarterdeck, and my father pointed him out, and he says to me, "Brian, my son," – Brian Doyle O'Dwyer, I was, before Omar Ibrahim was hatched out of a Mahometan egg – "Brian, that captain there, he's the famous Quinton that sailed with Drake and fought the Armada, no less. An earl of England, he is." Now, what was that title he bore? Near forty years ago, Captain, and my memory's not what it was. Some bird, I think. Eagleswing? Hawkscar?'

'Ravensden,' I said. 'The man you saw was Matthew Quinton, my grandfather, and I share his name. My brother is the present Earl.'

Musk snorted and rolled his eyes; he had been a persistently surly yet ferociously loyal retainer to my grandfather, father, brother and now to myself. But even then, I was not such a raw idiot that I could not see what this O'Dwyer (if such truly was his name) sought to do. Claiming a connection with a stranger at first meeting, and flattering their family name to the heavens, is a sure way of melting the heart of the gullible, especially if this gullible stranger has the power to put a noose round your neck. But it was hardly a story that the Irishman was likely to invent (how else could he have known the name and history of my grandfather?) and I knew from reading Earl Matthew's sea-stained journals in our library at Ravensden Abbey that his ship had indeed spent some weeks repairing in Kinsale harbour in the year twenty-five. Kinsale, the same haven where my first command was wrecked through my utter ignorance of the seaman's trade, costing the lives of over one hundred men.

The Irishman said, 'Brother to the Earl of Ravensden, by God! That lifts my spirits a little, Captain. To surrender at all, well, that's enough disgrace for a lifetime, and many of my fellow captains, the native

Algerines that is, won't even countenance it. But to surrender to a man of noble birth, and to an Englishman, not yon Knight of Malta – '

'Yes, my thanks, but enough, sir!' I blustered. 'Now, let us return to the matter in hand, namely your imminent hanging. When and why did you turn renegade and traitor, Irishman?'

O'Dwyer sighed, a little too theatrically for conviction. 'You'll not know Baltimore, I suppose, in west Cork? A grand village, Captain, just grand. We had a good life there, with the fishing and the like. I can remember that day in the year thirty-one as if I was standing there now, back down on the green shore with Seamus O'Sullivan, the brewer's son, and his sister Aoife. We saw the great galley come in from Clear Island, we did, and watched it with all the curiosity that fills youngsters of twelve or thirteen, as we were. It was only when their boats started to come ashore that we realised they were Turks. They carried off the whole village, that day, every man, woman and child. Upward of three hundred souls, all carried back to Algier and eternal slavery. Aoife went into the harem of the *dey* that ruled Algier, and bore him four sons before the plague took her.' The Irishman's eyes were suddenly distant, as is the way of his kind when they digress into matters of love and death. 'Aoife O'Sullivan.' Matters of love, at any rate, from the sigh that accompanied the name. 'Ah, now there's the thing, Captain Quinton. We were all slaves, you see. But Aoife was the greatest lady in the court. She died in comfort in the palace of Algier, in the full beauty of her youth, rather than as an ancient hag in the putrid hovel of the Baltimore O'Sullivans. That's played on my mind for near these thirty years, Captain. For if we talk of slavery, when in her life was she truly a slave?' This was a strange, unsettling man, this Omar Ibrahim, or O'Dwyer, or whatever he elected to be from one moment to the next. Then the Irishman's temper brightened in the blink of an eye, and he said, 'Seamus, though. A big, laughing lad he was. But, well, he was ever a stubborn one, Captain, the sort who can never accept their fate, you see. He swam for it one night, hoping to reach a French ship lying off Algier. The Turks' guardboat caught him, and they skewered him on a pike. I saw things differently, shall we say. I knew my chances of returning to old Ireland were as likely as there being a woman Pope, and I could see the corsair ships coming back laden with booty that made their crews rich. Not a difficult choice, in the end. I embraced the Prophet just before my sixteenth birthday, which was when Omar Ibrahim ventured out on his first voyage.'

Musk growled, 'And killed and stole from good Englishmen ever after. Damned from your own treacherous lips. Let's get the rope – '

Martin Lanherne entered the cabin, saluted, and spoke in his strong Cornish voice. 'Mister Castle's compliments, sir. The captain of the Maltese galley is coming across by boat.'

I said, 'No doubt to protest at our stealing his prize, or to demand the right to hang this renegade himself, or both. Whatever the upshot, Irishman, you'll hang this day. Say your prayers to whichever god you've currently elected to serve.'

'Ah, Captain, that would be a mistake, a most grievous mistake, that it would. Your king would be most angry with that, seeing how useful I could be to him.' Our trumpeters were already sounding their welcome to our imminent guest, and Musk was searching in my sea-chest for garments that could clothe me suitably for the occasion. The Irishman was casting about for anything that would save his life, that much was obvious, and would say anything to stave off his inevitable fate.

As I donned the clean shirt that Musk handed to me, I said, 'Desperate lies won't save you from the rope, O'Dwyer. Once I've talked to this galley captain, I'll see you dangle.'

His tone became more urgent. 'Not lies, Captain. No, far from a lie. The biggest truth in the world, instead. It's gold, you see, Captain Quinton – a whole mountain of gold. There, in Africa.' He pointed toward the distant shore, far over the horizon. 'Oh, it would make your king the richest monarch in the world, that mountain, *and I am the only white man who knows where it is.'* He was speaking very quickly now, aware that he only had seconds before I had to leave him to greet my fellow captain. Only seconds in which to preserve his miserable, worthless, renegade's life. He even clutched my sleeve as he spoke. 'One year when I was a young man, our corsair fleet was forced to stay in harbour by plague and an enemy's blockade. I took a caravan across the great desert, hoping to find plunder in the south. And that was when I met an old Arab merchant who led me to it, Captain. A mountain of gold. I'll swear it on every holy book of every faith under the sun. A mountain twice as tall as the old hills of Beara, and as broad again. A great rocky hill with streaks of gold along its length, each one catching the desert sun in its turn.' His eyes blazed, as though reflecting the gleam of that golden mountain. 'My old Arab, Captain, he says to me it's the prize that they've all sought, down the centuries. Alexander himself, the Caesars of Old Rome, David and Solomon alike, Prester John, the Grand Turk. All of them searched for it. And now King Louis and Emperor Leopold both seek it, for they know what it will bring its owner. Gold without equal, Captain Quinton.' His voice was now an insinuating, plausible whisper. 'Unlimited gold, and with it, unlimited power. No white man has seen it, other than your humble servant, here. No other white man knows where it is, and can lead an army right to it. Now wouldn't it just be the grandest shame if you strung up the man who could make your King Charles the richest and most feared sovereign in all the world?'

This was indeed a brazen, audacious speech, but even though I was then still but young and foolish, I knew enough of the world to remain sceptical of the Irishman's serpentine words. After all, I reasoned, why was this Omar, or O'Dwyer, but captain of a galley, and that not the largest, rather than the *dey* of Algier or the Grand Vizier himself?

So he would hang; but, perhaps, not quite yet. I donned my broad hat, and came to a decision for good or ill. 'Well, Irishman, as liars go, I have met few to equal you. But your lies have a certain diverting quality to them, and God knows, the Levant trade is tedious work, so I require a little diversion. You will tell me more of your imaginary mountain of gold after I have spoken with this Knight of Malta. Mister Lanherne, see this man chained in the hold.'

As we strode toward the quarterdeck, Musk began to berate me for a fool, but I cut him off. 'What matter can it be if he hangs now or in an hour? It's all fantasy, of course.'

But as I stepped out into the sunlight, the Irishman's plausible words had somehow already planted the thought in my head. *What if – ?*

$\mathcal{T}wo$

Musk had clad me in my finest silk frock-coat. In that heat, and despite the awning stretched a few feet above the quarterdeck, the sweat was pouring down my flesh well before my guest stepped onto the deck, where he was greeted by Boatswain Fuller's whistle. He seemed entirely oblivious to the heat, despite wearing attire even less sensible than my own. It was as though the thick black cloak with its single silver Cross of Malta somehow rendered him immune to the world around him. The gleaming hilt of a sword protruded from the cloak. This magnificent galley-knight raised a splendidly befeathered hat to salute the *Wessex* and its captain, and I stepped forward, doffing my own hat and bowing low in deference. He was a man of middling height and middling age, this Knight of Malta, so thin as to be almost skeletal. His long, watchful face betrayed nothing but disdain for this young captain and his man-of-war, so ugly and towering alongside the shattered but slender galleys. He looked about him with the unnervingly self-confident arrogance of those who are supremely aware of their own power, and with something else, too. Contempt, certainly, but more than that. He had the look of a priest-executioner, weighing up precisely how long it would take his latest batch of faggot-fodder to burn at the stake; and to this day, I retain the uncomfortable suspicion that this was exactly what he was doing. The dark knight looked me up and down. Although it was one of the hottest days I have ever known, I shivered.

He spoke at first in French, which was evidently his native tongue, then in Latin, then in Italian, all fluently, then in a somewhat more broken Dutch, and lastly in a halting and reluctant English. Too late, I realised that his linguistic recitation was occasioned by the simple fact that I had forgotten to order our ensign hoisted as soon as I came on deck. '*Monsieur*,' he said in his rasping voice, 'I am Gaspard, Seigneur de Montnoir, captain of the galley *San Giacomo* in the service of his Most Eminent and Serene Highness Rafael Cotoner, Grand Master of the Order of Saint John of Jerusalem, Rhodes and Malta. To whom do I have the honour of speaking?'

His tone made it entirely apparent that he did not consider it an honour at all, rather a task akin to cleaning a dog-turd off one's shoe.

Mustering as much confidence as I could, I replied in the flawless French that I had learned at the knee of my grandmother. 'I am Matthew Quinton, sir, captain of this ship the *Wessex* in the service of that most high and puissant prince, his Britannic Majesty King Charles the Second. You will take some refreshment?' I gestured vaguely towards the stern, knowing that Musk would barely have had the time to lay on my cabin table a flagon of Sicilian wine and two glasses.

But Montnoir was evidently not a man for pleasantries, nor did he display any surprise at my fluency in his native tongue. Reverting to French, he said, 'I thank you, but no, Captain. Our business can be concluded here and now, and very easily, I think. I seek only the delivery of our prize, and of the men that she carried.'

'Your prize, sir. And what prize would that be, pray?'

Montnoir's face was a picture. 'The corsair, Captain Quinton. The accursed heathen corsair galley that we came across by God's good grace as she was plundering an honest flyboat out of Malaga. My men and I fought that devil for six hours, at the cost of many lives and limbs. We seek our lawful prize, bought with the blood of good Christians, and the release of the benighted souls of our faith that the Turks have kept chained to their oars.'

I shrugged, for I had learned French mannerisms, too, at my grand-mother's knee. 'Good sir, I see no prize of yours. When we came upon the galley, she was disabled and sinking. With all possible respect, the like condition applied to yours, which was a long way further off, and I see you still have some considerable distance to close before you can even lie alongside this corsair again, let alone claim it as yours. Much depends, of course, on how many of the benighted souls of the Maho-metan faith that you keep chained to *your* oars can be whipped into enough effort to give you any sort of headway.' Ali Reis, who was cling-ing to the main shroud, smiled at that, and I recalled him telling me once that his brother was a slave on a galley of Malta. 'You had, and have, no prospect of making her prize, Captain, whereas we do. And our lawful prize she'll be proved, I don't doubt.'

Montnoir was dumbstruck. 'You deny my right?'

'*Monseigneur*, I gladly make over to you the poor galley slaves, for otherwise we would have to feed and accommodate them, and our cabins and victuals cannot bear so many. Besides, most of them are of your French race, I gather, or else Italians and a few Spaniards. None to give any concern to an Englishman, at any rate. But the galley itself and all its officers are now in the custody of His Britannic Majesty and his representative here present. In other words – myself.'

Despite my inward nervousness I was relishing this taunting of Montnoir, a man evidently much more the sea-veteran than myself. After all, I possessed the trump card, and if he forced me to play it …

The Frenchman was oblivious, and puffed up in all his splendidly cloaked arrogance. 'Captain Quinton, you are a fool. Can you really wish to bring about a breach between King Charles and those whom I serve, the Grand Master of Malta and the Most Christian King Louis?'

So we had it, at last. For all its eternal fame, the name of Malta was not enough to deter a captain and a ship of the King of England. But the name of *le Roi Soleil*, the king of the largest and most feared land in Europe, was a very different case. I determined on impudence for my reply, for I knew that the eyes and ears of my crew were upon me (and enough of them knew sufficient *port taverne* French to keep up a hasty and clearly audible translation for those who knew none). Both they and my far-distant King demanded a certain swagger in such a circumstance. 'Ah, so you serve two masters, then, *monseigneur*? How terribly confusing for you.'

A few of my men nodded gravely. Julian Carvell, who still bore the scars from a fist-fight with a dozen Frenchmen at Messina some weeks earlier, grinned broadly, and not a few smirked with him. But it was not merely a cheap jibe against Montnoir. I knew that the loyalty of the proudly international Knights of Saint John to their Order was superseded all too often by their abiding loyalties to the lands of their birth, and to the monarchs who reigned over them. Nowhere was that more true than with the French Knights, who dominated the Order and yet also somehow provided the backbone of King Louis' own ever-increasing navy.

For all his pride, Montnoir was no fool. He could see our battery plainly enough – he stood almost between two culverins, polished to a suitably warlike sheen, with a neat pile of eighteen-pound iron balls at the side of each – and he could see the lust for a second prize and a consequent augmentation of prize money that blazed in the eyes of my men. He would have known very well that against the fearsome broadside we could fire in an instant, upon my word of command, his proud but wounded galley was so much matchwood.

He turned to me and said, 'Very well, Captain Quinton. Your prize. So be it. But one thing only I request, sir. Let their captain, the heathen named Omar Ibrahim, be turned over to face the Grand Master's justice.'

I was on firm ground now. For all my apparent confidence, in truth the issue of what might or might not be lawful prize lay in the hands of those blood-sucking leeches and eternally avaricious parasites who infested the High Court of Admiralty in London. In other words, lawyers. But the issue of who might or might not be a renegade Irishman turned Turk, a natural-born subject of my King and thus one who had committed the most infamous of treasons, lay at that moment with one authority alone. I said, 'The man that you name as Omar Ibrahim, Captain, is the man that I name as Brian Doyle O'Dwyer of the Kingdom of Ireland, and thus a subject of *my* master, King Charles. Therefore his fate rests with me, sir, and not with you, nor with the Grand Master, nor with King Louis.'

Montnoir looked at me as though he was seeing an apparition. Then he did something entirely unexpected, something that made his cadaverous face even more ghastly than it had seemed at first.

He smiled.

'An Irishman. Omar Ibrahim is an *Irishman*?'

'I can bring him out to tell you that himself, if you wish.'

The Frenchman looked about him with a strange, far-off expression, as though transported from the deck of the *Wessex* to some distant fastness. He frowned. He smiled again, and frowned again. Then, quite suddenly and disconcertingly, Montnoir reverted to English and waved his hand dismissively. 'No, Captain Quinton, the word of the heir of Ravensden is sufficient upon the matter. I bid you good day, sir.'

With that, he doffed his hat once more, stepped out of the opening in our starboard rail, and descended the ladder to his boat. I waited until he was half way back to his galley before I threw my hat to the deck and tore off my silk frock coat and my so recently new shirt, all now wetter than my native River Ouse in flood.

As I returned to my cabin, I said to my grumbling clerk: 'Was that not strange, Musk? Aye, the whole affair, I'll grant – but above all, how could he know that I was the heir to the earldom? How could he know me for who I am?'

Phineas Musk had both the wisdom of his years (perhaps forty, more likely sixty; it was difficult to tell) and the impudence of a man who had spent most of his adult life discreetly abusing the great lords and ladies that he served. He said, 'Not strange at all, Captain. We've been in this sea for months. An English man-of-war captained by a certain Matthew Quinton – well, they'll know that name, won't they, certainly over in Cadiz and all parts of Spain. What did they call him, your grandfather, back in the old queen's day? *El diablo blanco,* wasn't it – the White Devil? So the stupid and credulous will assume that the White Devil has risen from his grave, while the noble and educated will examine the genealogies in their libraries and note against the name of Charles Quinton, tenth Earl of Ravensden, that his brother and heir happens to be a captain in the King of England's navy. *Quod erat demonstrandum.*'

The occasional flashes of Musk's unsuspected learning always unsettled me. We reached my cabin, and without a by-your-leave the cause of my discomfort poured himself a large glass of the neglected Sicilian wine. He continued, 'But there was that other strange matter, though.'

'Another matter, Musk?'

'Well, Captain, I see it this way. Suppose we were at war with the Dutch again, and we chanced upon a ship of theirs that was plundering a merchantman of ours, but our foe got away from us, and we pursued it.' He took another draught of wine, and said, 'Well, what I'd want to know is this, I suppose – how would you know the name of the captain you were fighting before you actually took his ship?'

* * *

Tangier.

As the *Wessex* beat up into the bay from the north-east, I studied this much-vaunted new jewel in England's crown. A city of low, white houses huddled together on a hill of bare, red rock, like all the land that surrounded it. A city baked by the sun: unceasing, unrelenting sun. There were walls, and forts, and at the summit, a castle, over which flew the

Union flag of Charles the Second's two kingdoms (this having replaced the flag of Portugal but the year before, when Tangier formed part of our Queen Catherine's marriage dowry). Soon, it was said, a great breakwater, the mole, would stretch out to sea, part of a grandiose scheme to turn this into a mighty port from which the king's fleets would roam the oceans, and England would dominate the trade of the world. What utter, unforgiving folly. Even as a young captain, ignorant in so many of the ways of the world, I could divine all too readily that this tiny outpost of our country, set down upon an alien shore, was fated to fail. I could see plainly the serried ranks of Moorish horsemen parading in front of the town, searching for a weak spot in the defences. I glimpsed red-coated soldiers upon the ramparts. An occasional matchlock-spark or puff of smoke betrayed the warning shots fired in the name of King Charles. The truth was that for all the great ambitions for it, Tangier was a city under permanent siege.

We anchored in what Lieutenant Castle proclaimed to be damnably foul ground that was bound to do for our best bower, and Coxswain Lanherne assembled the long boat's crew to row me ashore. The harbour, such as it was, contained no other ships, for the fleet was at sea and our convoy (with which we were meant to rendezvous in this roadstead) had been detained in Alicante by a leak to the *Paragon*. This was fortunate, for it gave me an opportunity to pursue the matter of the unbelievable claims of the Irish Turk who sat in my hold, secured to the deck by manacles.

I walked up the street toward the Upper Castle. This was my second visit to Tangier; we had called during our outward voyage, albeit very briefly, for the wind had been in our favour for a passage up the Straits, and no seaman (even one as raw as myself) will ever deny such a favourable breeze. Thus I had not then been able to pay my respects to the new governor, who in any case was leading a sally forth against the Moors of the hinterland, and my limited time ashore had been restricted to berating the victualler on the quayside. Now I had time to absorb the strange sense of this place, and of the even stranger collection of human-ity that had fetched up on this most desperate shore. There were Arabs, of course, bearded and robed in white, haggling with the Portuguese merchants who had stayed behind when their country abandoned them. There were soldiers, many of them evidently Scots or Irish, sweating in their rough red uniforms, some running with muskets in hand as they hastened to reinforce one of the outlying forts. There were clerks aplenty; Tangier in those early days was a very heaven for the attorneys, for whom the transfer of territory from one sovereign to another gener-ated endless disputes over title and, consequently, endless opportunities to line their pockets. There were urchins of indeterminate nationality, snapping at my heels from street to street and crying out for baksheesh (or, in one incongruous case, begging for a groat in an accent that was purest Norfolk). Every man of every race seemed to look over his shoul-der, fearful of what lay beyond the walls. Then there were women. Some of these, perhaps, might have been respectable; or at least, some of them might have been respectable once. But as I have observed many times in my life, heat, wine and a distance of several hundred miles from England conspire to transform many a cloistered maiden into the most brazen of wenches. It was as well that I was a married man, still newly married enough to be true to my vows.

By the time I reached the gate of the Upper Castle, I was a vision of sweat. I had removed my wig not long after leaving the boat, and ran a hand over the stubble of my hair (shaven partly for comfort, partly to conceal its premature loss), hoping by that means to reduce the torrent flowing into my eyes. It was with some difficulty that I persuaded the ser-geant at the gate that I was the captain of a king's ship, having legitimate business with the governor. My temper was not improved by learning that once again, the governor was not in his residence, but was down the wall, toward what was called the Catherine Port. I set off once more, praying silently for the sudden arrival of a proper English June day with its fine cold rain.

I found the governor of Tangier in the midst of a bevy of his officers, gazing out toward the wild mountains that overlooked the city, to the tiny, isolated forts that guarded the perimeter of this minute empire, and at the small groups of Moorish horsemen who rode back and forth across the barren ground, screaming obscenities in surprisingly vivid English. The younger men in the governor's company, Captain This and Cornet That, looked on me with more than a mild distaste. They were uniformed, and I was not; they were immaculate, and I was soaked like a galley slave; they had purchased their commissions, and thus possessed the inestimable arrogance that only a profound lack of merit can buy. I already found it hard to believe that until but a year before, my overriding ambition had been to join them; indeed, to be better than them, for these were mere infantry, and the King of England himself had offered me a commission in his Horse Guards, until so recently the summit of my own (and, even more, my wife's) ambitions for my destiny. A commission that I turned down to his face, having travelled a notably watery and violent Damascene road in the sea-lochs of western Scotland.

Fortunately, the governor was of a different metal to his subordinates, and readily granted my request for a private audience. General Andrew Rutherford, newly created the first Earl of Teviot, was a Scot of middle years, a large, bluff papist with an easy and open manner.

I told him of the business with the Irish renegade and the Maltese galley, and of the tale of the mountain of gold. At the mention of that, he stopped, and considered me gravely. 'A mountain of gold. South of those mountains yonder, south of the great desert beyond them. You're certain, Quinton?'

'You can interrogate him on the matter, My Lord. I intend to bring him ashore for that very purpose. All a ploy to save him from the noose, of course, but I thought I had best refer the matter to yourself or the admiral, whosoever I encountered first.'

Teviot frowned. 'I don't think any interrogation of mine would add to the case, Captain. But I can think of others who'll want to talk to this man. Our most gracious sovereign, for one.'

I was incredulous. '*The King?* My Lord, this man's a renegade and a liar. It's as plain as day, all he seeks is to save his own worthless traitorous neck. I thought a hanging here, in the public square of Tangier, would be more exemplary than killing him on the *Wessex* – '

'Captain Quinton, only I decide who hangs in this city.' Lord Teviot's eyes flashed, but in the next moment he reverted to his accustomed easy informality. 'Matthew, I have served far and wide for a quarter-century and more. In that time a man hears much, and learns much. Only ten years ago, the France that I then served was on her knees, torn apart by civil war. Many believed she would never rise again, but the young King Louis – he was no more than fifteen then – was entirely confident that a miracle to outdo Saint Joan would raise up France once more. You see, Captain, the young king had been convinced by one of his nobles, a man with mystical tendencies, that somewhere in Africa a great mountain of gold waited to be found. A new Potosi, no less, and a hundred times richer than the original.'

'Potosi? I think I have heard the name, My Lord – my uncle might have talked of it – '

Teviot pointed at the bleak land beyond the outlying forts of Tangier. 'See that, Matthew? All that sand and rock? Most of the soil of Old Spain is like that, or but little better.' I knew this to be true, for I remembered Old Spain well from my days in exile there. 'Yet for a hundred years,' Teviot continued, 'Spain was the greatest and most feared country in this world. She ruled an empire on which the sun never set. Her armies were invincible until my own day. Your own grandfather sailed against their Armada, the most powerful fleet on God's Earth. I grew up, and to a degree even you have grown up, fearing the Black Legend of the dread Spanish empire.' I nodded, for in my childhood nightmares the Inquisition had featured almost as often as Cromwell's Ironsides. 'And how did

26

poor, barren Spain achieve all that, Captain?' asked Teviot. 'Because one day, over a century ago, some of her soldiers chanced upon a vast mountain of silver in the wilds of South America. Potosi. The silver of Potosi paid for the armies I fought against, it paid for the great Armada that your grandfather battled, and it paid for an eighty-year war against the Dutch. *An eighty-year war.* Can you conceive of England fighting even an eighty-month war, Matthew? The King would be bankrupt within twenty.' I had to nod, for some truths are inescapable. 'So the chance, even the faintest, most improbable chance, that somewhere in the world there exists a mountain of gold, waiting to be claimed by the first nation that finds it – I ask you, Captain Quinton, would you really wish to be the man held responsible by your monarch for executing that most improbable chance in the market square of Tangier?'

He fixed me with a stare that gave me no opportunity to argue the case, a case rather too close in substance to that which had been argued by the renegade O'Dwyer himself. But there was one other thought; one thing that the governor had said. There was one question – 'My Lord, the French nobleman who convinced King Louis of the mountain of gold. Was his name Montnoir?'

Teviot shrugged. 'It was a long time ago, Matthew. I can't recall whether Turenne even told me the name. Why do you ask?'

'No matter, My Lord.' Even if the governor could not recall the name, I knew a man who might.

Teviot leaned on the parapet, looking down on a particularly bold party of turbaned riders. 'Look at them, Matthew. Look at this place. Oh, it will hold, because those Moors can shout all they wish, but they don't have the cannon to bring down these walls and they don't have the ships to starve us out with a blockade. But they will wear us down, strike at a fort at a time, kill good men by the score, and then by the hundreds, so the King will have to build more forts, and send more men, and one day, the whole place will become so expensive that our King will be glad to sell it to the Dutch or the Spanish. Or the French, as he did with Dunkirk.' Teviot knew that better than any man; he had been governor of the short-lived English garrison at Dunkirk. 'We are soldiers,' he continued, 'and we can look around at what we see in this place, and know that yet again, we will fight and die for a hopeless cause. But that, my dear Matthew, is what soldiers do. After all, isn't that what your father did?'

My father, who had fallen in glory at Naseby field, fighting for a king doomed to lose that battle, that war, three kingdoms, and his head. Just as Teviot would fall the next summer, leading out a raid against the Moors. It was an ambush, and My Lord Teviot fell in battle. When I was in Tangier again, years later – not long before King Charles abandoned the place by blowing it up, rather than selling it – Teviot's successor pointed out his bleached bones from the ramparts. They probably lie there still, crumbling into the red dust.

Finally, I asked the living Teviot, 'What, then, should I do with the man O'Dwyer?'

The governor said, 'I should sail with the tide, Matthew, and carry him straight to England and the King.'

'But My Lord, I have orders to await the *Paragon*, and the convoy lying at Alicante. I would have to await the return of the admiral – '

Teviot frowned. 'I will settle matters with Sir John, once he has vented his necessary rage at me, a mere soldier, for daring to overrule his command as an admiral. Be not afraid on that score, Matthew. But while you await the tide, you'll take some refreshment with me, perhaps, at the castle? It occurs to me that letters came for you in the last ship from England. God knows, I seem to spend half my time acting as postmaster to every officer in your damned precious fleet.'

The whitewashed governor's house within the castle precincts was blessedly cool, and Lord Teviot was generous in his hospitality. There was quite a bundle of letters, and I divided them by the easily recognisable hands of the senders. There were ten from my dear wife Cornelia;

significantly fewer than usual. There was one from my mother; significantly more than usual. There was one from my brother, the earl; ditto. There were the inevitable letters of duty from my Lord High Admiral, the King's brother James, Duke of York; and from Samuel Pepys, esquire, Clerk of the Acts to the Navy Board, who sometimes seemed to think himself the Lord High Admiral. There were several from friends, who would either be begging for money or reporting on loves won and lost. All of these, I decided, could be postponed; even Cornelia's letters, which were bound to raise my spirits with their bottomless well of good humour, loving endearments and scurrilous venom directed against my mother and most of the people that we knew, from the King downwards. Yet there was one letter which stood out: one that demanded to be opened first.

This letter was addressed as follows.

For The Honourable Matthew Quinton
Captain of His Majesty's Ship the Wessex
Copied to Lisbon, Cadiz, Tangier, Alicante, Malaga, Malta, Messina, Leghorn, Venice, Smyrna, Constantinople, Aleppo, Alexandria and Antioch.

I smiled, recognising my uncle's hand and his typically thoroughgoing efficiency in sending to every possible port-of-call that we could make, and to several that were entirely impossible. I broke his wax seal – the arms of Mauleverer College, Oxford, of which Tristram Quinton was a most unlikely Master – and read. Ever since I was a small, fatherless child, letters from my uncle were to be treasured, for he could transport me in a few words to lands beyond the limits of my imagining. And so it was on this occasion, though the new land that he conjured up could be found only in the imagination of Satan.

Dearest nephew Matthew.
I know not why I write, for what can you, fighting the Turks so very far away, do to remedy the disaster that has befallen the House of Quinton? God knows, by the time you receive this, the scheme will be well afoot, and I might be dead, driven to my grave by grief or the bottles that line my table

here in Oxford. But I feel a need to unburden myself, Matt, and since my brother, your venerated father, fell on Naseby field, who can hear my confession, if not you? There were several crossings-through at this point, after which my uncle's hand commenced a rather less steady progress across the page, as though the bottles that doubtless lay by his other hand were beginning to write their own story.

The truth is, as ever, the matter was put in train by that unnatural crone, my good-sister. Your mother. My Lady Anne, Dowager Countess of Ravensden. Call her what you will. This was strong, even by my uncle's standards; he loved my mother, after a fashion, but generally only in the hours between sleep and waking. *The truth is, Matt –* The paper was stained at this point, the colour suggesting spilt claret – *she has made a match for your brother.*

The walls of the governor's house swam before me, and only a brusque cry from Lord Teviot, who must have seen the blood drain from my face, saved me from the disgrace of fainting. *A match for your brother.* Charles, Earl of Ravensden, one of the most intimate (and by far the most discreet) of our King's very few close friends. My dearest delicate brother, twelve years older than myself, who had taken enough wounds for that king on Worcester field to kill many men with constitutions far stronger than his. Earl Charles, half of whose manhood had been shot away by Cromwell's dragoons, and the remaining half of which was pledged to a circumspect young actor of Betteridge's company. In short, my brother was as likely a candidate for the marriage bed as I was to be the next King of Poland.

Teviot's attendant brought me a glass of wine, which settled me a little, and permitted me to read on. *Of course, it is all to do with the two things that have ever driven our noble house, money and our bloodline. Let us be honest here, nephew. Or let me be honest, at any rate, with this pen and this piece of paper.* Imprimis, *money. We have none. We have had none for generations. Oh, our lands produce a fair income, but we are mortgaged several times over and in debt to every tradesman in Bedfordshire and to much of the City of London besides. The home of our forefathers, Ravensden Abbey, is a calamity. The roofs leak, and the rains stream down our walls to meet the damp rising to meet them from the floor. This much you know better than I, Matt, as you have lived there for some of the past three years, whereas I have been dry and drunk in my Master's lodgings.* This much, indeed, was perfectly true. Only the winter before, one of Steward Barcock's children had been killed when the entire north-east wall collapsed, taking two rooms with it. The Dowager Countess, my mother, had simply summoned our new vicar to utter some peremptory prayers over the rubble and then sealed off the entire wing.

I forced my pained eyes back to Tristram's text. *Your mother is convinced that only a marriage to a great fortune will remedy our situation. In that, perhaps, she is right; but methinks that sometimes a fortune can come at too great a cost. Now,* secundo, *our family line. We must be intimate and frank here, nephew. I have no wife. Many children, of course, but no wife, unlike our dear monarch, who has a wife and many children, but alas, none by her. Now, we know that I could have a wife with no difficulty.* (Modesty had never been a particular characteristic of Tristram Quinton's, especially when it came to women.) *But thanks to the perversity of my college's outmoded and byzantine statutes, that would mean surrendering my post here at Oxford, and necessarily the considerable income and perquisites that accrue from it, not least my cellar of old Bordeaux wines. So if the glorious earldom of Ravensden is not to perish, and pass into dust like old Hotspur and Mortimer, then either you or Charles must father children, as we have no collateral lines. Now, you have been married five years, Matt, and so far your Cornelia has not even managed an encouraging miscarriage.* My uncle could be brutal in his cups, but there was truth enough in this. Cornelia, the epitome of a rational, modern Dutch woman, had even begun to visit a wise-woman in the forest beyond Baldock, who convinced her that our failure to conceive was entirely my fault. As wise-women do. *Of course, it is possible that Cornelia will die, or that you will find a means to divorce her.* (My uncle could be *very* brutal in his cups.) *But your mother has calculated that you are too besot-ted with her to do the latter, and that our House is too unfortunate for God to facilitate the former. Thus she has convinced Charles that it is his duty to marry and endeavour to continue our line, regardless of his own inclina-tions (which we both understand amply enough, I think). What is more, and for reasons that I cannot fathom, the King himself is an enthusiast for the match. As we know, the noble Earl your brother can never refuse the wish of our esteemed monarch.* This, too, was true; their friendship dated back to the darkest days of the King's first exile, when he was but a pen-niless and titular Prince of Wales, and had been strengthened thereafter in ways of which I was then only dimly aware.

Lord Teviot asked me if I wished for more wine, and I asked for my glass to be charged, if only because I dreaded what might come next.

Our new Countess is to be Louise, Lady De Vaux. You might have heard of her, for she has a considerable name at court. Several names, indeed, of which 'harlot' is the one least likely to cause offence to the King of Spain's Inquisition if they intercept any of the copies of this letter. But she has an ample estate, it's said, thanks to two dead husbands. Now, Matt, some will say that two dead rich husbands are the will of God. Yet I have witnessed all the late troubles in this land, and have seen death come in a thousand ways or more, and I wonder – can two *dead husbands truly be the will of God, or the will of the Lady Louise? And thus, what intentions might she harbour toward her third? You will forgive me for such thoughts, for believe me, they are as nothing to the opinion of your own dear wife, who rode here to Oxford but yesterday to regale me upon the matter.* This was typical of Cornelia, who would not have balked at the surprised stares and caustic comments of those who witnessed a lady of breeding riding hell-for-leather (as was always her wont) the fifty or so miles between Ravensden Abbey and Oxford. I could also imagine her opinion. Indeed, I did not need to imagine it for very long; it awaited me on the pages of her many letters. Even today, in these rude and permissive times, I have rarely encountered an author who possesses such a richly diverse vocabulary of the obscene. If Tristram's concerns over potential interception by the Spanish Inquisition had any justification, and even if only one of my wife's letters had fallen into their hands, then the successors of Torquemada would have significantly enhanced their comprehension of human anatomy. Such were the consequences of Cornelia's childhood, much of which was spent avoiding her dull parents and mixing happily with the foul-mouthed sailors and fishwives who thronged the quays of Veere, her home town in Zeeland.

I returned to my uncle's peroration. *Forgive me, nephew, for I write importunely. You cannot possibly influence or deter what is to come to pass – what might already have come to pass, perhaps, by the time that you and your ship return safe to England's shore. Perhaps these are but the rantings of an old and bitter man, and your brother and the Lady Louise will indeed provide the longed-for heir to Ravensden. God knows, they may live in married bliss hereafter, to the glory and honour of our ancient lineage. But I write this to you now, as your father's son and the bearer of my father's name, knowing that you will not betray my confidence, and that you will share at least some of my fears for Charles and our most glorious, but most vulnerable, House of Quinton. God be with you, dearest nephew.*

Your most loving uncle,

T. Quinton.

T. Quinton; never Tristram. I put down the letter, and saw Teviot's eyes upon me. He asked me how I fared, or something of the sort. I cannot recall it, but I can recall my reply: '*The longed-for heir to Ravensden. But I am the heir to Ravensden.*' A responsibility I had shunned all my life; and yet the prospect of it being taken away by the issue of this unnatural marriage brought on a strange surge of anger. 'My poor brother. My poor family. This cannot happen. *This will not happen.*'

PART TWO

∞

Ravensden Abbey, Newmarket, and London

September to December 1663

*T*hree

'She is a murderess, and twice over,' said my wife. 'I am convinced of it. Tristram is convinced of it.'

My anger toward the marriage had been tempered in the long weeks that it had taken the *Wessex* to make passage back to England. It survived a great storm in the Bay of Biscay, then began to abate a little as we were driven back by contrary winds in the Channel, and finally blew over as we made our way round from the Downs to Chatham, where we had finally moored but a few days before. Musk had immediately resumed his old duties as steward of our London house, relegating to ancillary duties the youthful Barcock who had substituted for him during his absence at sea. Thus I had made my way north alone, returning finally to the ancient monastic pile that now passed for our family home.

Upon my return to the crumbling ancestral walls of Ravensden Abbey, I had certain matters of the flesh in mind. But Cornelia turned away, to stand in determined, cross-armed isolation at the window of our bare old room, looking out over the ruins of the old abbey church.

'And she is to be the Countess!' she continued, more sad than furious. 'Countess of Ravensden! Mistress of this house – *our home*, Matthew, until you finally have sufficient income from your pitiful naval service to get us some mean tenement in London. If you ever do, of course, and are not killed by a Turk, or drowned in a storm, leaving me a widow and at the mercy of your mother and this De Vaux *stoephoer*.' Cornelia had still not really forgiven me for turning down a commission in the Guards, and with it status, privilege, a splendid uniform, and above all a regular income. Nor had she reconciled herself to my chosen career in the navy, even though her own brother had been captain of a Dutch man-of-war for ten years or more (and had been on hand providentially to save my life during my second commission). 'Dear Lord, think on that, husband – she will be the Countess. She will have power over us, that *vuile teef* – ' Cornelia's vitriol began to translate into her native Dutch. I moved toward her, opening my arms in loving greeting once more, and hoping by that means to curtail the beginnings of another colourful diatribe against the Lady De Vaux. She turned from me and said, 'It is all your mother's doing, of course. All so that there may be an heir. All because we cannot – I cannot – ' The tears began, and I went to her, putting my arms around her. She turned to me and said, 'You must put me away, Matt. I will turn papist, become a nun at Brussels as your mother suggests. I will accept a divorce. You must marry another, who will give this house its heir. It will be better than forcing this unnatural marriage onto poor Charles – '

I lifted her face and looked into those dear, deep, weeping eyes. 'Never. No, never, Cornelia. We are one. Forever. I would rather forsake the King and the navy than forsake you.'

She cried much more, then laughed a little, and in but a brief time my thoughts of the flesh were made real.

Our splendid afternoon sojourn was short lived. It was not curtailed by my mother, who was unaware of my early return from the Straits and had thus decamped to nearby Buckden, the palace of the Lord Bishop of Lincoln, to lecture that unfortunate prelate on the manifest evils of the increasing number of dissenting congregations in Bedfordshire. Instead, it was one of the many sons of our ancient steward, Barcock, who knocked delicately on our door, informing us that the Vicar of Ravensden had learned of my return from sea and wished to present his compliments. Cornelia sighed, something she had done often enough in the last hour, but in this case it expressed her discontent rather than her pleasure. Until but six months before, my own reaction would have been even more vocal. Our previous incumbent, the Reverend George Jermy, had been so old and so dull that his continued presence on this earth was almost as much a mystery as the continued presence of his congregation. Faced with the tedium of his sermons, it was a miracle that the entire village had not decamped to the woods to join the dissenters who so alarmed my mother. But finally, and in the presence of myself, the Earl, and the Dowager Countess of Ravensden, Jermy had simply halted in the middle of the first verse of Chapter Twenty-Three of Deuteronomy, fallen gently forward in his pulpit, and given up the ghost to a maker who presumably had forgotten to reclaim him several decades before.

I dressed, descended the stairs, entered the grand porch of Ravensden Abbey, lined with the swords and armour of my ancestors, and greeted our new rector, a broad, strong man of close to fifty years.

'Captain Quinton,' he said. 'I rejoice at your return from the Straits, sir. In approximately equal measure, Matt, I regret that I could not accompany you and cleave my sword into the hordes of heathen Turks.'

At that he grinned, and we both embraced; for at my behest, on Jermy's death my brother had exercised his right of patronage over the parish of Ravensden by installing my former chaplain aboard the *Jupiter*, the Reverend Francis Gale.

I led my dear friend to the library, the octagonal room that had been the chapter house of the original abbey. It was one of the few large rooms still in a state fit enough to receive visitors, although a suspicious odour of damp was beginning to cling to many of the books.

Francis Gale was no longer the bitter and hopeless sot that I had first encountered on the *Jupiter*, a man consumed by the dreadful death of the woman he loved and their unborn child amidst the horror of Cromwell's onslaught at Drogheda. But nor was Francis Gale made to be an entirely abstemious paragon of sobriety. He still relished a bottle, though now he imbibed for good cheer and fellowship, not to drive away his tormenting demons. Thus he had rapidly become firm friends with my uncle; they spent many long hours in this very library, debating everything from the nature of the Trinity to the peculiar shape of Lady Castlemaine's bosom, with every discourse washed down by generous measures of old sack and some of the more ancient wines that my grandfather had brought back from France.

Another young Barcock brought us some flagons of good local ale, and we settled to discourse. Francis wanted every detail of my journey to the Straits, of my meeting with the corsair and the knight of Malta, and of the renegade Irishman O'Dwyer, who now sat in a cell of the Tower, awaiting the King's pleasure. He, too, was convinced that the man was a fraud, one of the many imposters and cunning men who had crawled out from under stones since the King's restoration, hoping to take advantage of a generous-hearted monarch and an inexperienced government. A mountain of gold? No, it was preposterous, Francis thought: a myth, or a mere story to divert young children.

We turned to other matters, and I asked how he was enjoying his new living. 'Ah, there's much to do, Matt. As you'll know better than I, my predecessor had not really been the most active servant of the Lord for many years. Decades, if truth be told. There are grown men yet unbaptised, and I have yet to find one villager who knows his Creed. Then there's the fabric of the church itself – apparently the choir boys have wagered on whether the bells will fall before the tower collapses, or vice-versa. And the parish registers are chaos.' Francis sighed and took a long draught of ale. 'Pieces of paper everywhere, some chewed by rats, some years not written up at all. Yesterday I found the page with the marriage record of your great-grandfather, the seventh earl, from the year 1557. It was in the vicarage's privy, ready for use, along with a whole set of transcripts that should have been sent off to the bishop in King James' time. But thankfully I have the lad, Andrewartha. He's a good worker, and his appetite for putting records in order is rather greater than mine. He shows a true vocation, and I hope shortly to secure a place for him at Emmanuel in Cambridge, my old college. He'll be a fine candidate for the Church.'

This pleased me; young Andrewartha had been an officer's servant on the *Jupiter*, and was saved from a court-martial and an almost certain hanging by the generous spirit of Francis Gale. But the mention of my ancestor's marriage brought me back to present concerns, and I said, 'Well, Francis. So what is your opinion of the proposed match between my brother and the Lady De Vaux?'

I had seen Francis Gale in many states. I had seen him drunk. I had seen him angry, I had seen him desperately sad, I had seen him deliriously happy. I had seen him kill men with rabid blood-lust in his eyes. But until that moment, I had never seen him embarrassed. Haltingly, he said, 'She – she is a fine lady, sir. She will be a countess to bring credit to this house – '

The library door was thrown open with such force that it struck hard against the inner wall, shaking loose some plaster from the ceiling. 'Oh, *kloten – bollocks*, Francis!' cried Cornelia, who was finally dressed.

We stood, and my wife made straight for my flagon of ale and drained a long draught. As the world knows, Dutch women come out of the womb crying not for their mother's milk, but for beer.

I said, 'My dear, perhaps Francis has a different opinion of her – '

Gale sat, but rather less comfortably than before. 'Oh, husband,' said Cornelia. 'Think on it! I will say what Francis dares not, but which should be obvious to the man who could be Earl of Ravensden in a heartbeat. For but a few months more, at any rate. In this country, any vicar owes his place to whoever holds the right of presentation to the living. Is this not so? Thus Francis remains our vicar only at the pleasure of the earl, although of course, that pleasure would also be shaped by the two women who bear the title Countess of Ravensden – the earl's mother and his new wife. And should there ever be any debate in the matter, the final judgment would rest with the Supreme Governor of the Church that Francis serves. The earl's friend King Charles, in other words. Now, what do all of those who hold power over poor Francis's position have in common? Ah yes. They all favour the marriage.'

For my part, I was increasingly uneasy that both my wife and uncle had condemned this woman out of hand, without fair trial and without even meeting her. But in one sense she was right. The Vicar of Ravensden's position was particularly delicate, perhaps because – 'Oh, Francis,' I said, 'surely you are not to officiate at this ceremony?'

Francis Gale essayed a little smile of relief. 'No, Captain. God places men in situations that are invidious enough, and He has not sought fit to inflict that additional punishment upon me, thanks be to Him. The ceremony will be at Saint Paul's, no less, and in November, so thankfully distant. It's as well, really, for Ravensden Church could never hold the congregation that's expected. What's more, the King himself intends to give away the bride, so I would not wish to be held to account if the roof collapsed in the middle of the service. Some might construe that as high treason.'

Ah, Francis, my old and long-gone friend; would that we all have the gift of second sight. For the roof, tower and bells of Ravensden Church are all still there and sound enough, more than sixty years on. They will probably still be there at Doomsday. Whereas, of course, old Saint Paul's was reduced to cinders but three years later.

Cornelia sniffed. 'Ha, Charles Stuart only chose Saint Paul's because no other church is large enough to accommodate his brood of mistresses and bastards. Then there will be the family and confidantes of our new countess, of course. A veritable multitude they'll be.'

Francis said, 'Not so, Mistress Quinton. It seems she has no immediate family of any sort.'

Cornelia and I leaned forward, almost in unison. This was news indeed. My wife said, 'No family? Who has no family, other than beggars, orphans and the very old? Most of us have too much family.' This was undoubtedly true of her own breed, the van der Eides: her parents, brother, sisters, uncles, aunts and cousins, spread across a large swathe of the Netherlands and Flanders, constituted a vast dynasty of tedium. It was less true of the Quintons, a line that was almost extinct; but even I had a living mother, a brother, a sister and an uncle (as well as innumerable cousins on my mother's and grandmother's sides of the family, including even a few who were both sane and not French).

Francis nodded. 'Quite, Mistress. But the Master has written to tell me that he has been conducting some discreet researches into Lady De Vaux's history. He has no conclusions as yet, but as he writes in a letter I received only today, neither does she. No conclusion to any branch of her family's history, for there seems to be no family.'

The juxtaposition of Master and Mistress confused me momentarily. Then I realised that 'the Master' could only be my uncle Tristram, the Master of Mauleverer. So Tris was looking into our new countess's past.

I looked at my wife, and at my friend Francis Gale, and knew in that moment that I was looking upon the beginnings of a conspiracy. My heart cried out to me to join it, there and then, but my head urged different counsels. *You have not spoken with your brother*, said my head, *and after all, it is his marriage.* My heart protested that it might indeed be his marriage, but that it was my inheritance, for good or ill, sought or unsought; my duty to the past and future of the House of Quinton. Besides, my brother was far away, inspecting the bleak and barely economical estate in Northumberland that a complex marriage-settlement had brought to our family a century or so before. *That may be*, said my head, *but neither have you spoken with the two who urge this marriage more than any others.* This was so, but I could hardly seek an audience of Our Sovereign Lord the King to demand to know why he wished my brother to marry a suspected murderous whore. But as for the other ...

As if summoned by angels or demons, the state coach of the Earls of Ravensden thundered into the stable yard beyond the library window, an unjustifiably extravagant team of six horses pulling it home. Two young Barcocks rushed forward to the door that bore our ancient blazon of arms, opened it, and helped a tall but stooped old woman to descend. Still clad in mourning black, some eighteen years after her husband's death, the Lady Anne, Dowager Countess of Ravensden, looked about her with a satisfied air and made her way slowly towards our old house, bent almost double, her two sticks striking the cobbles and giving her the unsettling sight and sound of a vast and ancient spider, moving relentlessly towards its next fly.

My mother had returned.

The crooked hand extended toward me, and I leaned forward to kiss it. Mother was seated in her room in the former monks' infirmary, a little way down the corridor from the one which Cornelia and I shared. Thus she, too, had a view over to the ruins of the abbey quire, but the demolition of part of the wall by Henry VIII's agents when the monastery was dissolved meant that she had an uninterrupted view down to the grave of her husband. James Quinton, Earl of Ravensden for less than half a year, lay there, forever in her view: poet, warrior, fallen legend of the Cavalier cause, and the father who had died when I was only five. My mother's chair was carefully positioned so that she did not have to look down upon the adjacent grave of my grandfather Matthew, the previous earl, whom she had hated with a passion equal to that with which she had loved his son. Or as I thought she had loved him until I had heard the enigmatic words of a dying man, in Scotland the year before.

'Matthew,' she said. 'You should have sent Musk or another ahead of you, to inform us of your coming.'

'There was much to do, mother. There always is when a ship pays off.' This was invention, for the end of the *Wessex*'s cruise was the first time I had paid off a ship in the normal way. My first command had been wrecked on the coast of Kinsale, my second almost blown apart in the Scottish isles. But there was also a truth in it, for the bombardment of paperwork which accompanied our return to Chatham had been almost as terrible as a broadside, and certainly more time-consuming. I had meant to write ahead and inform my family at Ravensden of my return, but by the end of each day I had written so many formal letters, read through so many muster books, pay books and manifests, dealt with so many officious time-servers from the dockyard and the Ordnance – after all of that, I could barely keep my eyes open for a jar of wine at the King's Head in Rochester before falling unconscious into my bed.

The Dowager Countess frowned. 'As you say, Matthew. The ways of the navy are a mystery to me.' (This was a blessing; her hatred of her father-in-law had grown into a profound lack of interest in the service that he had graced and to which I now belonged.) 'But you are so *brown*! Why, they will mistake you for a Moor when next you ride into Bedford – the people there will never have seen so dark a face – '

My mother was not adept at ordinary conversation. This was one of the chief reasons why relations were sometimes strained between her and Cornelia, who could extract a conversation out of a rock. So I came straight to the matter, and said, 'Mother, we must speak of this proposed marriage. Between Charles and the Lady De Vaux.'

The eyes narrowed. To be fair, my mother had learned suspicion at the court of King Charles the First, amid all the fevered rumours and hysteria that had culminated in civil war; like many men and women of her age, she carried suspicion on her shoulder like a vast but invisible bird of prey. 'What of the marriage?'

Time for diplomacy, for the King and the Lord Admiral his brother wanted their captains to be good diplomats. 'Well, it affects me, as the heir. Mother, all I seek is some explanation that will settle my mind in this matter.'

She looked on me with sadness and – and with something else, something that I could not quite identify. 'Yes, you are the heir, Matthew. And after you? Who is the heir then? When you married Cornelia, Charles and I saw it as the salvation of the bloodline. But five years on, you have no children. The line must continue. This family must continue.'

'But to put Charles through this – Charles of all men – and with this woman of all women – '

'Charles is – sanguine, shall we say. You can speak to him yourself, when he returns from Alnburgh. And the King's enthusiasm for the match weighs heavily with him. As for the Lady De Vaux, it's true that she has a certain reputation. But I have lived a long time, Matthew, and I have found that reputations are often unjustified. Particularly if, as I suspect, that reputation is founded upon jealousy of the thirty thousand that she possesses.'

'*Thirty thousand*? That much?'

'Some widows are fortunate in their inheritances, Matthew, while some are not,' she said, looking out to the grave in the ruins. 'I need not tell you what thirty thousand will mean to this house. And remember, I have met the lady several times, which you and Cornelia have not. I believe I can judge a character, and I judge hers to be – suitable.'

'But there are so many questions about her past – she has no family-'

The bird of prey preened itself, and pounced. 'And how do you know that? Oh, don't bother lying. Tristram, of course.' She was angry now, and my mother's anger was always cold and controlled, unlike the arm-waving tempers of Cornelia. 'Tristram will never reconcile himself to this, just as he never reconciled himself to me, nor to his king in his time of need, come to that. I could have proposed the marriage of Charles to the most saintly virgin in England, if any such can be found, and still my good-brother would have opposed it – for it would not have been of his conceiving, and that irks him more than anything. But then, if he had any true sense of family duty he would abandon his miserable little college, his wine and his mistresses, get a wife, and father the future heir to Ravensden himself.' She was furious now, and my mother furious was a sight to behold. 'But Tristram will always indulge himself first, then play his little games. So like his father, in all things. Thank God that he was the younger son, and thank God that is the way of it in the next generation, too. All the responsibility and sense of duty with the elder – '

'*Enough, mother!*' Enough of diplomacy, too; time for the broadside. 'Responsibility? Duty? You dare talk of those things, when you tell Cornelia to enter a convent? Oh, you'll gladly set aside my responsibility and duty to my wife to suit your own purposes. You chide my uncle for playing games, when you play them with the lives of everyone in this family?'

'You will not speak to me in this way. I have told you before, *you will not* – '

I was angry now, the rage blazing inside me like a burning magazine. 'Oh yes, mother. You have told me before. You told me when I questioned you about the early days of the late king's reign, in Lord Buckingham's time, when my father was away at the French wars – ' elusive hints of secrets buried deeply over thirty years before were an unexpected legacy of my voyage aboard the *Jupiter* – 'What else passed in those times, mother? *What else?*'

I saw something in her eyes …

It was gone in an instant, and the narrow, suspicious slits returned. 'Get out,' she hissed. 'Get back to your barren wife.'

'Better a barren wife than a whore for a countess,' I snapped as I turned away from her and strode from the room.

It was only when I stood outside, in the dark, damp corridor, that I realised two things. First, she had insulted Cornelia, but she had done no more than speak the truth; whereas I had made the fatal mistake of not distinguishing between the once and future Countesses of Ravensden. As I heard my mother's sobbing begin, I also knew what I had seen in her eyes when I demanded the truth of all that she had known and done at the court of the first King Charles.

It was fear.

* * *

I sat in a small private room of the old George Inn, just up from the river bridge in Bedford. It stank. As in all towns, the common sewer flowed down the High Street just outside, but in Bedford, it met the river's own distinctive stench right outside the entrance to the George. Moreover, the stables at the back were particularly close to the main body of the inn, and the innkeeper apologised for the presence of a noxious herd of unruly Irish horses with violent diarrhoea, en route for the royal races at Newmarket. Yet by the end of a second jug of good Bordeaux, the George seemed like a very paradise on earth, especially as it did not contain either my mother (still distraught) or my wife (attempting vainly to calm my mother).

My thoughts raced this way and that, although the wine progressively slowed and dulled them. I had been insufferably rude; of course I had. If my mother knew great secrets of state, well then, so be it. We are all entitled to our secrets, and besides, hers had to be of so very long ago; what possible relevance could they have, especially when the only matter of the moment was that of the unnatural marriage proposed for my brother?

I was beginning to contemplate the relative merits of a third jug of Bordeaux against riding unsteadily back to the abbey when a Barcock – Paul, I think, or it might have been Peter – entered my small, stinking world at the George Inn, and handed me a letter that had been delivered at Ravensden by a royal courier but an hour before. I thanked him in the vaguely profuse way of the drunk, and opened the letter. It was a script I knew well – clear, precise, a little pompous – and the message, too, was redolent of its author: just a little more long-winded than it needed to be.

Sir,

His Majesty having summoned me to attend him at Newmarket upon some concerns relating to the present state and occasions of the navy, His Majesty has seen fit to instruct me to inform you that he wishes your immediate attendance upon him in order to expedite the same purpose. I therefore desire that you will see fit to attend upon His Majesty and myself at your earliest convenience.

I am, Captain Quinton, your most humble and respectful servant,

S. Pepys

Clerk of the Acts to the Honourable Principal Officers and Commissioners of His Majesty's Navy

So I was to have my wish. True, I had mismanaged my interview with my mother. But now I would be able to see the King himself and have an opportunity to ask him why he wished to force this preposterous marriage onto my brother. That one thought drove all else before it, including the one question I should have asked; the one question that was hidden there, festering in the depths of Pepys' letter.

What purpose relating to the 'state and occasions' of the navy could possibly tear Charles Stuart away from the horse races and mistresses that took up all his time at Newmarket, and compel him to summon one of his lowliest captains to expedite it?

Four

The next morning was sunny, and despite the excesses of the previous night I rose very early, kissed my snoring Cornelia, and rode off for Newmarket; somewhat thick-headed and unsteadily at first, then with more confidence. It was a brisk, easy ride across the flat lands to the east, upon the firm roads of late summer. The harvest was being gathered in, and village folk were everywhere in the fields, singing hymns in the more devout communities and bellowing foolish songs about rude lads and wenches in the more profane. My steed was Zephyr, an old favourite who had once carried me uncomplainingly from Ravensden to Portsmouth in two days, a pace that would have done for many a lesser horse. Our passage was impeded only twice. Just before we reached Cambridge a football match between two villages degenerated into a great brawl; one player seemed to have been accused of feigning injury to gain an advantage, and was rightly kicked senseless by his opponents. And though Cambridge itself was quiet, for the university term would not begin for another month, beyond it the road gradually filled with more and more of the ruder sort of people, all bound for Newmarket to see the King and the great ones of the court. I spurred Zephyr on and bustled my way through, for unlike them, I had a summons to attend upon our sovereign lord himself.

The sovereign lord had a special enclosure on a knoll in the midst of the Newmarket heaths. This gave the best possible view of the circuit on which the horses raced; it was fenced off and guarded by soldiers in sharp red uniforms, half with pikes, the rest with muskets. It also gave the best possible view of the land all around, a flat land of green fields, windmills and church steeples, with the great octagon tower of Ely Cathedral just visible on the far horizon. Several large tents sheltered those who elected to ignore the view and the racing, or who simply preferred shade to sunshine. They contained tables that groaned with delicacies. I dismounted at the fence, showed my letter of summons to one of the guards, and was directed towards the largest tent. There I found a throng of flunkeys, several gaudily painted whores and a familiar, small, round man with a long face, perhaps thirty years old or thereabouts, sweating under an unfeasibly large wig (this being then the newest and highest of fashions; indeed, almost the only fashion of those times that has survived until this, and will doubtless remain the fashion for all eternity). The round man was looking keenly around him, and at first missed my approach.

'Mister Pepys,' I said.

'Ah, Captain Quinton,' said the Clerk of the Acts to the Navy Board. 'Welcome, sir, welcome. A most prompt response to the King's summons, if I may say so. You'll take a little refreshment after your ride?'

'I thank you, Mister Pepys. Yes, a little beer, I think.'

I had known Samuel Pepys for two years now. As Clerk of the Acts, a kind of secretary, he was the fulcrum for all the correspondence that passed between we captains and the Navy Board, and thus handled all the concerns relating to the daily management of our ships. This Pepys had only been put in to the place because he was some sort of kin to Montagu, the Earl of Sandwich, then one of the greatest men in the realm; for it was Montagu, Noll Cromwell's protégé and a general-at-sea, who had persuaded a suspicious navy to support the restoration of the King, and it was aboard Montagu's flagship that Charles Stuart was brought safe home to England. Naturally, the gratitude of a restored monarch cascaded rewards upon Montagu's rather jowly head, and one of the least of them was a place in the Navy Office for Montagu's creature, Master Samuel Pepys. He was an odd little man, this Pepys, and my opinion of him was not wholly formed. True, he could be a pedant of the worst sort, with a puffed-up pomposity to boot. True, he was a little too confident of his own worth for my liking, and a little too eager to proclaim that worth to all and sundry, especially those who were in positions of some importance. But he was also an enthusiast, endlessly curious about all manner of things; a man genuinely interested in the doings of other men (and women, too – that much was obvious as his eyes roved round the royal enclosure); and when he was in drink, an inestimably good companion, as he was now. This Samuel Pepys I could like, even love. The Samuel Pepys who had chided me in a most high-handed fashion for the inadequate keeping of receipts for certain stores aboard the *Wessex*, and had criticised me before the Lord High Admiral for the same – well, that Samuel Pepys I regarded as highly as the aromas of Bedford's George Inn.

As we drank our beer, I asked him how he came to be with the court at Newmarket. He explained that he, too, had been summoned to attend the King, but that this was no imposition for him: 'I am from these parts, Captain Quinton. My family were of Huntingdon – also the seat of My Lord of Sandwich, of course – and I was schooled there. So I can attend both to the business of the navy and my own family during the same excursion from London. A profitable use of time, I'd say. Now, sir, we should attend upon the King.'

'No, sir, I think we should not.'

Pepys' face fell; he had an aversion to being contradicted. 'But Captain, your summons was urgent – '

I pointed behind him. Beyond the flaps of the tent, out at the edge of the track, stood the unmistakably tall and dark figure of His Majesty

Charles the Second, King of England, Scotland, Ireland and France (the last in name only, to honour his ancestors who had wasted so many years of their lives, and so many lives of their subjects, invading that fair land in vain attempts to seize its crown). Our sovereign lord was red-faced, stamping on the ground, gesticulating at a distant group of horses and berating all around him – notably his oldest friend, the Duke of Buckingham, and the delectable maid of honour to the Queen, Lady Frances Stuart, who some said was destined soon to replace the formidable Countess of Castlemaine as the King's principal mistress. It was as well that her latter ladyship was in the last days of her latest royally-induced pregnancy and thus confined to London, for otherwise her unrestrained rage would probably have been heard across several counties.

I said, 'With respect, Mister Pepys, I have known the King much longer than you. Seeking him out when his horse has just lost badly is not necessarily conducive to our business here, whatever that business might be. I suggest that we remain here, drink more beer, and watch for the moment when His Majesty backs a winning horse. *Then* he will be receptive.'

Pepys' expression changed in an instant from annoyance to puzzlement to relief to happiness. In that moment, I realised that in one essential respect Samuel Pepys was very like me: for both of us, knowledge was all. He said, 'That sounds to me like most excellent advice, Captain Quinton. I shall remember that. Thank you, sir. Now, you were suggesting that we drink more beer?'

The restoration of His Majesty's humour took three races. Pepys and I finally approached the royal presence as the King roared with laughter, extolling the virtues of his own victorious filly over His Grace of Buckingham's inept nag.

'Damn me, George,' cried the Lord's Anointed, 'that'll teach you to wager fifty guineas on a mouldy pile of bone that's good only for dog food!'

The duke laughed, but it was the forced, artificial laugh of the mortified. George Villiers, second Duke of Buckingham (son to the great favourite of the first Kings Charles and James, the Lord High Admiral under whom my grandfather had sailed) fancied himself as a great wit, but somehow that quality of his always evaporated when the King turned the ferocious royal humour against him. They had been bosom friends since the cradle, these two, for King Charles the Martyr had brought up the orphaned heir of the first Duke with his own son. History records that after the second Charles' happy restoration, the second Buckingham sought to trade on that friendship by becoming the greatest commoner in the land, just as his father had been; but the King, who could see through most men (but curiously, not through most women, other than through their clothing at any rate), knew His Grace of Buckingham for what he was, namely a charming, indolent coxcomb, fit to entertain him in good times and bad, but suitable for about as much responsibility in the kingdom as the inhabitants of Bedlam. This made for some difficulty between my family and the great duke, because Buckingham never understood why the King preferred the quiet, serious friendship of my brother above his own, and entrusted Charles Quinton with matters of state that he would not have dreamed of confiding to George Villiers. Thus it was no surprise to me that Buckingham's eyes filled with suspicion and resentment as Pepys and I approached the royal party, bowing deeply as we did so, whereas the King's expression was happy and open.

'Matt Quinton! Pepys! At last. Now for the serious business of the day, by God!' A functionary ran up, bowed, and informed the King that the horses and riders were ready for the next race. Charles Stuart raised his hand, announced loftily that the next race would have to await his royal pleasure, and turned back to the rest of the party. 'Your Grace. My Lady Frances.' (A long glance at that good lady's ample and, perchance, amply displayed bosom.) 'You must forgive us, for this is a most pressing matter. I trust we will not detain you long. George, entertain them with a stanza, or something of the sort.'

The King beckoned us toward a bare patch of ground, between the royal enclosure and the impatient entrants in the next race. I caught His Grace of Buckingham's expression. It was that strange mixture of arrogance, puzzlement and downright anguish that one always sees on the faces of those who are never accorded quite the importance that they think they deserve. I saw it often on the face of our late and unlamented monarch, George the First, an obscure and stupid German princeling who somehow seemed to believe that people should take him seriously just because various peculiar turns of fate had bestowed upon him the wholly inappropriate office of King of Great Britain.

When he judged that we were far enough away from curious ears, King Charles turned to me and said, 'Matthew Quinton, by all the saints. My God, sir, you've become almost as dark as me. A second Black Boy, indeed!' The King was famously swarthy, a legacy of his grand-mother's Italian family. 'Now, this business of the Irish renegade that you captured. All this matter of a mountain of gold. You formed your own thoughts on that, I take it?'

There was little point in dissembling before the greatest dissembler then living. 'Your Majesty, it seemed to me but an arrant pack of lies, designed solely to save his worthless skin.' I made to change the subject, even though that was not the done thing when in the presence of royalty. 'Sire, if I may, there is also this matter of my brother's proposed marriage – '

Charles Stuart seemed not to have heard me, although of course, he had heard me perfectly well (a divine right to deafness being one of the most essential attributes of monarchy). 'An arrant pack of lies, you say. Well, yes, that does seem the most plausible interpretation, of course. And you, Mister Pepys? You have your own thoughts on this matter, too?'

Flustered, Pepys replied, 'Majesty, I – that is to say – well, my thoughts are at one with Your Majesty's – '

The King's expression was suddenly still, and when he spoke, his voice was different, and distant. 'Oh no, Mister Pepys. No man's thoughts are at one with mine. No man's.' Charles looked far away, as though searching for something well beyond the distant tower of Ely. But in a moment, his eyes brightened – methought when his gaze fell once more upon the distant spectacle of the Lady Frances Stuart – and he said, 'Look around you, gentlemen. All these people, gathered here on this dire and blasted heath, miles from any decent lodging. Why is that, exactly?'

'Why,' said Pepys, 'because of Your Majesty's presence – '

'Oh, yes, some of them, Mister Pepys. My courtiers, those who will always be where I happen to be simply because that is what they were born to do – His Grace of Buckingham for one – just as shit always attracts flies. Then there will be those like you, Mister Pepys, who have to attend upon the royal presence because it is a condition of the salary that I pay you, albeit several months in arrears. And, of course, there are men like Captain Quinton here who attend me in the hope of prefer-ment and honour. But there are many more here today than either of your kinds, or even His Grace's. Damn it, I've sighted at least two dozen rabid Cromwellians and Commonwealths-men who still hanker after the old republic. They'd rather eat brimstone than fawn over the man they regard as the agent of the Antichrist. Cambridgeshire men, mostly. God protect me from Cambridgeshire. But they've one weakness in common that brings them here today, a weakness that they share with myself and Buckingham and almost everyone else present on this heath.' Quite suddenly, the King turned, raised his right arm, and let it fall. The functionary who had attended him earlier waved his arms furiously, and in the distance, to a great cheer from the attendant throng, a dozen horses began to pound along the track, spurred on by jockeys in liveries that were all the colours of the rainbow. Charles said, 'Oh, the sport is one thing, gentlemen, but the gamble is quite another. You see, a loss is a loss – there are many horses in a race, so we know that loss is always the more likely outcome. We learn to live with loss, we can accept it. I lose a few guineas to His Grace of Buckingham – so be it. The poor men down there, they lose a few pennies – so be it. But oh, gentlemen, the sensation of winning! The thrill of the chase, and the thrill of the chance – the glorious, impossible chance that the outsider will win against the odds! I can live with ninety-nine defeats, if I can just have that feeling in the hundredth race! That, gentlemen, is what unites those who come here today.'

I had seen the King like this before: elevated to a state of sublime bliss. Such occasions usually involved the nearby presence of a disordered woman, but that day on the heath at Newmarket, Charles Stuart seemed to be in an ecstasy that went beyond the pursuit of the female sex. He was silent for a few moments, but even the ever-garrulous Pepys knew enough of court etiquette to realise that one did not interrupt the Lord's Anointed, and I knew that I could not broach the subject of the marriage until and unless His Majesty deigned to hear me out, if he ever did. Eventually, the King said: 'Sometimes, gentlemen, kings have to gamble with the highest stakes of all. We can make war, and send good men off to their deaths – men like those down there, or indeed men like you, Matt. But sometimes, kings gain unexpected opportunities to make gambles that they cannot lose. Thus it is with this business of the mountain of gold. If you're right, Matt, and this Irishman is a brazen liar seeking to save his pitiful life, then what do I lose if I humour him awhile? Nought, for I gambled no stake. But if we are all wrong, gentlemen, and there's even a grain of truth in what he says – Think on it. A mountain of gold. The greatest prize in all the world. What would I do if I gained it? I have thought much on that. To be the richest monarch of all, able to make my country the greatest empire that the world has ever seen, able to do anything that I wished.'

He looked down towards the enclosure, towards the lithe shape of the Lady Frances. Of course, history records that the King's pursuit of her would never be fulfilled; one of his very few pursuits of that sort which failed, if truth be told. Instead he immortalised her as the model for Britannia, stamping her image on his copper coins. She is there still, and there she will probably remain until the end of time. Why, the other day I even heard the feckless son of my upholsterer, old Arne of Covent Garden, singing some idle new ditty about her.

The King's gaze returned to the distant horses, thundering around a bend in the course. 'Spur him on, Garside! Harder, man! Use your whip, for God's sake – Ah, that's more like it!' Turning back to me, he said, 'And O'Dwyer is not our only witness, after all. Why, I first heard rumours of this mountain of gold when I was in Paris in, what, forty-nine? Not long after my father's execution, at any rate. The late Cardinal Mazarin was quite taken by the prospect of it, despite the civil wars which then ravaged France.' *The French again…* 'My cousin Rupert, too, has always been particularly intrigued by the possibility. Forever whispers of it in my ear, in fact – well, what passes for whispering from His Highness, at any rate.' The Prince Palatine of the Rhine, the famous general in our civil wars, was not noted for his subtlety. 'He learned of it and searched for it when he and Holmes were in the Gambia ten years or so ago, before my little navy-in-exile was disbanded. No success, of course, but after all, gentlemen, even if the conquest of a beautiful woman fails at the first attempt, the eventual reward can ever make it worthwhile to continue the chase!' He laughed, and I joined in dutifully, Pepys rather more nervously. The King placed a hand on my shoulder and said, 'Well, Matt, now you see my game. You are my racehorse in this, by God. For who else can I entrust with this task, other than the man who brought the prospect of the mountain of gold once more before my eyes?'

The race ended at that moment. There was a great cheer from the concourse, and it was clear that the horse bearing yellow, the King's colour, had won. Charles Stuart smiled with satisfaction, waved triumphantly to the downcast Duke of Buckingham, and said, 'Another gamble won. You know, Matt, I think my luck has turned at last?' He stepped closer to me and whispered in my ear. 'And so has that of your noble house, with this marriage to the Lady De Vaux. Trust me upon that, for I can say no more.' The King turned and beckoned to Pepys, who handed him a leather pouch. Charles took it without a word, handed it to me and said cheerfully, 'So, Matt. In that pouch, you'll find a commission from my brother the Lord Admiral appointing you Captain of the *Seraph*, Fifth Rate frigate, thirty-two guns, currently lying at Deptford. Not as large as your *Wessex*, it's true, and thus not as much pay for her captain. But she's new, fresh out of a private yard at Blackwall. The builder assures me that all his ships are blessed by Merlin and the fairies of the dawn, who tell him where to position the futtocks. He may be as mad as the Duke of Norfolk, but he builds damnably good frigates. She can outsail anything on the world's oceans, Captain, and I'll vouch for her because I took her whipstaff in a brisk northerly on passage from the Hope to the Nore and back again. She answers the helm better than any of my yachts, Matt.' This king was ever a frustrated sailor, who lived vicariously through every moment of every one of his captains' voyages. 'You'll fly to Africa and find my mountain of gold. Your sailing orders and your less public instructions are in the pouch also. You will see that you are to be part of a larger expedition, with larger aims, but you will detach from that at the Gambia. I have also provided you with some additional, confidential instructions concerning your passenger, to be opened if the need arises.' I had a sudden dread – 'I don't doubt that you, like every one of my ministers, will damn me behind my back for a trusting fool who puts too much faith in leniency. Perhaps you will all be proved right, in which case these additional instructions should amply cover the case. But I have found that if we place our faith in scoundrels, then at least we are never disappointed when they revert to their nature, unlike the case when men who assume the pretence of goodness later show themselves to be even fouler villains.' That was how it was with this king: in the blink of an eye, he could both assume the overweening, unanswerable royal 'we' and become the arch-cynic that history records. Of course, I did not know then that this king would even forgive the man who stole his crown jewels, but I do not think that such knowledge would have shocked my young self. So when the King's peroration came, it was no longer a surprise. 'Your passenger, Matt, will be the newest Lieutenant-Colonel of my Irish army. That is to say, Colonel Brian Doyle O'Dwyer of Baltimore in the County of Cork.'

I began my journey back to Ravensden in the foulest temper imaginable. I scowled at smiling country lads as they returned from the harvest. I almost had Zephyr trample the bride as I rode angrily through a cheerful wedding party. The sun continued to shine, but my heart was the deepest, darkest place on God's earth, and I became fatally unaware of my surroundings and of the pairs of eyes that might have been viewing my progress. I had learned nothing of my brother's marriage, other than not to question it. True, I had been granted a new command. But a voyage to the coast of West Africa, a shore notoriously fetid and the killer of many a good captain and his crew? Moreover, a voyage that was bound to be the wildest goose-chase in the history of England, promoted by a devious time-serving renegade who would probably jump ship to rejoin his murderous corsair friends the moment we touched our first African landfall? A renegade whom His Majesty had seen fit to promote to a rank far above my own. The more I thought upon the words and actions of Charles Stuart, this man whom I had been brought up to revere almost as a god, the anger swelled inside me. *I gambled no stake* – true, Your Majesty, none beyond the lives of several hundred men, Matthew Quinton among them.

As I rode, I began to harbour increasingly wild thoughts. Perhaps I could decamp to the French service; I was certain my friend the Comte d'Andelys could arrange it. Or I could abscond to the Americas and go off into their wild, empty hills to escape the world. Or else I could become a boucaneer of the Caribbee, or whatever they called themselves. What was left for me in England, if I was to be displaced as the heir of Ravensden and entrusted by the King, not with his reasons for thus displacing me, but with a voyage born of his avarice and his fatal determination to place faith in those that the rest of the world rightly condemned as faithless? Cornelia would soon find another, one who could provide the children she craved …

My temper was so vile that I finally mistook my road and found myself on a poor track. I cared but little when I realised my error; the sun in the sky told me I was still riding west, I knew I was close to the Bedfordshire border, and I would hardly go astray when I reached the great road from London to the north. All too quickly, I sank back into my dark reflections, ruminating on the injustice of it all, casting silent curses down upon the heads of a duplicitous king, an arrogant mother …

I thought I heard a cry – '*Ride hard, boy!*' – and my horse seemed to begin its gallop the faintest fraction of a moment before I gave it the spur. Thus I rode fast and hard into the thicket ahead, where the lane narrowed almost to a path. As well that I did, for if I had still been going at a canter I would have been easy prey for the gang that sprang out from the trees on both sides. Eight or ten of them, I reckoned, although I passed them in a blur. They had clubs, and one of them managed to strike my horse's haunch. The blow did no real hurt and only emboldened my mount to find yet more speed. Two of them called out, including the last one that I passed. Then I was beyond them, back out into open country.

I rode until I was almost within sight of Ravensden. As I slowed, I could finally reflect on the attack. Of course, the land was full of broken men and sturdy beggars, waiting in thickets to attack unwary travellers who foolishly strayed from the main roads. Such was life, and I had been a fool to come so close to falling into their clutches.

But the more I thought upon it, the more I wondered whether this was truly just another wayside robbery. I was not so concerned with the voice that might or might not have called out to hasten me; the same inner voice had spoken to me before, when I stood in mortal danger on the deck of my enemy's ship, and I had no reason to fear it. But I could still see that last man of the robber band. I could see the great scar on his face, and the left eye that was no longer there. I could see that he bore a sword, hardly the weapon of a beggarly roadside thief. And I could still hear what I thought was the shout from one of his lackeys, as well as what might have been the scarred man's reply.

'Quinton's escaped us, sergeant!'

'Aye, but he'll not run from us forever, boys!'

$\mathcal{F}$*ive*

My mother was a misanthropic old vixen. She disliked the common herd of humanity with a venom that in my younger days I reserved solely for lawyers and the Welsh. She was also unpredictable in many things, but in some, she could be as set in her ways as Stonehenge. One of these, and to my mind one of her more creditable traits, was that she had a powerful regard for tradition, especially the traditions of the Quintons. Thus she decreed that the new countess should be introduced to the broader family, our neighbours and our tenantry at a grand reception in the grounds of Ravensden Abbey, for that was how Quintons had behaved since our chain-mailed ancestors sat within their wooden walls on the mound across the valley. Legend had it that the first earl's betrothal was celebrated by a crowd of five thousand, including his good friend King Henry the Fifth of blessed and immortal memory, with whom he had fought at Agincourt. Not quite so many attended my mother's induction into our family forty years before, but at least she abided by the family custom. Indeed, one of her grievances against my long-dead grandfather was that he had been the only Quinton to neglect such niceties, choosing instead to marry his much younger French bride in a hasty ceremony on his estate in the Val-de-Loire (long sold) and not actually bringing her back to Ravensden until she had borne him three children. The fact that Earl Matthew's marriage occurred before she was born, and thus could not have been of the slightest concern to her, did not prevent my mother adding it to her endless litany of grievances against him.

Much as I resented the occasion for the grand entertainment, I secretly approved of my mother's reverence for our old traditions. (My approval had to be secret, not because my mother and I were still not on speaking terms – we were, in a strained and formal fashion – but because inevitably, Cornelia's disapproval was vehement and prolonged, and I sought a quiet life.) No, my objections to the great Quinton reception were more immediate and distinctly more practical. First, we could not afford it. True, I had no detailed knowledge of our balance sheet, but one does not need to be near a sewer to know that sewers stink. Second, my mother proposed to hold the grand event outdoors, so as to accommodate more people. In October. In Bedfordshire. Now, one of the few joys of my fatherless childhood had been to study atlases; it was better to think of faraway lands than of my own, which was still ravaged by civil war. I think it was on a December day, perhaps in that winter when they killed the king and the snow lay four feet deep on the fields of Ravensden, that I looked at a map of Europe and realised that no mountain range, no obstruction of any sort, lay between us and the wastes of Muscovy. So when the east winds howled, as they often do in October in our parts, the Russian snows frequently came with them.

And thus they did, unexpectedly early and heavy that year.

This simple fact would have defeated lesser mortals, but not my mother. Instead, she hired every brazier in the county, erected flaming torches all around our grounds, ordered vats of mulled wine so vast that they could have floated a small ketch, and awaited the great day. That day was to be crowned not only by the debut of our new countess-to-be, but also by the long-awaited return of the Earl of Ravensden himself.

Charles had found several apparently pressing reasons to detain him for an inordinate period of time on our Alnburgh lands, and had then gone on to the estate in Wiltshire that Lady De Vaux had inherited from her second husband. Charles' letters to me during this time had always been brief, as was his wont, but containing endless promises to take me into his confidence on his return, which was not. Indeed, he contrived not to come back to Ravensden until the very day of the reception itself, sending ahead to say that he and his lady had been detained in their journey by a broken wheel on their coach. Thus I was destined to meet my new sister-in-law in public, at the same time as our legion of guests.

I have never forgotten my first sight of the grand reception. Mother had arranged that we of the immediate family, and certain other notables, were to be admitted formally, and had thus arranged for the grand steps from the hall into the gardens to be brought back into use. This involved opening a set of doors that had probably not seen their key since her own betrothal reception. The doors in question promptly fell off their hinges, which crumbled into rust, forcing us to send to Bedford for carpenters. They were now pulled open by two Barcocks, and I strode out on to the steps, resplendent in a cloak and a broad, feathered hat, my sword at my side and my breastplate strapped across my chest. The last was at Cornelia's insistence, on the grounds that it made me look more martial and would also protect me against a further assassination attempt by the scarred man, though I was no longer wholly convinced that I had heard what I thought I had heard after the attack on the road back from Newmarket.

'*The Honourable Matthew Quinton, Captain of His Majesty's ship the* Seraph, *the heir presumptive to the Earldom of Ravensden!*' cried the steward-designate of that same man-of-war, for Phineas Musk had been pressed into service as master of ceremonies. This was much to the chagrin of old Barcock, the steward of Ravensden Abbey, but the easterly winds had brought him his first cold of the winter and taken his voice away. Besides, he was needed in the kitchens, supervising the chaos engendered by his formidable goodwife, out of which somehow he managed to deliver a reasonably regular supply of food and drink to the shivering masses outside.

For shivering we most certainly were. It was like the depths of January: the great snowstorm of the morning had abated, but flakes were still falling, and the hundreds of guests were broken up into small groups huddled forlornly around braziers or torches. All the men wore cloaks or thick coats (several coats, in the case of some), and many of the more genteel sort wore gloves. Three earls – our near-neighbours Bedford, Kent and Manchester – stood together, perhaps reckoning there was strength in numbers ahead of the inevitable moment when my mother would descend on them and berate them yet again for supporting the Parliament's cause during the late civil wars. The women stood around disconsolately, ruing the fact that their lavish dresses had to be concealed beneath the thickest coverings available to them, their splendid décolletages hidden away to prevent frostbite of the bosom, their exquisite hemlines acquiring more and more mud as the hundreds of feet turned the snow into slush and our lawns into a swamp. Cornelia should have been among them – indeed, she should have stepped out by my side – but her disgust at the purpose of the event had made her take to her bed, proclaiming loudly that she was ill. Mother would have none of it, of course, and a most terrible scene passed between them; or at least, there were the beginnings of a most terrible scene, averted immediately and entirely by Cornelia's suggestion that her symptoms might be morning sickness. Mother changed in the blink of an eye from screaming vulture to clucking hen, insisting that Cornelia should rest, sending her plates of jelly and other delicacies, and summoning no fewer than three doctors to attend her. In some matters Mother could make Machiavelli look like a milksop, but in others, she could be as naive as a new-born. For as we left the room, Cornelia winked outrageously at me.

I went down into the crowd, and was fortunate to find Francis Gale near the foot of the steps.

He said, 'Matthew. Grand event, this. Good punch. Better mulled wine. Now. You'll be needing a chaplain for your forthcoming voyage, I presume?'

The Reverend Gale was already well into his cups, but even so, this was direct even by his standards. I said, 'Good God, Francis, you're not tired of Ravensden already, surely? Jermy's legacy hasn't ground you down?'

'Not at all, my dear Matthew! Francis Gale is made of stronger stuff.' The vicar of Ravensden belched loudly. 'But during her recent visit to the Lord Bishop, your mother impressed on him the difficulty of the task facing me, the manifold backslidings of the dissenters of the parish, and so forth. In fact, she impressed all of that so well onto his Right Reverend Lordship that he has just sent me a young curate, an eminently serious and hard-working Oxford man, who insists on doing absolutely every piece of work connected with the parish, no matter how trivial. You'll see him at church on Sunday, for he has offered to take the service in my place. I think he has ambitions to be an archbishop.' *As did the young Francis Gale, once, I thought.* 'But it struck me that a voyage might be beneficial to us both. We can see if my curate can sink or swim, and I can have a last moment of excitement before I settle down to long years of delivering dull sermons from the pulpit of Ravensden Church.'

'Well of course, Francis,' I said, 'if the Archbishop consents to you taking a leave of absence – '

'*The Most Honourable Sir Venner Garvey, Member of Parliament for the borough of Rievaulx, and the Lady Garvey!*' bellowed Musk.

My beloved sister Elizabeth stood at the top of the steps, clad in a rich green cloak. Almost as tall as I, she towered above her minute (and far older) husband. Lady Garvey was one of the most elegant and beautiful women on which a man – even her brother – could cast his eyes; or at least, so she was when she stood still. For when she began to descend the steps, as at all other times, my dear sister had the gait of an elephant. By contrast, Sir Venner Garvey, the carbuncled and devious time-server who had been such a staunch supporter of our late Lord Protector, moved so daintily that one could have sworn he was suspended in the air by invisible strings.

I had seen Elizabeth when they arrived a little earlier, but she was late (as ever) and shrieked something about needing at least three hours to prepare herself before rushing off to her childhood room to commence the process. Now, though, the Garveys came at once to my side. Elizabeth kissed me in her usual uninhibited way, Venner congratulated me on my new command, and I introduced them both to Francis.

Elizabeth said, 'So Cornelia's taken to her bed, then? Promising signs of a pregnancy, Mother says?'

'Umm – well, we pray so – '

'Oh, for Heaven's sake, Matt. She might be able to fool Mother, but she can't fool me. If Venner hadn't dragged me here, I'd probably have done the same as her.'

It was rare that I exchanged a glance of knowing fellow-feeling with my good-brother Sir Venner, but this day was an exception. I heartily disliked Venner Garvey – I disliked his Cromwellian past, I disliked his hypocritical mock-Cavalier present, I disliked the fact that the king seemed to feel a need to fawn on Venner and his kind. Above all, I disliked the fact that the prosperity of his Yorkshire estates had persuaded our mother to insist on my dear elder sister's marriage to him. But on occasion, Venner could be strangely diverting company. I was about to ask how their children fared – young Venner and Oliver, my nephews – when the doors of the abbey were flung open once more and Musk proclaimed, '*The Most Noble Lady Anne, Dowager Countess of Ravensden!*'

My mother had briefly forsaken her accustomed black, and as was usual in her case, she had gone to the opposite extreme: she was clad all in white.

Mother descended the steps slowly. She had forsaken her sticks – she almost never produced them in public – and had straightened her back as far as it would go, even though I knew that would keep her in agony for as long as she held the position. But she did not show it. Hundreds of eyes were upon her, and she knew it. At moments like this she was once more the young Lady Anne Longhurst, one of the beauties of the court of the first King Charles, and the Lady Caldecote, the fearless Cavalier termagant of the great civil war. So she was still, in her mind's eye.

She paused at the foot of the steps, looked around her, and as I had predicted, she made directly for the three noble earls, who bowed at her approach.

There was no time for me to resume my conversation with Venner and Elizabeth. Musk was in position again and cried with especial pride and volume, '*My Lords! Ladies, gentlemen, esquires, yeomen, and those of other estates and conditions! I give you that most high and noble lord, the Right Honourable Charles Quinton, tenth Earl of Ravensden, Baron Caldecote, Privy Councillor of the Kingdom of England!*'

My brother looked pitifully small and wasted against the great grey walls of the abbey. His pallor resembled the snow that lay all around, but even so, he had evidently rejected a cloak in favour of a modest frock coat. He wore no wig. Charles hated ostentation of any sort, and to be standing thus, at the top of the stairs and with hundreds of eyes upon him, would have been mortifying indeed. He descended slowly, favouring his right side; for it was his left that had taken three musketballs for the king at the Battle of Worcester, leaving him barely alive.

He made his way toward our little group. Elizabeth ostentatiously nudged Venner Garvey, who said, 'Ah. Yes. You must forgive me, Matthew, but I have some matters of parliamentary business to discuss with Sir Samuel Luke, who I think I just spied by yonder brazier.' He made to move towards the distant Luke, but that path took him directly past me, and as he brushed my arm he whispered, 'You and I must talk, shortly. And alone. The undercroft, say, in an hour? About this business of the mountain of gold.'

Venner's words shook me to my toes, for who but a close circle around the King knew of my mission? But there was no time to dwell on the matter, for no sooner had Venner left our circle than Francis Gale, too, excused himself. He had just sighted the Dean who presided over the parishes of our region, a pompous, prating little man whom he heartily despised and thus wished to avoid at all costs.

So, finally, the three surviving Quinton siblings were alone together. Elizabeth kissed Charles profusely, and I offered formal congratulations on his betrothal. My brother seemed embarrassed by that gesture, and said, 'Matt – yes, thank you, of course – I'm sorry that we haven't had a chance to talk, or for you to meet My Lady informally – '

Elizabeth said, '"My Lady", indeed! Not "Louise", then? It is common for a betrothed couple to be on first name terms, brother.'

Charles blushed at that. He looked downcast and lost, and in that moment I knew that he was truly troubled, for the Earl was ever a man in command of his emotions. He whispered, 'It will be for the best. Yes, for the best.'

Musk was ready to announce another; his most important introduction of all, in fact. But the man who had bellowed the names of the rest of us showed his feelings on the matter by almost mumbling, so that only those of us who were still close to the steps could have heard his words. *'Lords, ladies… etcetera, etcetera… the Lady De Vaux.'*

Those who did not hear him continued their hubbub of conversation, but gradually that stilled as more and more became aware of the startling apparition that stood at the top of the steps. Even I, who was predisposed to be unimpressed, stared at her in undisguised astonishment. Elizabeth's jaw had fallen. And over by the three earls, my mother smiled.

The Lady Louise had eschewed a cloak or winter garb of any sort. Instead, and seemingly oblivious to the bitter Muscovite wind, she was clothed in a vast, billowing satin gown of the brightest red, cut so low in the bosom that her decency must surely have been imperilled with every breath she took. A great stiff collar at the back, something like the unfeasibly vast ruffs of the old queen's days, framed her jet-black hair, set high above her face. Even from a distance, I could see strong features, a wide mouth, and eyes that seemed to penetrate to the most distant parts of the great assembly. Individually, none of her features were truly remarkable, but taken together, they gave her an aura of serenity and duplicity, arrogance and power, that I have only ever observed in the features of two other human beings; and both of those were kings.

The lady came down the steps slowly, but even so she did not do what all the rest of us had done, discreetly checking our footing on each icy, slush-bound step in turn. She looked only ahead, imperiously. Every eye was upon her, and she knew it. More eyes, indeed, than were present at the reception, for I could see my own bedroom window, and Cornelia was framed in it, remarkably recovered and looking down upon the scene below. Her face was a picture; indeed, could have been taken from a picture. When I lived in exile in the Low Countries, I saw many paintings by an old Flemish artist called Brueghel. He often chose scenes of horror and death, portraying men and women with twisted screams of death-agony distorting their faces. That afternoon, my Cornelia could easily have modelled for him.

The Lady De Vaux knew the duty of her rank, that much was certain. While her husband-to-be entertained his insignificant siblings, the future countess made directly for her predecessor and the three earls.

Very quietly, and seemingly not to either Elizabeth or myself, Charles said, 'She will suit. If God wills it, she will suit.'

A familiar voice, restored this time to its full volume, called out once more. No-one had expected Phineas Musk to make yet another announcement, so every eye turned to the top of the steps, and to the quite astonishing spectacle that stood there. Nor had they expected any further announcement, if there had to be one, to be in Latin. '*O domini honoratissimi dominaeque honoratissimae, nec vos omitto, o qui honorem minorem meretis!*' cried Musk, whose command of the tongue of Cicero, Tacitus and the Caesars was surprisingly fluent.

'Oh Christ in Heaven,' hissed Elizabeth. 'Not even he would dare this, surely? To upstage a new countess on this of all days – '

But Musk was into his flow. *'Vobis praesento doctorem illum sapientissimum et inlustrissimum, Tristram Quintonem magistrum collegii Mauleverensis in Universitate Oxoniensi!'*

Two page boys held up Uncle Tristram's vast black-and-gold gown as he descended the stairs slowly and grandly, as befitted the Master of an Oxford college. He made his way through the throng, bowing left and right as though he were the king, doffing his broad doctoral cap to all and sundry. I caught my mother's wrathful stare: it made the Medusa seem like a blinking rural innocent.

Doctor Tristram Quinton stopped before us, brushed down the shocking green-and-gold frock coat that lay beneath his magisterial gown, and said mischievously, 'Sorry I'm late, children. Have I made a scene, do you think?'

He looked utterly unlike his brother, my late father, or so the latter's portrait in the hall and my dim childhood memories attested. Instead, he bore a remarkable resemblance to Holbein's painting of the sixth earl, who (it was said) had made a pact with the devil and still rode the local highways by night, seeking virgins to defile. Then approaching his fiftieth year, the Master of Mauleverer was an ugly, angular man with unkempt grey hair; he refused to wear wigs, which he detested. A florid face framed by a great nose and ears gave him something of the appearance of the hobgoblins of ancient legend. His interests in the sciences, especially alchemy, were well known, and added to his sinister reputation. I had already seen a few of our older tenants cross themselves surreptitiously as he passed by, a full century after England ceased to be popish.

I said, 'I'd assumed you would stay away today, uncle. We all had.'

Tristram glanced over at the Lady De Vaux, who seemed to be staring at him with an oddly detached mixture of curiosity and hostility. He said, 'Had to come and have a look at the murderous harpy. Know thy enemy, and all that. Damn me, though, that's not a bad body.'

'*Uncle!*' hissed Elizabeth.

'Oh for God's sake, Lizzie, I'm Master of Mauleverer, sworn to celibacy thanks to collegial statutes that haven't been revised since Cardinal Pole was in swaddling clothes.' He grimaced. 'Well, sworn to not marrying, at any rate – which isn't quite the same thing, so my eyes can rove wherever they wish. Other organs, too, come to that. Anyway, Matt my boy, where's that bold wife of yours? I'll need some of her cheery and obscene conversation after an hour among these drones.' I told him, and he grinned. 'Good girl. That's Cornelia to the life. I'll inspect her later – after all, I am a Doctor. Philosophy, Medicine, it's all one at the end of the day. Hell's bones, though, there's that old fart Montagu of Manchester. And Kent. And that's not Bedford behind your mother, is it? Oh sweet Jesu, so it is. What a holy trinity of tedious, sanctimonious old bores. Belted earls be damned. I'd belt them all from here to Stamford!' Tristram's head swivelled, his gaze falling on members of the throng in their turn. The members of the throng gazed back with hostility, dread or pity, depending on how well they knew my uncle. At length, both recognition and relief softened the Master of Mauleverer's diabolic visage. 'Ah, by God, there's Franny Gale! Now that's an improvement. A man of God with a heavenly capacity for drink. I'll – oh Lucifer's shit, here comes your mother and our brood mare – '

Elizabeth and I dutifully kissed our mother on both cheeks. Even Tristram and she exchanged the courtesies of good-brother and good-sister, although their kisses were as charged as that which Judas planted on Our Lord. Elizabeth was then the first to kiss the Lady Louise, followed by myself. I did so with all the enthusiasm of a man kissing a serpent, but was surprised to find the experience not unpleasant. In close company, the soon-to-be countess appeared demure, even innocent, an impression belied by her fantastical choice of garment and by her clear, cold eyes. She was shorter than Lizzie but rather taller than Cornelia, and her raven-black hair still bore no hint of grey, although she was clearly well past thirty; she was mightily perfumed, as though to obscure any stench of murder that might still cling to her.

Her voice was winsome but strangely clipped: a tone I have heard often, usually in courtiers who affect a new accent to conceal the one they were born with. 'Dear sister and brother!' she proclaimed, after the manner of a Drury Lane diva. 'Oh, what delight this moment brings me! I rejoice that my happy betrothal to your dear brother the Earl will make us one joyous family ere long!' But her eyes did not speak of delight, happiness and joy.

Uncle Tris swayed a little, and I thought he would be sick. But he recollected himself and kissed her hand with grave formality, even managing a 'My dear lady.' I could tell from the direction of his gaze that even Tristram's bitter hostility to our new countess was somewhat assuaged by the close proximity of her formidably impressive cleavage.

The countess-to-be dutifully enquired after the health of Elizabeth's two boys, who were as all boys are – 'too prone to snot and inexplicable grazes', as Lizzie said, for she had few of the illusions that can accompany motherhood. Our mother, who had possessed illusions aplenty (and still did) raised her eyes to the heavens, but kept her peace.

Then it was time for the unsettling blue-eyed gaze of the Lady De Vaux to focus on me. She said, 'So, Matthew. You have a new commission, I gather? A Fifth Rate frigate mounting thirty-two pieces of ordnance, but lately completed at Blackwall?' Unsettling indeed. Encountering a woman who knew anything about ships of war was like encountering a haddock that could ride a horse. I mumbled something, and she said, 'Now, dearest brother-to-be, you must tell me everything about your voyage in the *Jupiter*. There are so many rumours at court about what really happened. Empty tales, probably, but it is so good to know the truth behind the dark fantasies of conspiracy that foolish men conjure up, is it not?' At that, Uncle Tris choked and began to cough violently. I slapped his back, and the lady said, 'Oh, *poor* Uncle Tristram! I shall return to talk to you when you are composed, sir. Now, sister Elizabeth, you really must introduce me to your dear husband, Sir Venner...'

As the Lady Louise took Elizabeth's reluctant arm and steered her away, Mother moved to Tristram's side and hissed, 'I hope you choke to death, you treacherous, rebellious, preposterous old devil.'

Despite being purple in the face, Tris managed to spit out, 'Oh, go and boil in your own juices, you unnatural harridan. And I'm younger than you, you decayed ancient bitch.'

Ours was indeed a contented family.

The undercroft of Ravensden Abbey was a low, dark, vaulted room that had once served the monastic infirmary above. Now it stored the hogs-heads that kept the Quinton family supplied with beer and wine, but their number had been diminished significantly by the festivities proceeding apace outside, and there was ample space for a young man and his far older brother-in-law to discuss what should have been the most closely guarded of all secrets of state. Or so the young man had erroneously assumed.

Venner was already in the undercroft when I arrived, contemplating some ancient piece of monkish graffiti on one of the pillars by the thin light from the single fireplace at the one end of the room. He turned to me, and did not prevaricate in the slightest: Venner Garvey had only two conditions, the blunt plain-speaking for which his native Yorkshire is renowned and a mastery of dissembling and deceit that matched the two acknowledged masters of those arts, Lucifer and King Charles the Second. Today was evidently to be a time for plainness bordering on the brutally abrupt. 'So, Matthew. The mountain of gold. You're in favour of this mission, I presume?'

Knowing the question would come, I had spent much of the past hour of tedious introductions and dull conversations mulling over an answer in my head. 'With respect, Sir Venner, my mission is a secret entrusted to me by the King and His Royal Highness. I am honour bound not to talk of it to any man, not even my good-brother.'

'Whom you do not trust in any case.' Venner Garvey's breath came out in a little cloud, for despite its fireplace the undercroft was little warmer than the gardens beyond. 'But you see, good-brother, *I* trust *you*. I also respect your sense of honour and duty, Matthew. You can believe that or not, as you wish, but it happens to be true. However, I do not respect the ability to keep secrets of those in the immediate circle of His Majesty and the Duke of York. The whole court leaks like an incontinent whore, Matt. Take your commission in the *Jupiter*, for instance. That business of the attempt to overthrow the King, and the great battle that you fought off Ardverran Castle.' I felt myself sway. The King himself had assured me that this would be the most guarded of all state secrets – or at any rate, the most guarded before this of the mountain of gold. With equal effect, it seemed. 'Oh, don't concern yourself with that, Matthew, I raise it merely to illustrate my point. Many of us who loyally served the late Commonwealth have absolutely no interest in trumpeting the treachery of another of our kind – God, how some of the rabid Cavaliers across the chamber from me in the Commons would love to have that knowledge, to throw it back in my face! No, on that matter I concur entirely with His Majesty's concern to keep it a secret, or at least as much of a secret as it is possible to sustain within the cesspit that is Whitehall. But the mountain of gold is quite another thing.' He moved away, seemingly intent on examining an unusual mason's mark in the vaulting. 'Tell me,' he said, 'you know your history, Matt. You know the history of the late troubles in this land, too – how could you not, as the son of a great Cavalier martyr? So, good-brother, where do you stand on the issue of absolute monarchy as against limited monarchy?'

This was an abrupt change of direction indeed, especially in that place and that time: coming to us clearly from but a very few yards away was the laughter and conversation of men whose families had recently killed each other in the cause of one form of monarchy or another. But I was used to such switchback debates; after all, I had been trained in the arts of rhetoric and philosophical discourse (and much else besides) by Uncle Tris, who once trounced that much cried-up old charlatan and alchemist Isaac Newton in public debate – only to spoil his case somewhat by triumphantly punching his opponent on the nose, an incident strangely unrecorded in the many panegyrics written in honour of *Sir* Isaac upon his relatively recent demise. So I thought for a moment, then said, 'Absolute monarchy is an unadulterated monstrosity, fit only for the likes of the French and the Russians, who enjoy being bullied by their rulers. History undoubtedly teaches us that, as do the present times. Whereas England was always a mixed monarchy, with king, Lords and Commons all working together for the common good. Until the year forty-two, at any rate.'

'Ah yes. The year forty-two. I had the misfortune to be there as a grown man, of course, and to have to make a choice, whereas you, Matthew, were barely – what? – two years out of the womb? So tell me of the year forty-two, and of the choices that your father and I made.'

This was dangerous ground, but there was little point in dissembling; not that I ever could on the matter of my father. 'My understanding, good-brother Venner, is that you and your kind sought to hem in the late king, to take away his powers, to make him a puppet king little better than a Doge of Venice, a mere figurehead. Whereas my father and the Cavaliers sought to preserve the kingly authority – '

'And to do away with Parliament?'

'No, sir, most certainly not to do away with Parliament, but to keep a proper balance between the powers of Parliament and those of the king.'

Venner turned sharply towards me.

'Indeed. And that, then, was the cause for which his late Majesty King Charles the First also fought?'

Trapped. 'I – I believe – my uncle told me – '

'Ah yes, your uncle, the esteemed Doctor Quinton, who supported the Parliament's cause so notably in print, even if he did not actually take to the field in its behalf. He told you what, exactly? Or shall we go outside and ask him?'

I swallowed hard. 'He – well, he told me that my father came to share his own doubts about the king's motives. Claimed that the king was truly bent on creating an absolute monarchy in England, and that the war was the means to that end.' They were terrible words, and I felt shame as soon as I had uttered them.

Venner's face betrayed no sign of triumph. 'Quite. In other words, your father, your uncle, the three noble earls out yonder and many others beside all agreed about the England we wished to see – a mixed monarchy of the three estates. Our only disagreement was about the precise distribution of power between the three, and by no means all of my colleagues in Parliament sought the complete diminution of the king's role that you expounded just now.' Venner Garvey sighed. 'Whereas the late king, of course, had a different agenda. He misled many of those on his own side, your father among them, in his bloody quest for absolute power. That was the tragedy of the late troubles, Matt. Both sides were fighting and killing each other in the name of King and Parliament, you see – all of us except the king himself.'

I was a little calmer now and said, 'Sir Venner, I have had similar conversations with my uncle. But how can this history of the late troubles affect my forthcoming voyage?'

My brother-in-law looked directly at me (something he rarely did) and said, 'Bear with me if I put to you some assumptions that you might not wish to hear, Matthew. First, let us assume that our present monarch has inherited at least some of his father's craving to be absolute. After all, any such inheritance might have been reinforced by those long years spent in exile in the likes of France and Spain. It is an open secret that he particularly admires his cousin King Louis and the power that he wields. Is that not so?' I had to nod, for I knew Charles Stuart well enough to know the truth of it – had seen his undisguised, childlike awe at the splendours of Fontainebleau and Chambord, and his knowing admiration of Louis the Fourteenth's government. Moreover, my brother, who knew King Charles better than any man, had often confirmed this to me. Sir Venner continued, 'Second, let us assume that as a result of the first, the King simply tolerates the present Parliament – tolerates it because he relies upon it for money, and thus cannot be rid of it even if he wishes. This is especially so if the King seeks a war with the Dutch and the funds to pay for it, as perhaps you know better than I.' Indeed I did. The city was full of war-talk, the merchants contending that driving down the Dutch once and for all would give England all their trade and make her the dread and envy of the world. Unlike Venner Garvey, too, I knew the full scope of the mission on which I was embarked, for it was laid out explicitly in the detailed orders the King had given me at Newmarket: regardless of the outcome of the hunt for the mountain of gold, my *Seraph* and the senior warship in company with us were to harry the Dutch trading posts in West Africa, to fight their forts and ships if they challenged us, and to replace the flag of the Seven Provinces with that of Great Britain wherever we could. In short, we were to be the instrument that would bring about a new and final Dutch war. 'Now of course,' said Venner, 'I have no quibble with the notion of another war against the Dutch.' Naturally he would not, given how mightily he had profited from the Commonwealth's war against that enemy; whereas I, who had a Dutch wife, had quibbles aplenty. 'But,' he continued, his voice increasingly urgent, 'let us further assume that regardless of whether or not we have a war, the King suddenly acquires a vast new source of income, far greater than anything Parliament can vote him in a generation. Enough to pay for wars against the Dutch, and the Spanish, and the Sultan, and whoever else takes his fancy; even against his own parliament, say. Why, then, should he continue to put up with a quarrelsome institution that causes him so much trouble? Why not emulate the example of his French cousin? What greater triumph for a man who venerates his father's memory than to achieve his father's dearest ambition?'

I struggled for words. 'Sir Venner, this cannot be the case – I trust the King – I hold his commission, I serve him in honour and duty – ' But even as I spoke those words, I recalled Charles Stuart's own words to me on Newmarket Heath. *To be the richest monarch of all, able to make my country the greatest empire that the world has ever seen, able to do anything that I wished.* And in that moment, I came to a terrible epiphany. I had always revered Charles, the King. But suddenly I understood that it was possible to serve the office of King while mistrusting the man, Charles Stuart; and in that moment I seemed to feel the presence of my father, who had reluctantly fought and died for the previous holder of that same office, a man whom he knew to be arrogant, duplicitous and incompetent.

As if he could read my thoughts, Venner Garvey said gravely, 'Think on the cause that your father believed he was dying for, Matthew, rather than the false one that he truly served. Then ask yourself if you, too, wish to serve the false cause of ending parliaments forever, and bringing down our good old English constitution. Oh, this mountain of gold is probably a chimera, good-brother, merely the wild fantasy of a desperate man. But in the name of Parliament, I tell you this. If such a mountain really exists, then you must not find it.' He leaned toward me, half his face red from the undercroft's firelight, the other half in black shadow. He whispered, 'This mission must not succeed, Matthew. This mission *will not* succeed.'

Six

The snows were gone within a week, leaving behind a sea of mud that choked the roads from Bedfordshire to London, and then from London to Deptford. Musk and I rode out from Ravensden House, my family's crumbling old town house on the Strand, struggled past the herds of cattle and people thronging London Bridge, and rode east, entering open country at the edge of Southwark. The fitting for sea of my new ship was to proceed, and I had decided that it was time for me to inspect her. Venner's dire warning had made me wary of sabotage, and I wished to reassure myself that the security provided for my ship by the officers of Deptford yard was adequate. But leaving London for Deptford, no matter how briefly, also removed me from any prospect of an unwelcome encounter with Colonel Brian Doyle O'Dwyer, who had become something of a celebrity at court thanks to his sharp wit and exotic history, or a reencounter with My Lady Louise, who was also about the palace. Of course, fitting-out was by no means a prelude to the immediate departure of the *Seraph*, although I have met very many who believe that sending a ship-of-war to sea is but a trivial matter. An order is given – let us say, by the King; let us say, during a race meeting at Newmarket – and behold, the very next day His Majesty's ship the *Utopia* is under sail, *en route* for foreign climes and untold glory! Many of those who hold to such opinions are poor innocent souls who cannot be expected to know better: for instance, women and soldiers, and these days that new-fangled beast, His Majesty's Prime Minister.

In truth, preparing a ship for sea, and especially for an expedition to far distant shores, is not a matter of a day's jollity, with cheerful tars singing songs as they hoist sail and put to sea as soon as their captain comes aboard. Would that it were. The ship has to be fitted, and that means endless orders to and from the Navy Board, the master shipwright of the dockyard, the master caulker, the master attendant, the master dogsbody, and so forth, followed by several weeks during which the works are carried out wrongly, and finally made good again. Then the ship has to be armed, which in the case of the *Seraph* meant prising thirty-two good and true pieces of ordnance out of His Majesty's Master of that deadly commodity, ensconced at Tower Hill. The Master of the Ordnance claimed to know nothing of it, protested that he had no demi-culverins in store, and sought sanction to have new ones cast at the furnaces in the Weald of Kent. The ship still has to be victualled, and the victuallers are accustomed only to supply those ships that put to sea in the summer; a sudden and unexpected decision to put out ships in the winter makes the clerks of the victualling office turn white in the face and protest that this is a matter beyond all human comprehension. Then there is the not inconsiderable matter of the other ships meant to sail in company with one's own. In our case this meant the *Jersey*, one of England's finest and strongest fourth-rate frigates, and a hired merchantman carrying a party of sixty soldiers, considered essential for the security of the landward part of our expedition to find the mountain of gold.

Even when all of these obstacles have been overcome, the ship has to be manned. The year sixty-three was a year of dead peace, so there was no possibility of press warrants being authorised – the King, then in the early days of his rule, still courted popularity, and pressing in peacetime would have sparked riots in every port in England. Thus I would have to depend on volunteers, and who but madmen would volunteer for a voyage to Guinea, a coast notorious for fatal sickness? It seemed almost unnecessary for my good-brother to put any more obstacles in the way of the voyage of the *Seraph*, but I knew him too well to believe that he would not do so somehow and at some time.

Thus I rode for Deptford in a state of cloying unease. Musk did not share my sentiment; indeed, by his own standards he was unsettlingly brisk. Presumably he wished to inspect our ship to establish exactly where large quantities of illicit imports from West Africa could be stowed without attracting the attention of the customs officers. However, the encounter with my scarred would-be assassin on the road from Newmarket meant that at Cornelia's behest, Phineas Musk was now also my personal guard, his commitment to the task cemented by a purse of twenty guineas. Being Musk, he complained bitterly about the responsibility and yet carried out his duties with an almost fanatical enthusiasm. Thus he horsewhipped a clergyman who rode a little too close to me in Horsleydown ('thought I saw a scar,' Musk explained), and it was only with considerable difficulty that I dissuaded him from shooting dead a suspicious-looking beggar. All in all, it was an uncomfortable journey, made doubly so by the bitterly cold east wind and the roads that resembled quagmires; we must have passed a dozen carts or coaches stuck in the morass, and resisted all the cries of their crews to come and help them, for pity's sake. All told, I was doubly relieved when we finally came within sight of Deptford yard, beyond which stood the ruinous old palace of Greenwich where Harry the Eighth had been born, all those long years before. The crumbling buildings were nestled between the bare hill of the Black Heath and the river, on which ships, barges and boats of countless sorts jostled each other for passage to or from the port of London.

We rode by the side of the dockyard wall up to the gate, where the porter informed us that the master shipwright was already aboard the *Seraph*, moored in the wet dock. This was to the left as we entered the yard. A great storehouse directly ahead of us dominated the entire site and towered above the dry dock to our right, sealed by wooden gates from the high tide on the hull-crowded grey waters of the Thames. Dockyards produced arguably the most prodigious stinks in England, for no other site of comparable size encompassed the smoke from coal furnaces and forges, the smells of wet and dry wood, boundless quantities of tar and rope, and that final indispensable ingredient, the stench of several hundred men. Around us, all was bustle: or at least, what passed for bustle in a royal dockyard, those very Edens of sloth. Shipwrights were at work on an old Third Rate at the head of the double dry dock, some taking down decayed timbers, others hammering new ones into place at an approximate rate of one treenail every fifth minute or so. A few caulkers and labourers stood at the head of the dock, listening to a harangue against their gross idleness from their foremen. Two men painted a boat, lingering over each brush stroke as if they were Titians capturing a Madonna. The sound of sawing rose from the various sawpits scattered around the yard. Great piles of wood were stacked in every available space: huge trees stripped of their branches, that would soon make masts; strange curved pieces that would make futtocks, the bends in a ship's hull; and planks galore, ready to enclose a ship's side. A few men were sawing away at some of these piles, cutting them expertly into pieces almost exactly three feet long.

'Chips,' I said to Musk. 'Pepys once told me that by tradition, men can carry out of the yard left-over pieces of wood up to three feet long. They can sell them, or use them in their own homes, or whatever they will.'

Musk frowned. 'Three feet's a damned big chip, I'd say. And those don't look like left-over pieces. If I didn't know better, I'd say they were cutting them deliberately to that length.' A man walked past us, weighed down by the great piece of oak that he carried. Musk snorted. 'Chips so large, they have to carry them on their shoulders!'

I laughed. 'Don't impugn the good name of the Deptford shipwrights in their hearing, Musk. We want to get out of here alive, remember.'

The *Seraph* was berthed as the outermost of three ships tied to the east wharf of the wet dock, so we had to cross the decks of a Fourth Rate and a Fifth to get to her. The King was quite right about my new command. I was starting to know enough of ships to recognise those that looked the part and those that lumbered sluggishly around the oceans. The *Seraph* was trim, riding high in the water because the guns were yet to be put in her. She had finer lines than my old *Jupiter*, which had been about the same size; her masts were stepped a little further back and had more of a rake. Old Shish, the master shipwright of Deptford, was on the quarterdeck, seeing to a problem with the starboard rail. He and I were acquainted vaguely of old, for my first command, the doomed *Happy Restoration*, had been fitted out in this same yard. He bowed as I approached, but I had forgotten that it was always a mistake to approach Jonas Shish from leeward, for he reeked prodigiously. I introduced him to Musk, the ship's steward-to-be, and they nodded curt acknowledgment to each other.

'Well, Captain Quinton,' Shish said. 'Glad they've given her to you, sir. She's a good ship. Almost as good as any I could build myself, indeed. Now, you'll wish to see your cabin?'

'In due course, Master Shish. I'd be grateful for an introduction to the ship's standing officers first.'

The bluff and pungent Shish seemed nonplussed. 'You've not heard of the funeral then, sir?'

'A funeral?'

'Indeed, Captain. Old Graves, the boatswain. Appropriate name, that. Appropriate when you're dead, that is. Laying Graves in the grave, as it were. Anyway, they're burying him over at Erith today, and all the rest of them have gone over there. That's Lindman the gunner, Harrington the purser, Bradbury the cook and Shish the carpenter.'

'Shish? A relative of yours, Master Shipwright?'

''Sakes no, sir. Well, probably at some distance, but there's enough of us in these parts, you see. Every second man from here down to the Nore is a Shish or a Pett.' As Shish began to show Musk and myself around the upper deck, I began to think on this matter of the boatswain's death. A previous voyage had begun with the unexplained death of a ship's officer – her captain, in that case – and that parallel, alongside the recent experience with the scarred man, had perhaps made me unduly suspicious. With as much insouciance as I could manage, I asked Shish how the man had died. 'Oh, Graves had the pox, sir. And griping of the guts. And you should have heard the man's chest. But that's not what did for him in the end. Got into a brawl with some Hamburgers in an alehouse down at Gravesend – over some lewd serving wench, they say. He did for two of them before the third put a knife in his ribs. Even then he lingered five days.' Shish sighed. 'An example to us all, really, considering he was seventy-eight.'

With my suspicions assuaged, a calculating proposition took shape in my head. The office of boatswain was vacant. No doubt a crowd of solicitants for the place were already thronging the Palace of Whitehall, hoping to lay their merits before the Lord High Admiral, the Duke of York. But the captain of the *Seraph* had a worthy candidate in mind, and all matters relating to this voyage were the prerogative of the King, whose ear the said captain had in ample measure. *Ergo*, just as in card games kings trump all lesser cards, so in life kings trump all lesser mortals.

With these thoughts spinning in my mind, jostling for attention against recollections of Sir Venner Garvey's warning and uncalled-for remembrance of the Lady Louise's look and smell, I began my inspection of my new command. The shipwright might have been a moonstruck lunatic, but his creation was anything but insane. Like all Fifth Rates, she had but the one fully covered gundeck, with eleven ports cut into each side. There were another three on each side abaft, beneath the quarterdeck and the small poop at the stern, and another two on either side of the forecastle. The latter was somewhat more truncated than it had been on the Fifth I had commanded most recently, the *Jupiter*, but the quarterdeck was a little longer, which promised more space for the captain's perambulations. The only sign of the shipwright's peculiarities came on the main gundeck, where a bizarre gallery of animals and astrological symbols had been carved into each beam; at the centre of each was the familiar face of a man with foliage sprouting from his mouth, so alike their fellow Green Man that adorned the porch of Ravensden Church.

At last we came to the great cabin – *my* cabin. But even three months ashore had been sufficient to make me forget one of the essentials for the comfort of Matthew Quinton's life in the navy, especially when so many other thoughts served to distract him. I stepped through the door, straightened up, and immediately struck …

'Beam,' said Musk, helpfully but belatedly.

Shish said, 'Ah. I think we may need to raise the deck a little, Captain. Six inches should suffice, I think? I'll order Bagwell and a party of men off the *Nonpareil* to attend to it. But you're not due to sail until, what, the end of the year? Ample time.' I felt the beginnings of that throbbing in the forehead which is familiar to all tall men who have to inhabit low structures. Shish continued, 'So, Captain Quinton. What would you fancy for decoration, sir?'

I had no opportunity to reply, for at that moment there was a commotion on the deck. The yard porter, whom I had encountered earlier – a low, squinting creature of no breeding – admitted himself, bowed perfunctorily to me and spoke to Shish in a hushed whisper. The Master Shipwright seemed immediately discomposed by his tidings. 'Sir, it seems we have an invasion.'

An invasion? Great God, had King Louis or the Dutch chosen this moment to exploit England's craven weakness? I felt for the hilt of my sword – 'A host of ungodly foreigners is warring in the town, says the porter, here,' said Shish. 'Warring with my shipwrights, Captain Quinton! The women say they are Turks, or some other breed of uncivilised heathen – Russians, perhaps, or worse. They have attempted to seduce honest goodwives, and my shipwrights won't have it! No, they won't have it! But there is a strange thing, sir. A very strange thing, indeed. They seem to be calling your name, Captain Quinton.'

A cold chill gripped my heart like a vice. Quite equably, Musk said, 'Well, Mister Shish, you're right in one thing, at any rate. Much worse than Turks or Russians.'

We ran out of the dockyard and up the High Street of Deptford. Ahead of us, only a few hundred yards from the dockyard gate, lay the venerable Gun Tavern, where my grandfather had got horribly drunk with old Howard of Effingham, the Lord High Admiral of England, before they both ventured out against the Spanish Armada. Now it was the scene of another great battle. A bloodied shipwright lay in the door, moaning; another came through a window as we approached. I halted and sighed. With as much authority as I could muster, I shouted, 'Cornishmen! In the names of your King and of Captain Matthew Quinton, I order you to desist! Lanherne, where the hell are you, man?'

The sometime coxswain of the King's ships *Jupiter* and *Wessex* appeared in the doorway, holding a shipwright in a tight arm lock. Reluctantly he released the man and saluted. 'Cap'n.'

John Tremar, a behemoth of strength and unutterable violence crammed into a miniscule frame, came up beside him and smiled contentedly. 'Cap'n,' he echoed.

'What is the meaning of this riot, Mister Lanherne, in the name of all that's holy?'

Lanherne, who had served notably as a soldier in the land's dreadful civil wars, looked sheepish and said, 'They were rude, sir. We merely asked them to toast with us.'

'Quite exceeding rude,' said Tremar. A piercing scream came from within the Gun Tavern: it was accompanied by a plea for mercy, cried in a pitiful Kentish voice. There were unmistakeable sounds of large men falling against tables or walls.

'And what toast did you ask them to drink?'

Lanherne brightened. 'Why, sir, this place, Deptford – well, it's sacred to all Cornishmen, you see. It's where our forefathers fought and died, in the year ninety-seven.'

Now, I knew my history of Queen Elizabeth's reign; naturally, for my grandfather had done so much to shape that history. But – 'I don't recall any Cornish action here in 1597, Lanherne. And with respect, we are quite some way from Cornwall.' With that, another of my old coterie, the man-ape John Treninnick, fell through the door, rubbed away a punch to his chin, saluted, screamed with rage and threw himself back into the fray.

Lanherne ignored the intervention entirely. 'Oh, not *Fifteen* Ninety-Seven, sir. *Fourteen* Ninety-Seven. When our proud Cornish boys led by An Gof the blacksmith and Flamank the lawyer marched all the way across England, to London itself. Twenty thousand of them, sir. Got all the way to Deptford Bridge, then took on the king's army. A close run thing, Captain, but the Tudor's men fought an unfair battle – well, at any rate, they had cannon and cavalry, and our great-grandsires had only pitchforks or their bare hands.'

I sensed the impatience of Shish, at my side, for we should have been about our task of quelling this riot, but this was a history unknown to me, and curiosity won out. 'So this was some great cause the Cornish-men were about? To overthrow Harry the Seventh and restore the line of York, perchance?'

Lanherne and Tremar looked at each other. 'Aye, sir, the greatest cause of all,' said Tremar, gravely. 'They didn't fancy paying their taxes that year.'

'So we asked the shipwrights to toast their memory with us, sir, all politely, of course. To toast An Gof in his own words, *a name perpetual and a fame permanent and immortal*. Uttered just before they hanged, drew and quartered him. A request modest enough, Captain.'

'But they were quite exceeding rude.'

It was Musk who asked the obvious question: the one that I should have asked at the very beginning, but to which I already knew the answer. 'And what, exactly, is your business in Deptford, Mister Lanherne?'

The coxswain looked nonplussed. 'Why, Mister Musk, word got down to Cornwall that the captain had a new ship. We beat drums from Penrhyn up to Bude, and there's sixty or more of us here, good and true, ready to list with Captain Quinton once again.'

Another of my old Jupiters, a dark lusty fellow called Summercourt, came through the door at that moment, falling into the gutter in what appeared to be a wrestling match to the death with a hirsute shipwright. I nodded to Shish and drew my sword, for it was time to restore the king's peace to the good people of Deptford. But at least I had the answer to the question that had vexed me during my journey to the yard.

Who but madmen would volunteer for a voyage to Guinea?

Of course.

Cornishmen.

Seven

I still had several weeks of grace before the *Seraph* finally got under way in its pursuit of the mountain of gold. Weeks during which I could attempt to avoid meeting my dreaded passenger-to-be, a feat that I had managed with success thus far. Weeks during which I certainly could not avoid attending the apotheosis of the Lady De Vaux: her marriage to my brother in St Paul's Cathedral. Weeks in which I could reflect fully upon the warning given by my good-brother Sir Venner, and think upon those others who might seek to prevent the voyage of the *Seraph* – or at least, to prevent the continued living of her captain. The scarred man, for one, though there had been no further sightings of him, and increasingly I questioned what I might or might not have heard on the road from Newmarket. The other I had almost forgotten, until a letter came to me one day at the beginning of November. The winds were howling around the ancient abbey – indeed, such was the nature of our home that many of them were howling straight through it – and I was in the library, writing what I calculated to be my fifteenth letter of the day to some functionary or other who had a part to play in getting my *Seraph* ready for sea.

Cornelia brought the letter to me; she always reached the mail first, for invariably most of it was for her. (Letter-writing seems to be one of the national religions of the Dutch, presumably because in their country there is little else to do, and every post brought endless epistles from her parents and her obscure cousins in Gelderland, Friesland and every other 'land' in that muddy nation.) She was in ill temper. Even by our standards, we had been making particularly vigorous efforts to pre-empt the forthcoming debacle at St Paul's by getting Cornelia pregnant. Regrettably, a position recommended by the wise woman of Baldock Forest succeeded only in spraining her back, and she was bent almost double as she handed me the letter. She was still seething at a comment overheard in Bedford, where she and my equally bent mother had gone to purchase some horses – only for a somewhat short-sighted alderman of the town to enquire whether they were sisters.

She said, 'It's from Roger, by the looks of it. He's close to King Louis these days, isn't he? Can't he persuade him to invade before the wedding? That would well and truly thwart My Lady De Vaux – a few hundred French guards and a cardinal or two parading up the nave of St Paul's! *God in hemel*, I'd like to see your mother's face, too, if King Louis' musketeers turn up and cancelled the wedding in favour of a full papist *Te Deum*!'

I sighed and took the letter. Cornelia sat down opposite me (very, very slowly) and picked up an old anatomy book by Galen that had belonged to the alchemically-inclined seventh earl.

I broke open the hugely impressive wax seal of the Comtes d'Andelys, its crest unchanged since the times of Charlemagne, and began to read.

'*Mon cher ami* – ' To render it in the original French is the height of folly, of course, for in these days when the German tongue pervades our court and country, who but the near-dead like myself could comprehend it? In English, then – *'My dearest brother-in-arms! Oh, my esteemed and noble friend, Matthew Quinton! My fellow warrior in the time of greatest adversity –* 'There was much more in the same vein, for although Roger-

Louis de Gaillard-Herblay, seventeenth Comte d'Andelys, was a good man and a true friend, he was, at bottom, French, and alas, brevity is not a characteristic of that mighty race. When the endless expressions of undying affection toward my person finally ceased, there was much on his search for a wife (as yet unfruitful, although a prodigiously plump daughter of the prodigiously rich Duc de Montreuil was said to be a promising candidate), a long discourse on the doings of King Louis and his court (the queen and at least one mistress reportedly pregnant), much on the splendid harvest brought in by cheerful peasants from the fertile soils of his endless fields… and so on. Finally, though, not even a Frenchman could further postpone the matters of substance.

'*My thoughts turn increasingly toward the sea, Matthew, and to the times we had in the old* Jupiter. *As you will already know, my King seeks to make France a greater power at sea, and is ordering a new fleet of ships from our own yards and those of Holland. This is no threat to England and your great navy, of course, but it is shaming that a country the size of France should have no more than a few ancient tubs carrying her proud fleur-de-lis ensign to sea. The King is commissioning great nobles to command his new ships – men with far less experience at sea than my own, though I will confess that my experiences were, shall we say, unconventional.*' (Escaping the wrath of King Louis' minister Fouquet, whose wife he had seduced, the Comte d'Andelys had enlisted aboard the *Jupiter* as a sailmaker's mate named Le Blanc, and I inherited him with the ship.) '*Thus I am tempted to solicit a command. Who knows, my dear brother-in-arms, one day we might sail alongside each other, side by side against a common foe!*' Ever the optimist, Roger evidently had not contemplated the possibility of us fighting *against* each other.

'*Now, Matthew, I turn to this matter of the Seigneur de Montnoir. I have never met this man, but some of my friends at court know him. He is a strange and secret creature, it seems – part warrior, past mystic. Some say he is a descendant of the old prophet de Nostredame, but our court is ever home to a feverish terror of the occult, and I would place little weight on such tales. He has great lands in the Auvergne that have allowed him to indulge his passions. These do not seem to include wine and women, as is the way with most of us in the Second Estate. Instead, my friends inform me that Montnoir is a fanatic. He seems to have convinced himself that he committed a mortal sin by fighting against Spain during our late wars with that kingdom, believing that all of Catholic Europe should be united in crusade against the Turks and the Moors, as well as those notorious and unrepentant heretics, the English and the Dutch. As we know, my friend, there is only one thing more dangerous than a fanatic, and that is a wealthy and well-connected fanatic. Thus Montnoir serves the Order of Malta because it gives him a licence to kill heathens indiscriminately, and in the hope that one day he will become Grand Master, a sovereign prince of Europe and keeper of much of the supposed secret knowledge of the ancients. But he also has the ear of King Louis, who detests mystics unless they tell him what he wants to hear –* '

'Well?' asked Cornelia, looking up from the gruesome illustrations in Galen just as a particularly vicious gust of wind carried a dead bird and some branches hard against the window.

'Roger's thinking of taking a command at sea,' I said, summarising the letter to rather less than its bare bones.

'Oh sweet God, not another one,' my wife said. 'Another sea-captain. Thirty years from now, there you will be, husband. You and Roger and my brother, the admirals of England, France and *Nederland*.'

She chuckled, and took up another book from the table: Foxe's *Book of Martyrs,* a fine source of potentially grisly fates for the Lady De Vaux, most of them involving searingly painful immolations. Within moments, she was engrossed.

I returned to Roger's letter. *'He is convinced that he has two certain routes to the Grand Master's throne. One is to be the discoverer of an unlimited source of wealth, either the philosopher's stone of the alchemists or a great golden hill that is said to exist somewhere in Africa, or better, both.'* I felt a sudden chill as I read that sentence. *'The other is to bring about the restoration of the Order's English and Scottish lands, lost during what you call your Reformation. Thus he takes a close interest in the affairs of your country, Matthew; almost as close an interest as he takes in promoting his dark ambitions. Indeed, it is said that he has an agent or agents in England even now. So beware of this man and those who serve him. From what I have gleaned of him, it would not surprise me if he sought to burn the entire population of England as heretics, whether or not they stand between him and his goals. But while England has such gallant swordsmen as Matthew Quinton to defend her, she need never fear...* (There were several more paragraphs in this vein before Roger eventually reached his valediction.)... *May both the Catholic and Protestant Gods watch over you, old friend, and my undying love to your dear Cornelia.*

    d'Andelys.'

I closed the letter, and as the wind again rattled the windows with a fury carried from the gates of Novgorod, my wife looked up with interest and anticipation.

'Well?' she demanded once more. 'There must have been more than him seeking a command, surely?'

'He sends his love,' I said.

My first moment of reckoning had come. A few days after the arrival of Roger's letter, a nondescript summons from Pepys took me to the Navy Office for a meeting to discuss the progress of preparations for the Guinea expedition; a meeting that would be attended by my new commanding officer and by the man who had inspired the entire scheme, the repugnant O'Dwyer himself. Thus it was a wholly miserable Captain Matthew Quinton who rode the short distance from Ravensden House on the Strand (whither I had moved to oversee the fitting of my ship) to the Navy Office, then housed in a rambling warren of buildings at Crutched Friars on Tower Hill. A torrential downpour in the shadow of Paul's Church did nothing to ameliorate my temper, for it brought to mind a troubling daydream of the Lady Louise standing at the altar within, waiting to be wed: not to my brother, but *to me*. Nor did the fact that almost an hour after the time specified for the start of the meeting, we were still awaiting the two men without whom it could not proceed. I occupied the time by making polite and inconsequential conversation with Pepys, but stole more than a few glances at his colleagues, the others of His Majesty's Principal Officers and Commissioners of the Navy. There, at the head of the table, sat old Sir John Mennes, the Comptroller of the Navy, a man so venerable that he had even commanded ships under my grandfather. Mennes had apparently been quite the handsome peacock in his younger days, or so my mother said, and he still had a face and eyes that betold the shadow of a witty, lusty man. He was a man of poetic bent; a rarity among our sea-officers, most of whom could barely tell one end of a quill from the other. Alas, time and the civil war had not been kind to John Mennes, who could now barely comptrol his own bowels, let alone the King's Navy. He was engaged in conversation with the man who ever led him by the nose, namely Sir William Batten, the Surveyor, a crafty, foul-mouthed old scoundrel who had defected from the Roundheads in the great revolt of the year forty-eight. Every now and again, Batten cast a hostile glance towards Pepys, whom he detested (chiefly because the righteous Pepys was particularly astute at exposing the Surveyor's embezzlements and incompetence alike). Pepys, still relatively inexperienced and in awe of the company, smiled nervously in return, especially when the talk of the great men turned to the growth of buggery amongst our gallants, so much so that pages began to complain against their masters for it.

'Captain Quinton,' whispered Pepys, 'I hear much mention of this word "buggery", but I have no notion of its meaning. Do you, sir?'

That a man perhaps seven years older than myself should be so ignorant (and innocent) was remarkable indeed. 'A matter best kept for another time, I think, Mister Pepys,' I said, as charitably as I could.

Across the table sat Sir George Carteret, Treasurer of the Navy. Sir George was sumptuous in every way: he still affected the dress of a young Cavalier, although he was well past fifty, and both his trim little beard and unwigged locks suggested a man trying desperately to preserve the fading remnants of his youth. He had been little better than a pirate in the civil wars, I had heard, and evidently prospered sufficiently to acquire a parcel of forest in the Americas, which he then somehow managed to elevate into a royal colony. He named it after the Channel island of his birth, from which he had plundered indiscriminately the trade of all nations; but they say it is never likely to prosper, this 'New Jersey' of his creation. Next to Carteret was the most distinguished of the company. This was Sir William Penn, no less, one of Cromwell's legendary generals-at-sea, now all too evidently chafing at the tedium of his shore-bound role as a commissioner of the navy. Penn was still quite a young man, barely forty (although impossibly ancient to my twenty-three-year-old self), and had the nondescript broad face of a provincial choirmaster. Yet he had been a hero of the Commonwealth's war against the Dutch, almost ten years before, and later commanded a mighty expedition of conquest into the Caribbee, duly liberating Jamaica from the tyrannical yoke of Spain, placing it under the tyrannical yoke of Cromwell instead. A timely defection to the royalist cause just before the Restoration ensured Sir William's place as one of the most valued naval advisers to our King and Lord High Admiral. On this day, though, Penn's features were creased with anguish. This might have been due in part to his annoyance at the delay of our proceedings, but it was more likely thanks to the gout; his foot was bandaged and resting upon a stool, and even the slightest movement made him wince as though he was skewered by a death-wound.

There was a disturbance beyond the door. I heard the voice of one of the clerks, low and respectful, followed by an almighty explosion of Irish-accented wrath: *'Hell's arse, boy, do you not know who I am?'* The door was thrown open with great force. Framed within it was an embarrassed clerk (young Hayter, who would become Secretary of the Admiralty) gripped at the ear by a square-shouldered, sharp-nosed man of forty or so. His chin was scarred and he sported a great wig, but the most remarkable thing about him was his hands, which were truly vast in proportion to the rest of him. Penn said mildly, 'You're late, Major Holmes.'

The commanding officer of the Guinea expedition released the clerk, who retreated in disarray, and bowed to the assembled company. 'I crave your indulgence, esteemed sirs all. A matter of honour. A wholly impudent captain of the dragoons. Just ran him through in the Convent-Garden.'

Only Mister Pepys was discomforted by this information – remarkably so, for his cheeks lost all their colour. The rest of us were, at bottom, swordsmen, albeit of the maritime variety, and we could all appreciate and sympathise with the veritable host of reasons that a gentleman like Major Robert Holmes might have had for fighting a duel with a fellow officer (albeit in express disregard of all the dire injunctions against duelling issued by the monarch whom we all served). This Holmes was already a legend among the Cavalier fraternity, although my brother and I looked upon him with a certain ambivalence: for he had always been the loyal lieutenant by land and sea of Prince Rupert of the Rhine, the King's cousin, the very man that our mother blamed for our father's death on the battlefield of Naseby, eighteen years before. Even so, I had got to know him well during the summer, when his *Reserve* had been in the Middle Sea at the same time as my *Wessex*. My initial wariness had evaporated upon true acquaintance; indeed, we had got memorably drunk together at Leghorn. Thus I knew, as Pepys did not, that for all his blustering arrogance and hubris beyond measure, Robert Holmes was a man who would stand and fight for his friends, his country and his king to the last drop of his blood. Better, he had the rudest humour of almost any man I ever knew.

Mennes suggested that Holmes might wish to take his seat for the meeting. The major grunted, looked around in irritation and shouted, 'O'Dwyer, you pox-ridden renegade turd! Where the hell are you, man?'

My heart sank as my old prisoner appeared in the doorway, grinning broadly. He had buried Omar Ibrahim as entirely as he had once buried the young Brian Doyle O'Dwyer. He wore a red military coat with an opulent black baldric; his swarthy face was capped no more by a turban, but rather by a fashionable periwig. 'Pox-ridden renegade turd of a *colonel* if you please, *Major* Holmes!'

My heart now had no further to sink, but still it made the forlorn effort to batter its way out of my heel. Holmes and O'Dwyer had become friends. Of course they had. Two godless Irish rogues, out for themselves and the mountain of gold; the only surprise was that I had not anticipated it.

Fortunately, Holmes sat down between me and O'Dwyer, but not before the renegade had greeted me with insufferable good cheer: 'Captain Quinton! My saviour, no less! It truly gladdens my heart to see you, sir, and to know that we will be comrades-in-arms on this expedition.'

I bowed my head (for he was my superior officer, after all) but made no reply; it is always advisable to say nothing when there is a danger that opening one's mouth might project a torrent of vomit over the assembled company.

Thus the meeting finally began, although at first I was too engrossed in my own discomfort to take much notice. Batten insisted on reading out a long account of the condition of my *Seraph* and Holmes' *Jersey*, although we all knew that these were merely the reports from the master shipwrights recited verbatim, and that as there were no defects of note in either ship, there was precious little point in detaining the meeting with such an account. But Batten would have his say, for was he not His Majesty's Surveyor of the Navy, and should not such an elevated gentleman say his piece at such a meeting? I caught Penn's eye more than once, for he, the most distinguished and recently active seaman at the table, evidently felt as I did (perhaps because Batten's droning seemed to exacerbate his gout, causing him to fidget and shuffle in his chair). Holmes, too, thought thus; that much was clear from his frequent fidgeting, farting and picking of lice out of his wig. O'Dwyer, though, appeared serene, nodding sagely as Batten spoke, seemingly unaware of the fact that every man in that room would have gladly run him through if the King would but turn a blind eye to it.

Then it was Carteret's turn, and thankfully, he was briefer. But after all, Sir George had ten times Batten's intelligence and at least a hundred times his purse, so he had less need to assert his distinction. Penn, too, spoke briefly and to the point, for his interest was entirely in the military side of our expedition. With a large map of West Africa laid out upon the table, he leaned forward awkwardly to point a stick at a long estuary, almost half of the way down the west coast.

'I see the need for Captain Quinton's passage up the Gambia river,' he said, 'if Colonel O'Dwyer's mountain of gold is, indeed, but a few weeks' march from the navigable head of it, as he says.' Penn's glance at O'Dwyer expressed a boundless well of scepticism, but the ruddy Irishman merely nodded contentedly. 'My concern would be with the fort, here – ' Penn pointed at an island, some miles up the river and in the very middle of the great stream. 'Do we know its current strength?'

Holmes said, 'I know that fort, Sir William. Sailed past it back in the year fifty-one, when the prince and I first got wind that there might be such a thing as this mountain of gold. Before we had the advantage of Colonel O'Dwyer's services, here.' He smiled at his fellow Irishman, who bowed his head in acknowledgment. I felt a surge of bile in my throat. 'It was still ruled by the Duke of Courland, then, before he sold it to the Dutch – although I hear he now disputes the validity of that sale. Jakob's fort, it was called. But I'm told the garrison hasn't changed much, if at all. A rag-tag of Dutchmen, Courlanders, God knows what. Hardly a concern to us. And if they challenge us – well…'

He left the sentence unfinished, for all in that company knew the ending full well. It was the ending that I had discussed with my serpentine good-brother, Sir Venner Garvey. The mountain of gold was not the only objective of our present expedition. If the fort in the river challenged us, we would take it. Meanwhile, Holmes was to sail along the coast, ostensibly to give all possible assistance to the trade of the Company of Royal Adventurers for Africa. This innocent-sounding instruction concealed a very labyrinth of subtleties. For the head of the Company was the King's brother James, Duke of York, the Lord High Admiral; its directors and shareholders were the greatest ministers and courtiers in the land. In other words, the Royal Adventurers were the political elite of the state masquerading as an innocuous private company. Moreover, no man attending that meeting in the Navy Office had any illusions about the nature of the 'assistance' that Holmes was to offer the Company, which had been granted possession of almost the whole coast of Africa, from Morocco down to Good Hope, for a thousand years – regardless of whether anyone else was already in occupation. Consequently, Holmes was to take every Dutch fort and ship that he could, all the way down to Cape Coast and beyond. If the Dutch objected, the outcome would be that desired, not-so-secretly, by most good and true Englishmen from King Charles down to the humblest street urchin. We would give the Dutch a war, and this time, we would finish them off.

O'Dwyer, who had been quite silent during all the seamen's talk, finally asserted himself. 'The fort's the least of the concerns, Sir William. The kings of those parts, and the Portugee f- factors who sell their slaves for them; they're the men.' His Irish lilt faltered from time to time, as though he was searching for an English word that he might not have spoken in thirty years. Quite suddenly I saw him as a mere boy of twelve or thirteen, snatched from his native shore for ever; I felt what might even have been an unsought glimmer of sympathy. 'Armies fifty thousand strong, some of them have got, and we're going up there with two ships. I said to the King, I said he should send at least the *Sovereign of the Seas* and a fleet of fifty – '

'Quite so,' said Holmes, 'but from what I observed, Colonel, all the kings of those parts are at each other's throats, and hate the Dutch, who hate the Courlanders, who hate the Portuguese, and so forth. Divide and conquer is the method, sir. And a gratifyingly cheap method it is, at that, as His Majesty had cause to say to *me*.'

'With respect, Colonel O'Dwyer,' said Pepys, 'I have read not a little about those parts, and have discoursed with some who have sailed in those waters, and I have never heard of one of the kings having an army as great as fifty thousand – '

Holmes flashed his most terrifying scowl in the direction of the Clerk of the Acts. 'Why, Mister Pepys, if the good colonel here talks of armies that large, then it must surely be true. Must it not, Mister Pepys?'

The Clerk glanced nervously from Holmes to O'Dwyer and back again, muttered something about it being so indeed, and blushed prodigiously before staring down at the floor. I felt not a little sympathy for him, partly because I, too, had drawn a similar conclusion from O'Dwyer's confident speech. Moreover, I could not forbear to wonder why such powerful kings as the renegade spoke of, with such large numbers of armed men and slaves available to them, had not long ago found and mined the mountain of gold, especially if it lay so little distance from the Gambia River. But this seemed to have occurred to no-one else, not even our supposedly omniscient sovereign, so I held my peace. Indeed, I had done little else the whole meeting; like Pepys, I was more than a little in awe of these great men with their grand titles, and I was but the second in command of the expedition, or perhaps even third: the King's instructions, so precise on such matters as how the gold was to be mined and shipped back to England, were disconcertingly vague on the matter of the relative authority of Brian Doyle O'Dwyer and myself.

Penn returned to the perusal of his map, and pointed his stick slightly further north. 'It is indeed a complicated region, gentlemen,' he said. 'Dutch and Portuguese, as we have heard; Courlanders, and all the rest of them. And these native kings, of course. But I have a somewhat greater concern. Look here. Fort Saint Louis, an outpost of the Most

Christian King. Not so many miles from the mouth of the Gambia. We would do well to avoid – eh – entanglements with the French, whatever we might do to the Dutch.'

O'Dwyer grinned. 'Ah, God bless the French, Sir William. But their fort, there – well, it's just a feeble place, established not five years back. I sailed past it on a Sallee rover but the last summer. The French have no stomach to compete with the Dutch or ourselves for dominion over Africa, good sirs.'

Pepys seemed about to say something, but one glance at Holmes' ghastly smile deterred him. Instead, we passed on to the matter of the manning, arming and victualling of our ships; the only matter in the meeting that was likely to be of interest to me, if truth be told. This was ostensibly the domain of the Comptroller, yet old Mennes made but a poor fist of it. He had muddled his papers, and confused *Jersey* with *Seraph*, even myself with Holmes. After a few minutes he stuttered to a halt, and Pepys, who had been longing to intervene since Sir John began, seized his opportunity.

'If I might assist, Sir John?' he enquired helpfully. Batten rolled his eyes to the heavens, Holmes yawned theatrically, but Carteret, whose office of Treasurer gave him precedence at that table, nodded encouragement. Pepys began a confident peroration on the issues in hand; too confident, for no man likes to be upstaged by one who is so much their junior, and among that company of seamen (myself and the former Omar Ibrahim included), every single one of us resented sea-affairs being expounded with such masterful lucidity by a complete landsman. Holmes in particular chafed at the Clerk's account of the manning of the *Jersey*, which he said should be furnished with one hundred and fifty men when Holmes contended that she should have two hundred. After but a short exchange, Pepys conceded that the matter should be referred to the Lord High Admiral. Not even Holmes could openly challenge the authority of the King's brother, yet he glowered at Pepys like a child denied its favourite toy.

'Turning now to the manning of the *Seraph*,' said Pepys (avoiding Holmes' eye), 'we have the sixty-two men already entered by Captain Quinton at Deptford yard. I understand there is some dispute with the constable of the town over releasing five of them from the lock-up –'

At last, it was time for a Quinton to speak out. 'That matter has been determined satisfactorily, Mister Pepys,' I said. 'A warrant from one of the Justices of the Peace for Kent has entirely resolved it.' I did not add that the warrant had been obtained by means of a letter from the Right Honourable the Earl of Ravensden, Privy Councillor of the realm, who had used his authority unilaterally in the (correct) belief that his friend King Charles would not overrule him if and when he eventually learned of it.

Pepys inclined his head in gratitude. 'Thank you, Captain Quinton. That is satisfactory news. Meanwhile the lieutenant of the *Seraph*, Mister Castle –' (to my gratification, my old lieutenant from the *Wessex* had agreed to sail with me again) – 'Mister Castle is raising men in his home town of Bristol, but writes that despite his credit with the seamen there, he has so far raised only fifteen. However, the new boatswain of the *Seraph* passed his warrant here at the office but this morning, and set off directly for Wapping to beat the drum on Captain Quinton's behalf.'

This was news indeed!

The new boatswain of the *Seraph*; in other words, Kit Farrell, the bluff young tarpaulin who had once saved me from a watery death, and who had since endeavoured intermittently, and with but intermittent success, to turn me into a proper seaman. (And in return, I had taught him the mysteries of reading and writing, which he had mastered rather more swiftly.) So Kit was returned from his voyage, and had immediately set about his new task without waiting for his captain's behest. That was the man, to the very heart. I vowed to ride directly from the Navy Office to Wapping upon the conclusion of our meeting.

Fortunately, there were few more formalities to conclude, and ere long we emerged into the light of day. The rain had stopped, but the clouds behind the tower of St Olave's were still dark and threatening. As we walked to our horses, I asked Holmes why Pepys seemed so fearful of him, and why he, in turn, seemed to take such delight in baiting the Clerk of the Acts.

'Oh,' said the Irishman cheerily, 'well, for one thing he's a mere jumped-up quill-scraper from the Fens, and why should he presume to lecture men of honour and the sword on their business? For another, he tried to fob me off with an incompetent creature of his as Master of my *Reserve* in the Middle Sea – you remember I talked to you of it, when we were at Lisbon?' I nodded noncommittally, for Holmes had got me quite astonishingly fuddled on that occasion. 'And for yet another thing,' said Holmes as he mounted, 'he thinks I've had his wife.'

This was a revelation; for one thing, I had not known until then that Pepys was married. 'And have you?' I asked as I, too, climbed into the saddle.

Holmes shrugged. 'Do you know, Matt, I honestly can't remember? So much wine, so many women. A man forgets.'

Holmes and I rode east, by Crutched Friars into Woodruff Lane, then alongside the north moat of the Tower and into East Smithfield: the major for an assignation with a goodwife of Bow (a matter on which he was graphically explicit) and myself in quest of the new boatswain of the *Seraph*. O'Dwyer went west toward Cheapside, accompanied by two burly crop-headed lads. Holmes told me that the renegade had hired these to guard him against attack or abduction by his many enemies. Holmes was dismissive, but I recalled that oven-hot day on the deck of the *Wessex* and the skeletal, black-cloaked figure of the Seigneur de Montnoir, with his interest in the fate of the corsair captain then known as Omar Ibrahim, and I was not quite so certain.

We rode along the Ratcliffe Highway. The road was busy with carters, seamen and all sorts, bound hither and thither, so Holmes and I confined our talk to the doings of mutual friends and acquaintances. As we came near the turn for Wapping, where we were to part, Holmes suddenly looked all about him, searching for eyes and ears that might be able to report on us. Satisfied that we were quite far enough from any man's ken, he leaned over in his saddle and said conspiratorially, 'You know one of the best recent proofs I've had of the existence of God, Matt? The King decreeing that O'Dwyer should sail on your ship, not on mine. Damn me, if he set foot on the *Jersey* I'd probably skewer him inside a day.'

'But I thought – '

'You thought he and I were friends?' Holmes smiled. 'Ah, Matt my boy, never let outward appearances deceive you, especially outward smiles. I detest that renegade fuckwit and every breath he takes. But our Sovereign Lord humours him awhile, and I am ever His Majesty's faithful servant.' As I took in this startling revelation, Holmes bowed, as though to a regal version of myself. 'Besides, if his tale turns out to true, our Colonel O'Dwyer will be a quite remarkably rich and powerful man, and Robin Holmes here has a mind to be the great friend of the rich and powerful.' Holmes smiled. 'But then, if his tale turns out to be true you can call me the Caliph of Baghdad. For unlike all the rest of them, Matt, from the King down to our Mister Pepys and even your good self, I have been to the Gambia River. I've hunted for this mountain of gold before, and I know the great truth that nobody in that meeting was prepared to utter.' Holmes shook his head wearily. 'There's no such thing, Matt. You know it. I know it better than any man. We all know it, deep down. But the King wishes to believe in it, because God knows, he needs to get himself a mountain-full of gold from somewhere, so the rest of us go through the motions – and if those motions just happen to bring on a war with the Dutch, well, perhaps that's not too trifling a prize in its stead. Not least for the likes of you and me, Matt. War is always the best friend of our kind. An admiral's flag for me, I think, and a title; I have a mighty urge to be the first Lord Holmes of Mallow, you see. A great command for you, Matt Quinton, who will be an earl anyway. In any event, glory, honour and enough prize money to buy each of us a county or two. Aye, old Robin here will gladly bring on a war, if that's what His Majesty wants.' We reined in our horses, for we were at the crossroads where I was to turn right for Wapping. 'I tell you this, though, Matt. The moment O'Dwyer's mountain of gold is exposed for the giant lie it is, we'll take turns at running him through, you and old Holmes here, side by side. How does that prospect suit you, Captain Quinton?'

Despite myself, I grinned. 'It suits me very well, Captain Holmes,' I said.

Eight

All sea-towns smell. About all of them, there is the inevitable stench of the sea: mud and brine, salt and fish, their natural fragrances, and usually the sweat of seamen too. But I have observed that each also has its own, distinct stink, meaning that even a blind navigator might recognise each new port by its odour. Old Cadiz always stank of pine. Port Royal seemed to have a faint whiff of gunpowder upon the wind, as if a hundred buccaneers had just discharged their muskets all at once; which, perchance, they often had. Amsterdam reeked of sheer unconcealed luxury, its thick airs sensuous with all the spices of the orient and the perfumes of very rich men and their whores. Closer to home, I always found entering Portsmouth akin to walking into an overflowing latrine, for the tides rose and fell too little, and the harbour mouth was too narrow, to wash away all the excrement from the town and the ships in the haven, especially when a great fleet was manning for the wars. And Wapping: well, Wapping's distinctive odour was that of decaying human flesh. It did not matter if there were no pirates' corpses strung up on gibbets along the river (although if truth be told, it was a rarity if there were not); it counted for naught if no dismembered torso had been washed up on its foul Thames shore for months. Wapping always seemed to stink of an open grave.

All the rich scents of the place assaulted me as I rode into the street called Wapping Wall, heading east through the throng of two- and three-storey lodging houses, inns, warehouses, timber yards and roperies that lined both sides. Down some of the alleys to the right, I could spy the wharves that lined the Thames and, sometimes, the great river itself, though the tide was low. The road was filled with long trains of horses and donkeys laden with bales, and carts filled to overflowing with offloaded cargoes, all going in the direction opposite to my own, toward London and the men who would grow rich from their coming. I attracted much attention, and not only because I was one of the few travellers on that road heading away from the city. Men of quality did not generally stray into these strange, private worlds along the river, and I received my fair share of profound Thames-side wit: 'fuck off, you sodomising Frenchie!' was perhaps the politest barb flung in my direction. This was the anniversary of the accession of Her Most Illustrious Majesty Queen Elizabeth of glorious and immortal memory, the second of the great national feast-days in the month of November. It was ever an occasion when the senses of Englishness and Protestantism were at their highest among our ignorant masses, and it seemed that at least some of the denizens of Wapping shore might not have been sober since the festivities for Gunpowder Treason day, twelve days before.

The sight of the sword at my side sufficed to keep the ruder brethren of the shore at bay. I was bound for almost the edge of Wapping, where even all those long years ago, it was already starting to merge indistinguishably into Shadwell. That was where I knew I would find Kit Farrell, saviour of my life in my first command, my teacher in sea-craft in my second, and now the new boatswain of my *Seraph*; his mother kept an alehouse in an alley near the Pelican Stairs.

As it was, I heard Kit's voice long before the road twisted round and I caught site of his family home, the Slaughtered Lamb. His shouts punctuated the beating of a drum, the traditional means of attracting volunteers to the king's colours. '– aye, the son and grandson of true heroes, my lads! What better day to list for the *Seraph* than today, the feast-day of Queen Elizabeth, whom the first Matthew Quinton served so mightily? What better omen could you want, friends? Who better to serve under in our present times than the second Matthew Quinton? Brother to the King's closest friend, my brave boys! So come, take the king's bounty and make your way to Deptford yard! The *Seraph* will bear you south to glory – '

'To the grave, more like,' cried a rough London voice. This was greeted by growls of approbation.

'*Seraph* be damned,' another shouted, 'I'll take my chance on the next Levanter out of Erith Reach!'

'Aye, that'll be a better wage than the King'll pay this side of the next century!' These cries, too, were greeted with approbation.

'Quinton?' shouted another. 'Another of the king's cursed gentlemen captains, put in by his papist friends and his painted whores. Popinjays, the lot of them. I'd rather sail under Old Nick!'

'Lost his first ship, too – the *Protector*, as was. And God knows what he did with the *Jupiter*, last year – they say she'd been holed twixt wind and water, and but rudely repaired before they brought her back into Woolwich – my brother's a shipwright down there – '

The murmuring and clamour of hostility grew apace. I was torn. My heart told me to ride forward boldly to the aid of one of my officers; and more, to that of a good friend. But my head gave other counsel. My appearance among the hostile throng at that moment would surely do nothing to change the mood. If anything, it would probably worsen it, for I somehow doubted that the entrance of Captain Matthew Quinton, stage left, would have been greeted by an enthusiastic ovation. Worse, it might diminish our prospects of raising men at another time, among the better disposed (or more desperate) who thronged the tidewaters of the Thames. And worst of all, my entrance might undermine Kit; and if I knew anything of Christopher Farrell, it was that he could fight his own cause.

My decision made, I turned my horse toward an alley on the left. There was rough, open ground at the back of the houses, and I made my way down to the rear of what was obviously an alehouse of modest proportions. I dismounted, tethered my horse and made my way towards the back door. As I did so, a formidably large and pungent woman emerged from within.

''Sakes,' she cried, 'it's the captain! John! Get your brother – '

I raised my hands to quieten Mistress Farrell, Kit's mother, whose speech still betrayed traces of her native Lancashire. She was a woman of little intelligence, but when it came to the rough protocols of the foreshore, there were few to equal her, and she caught my gist at once. She led me within and deposited me in a small side room, well away from the front windows and from the other customers, who were already far advanced in their lusty and liquid commemoration of the Virgin Queen. John Farrell, one of my friend's numerous elder brothers, served me a mug of Hull ale with a surly nod and a grunt.

I waited perhaps half an hour for Kit to abandon his unequal struggle with the recalcitrant mariners of Wapping shore and retreat back to the embrace of his family's alehouse.

'Captain Quinton!' he cried as he came into the room. 'I had not expected you to wait upon me!'

We shook warmly and toasted both each other and good success to the voyage of the *Seraph*. 'Good success indeed,' I said, 'though from what I could hear, you were having but little success in persuading men of the merits of listing with us?'

Kit Farrell shrugged. 'It's hard enough to persuade a man to take a passage to Guinea at the best of times, sir. But with the winter coming on, and so many men already abroad or looking for a fat voyage in the spring, long before we'd be back from Africa... And if truth be told, Captain, trying to raise men on a holiday was arrant folly on my part.

My mother said as much to me, this morning. But I had a mind to be about our business, and idling away even Queen Elizabeth's day is not my way.' That was Kit, above all. I do not think I ever met a man of more purpose, for whom every hour was to be employed to best advantage. Of course, much of this derived from the Puritan faith of the Farrells, and from sermons drummed into him by the dissenting ministers who thronged Wapping and all the other Thames-side towns, fighting their endless battle to turn this least promising of congregations from drink, fornication and fist-fighting to the ways of Our Lord.

I said, 'I think your first instinct was correct, Boatswain Farrell. Tomorrow, we shall both resume the business of the *Seraph*. Today, I think we should fall in with the common herd. From what I have gathered of the great Gloriana, she would have demanded nothing less of us.' I raised my tankard, and we both toasted the immortal memory of Elizabeth the Great, Queen of England.

We were not too far gone on drink – our toasting had reached the memories of both of our fathers, and had not yet descended to wishing damnation upon the Pope, the French, the Dutch, the Spanish and all other foreigners (as it had in the larger rooms elsewhere in the alehouse) – and we were discussing our respective recent voyages, mine in the Middle Sea aboard the *Wessex*, Kit in the Caribbee aboard the *Caroline Merchant*. The sun was down, for we were on the cusp of winter, and Mistress Farrell had John bring us more candles, and sea-coals for the fire. The hubbub in the Slaughtered Lamb grew ever louder, for the burning of the Pope was imminent, and men were beginning to throng the windows and to spill out into the road to watch the procession pass. The cacophony of rough trumpets and drums heralded its approach. There were songs galore, a dozen or more sung at once, all of them tunelessly. And yet, in the midst of all that, I thought I heard a child's cry: 'The dockyard! There's a fire at Deptford!'

Kit and I ran to the front of the Slaughtered Lamb, but it was well-nigh impossible to go any further. Both sides of the street were lined by an almost impenetrable throng of laughing, drunken spectators. Between them, a great river of people flowed triumphantly toward the east, singing and shouting as they went. Near to the head of the procession was the focus of it all, transported in mock-state upon a bier: a dummy dressed up in clerical alb and chasuble, adorned with a gold-painted wooden replica of the papal triple tiara.

Kit and I pushed our way through the crowd, but it took a seeming eternity to reach the procession itself, and even longer to steer a crazy course through the laughing, dancing, drunken revellers within it. The crowd on the river side was smaller, and we had less difficulty shoulder-charging our way through the whores and children who had congregated there. Through, then, and down an alley to the foreshore – to see the houses along the shore of Rotherhithe illuminated by flames a mile or more to the south and east of them. The bend of the river made it impossible to see the source, but Kit and I both knew that there was nothing beyond Cuckolds Haven, at the east end of Rotherhithe; nothing until one came to the royal dockyard at Deptford.

'We'll not find a horse-ferry at this time of night,' I cried to Kit, 'even if the ferrymen aren't all filling their bellies with ale!'

'Aye, sir,' he said, 'and the procession will block the road down to Shadwell and Poplar, else we could have ridden down the Isle of Dogs and hoped for a boat at the bottom of it. One thing for it, Captain, though there's no wind to sail with, and the tide's against us!'

We ran down to the river's edge, where Kit picked out one of the smaller boats that lay in the mud and began to push it down the mud toward the Thames stream. I joined him and promptly fell face down into the mud for my pains. We pushed again, and got the boat into the water. It was a bitter night, and frost was already forming on the banks and on the wales and planking of the boat itself. The tide had but recently turned, so as we settled to the oars, we both knew that we faced a hard row against the flood. So it proved. It would have been a struggle for a decent crew, but Kit and I were an ill-matched pair of oarsman; he had been born to this, whereas I was the landsman personified, splashing water clumsily with every stroke I took. Thus, with Kit to larboard and me to starboard, my inadequacies and the tide meant that we often veered alarmingly for the Surrey shore. This would have been a sufficient problem in an empty river, but the Thames has probably not been empty since first it bubbled its way to the sea. The narrow channel was full of ships and lighters at anchor, and as the tide came in, more and more of those that lay on the mud floated free, their cables placing a web-like succession of new obstacles in our way. My oar struck buoys or became entangled with cables more times than I can now recall. Yet on we went, for livelihood and honour depended on it. My hands and face were numb with cold, my shoulders and arms screaming with pain, yet like one of O'Dwyer's galley slaves, I rowed as though driven by the lash. As we made the turn in the river at Limehouse, I glanced behind me and saw over our bow the flames reaching up from Deptford yard. I was relieved that it seemed to be contained in the west side of the dockyard (the great storehouse was not ablaze, and I could see the outline of a great ship in the dry dock, which was obviously safe). But then I recalled that our *Seraph* lay in the west part of the yard, on that side of the wet dock, and …

'It's a bad fire,' said Kit, who had also glanced over his shoulder. 'Pray God they can contain it. If there's too much timber and tar and pitch scattered around the yard, the whole place could be consumed. Every ship in it too, by God.'

Just then, flames erupted behind us, too; directly in my line of sight. I could hear shouts, and singing, and saw the tiny shapes of men dancing, silhouetted against the flames of a great bonfire. The procession had reached its end, down on the Poplar shore, and the pope was being burned. All was well in drunken Protestant England.

We rowed on, although all of my sinews were now joined as one in a loud chorus of pain and protest. At last we were into Greenwich Reach, and made for the dockyard wharf itself.

As we clambered ashore, I saw the true extent of the fire. Much of the area on the west side of the wet dock was ablaze, and the flames were already consuming the Fourth Rate that lay alongside the quay. To give credit, lines of dockyard men were hard at work bringing up buckets of water from the dock; others manned pumps as though their lives depended on it, or played the hoses connected to those pumps onto the flames. But most of the men were clearly concerned with dousing the fire at its source, thus saving the rest of the dockyard – as, indeed, they were right to do. Almost none seemed concerned with saving the three ships that lay alongside the west wall of the dock, the outermost of which was my command, the *Seraph*.

Kit nudged me and pointed to a man whom we both recognised: Cox, the Master Attendant of Deptford, and thus the officer responsible for the safety of the ships in the yard. We ran to him, and asked him what he proposed to do to save our ship.

Cox scratched his head. 'Not much we can do, Captain Quinton. The *Harlingen* has already gone, God help her, though we tried to cut her free. We can't get men across her to save *Antelope* before the flames reach your *Seraph*.'

'Good God, man,' I cried, 'surely we should be getting men out in boats and cutting *Seraph* and *Antelope* loose, rather than just standing here and letting all be lost!'

'No men to spare, sir. We have to save the yard – '

Now, it was true that the fate of three ships, and relatively expendable ships at that (for *Harlingen* was an old Dutch prize, and *Antelope* a mere Fifth Rate like *Seraph*) was as nothing to the fate of the entire dockyard. Yet the loss of *Seraph* would postpone my mission by many weeks, if not months, the time it would take to ready a new ship to be made ready to replace her. If, indeed, she was replaced at all. King Charles the Second was as fickle as the English weather, and by Christmas he might have forgotten all about the Mountain of Gold, especially if by then he was newly ensconced with Mistress Frances Stuart. And then how long it would be before Matthew Quinton found a new command, with pay and honour? I could see my good-brother Venner's face, and hear his prophetic words: *this mission will not succeed.*

The thought struck me in that moment. *Sabotage?* But surely not even Sir Venner Garvey would risk the destruction of Deptford yard and the deaths of perhaps scores of men in this way?

Such suspicions could wait.

'Captain,' said Kit, 'I recall that you can swim, sir.' He had learned as much when we survived the wreck of the *Happy Restoration* off Kinsale two years before. It was a precious rare skill for a sea captain in those days, and even rarer among our glorious English aristocracy; but I had learned through necessity, diving into Ravensden pond when I was eleven to save my beloved twin Henrietta from drowning. (Much good it did her, for the consumption took her but two years later.) Kit pointed to the axes that were strewn around the quayside from the attempt to cut free the *Harlingen*. He said, 'Do you think you can swim with one of those?'

I stripped off my shirt. 'One way to find out, Mister Farrell.'

We both tucked axes into our belts and breeches, and lowered ourselves down the planking that lined the dockside. And came to the water. I cried in pain, for my limbs still ached from the row, and now they were assaulted by the bitterest cold I had then known in my life. For this was a hard frosty night in an English November, and only a madman would think it a good time to swim in the wet dock of Deptford.

Somehow I struck out for the *Seraph*, with Kit a little ahead of me. My heart raced. The cold seemed to be biting through my teeth. The axe was heavy and threatened to pull me under. Yet youth and desperation are powerful counterweights, and in truth, it was but a short swim. I took hold of a cable and hauled myself out of the water, climbing the larboard side of *Seraph* to her main deck. Kit was already there, and we both turned to see that the flames from the *Harlingen* were already creeping along the larboard rail and onto the main deck of *Antelope*.

Pray God that neither ship had powder aboard, concealed by embezzling gunners.

Even if we were not blown to glory, we had precious little time. With gusto, Kit and I set to the task of hacking at the cables that secured our ship to the doomed *Antelope*. But Master Attendant Cox's men had been unduly scrupulous in making the ships fast. A myriad of cables fastened us to *Antelope*, and they were evidently of good, strong rope, not the poor stuff that the roperies often fobbed off onto the navy.

I glanced up, and saw the flames creeping closer across the deck of *Antelope*. The *Harlingen* was already well ablaze, flames roaring from her deck and the single stump of a jury mast that served most of the ships laid up in ordinary.

We had no time. Two men, alone, would never cut all the cables and free the *Seraph* before the flames reached her. Kit must have had the same thought, for he looked at me and shook his head.

A sudden shout – '*Kernow bys vyken!*' – and I saw the enormous shape of George Polzeath rearing up out of the night onto the larboard wale of the *Seraph*. Behind him came Julian Carvell, brandishing an axe with the relish of a man who was more accustomed to using it as a weapon. Behind him, Ali Reis the Moor and another five of my men.

Polzeath saluted. 'Saw you and Mister Farrell by the light of the flames, Captain. Master Shipwright ordered us not to leave the dousing of the tar-house, but we don't take orders from the likes of him, sir.'

Carvell grinned; his accustomed condition. 'We're the ones who can swim, Captain,' he said in his slow Virginian drawl. 'Not many, but we should be enough.'

At that, we all set to the cables. The larboard side of *Antelope* was well alight now, and *Harlingen* was all but gone, a blackened, blazing hulk. A new danger to us, indeed, for as she burned she began to settle toward the dockyard wall, pulling *Antelope* over toward her. I could already feel the new strain on the cable I was hacking with fury; very soon, *Antelope* would begin to pull us over, into the flames. The row, and the swim, and the cutting, had all produced an exquisite concoction of pain throughout my body, but I drove myself on, chopping at the cable with as much vigour as I could muster. Seeing my weakness, a cheerful youth of Mount's Bay named Penhallow joined me at the cable, hacking at it with all his might.

'Hot work, this, Captain!' he cried.

Indeed, the heat from *Antelope* was reaching us now. Sweat ran down my naked torso, and I could feel my brow begin to burn. For we were now at an angle, and it was growing with every minute – it was harder to keep a footing …

My cable broke, and almost decapitated me as the end sprang back. Penhallow grabbed me and prevented me from falling. Almost at once, Kit and some of the others severed their own cables, and others broke of their own accord. The balance had suddenly switched in our favour, and I was flung bodily onto the deck as *Seraph* righted herself. We were free of the *Antelope*.

Free from her, aye; but not apart from her. A wet dock is sealed against the tide, and has no current. Opening the gates would have taken too long, and besides, the tide was flooding. We needed to put distance between ourselves and the *Antelope*, but how?

'Trewartha, Reis, Polzeath – with me!' cried Kit. 'Carvell and the rest of you, unbatten the main hatch!'

At that, Kit and his three men raced below deck, while Carvell and the others hastened to open the large hatch in the middle of the main deck. Within barely a minute or two, a large wooden beam was being thrust out of the hatch to the waiting party on the main deck, Penhallow and I at the fore; a yard, and by the size of it, probably that for the foretopmast. Another followed in short order; a little smaller, so probably for the mizzen. Thank God we already had many of our stores aboard, these yards among them.

Kit and his men came back to the deck, and I saw his purpose. We divided into two parties, each taking one of the yards, and pushed them out over the side, resting them on the larboard rail. I joined the party with the foretopyard; no time to stand on dignity. With our makeshift poles, we shoved ourselves away from the flaming hulk of the *Antelope*. Inch by inch, we began to separate from that hellish conflagration. Our hull and our faces were scorched. But would it be far enough – ?

With relief, I saw four boats coming out to us from the head of the dock. Master Attendant Cox was finally coming to our aid. We caught the lines as they were thrown up to us, and the boats took the drifting *Seraph* in tow, bringing us safe over to the east side of the dock and a berth alongside the old *Nonpareil*. Behind us, I could see the Master Shipwright's teams suppressing the last remnants of the fire in the yard itself. *Antelope* was burning hard, her upperworks all but gone, and beyond her, it was just possible to see the blackened bow of *Harlingen*, burned almost to the waterline.

But we had saved the *Seraph*.

Only later, as I was clad in dry clothing and took soup and wine in the Master Attendant's house, did I consider exactly what we had saved. My employment and my pay, certainly. A good new king's ship, true. But we had also saved the lunatic quest for the apocryphal mountain of gold, and ensured that the next few months of my life would be spent in the company of the renegade O'Dwyer. That night, and so many times since that night, I have wondered whether I would have done better to have ignored the half-heard cry of 'fire!' from that child in Wapping, and allowed the *Seraph* to be consumed by the flames.

Nine

One of the abiding consequences of Doctor Tristram Quinton's unexpected and (from my mother's perspective) entirely unwelcome appearance at the introductory reception for the soon-to-be-Countess Louise had been a reluctant edict from the Earl prohibiting the Master from visiting his family home, Ravensden Abbey. This was certainly not of Charles' conception; in executing it, he was merely the mouthpiece for his mother and his bride-to-be. My dear brother was perhaps the bravest man I ever knew, but alas, his bravery extended only as far as the male sex. When it came to women, he ever surrendered with greater haste than old de la Palice when faced with Henry the Eighth's array of knights at Guinegate. I found the whole business shaming, for what authority did my mother and brother possess to deny my uncle the right to visit the graves of his own father and brother? In truth, I need not have concerned myself: Tristram being Tristram, the edict was a dead letter from the beginning. A sudden increase in nocturnal sightings of the spectral sixth Earl of Ravensden suggested the means by which my uncle paid his respects to the eighth and ninth of that ilk. By day, the Master of Mauleverer College took great delight in turning up at the kitchen door, disguised as a beggar, to be taken in by a happily colluding Goodwife Barcock. However, the edict created certain difficulties for those of us who were uneasy about our prospective Countess Louise. We could not meet in person at the abbey, and Francis Gale's vicarage was rather too close to Ravensden and thus to the prying eyes of my mother. Mauleverer, over which Tristram Quinton ruled almost as a feudal monarch, was too distant for frequent visits; and with the fitting out of the miraculously preserved *Seraph* now in its final stages, I was taking enough of a liberty by being away from the ship at all. Thus it was that on a bitter day at the very beginning of December, Cornelia, Francis Gale and I found ourselves on a punt, being steered by a reluctant Phineas Musk through the thin ice that encrusted one of England's last undrained fens.

After a quarter-hour or so, our destination appeared gloomily through the freezing fog that enshrouded the hoar-crusted reeds on all sides of our craft. A small, ancient building with ruined arches and columns abutting it, the farmhouse of Skelthorn had once been a Dominican friary, and was virtually unaltered from its monastic function as the institution's refectory. At the Dissolution, the decayed friary fell into the hands of Earl Harry, my ancestor; and his grandson, Earl Matthew, in turn had made it his chief bequest to his younger son. Tris obtained a small but useful income from the estate, but more importantly, it provided him with a refuge far from both my mother and the disapproving glares of the Fellows of Mauleverer; perhaps by way of compensation for their unfashionable and uncomfortably popish prohibition on marriage, the college statutes permitted the Master a quite remarkable degree of latitude in the residence requirements. Consequently, here at Skelthorn my uncle could indulge his passions to the full; both his passion for women (or at least, for such women as could be tempted to such a remote place by such a strange man) and for what he termed the exploration of all human knowledge, physical and metaphysical, but which was described by most contemporaries rather more crudely as mere alchemy.

As the punt approached, we could see the dim light of candles through the thick glass windows and a thin pall of smoke struggling to free itself from the chimney and fight its way through the low, chill fog. Tris's steward, a silent, bent old man named Drewett, came down to the water's edge to greet us in his unsmiling way. He led us into the main room of Skelthorn, the vaulted former refectory. We were all used to the sight, of course, but I still wondered how strangers would react upon seeing it for the first time. It was not so much the chaos of books and jars strewn on every available surface, nor the unmistakeable odour of sulphur, which seemed to be the essential ingredient of most of my uncle's experiments. Rather, it was the fact that the whole of the far wall was taken up by skulls. Shelf after shelf of skulls. During the chaos of the civil wars, Tris had apparently 'liberated' an entire medieval ossuary from a church somewhere in the wilds of Derbyshire. Quite what earthly, or indeed unearthly, purpose they could serve on this remote isle in the Fens, only Our Lord and Doctor Tristram Quinton knew.

The Master of Mauleverer greeted us with his customary cheeriness and somewhat chaotic domestic arrangements; Drewett produced jugs of good Malaga sack, claret and ale, hard cakes of indeterminate age, and some plates of coffee, though quite how (and why) this newest and most fashionable of London commodities had made its way to the remote fastness of Skelthorn was a sublime mystery.

Francis, Cornelia and I settled onto ancient and precarious stools, while Tris sank into his vast carved and cushioned chair, somewhat resembling the throne of an oriental potentate; no doubt another appropriation during England's age of blood. Drewett disappeared, while Musk took up a watchful position as far from the unsettling wall of skulls as he could possibly be.

So we began. I was made to repeat the story of the Deptford fire, although Cornelia, Musk and Francis were well enough versed in it. But Tris was never a good listener, and fidgeted throughout. Besides, we were all there to discuss rather different fare; a subject that my uncle began to address in an unexpectedly oblique way.

'The mastership of an Oxford college,' said Tris expansively, 'gives a man many advantages. Status and prestige, naturally. A fine wine cellar, of course.' He took a sip of his claret. 'But perhaps the greatest advantage of all is that he has an ever-growing corpus of present and former students, drawn from all parts of the land and from most ranks and conditions. Now, if a college master is minded to use it in such a way, my friends, then he has at his disposal a web of agents as all-pervasive as old Thurloe's.' And Tris would have known that better than anyone, I thought; there were persistent, though always unconfirmed, rumours that he had served John Thurloe, Cromwell's spymaster-general, in certain important but never entirely specific ways. These rumours provided an intriguing counterpoint to the undoubted fact that Thurloe's remarkably efficient organisation had never quite succeeded in capturing one of the most sought-after royalist agents of the day, namely Tristram's nephew, my brother, Charles Quinton, the tenth Earl of Ravensden. 'Thus it is in the present case,' Tris continued. 'Our Lady De Vaux has been markedly adroit in covering her tracks, but not quite adroit enough, perhaps. Although we are clearly still some way short of possessing sufficient evidence to convince even the most venal of magistrates.'

'English law,' said Cornelia dismissively. 'I will never understand it. The plainly guilty go free and become rich while the plainly innocent are hanged.'

'That is why it is called common law, my dear,' I jested, 'for it is applied only to the common people.'

My wife was evidently in no mood for such humour, and cast me the blackest of looks.

'Let us consider what we now know about the lady,' Tris said. '*Imprimis*, the matter of her first marriage to Sir Bernard De Vaux, in the year forty-five. Now, this Sir Bernard was a staunch cavalier, whose seat lay at Billringham in the county of Lincoln. A remote and blasted place,

I'm told by the young exhibitioner of Bourne who has made enquiries for me in those parts. Forty-five was the bloody climax of our civil wars, of course – the year that claimed my dear brother, the late earl.' My father, in other words, fallen in glory upon Naseby field. 'And yet in the midst of all that slaughter, Sir Bernard De Vaux, a lifelong bachelor aged fifty-nine, discovers for himself a new bride, and a bride of no more than sixteen or seventeen summers at that. De Vaux had been a notable commander for the King in the south, where he harried Dorset quite mercilessly, and had returned to Billringham to recover from wounds. He brought the girl with him – several thereabouts can recall the day – and they were wed within a week.' Tris paused and took an exceptionally long draught of wine, even by his catholic standards. 'A strange thing, then, that no record of the marriage exists. No entry at all in the parish register, for the page for that year has been torn out. A pity, for the then vicar of Billringham was most assiduous in providing details of a bride's parentage, and of her native parish if not an inhabitant of his own.'

'What was she hiding?' cried Cornelia. 'Answer me that!'

'It need not be suspicious, and it need not be her doing' said Francis reasonably. 'It was the height of the war, and many such records were mutilated or lost when the fanatic brethren turned their wrath upon the churches.' That had certainly been true at Ravensden, where some rude Puritans of Bedford had smashed the ancient stained glass and shot at the wooden angels on the roof. 'But the matter can be addressed easily enough. A transcript of the register should have been sent to the bishop at the end of each year, and even during the war, the record-keeping of this diocese was exemplary. I shall visit the archive at Buckden before I come down to join the ship – it will be easy enough for me to find a pretence to pay a respectful farewell to the Bishop.' Like every incumbent of Ravensden since the Conquest, Francis Gale was a clergyman of the vast Lincoln diocese: a territory so extensive that its palace had to be at Buckden, not far from us, as the Lord Bishop had cause to regret whenever my mother's coach passed through his gate.

Cornelia accepted Francis's argument with good grace; she both trusted and respected the soon-to-be chaplain of the *Seraph*.

Tris bit into a slice of cake, looked at it disapprovingly and put it down. 'Quite so. The matter of the marriage entry might be all or nothing. But the law might take a rather keener interest in the death of Sir Bernard De Vaux. It seems that this valiant cavalier was ignominiously hacked to death on the common highway in the winter of forty-seven, an event followed in short order by the disappearance of his grieving young widow, still no more than twenty years old or thereabouts.'

Musk whistled loudly to himself, but I remained sceptical. 'The winter of forty-seven,' I said. 'I can just remember it. Was it not a time of dearth? Of the disbandment of much of Parliament's army? Of desperate men roaming the country, seeking a way to sustain themselves?'

'Aye, what a precocious and observant seven-year-old you were,' said Tris, who had most of the credit for making me so.

'Then,' I said, 'is it not probable that Sir Bernard was fallen upon by such men, and done to death for his purse?'

'Of course, husband,' snapped Cornelia, 'but it is also quite possible for a soon-to-be-rich widow to hire the men who bring her husband to his fate!'

'Not so rich, it seems,' said Francis. 'Sir Bernard had been punished most severely for choosing the losing side. Fines, compounding, sequestration of many of his lands – the full panoply of godly Parliamentarian wrath against a known malignant, as they termed us who loved the king. True, the lady was sole heiress of the estate, and true, she eventually exercised her right to sell what was left of it. But it would have brought her but very little; a hundred or two, perhaps.'

'Two hundred,' said my wife. 'The dress she wore at the reception cost more than that, I'll wager. Whither, then, comes the thirty thousand of which your mother speaks so often and so loudly, husband?' Cornelia enquired triumphantly.

'Ah yes, the lady's allegedly great income,' said Tris. 'My good-sister, your mother, seems fixated by that lustrous figure of thirty thousand, but it seems to me to have been conjured from thin air. Your mother was ever a calamity when it came to money, Matt – and she has the gall to blame my father for squandering the family fortune!' Tristram Quinton sighed. 'Though she has money, that much is certain; how much, and from what source, remains a mystery. We have many more enquiries to pursue in this regard – if the heir to Ravensden permits it, of course.' A tactful nod in my direction, which I acknowledged in a way that could have been construed as consent. 'Which brings us to the rather peculiar matter of her second marriage. Francis?'

Francis Gale took up another paper from the table, and began to paraphrase. 'For almost ten years, the Lady De Vaux disappeared from the face of earth. We have no reports of her. She was not with the royalist court-in-exile, that much is certain. But there seems to be no word of her in England either. The intelligence reports gathered by Mister Thurloe's agents are entirely silent on her doings – ' Tris, the likely source of that information, was impassive – 'until, that is, she suddenly appears in the year fifty-six as the new wife of Major-General Uriel Gulliver.'

'Gulliver?' I gasped. '*That* Gulliver?'

'Quite so, Matt,' said Tris. 'That Gulliver. The man who ruled much of the Thames Valley in the name of the Lord Protector. Cromwell's right hand man, some said. Cromwell's likeliest successor, others said. In any event, the Gulliver who banned Christmas and closed most of the alehouses from Oxford to Richmond.'

'A most judicious change of sides by the Lady Louise, then,' I said.

'A most prodigious change of beds, rather, husband,' said Cornelia. 'She moved from a stout cavalier to a foul rebel to advance her own vile ambitions. Yet her general knew of her previous marriage, and accepted her. Who would credit it?'

I did not speak the thought in my head, which was that most men probably could credit it; the sight of the Lady De Vaux in the gardens of

Ravensden Abbey would surely have melted the heart of even the sternest Puritan. It was certainly not a thought that the husband of Cornelia Quinton could utter in her presence.

'So it seems,' said Francis. 'The reports from the time make much of her previous title. Indeed, she seems never to have ceased to use it. She must have had a certain curiosity value, at the very least, at the Protector's court.' He picked up the paper again, squinting at its contents in the fading light. 'Like most of Cromwell's generals, Gulliver did notably well out of our late troubles; a bleacher's son who ended up with a large slice of Wiltshire to his name, largely due to appropriations from honest cavaliers and the generous patronage of the Lord Protector. It would have not been unlikely for him to be worth thirty thousand.'

'Well, perhaps four or five years ago, at any rate,' said Tris. 'But as we all know, the Lord Protector did not last, and neither did his major-generals. The restoration of the present king's fortunes brought down in turn the fortunes of many of those who had depended upon the old regime. And that is where we come to the next of the curious matters in the career of our countess-to-be. For it appears that an arrest warrant had been issued against the very much former Major-General Uriel Gulliver, but not served, on the day that he died. Of an apoplexy, the coroner's jury decided, although there seems no evidence that the body was ever subjected to proper medical examination. Thus rather than being forfeit to the crown, the estate of Lyndbury passed to his grieving widow.'

'A damnably convenient apoplexy for his widow, then, I'd say,' said Musk, scratching himself in the far corner of the room and seemingly bored by the entire business.

'Very much so, Musk. Very much so indeed,' said Tris.

'Well, is *this* not evidence fit to lay before a judge?' Cornelia demanded impatiently.

'Alas, I think not, Mistress,' said Francis gently. 'No judge or jury in England would reopen a case that was closed three years ago, and in which the only evidence has been rotting in earth all that time.' Tris nodded vigorously at that.

'Then at the very least,' said Cornelia, 'is this not evidence that we should lay before the Earl?' She was relentless now. 'Two suspected murders – who is to say there will not be a third? If a child is born, what need then of the tenth Earl of Ravensden? Without Charles, this bitch could control the estate for near twenty-one years, and God knows what will be left of it at the end of that time.'

Tristram's face indicated his concurrence; the same unspoken fear had been present in his letter that first brought me the news of the marriage. Deep in my heart I shared that fear, but publicly I had to be more circumspect.

'Cornelia, my dear love,' I said gently, 'we have no proof of anything. Tristram's discoveries create suspicions, but that is all they are. We all seek to defend my poor brother and the honour of our ancient House, but do we really serve any purpose by trying to poison his heart against his bride even before they are married? Aye, let us try and answer the mysterious questions that lurk in this lady's past – but let it be done discreetly, so that Charles does not know of it! If there is nothing to be found, then let him not know even that such finding was attempted. After all, Goodwife Quinton, what if some third party had investigated our lives before we wed, and revealed their discoveries to us?'

Cornelia blushed, for I doubted she had been a young nun in Veere, and I had certainly been no monk in England, France, or Spain. Or Flanders. Or Holland.

'Nevertheless,' said Tris, 'we have a number of enquiries to pursue. A most promising young man graduated from Mauleverer last summer, and he is now a curate in Wiltshire, not far from Lyndbury, the estate currently owned by the Widow Gulliver, alias the Lady De Vaux, alias the Countess-to-be of Ravensden. He informs me that there are many dire rumours of the true worth of the estate. The rentals have been devastated by the wars and General Gulliver's mismanagement, it's said, and there is much talk of great mortgages upon the land. Of course, that sort of tittle-tattle can be heard in every ale-house in the realm, especially among rude yeomen and farmers who covet the fields of the great estate next door to theirs. But I shall make establishing the truth or otherwise of these claims my particular task, my friends.' Tris beckoned to Musk to light another lantern; this day that had never been was dying in a grey death-shroud of fog. The lantern had but little effect, and the room remained dark, cold and smoky. 'It will take time, of course, for there is no business more damnably opaque in England than establishing the worth of a great personage. That way lie countless rogues and charlatans, notably lawyers and those devils incarnate who own the banking-houses, so I'll wager I am embarking upon a journey nearly as perilous and prolonged as your forthcoming voyage, Matthew.'

I thought upon the quest for the mountain of gold, the warning from Venner Garvey and the grinning, arrogant face of Brian Doyle' O'Dwyer, and somehow I doubted it. Yet the thought of leaving Cornelia and Tristram behind, fighting a battle on what they believed to be my and my brother's behalves, troubled me deeply. Moreover, it was a battle that ran the risk of offending the most high, for I could still hear my king's words in my ears: *trust me*.

I looked about me, and saw thoughtful, resigned faces. Cornelia's was the gloomiest, evidently seeing no way now of preventing the marriage and thus the ascendancy of the Lady Louise. Francis's eyes were closed as though in prayer. Tris was staring deeply into his jug of wine as though seeking inspiration in the dregs. Only Musk was active, shuffling nervously from one foot to another and endeavouring to attract my attention. No doubt he wished to leave this eccentric, unsettling place as quickly as possible.

'Yes, Musk?' I said.

'There's that other matter, too,' he said.

We all looked at him curiously. 'Another matter?' said Tris.

The old scoundrel shrugged. 'Her daughter,' he said levelly. 'The one she had by Sir Bernard. Sorry. Thought you knew…'

Tris coughed violently. Cornelia stared open-mouthed at Musk. Francis and I exchanged astonished glances.

I was the first to recover my voice. 'How in the name of Heaven did you come to know of a daughter, Musk? Does she live? Where is she, man? Why did we not know of this – '

'I did,' said Musk sheepishly. 'A man learns things in all sorts of places. Hears all sorts of things. Especially a man in my position, a mere servant.'

Tris scowled at him and said, 'Mere servant is the last thing you will ever be, Phineas Musk. Thus you were to my father, even at his end and your beginning – a brazen, secretive rogue, by damnation!'

'You overheard a conversation,' I said tentatively. 'Between my brother and either his lady or my mother. It could only be one or the other.' *Unless Charles had told him directly* – but if so, why Musk ahead of his closest family?

'But this could be the key to all!' cried Cornelia. 'What became of the child, Musk?'

'Don't know everything, do I? Haven't got a degree or two, have I?' He cast a hostile glance at Tristram. 'But I'll tell you this gratis, that I will. Seems to me you've all been barking up the wrong trees. Maybe the lady killed her husbands, maybe she didn't. Maybe she's as rich as Croesus, maybe she isn't. But seems to me the questions you should be asking are these – why are the Earl, the Dowager and the King all so keen on this marriage, and why are they all so convinced it'll produce a child? Seems to me that if there's proof she produced a living child before, it could explain why they all think she'll do so again. Proven breeding stock, and so forth. But if that's so, why is nobody trumpeting it? Why's the lady hidden the child's existence all these years?'

Once again I heard my king's words: *trust me.*

There, in the gloom of Skelthorn, I looked upon Tristram's rows of skulls, their blank eyes seeming to stare back at me, their mute mouths seeming to utter the names of Louise de Vaux and Brian Doyle O'Dwyer. Thus I came at last to a realisation of the shocking truth. Matthew Quinton had reached a place where no cavalier could in honour abide.

Trust me?

No, Your Majesty. That, I do not.

Some days later, I stood on the quarterdeck of the *Seraph*, watching intently as we inched our way toward the open gates of the Deptford wet dock. Of course, we had no sail aloft; two of Master Attendant Cox's boats were towing us, and we also had cables attached to both shores, warping us toward the open river beyond. It was another bitter day, but dry, and for the first time, nearly all of the officers of the *Seraph* were together aboard the ship, along with most of our crew. The only two missing were Francis Gale, delivering his final Holy Communion at Ravensden before going on to pay his farewell call upon the Bishop of Lincoln (and using the visit to examine the transcripts for Billringham); and Martin Humphrey, the surgeon, a young Londoner who was due to come to the ship in a day or two. Three of the officers were below decks, attending to their various responsibilities. Ludovic Harrington, the purser, was an old Cavalier who looked upon the son of the martyr-hero James, Earl of Ravensden, almost as an object of veneration. More importantly, he was competent and honest; a rarity indeed in a purser. Bradbury, the cook, was a maimed seaman, as were most of his breed. His meals proved to be most terribly overcooked. Only I, who had grown up with the cuisine provided by Goodwife Barcock at Ravensden Abbey (who opined that meat was edible only if cremated), could eat Bradbury's fare with some degree of enthusiasm. Then there was Tom Shish, the carpenter, who might or might not have been related to the Master Shipwright of Deptford. This Shish seemed an enthusiastic, open young man, determined to make his way in his profession so that one day he could build a truly great ship to outdo even the vast *Sovereign* herself, the mightiest man-of-war in all the world. He had already reported to me earnestly that for a new ship, the state of the chain pumps fell far below his expectations. Of course, I was not then such an ignoramus that I did not know the ship used pumps to expel the water that would otherwise fill her (for with the best will in the world, even the best-caulked ship in the world leaks); but my knowledge of how chain pumps worked was not necessarily complete. But in the same breath that he brought me the problem, Shish also brought me the solution; would that the same could be said of every subordinate I have ever commanded. He would go to the great storehouse at once, he said, and procure an additional supply of spare esses, these being the links used within the chain mechanism. I nodded in approbation as I would to an amenable but incomprehensible Chinaman, while also realising once again how many more leagues I had to travel to master this unfathomable sea-business.

I looked down upon the relatively few men who were actively engaged, attending to the warping cables or our end of the tow ropes. Very soon, we would have to divide this crew into the obligatory naval equivalent of the sheep and the goats, that is, by rating them as able or ordinary seamen. This was one of those arcane naval mysteries in which I had not previously participated. Indeed, it seemed even to my young and ignorant self to be a very pinnacle of perversity, for the new general instructions of the Lord Admiral to his captains, issued but a few months before, followed time-honoured tradition by insisting that men should be rated at once upon joining the ship. Now, even at the tender age of twenty-three, and with less experience at sea than many a fishwife, I wondered how it was possible to judge whether a man was fit for helm, lead, top and yards, the definition of an able seamen, *long before the ship put to sea at all*. Kit Farrell, bustling about the forecastle with the unconfined happiness of a man returning to his natural element, had told me that the practised eye of the veteran mariner made the task as easy as judging men from women, but I found this analogy a little too carefree for my comfort.

* * *

I sought the opinion of the man alongside me on the quarterdeck, standing a little closer to me than the familiar bulk of Lieutenant Castle: Valentine Negus, the ship's master for this voyage. Thus far in my naval career, I had been markedly unfortunate in my masters. The master of my first command, the *Happy Restoration*, had been an inveterate sot whose drink-sodden arrogance had contributed at least as much to the destruction of that unfortunate vessel as the ignorance of her captain. The master of the *Jupiter* had been a vicious, surly brute, whose contempt for me had been matched only by my loathing of him. The master of the *Wessex* was such a feeble nonentity that now, over sixty years on, I cannot even recall the man's name. Negus seemed to be of a very different metal, thank God. A thin, dark Yorkshireman, he had made many a voyage to the coast and islands of Africa on merchants' business. Sober, clean and respectful, Negus evidently knew his business, and seemed to bear no resentment toward his young gentleman captain or toward Lieutenant Castle, a seaman as able as himself and thus a potential threat to his position.

I said, 'Well, Mister Negus, what do you make of our crew, thus far?'

'Good enough, I think, Captain,' he said in a voice not unlike that of my good-brother Garvey. 'Your Cornishmen are proven, and most of the men Mister Castle drew from Bristol are decent enough, I reckon – though God knows, there's likely to be bad blood between them. Always is, between Bristol and Cornwall.' He smiled, as though relishing the prospect of blood-sport. 'Reckon Boatswain Farrell will be busy enough with the cat and the cane, this voyage. The London men – well, they'll be a mixed bag, as London men always are. A few scrapings of the shore, I expect. Time will tell.'

'You're confident of rating them all before we sail, Master?'

Negus nodded. 'Before we reach the Nore, I'd reckon. Time enough to judge most of 'em. Quite what they'll be like on the guns, of course, is a different matter – uh, Gunner?'

Marcus Lindman, gunner of the *Seraph*, turned in our direction and grunted. '*Ja*, Master. *Ja*, Captain,' he said in his guttural Swedish accent.

'But a voyage to the Gambia gives time enough, I think, to make this crew sufficient upon the great guns. With my training, of course!'

A stout man with an unnaturally large and entirely shaven head, the dour Lindman was one of the many Swedes who served in our navy in those days, just as many of our men often served in the fleet of King Karl. The Dutch made friends with the Danes; *ergo*, we English made friends with the Swedes, the natural enemy of the Dane, and if one of us was at war and the other was not, what more natural way could there be for a man of action to spend a summer or two than to offer his services to our friends? Lindman was a veteran of the Battle of the Sound, a ferocious fight between the Swedes and their Danish and Dutch enemies in the year fifty-eight, so he knew his trade, that much was certain. That he had come to ply it in England upon the conclusion of the last Northern War proved to be a blessing for his captain aboard the *Seraph*.

We were edging ever closer to the open gate, and to a welcome escape from the noise and stench of Deptford yard. Cox, on the quayside, seemed as nervous as if he was trying to con the *Sovereign* herself out of dock, but in truth, a mere Fifth Rate like the *Seraph* had ample room to spare. Lieutenant Castle raised his hat to Cox in cheery salute as we passed. Up forward, our parties hauling on the warping ropes were markedly brisk, taking advantage of this early opportunity to prove themselves to the ship's officers: I recognised Polzeath and Tremar (ever useful men on a rope's end), their boisterous friend Trevanion of Crantock, Ali Reis the Moor, and the red hair of Macferran, the young Scot who had attached himself to me during the fateful commission of the *Jupiter* and who now had a mighty ambition to be rated Able Seaman ere long. The others were new faces from the Bristol and London drafts, some of them casting surly, suspicious glances upon their fellows and their officers; *pray God that Negus is wrong*, I thought, *and that we have no warring between our different English tribes this voyage.*

Our bows edged out into the Thames. The timbers of the *Seraph* gave the gentlest of groans as she met tidewater once more, and I felt the motion of the sea. I caught Kit Farrell's eyes upon me from the forecastle, and realised that I was grinning like a child with a new toy.

We continued under tow; there was no point in hoisting sail for this briefest of voyages. Down past the mouth of Deptford Creek, and after but a few hundred yards more I gave the order to drop anchor. *Seraph* came to her resting place almost in the shadow of the ancient ruins of Greenwich Palace, behind which the park stretched up to the Black Heath. We were close inshore and thus well out of the main stream and its ceaseless procession of merchantmen bound up or down the eternal Thames. Men set about securing the ship, for here we would lie until the ordnance barges brought down our arsenal, and the victuallers' lighters brought down our stores, both from the wharves adjacent to the Tower. I was reliably informed that all was ready – would have come down sooner, but for the fire in the dockyard – and that it simply had to be shipped down to us, a matter of a mere day or two's lading. I had nodded politely in the presence of the ordnance and victualling agents, but I had already experienced enough of their empty assurances during my brief naval career, and would truly believe it only when the last demi-culverin was on its carriage and the last barrel was in the hold.

I looked about my quarterdeck, and out over my ship, and for the first time in my life, but by no means the last, I experienced a strange sensation. I loved my wife. I relished my life ashore, and the company of friends. But at that moment, there on the deck of the *Seraph*, I knew that I desired nothing more than to remain there, in that little wooden world, and to face whatever untold storms and disasters and awaited us, rather than going ashore to face …

Ah, yes. To face *that*.

I turned and said reluctantly, 'Mister Castle, the ship is yours, sir, for the time being.' He and Negus raised their hats in salute, and I raised mine in turn. 'I take the leave granted me by His Majesty and His Royal Highness. After all, gentlemen,' I said, attempting to muster a levity that I did not truly feel, 'I have a wedding to attend.'

$\mathcal{T}en$

My last morn at Ravensden.

The last for many months, at any rate; perhaps the last of all, if the fevers of Guinea did for me. My sea-chest was already filled and ready to be moved to Ravensden House, as were Cornelia and myself. The wedding was but three days away, and after that I would immediately rejoin my ship in Greenwich Reach, awaiting a fair wind and tide to take us out to sea. Cornelia was still asleep.

I went out into the ruined quire of the abbey church, where the tombs of the Quintons stood. It was another chill morning, with a harsh frost and a mist that settled upon the entire valley like a shroud. I intended to pay my respects at the graves of my father, grandfather and others of my name; but another was there before me. Standing in silent reverence at the austere table-tomb of our father was my noble brother Charles.

He half-turned at my approach. 'Matt,' he said, simply. 'A cold morning for the contemplation of the dead.'

I came up beside him and looked down upon our father's monument, which (unlike myself) he visited so very rarely. 'Perhaps the dead are contemplating us,' I said.

'I never doubt it,' said the earl, sadly. 'The dead ever enslave us from their tombs.' We looked about us. A niche in the ruined north wall contained a splendid stone effigy of an armoured knight: the first earl. His successors were scattered all around us, either in table tombs in the middle of the church, or in alcoves at the sides. It was easy in such a place to feel the weight of history, and the sense of one's own small and worthless place in the endless story of this mighty but fragile family. One day, Charles would lie here among our ancestors. Perhaps I might also – if my fate was not to be that of a hasty interment at sea, slung over the side in sailcloth and weighed down by a cannonball.

Time for boldness, I decided. After all, the matter could no longer be halted, and I was bound for sea and perhaps for that self-same watery grave. 'I wonder,' I said. 'I wonder what they would have made of this marriage of yours?'

There was no change whatever in my brother's expression or tone. 'They would have understood duty, I think. Some of them, at any rate. Old Countess Katherine there, for certain.'

'Our father and grandfather? Would they have understood it?'

A slow shake of the head – 'Better than you know, I think, Matt.'

Impatiently, I replied, 'Yes, of course, My Lord. You knew them, and older times, as I who am so much younger did not. But I know enough to recognise how much this troubles you, brother. You are not content in this, no matter how you try to conceal it.'

Charles looked away. I felt an overwhelming urge to tell him all that I now knew – of the daughter whose existence Musk had blurted out, of the doubts over the new countess's income, of the marriage record that had also mysteriously vanished from the transcripts at Buckden, as Francis had reported but the previous day – but to do that would have been a dishonourable act. After all, what right did I, or Tris, or any of us, have to question the judgement of the Earl of Ravensden, and seek evidence to damn his bride?

'This marriage...' the Earl said tentatively. 'It is not what you think, Matthew. *She* is not what you think.'

We stood before the tomb of our grandfather Matthew Quinton, eighth Earl of Ravensden, as overbearing in death as he had evidently been in life. It was plain that on this matter of his marriage, Earl Charles was going to remain unmoving and unmovable; better then to attempt a different tack. But to my surprise, my brother went onto that tack before me. It was so rare for him to initiate a topic of conversation with me that I felt a sudden frisson of shock.

'The House of Quinton,' he said slowly, choosing his words with great care, 'has long been privy to – let us say, to certain secrets of state. God alone knows why our line has been so honoured or so cursed. Earl Matthew, here, was perhaps the most inveterate intriguer of them all, no mean claim for a Quinton. Even at the end of his days, well after the civil war began, the old man was plotting away...' We looked down upon the exuberant armour-clad effigy of the old man, a style of funerary monument unfashionable for many years before Earl Matthew had it erected over him. 'There is a burden upon us, Matt,' my brother said. 'A mighty burden upon our family. There is a burden upon *me*. And I would spare you that burden. One day, undoubtedly, you must come to know our truths long concealed. Yes, mine among them.' The Earl looked me directly in the eye; a significant rarity. 'But this is not that day, my brother. You have sufficient concerns of your own, with this voyage of yours and its manifold troubles. The burden will be yours in time enough.'

I was angry, and bitter, but I knew full well that there was nothing to be gained by losing my temper, and demanding the revelation of these mighty truths there and then, in the chill ruins of the abbey church. But perhaps there was one thing I could do, one thing alone, that would both convince my brother of my determination and content my own mind upon the matter, for the present at least. 'You swear upon a grave of my choosing that you will reveal it all to me, one day?'

This took him aback, but typically, he reacted quickly and decisively. 'On any grave you choose.'

I looked about me; there was no shortage of candidates. But for all the force exerted by the graves of our father and grandfather, there was really only one grave that would serve. I led Charles over to the small, pitiful slab in what had once been the south transept, and we looked down upon the inscription.

This small monument is erected to the memory of his dear and virtuous sister Henrietta Quinton who dyed the 29ᵗʰ day of December in the Year 1653 by her most affectionate brother Matthew, who prayeth

That this stone may lie until she rise

To see her saviour with her eyes.

My choice evidently had a profound effect upon Earl Charles, who seemed to shudder. For a moment I feared that he would lose his balance, which his old wounds had made forever unsteady. But he collected himself, and said clearly, 'I, Charles, tenth Earl of Ravensden, promise that in the fullness of time, all the truths to which the Quinton family has been and is privy will be revealed to Matthew Quinton, here present, the true and rightful heir of Ravensden.'

Well, the true and rightful heir for now, at any rate – until the womb of the Lady Louise bore yet more fruit, albeit some sixteen years since its last flowering.

Charles turned to me, took my hand, placed his other hand upon my shoulder, and said, 'Amen to that, then.' He looked at me, a profound distance and yet a powerful sympathy in his eyes. 'God bless and keep you in your perilous voyage, Matthew.'

'And you in your perilous marriage, Charles.'

At that we parted, and made to return to the house; but as we did so, we both glanced up, and saw our mother, the Dowager Countess, looking down at us from the window of her room.

* * *

That same day, Cornelia, my mother and I left for London in the family's state coach. With Charles, who had some estate business to attend to, following the next day, all of us would be cooped up in the same small space of Ravensden House for the few days that remained before the travesty at Saint Paul's. By the second evening, this was already too much of a trial for us all, especially following a visit from the Garveys during the course of that afternoon. Thus Mother decided to pay court to her old friend the Queen Mother in Somerset House; oh, to have been a fly on the wall at that conversation! Charles spirited himself away on what he claimed to be parliamentary business, though how this could be so was a mystery, for Parliament had not been in session since July. He did not wish for a last evening's carousing with friends, for he had almost none, and he wished for it even less with his brother. Even Cornelia abandoned me; her old friend and fellow Dutchwoman Aemilia, the Countess of Ossory, was at court, and the two embarked on a happy promenade through the galleries of Whitehall, shamelessly eyeing all the rakes. Fortunately, a brief sojourn at the palace also produced companions for me. Beau Harris and Will Berkeley, these; my fellow gentlemen captains. Making our excuses to the ladies, we headed back along the Strand, intent on some properly serious carousing in the City. They were good company, these two. Beaudesert Harris was from a stout Cavalier family of Warwickshire, but he was hardly of the old blood; his father had been a merchant who prospered from a monopoly in King James' time and was able to buy out the lands of a decayed gentry dynasty, acquiring a baronetcy in the process. Harris, a cheerful and irreverent soul, had commanded the *Falcon* on the Irish coast two years before, when I served there in my ill-fated first commission, and we became firm friends at that time. Will Berkeley was of a very different metal. For one thing, he was a serious man, determined to learn the sea-business (unlike Beau, who thought such menial knowledge beneath him). For another, there were few names older or grander in the history

J. D. DAVIES

of England than that of Berkeley; after all, it had been in the ancient castle of that name that King Edward the Second was done to death with a hot poker up the fundament, so that none might suspect a more visible death-wound. Will's father was the treasurer of the King's household, and his brother Charles, then the Viscount Fitzhardinge of Berehaven, was one of the King's great favourites. These connections had already procured for him the command of two of the kingdom's best and largest fourth-rate frigates, and he was but recently returned from the Straits in the *Bonadventure*, with a new commission already promised him by the King and the Duke of York. With his long nose and pointed chin, Will Berkeley looked every inch a lawyer, and as we approached Chancery Lane on our debauch, the resemblance seemed to grow ever more marked.

Our conversation was increasingly ribald (it was difficult to have a conversation without ribaldry in those early days of Charles the Second's court), and we had got to that stage of the evening where wagers were being made and drinking games commenced. The Mitre Tavern on Fleet Street was ever a good venue for such activity, and we crossed the threshold in the best of spirits ...

Which evaporated in an instant. For there, standing in the middle of the largest room of the inn, was Colonel Brian Doyle O'Dwyer, no less, seemingly unarmed, surrounded by an ugly coterie of ruffians with knives and cudgels in their hands, all evidently intent on doing him some ill. Their leader was known to me, too. He had a great scar upon his face and no left eye.

Now, there are some who will damn this as a mightily preposterous coincidence. There are others, no doubt, who will see this as a misremembering on the grandest scale, and thus as final proof of my dotage. As for the latter, I will permit God to be my judge; God and my twenty-six-year-old lawyer, educated at Oxford and the Middle Temple, whom I comprehensively outwitted on the matter of some mortgages but the other day. As for the former, it must be remembered that London was a much smaller place then, over sixty years ago, before the Fire. Moreover, although the city was crowded with drinking dens of all sorts, there were relatively few that were suitable for gentlemen of breeding (or who pretended to such breeding, no matter how presumptuously, as was the case with my 'friend' O'Dwyer). As for our arrival at the moment of a deadly assault on him by my own erstwhile assailant; well, I have experienced more than enough of life to be able to say with some authority that such things happen, and are perhaps the best proof that we have of the workings upon Earth of the Lord God (or perhaps more likely, of his disgraced archangel Lucifer). I still recall with a shudder the significant embarrassment and very nearly dire consequences to our realm's foreign policy caused by my quickshit-impelled arrival in a Deptford alehouse privy at exactly the same moment as His Late Majesty the Emperor Peter, Tsar of All The Russias.

'Damn me,' said the scarred man, 'Quinton as well. God in his Heaven smiles on us tonight, boys.'

'You have some damnably unpleasant acquaintances, Matt,' said Beau Harris, drawing his sword.

'A good thing for this gentleman of the army that the navy just happened along,' said Will Berkeley, drawing his.

Drawing my own blade, I said, 'Permit me to name Colonel Brian Doyle O'Dwyer, my intended passenger aboard the *Seraph*.'

'Oh, him,' said Berkeley, dismissively.

'The turncoat heathen?' cried Beau Harris.

O'Dwyer bowed his head slightly in mock salutation. 'As you say, gentlemen.'

The scarred man snorted derisively. 'Introductions, is it, by God! How very courtly. Well, as we're in the habit, gentlemen, I'll introduce myself, too. Habakkuk Leech, nobles and gentles all; late sergeant, Hewson's regiment, New Model Army. I won't bother with introducing the rest of my companions, here, for most of them either don't know their names or go by false ones.' Some of the gang – eight strong, no less – sniggered at that.

'Well, then,' I said, 'and what would be your business with Colonel O'Dwyer, here, Sergeant Leech? The same business perhaps that you attempted upon me on the road from Newmarket?'

Leech sneered dismissively. 'A related business, let's say, Captain Quinton. But with very different intended outcomes, I assure you. But I'd make you a proposition. Now, we both know that you have little love for the good colonel, here. So why don't you let the boys and I take him away with us, quiet like, and no more to it?' He looked about him. 'After all, Captain, there are nine of us here, all armed men who know our trade – learned it in the wars, most of us, unlike you fine but so young gentlemen. Nine of us, and but three of you. Four, if you count the Irish Turk. Still better than two to one for our side, Captain Quinton.'

I glanced at Harris to my left and Berkeley to my right, but I knew I need not have done so; we were of one mind. 'Men of honour don't bargain with the likes of you, Leech,' I said. 'And O'Dwyer, there, might be a damnable renegade, but he holds our King's commission and wears his uniform. We are bound to defend our fellow officer.'

'Fellow officer be damned,' snarled Leech. 'We should have chopped the heads off all you fucking Cavaliers when we had the chance.'

With that he and six of his men advanced toward us three captains; the other two circled O'Dwyer, who was evidently to be taken alive.

'Remind me,' said Beau Harris, 'to bring an entire regiment with me, the next time I come drinking with you.'

At that, Leech's men rushed us, two on each, with the sergeant himself hanging back, no doubt waiting to see which of us weakened first before administering the *coup de grace* himself. The odds were not good, it was true. But fighting in a confined space always has a dampening effect upon even the worst of odds, and we had swords, which would keep our knife-wielding adversaries at bay for a time, at least until we tired. Harris's two went for him first, perhaps sensing from his grip and posture that he was the least able swordsman of us; one learned his mistake by means of a deep slash across his hand, the other by a snick to the cheek. I barely saw the attack on Berkeley, for my two came for me in that moment, edging forward with their bare blades held out. They were big rogues, both of forty years or more – no doubt New Model veterans like Leech. But as New Model men, I calculated, they would have been happier with pike or musket than with knives, and they might have that innate fear of a sword which so many infantrymen possess. I described a swift figure-of-eight with the point of my blade, and they both flinched as they would have done if it was a cavalryman's rapier bearing down upon them. As they regrouped, I saw Berkeley grappling with his two, who had got close to him (for, in truth, Will was the weakest swordsman of us three). He thrust them away before they could stick their knives in him, giving one a thrust in the forearm for his pains. As I prepared for the next assault from my two, I caught sight of O'Dwyer, standing stock still behind Leech. He was smiling. Sweet Jesus, the infernal scum was not even thinking of raising a finger to help us, who were fighting – and, if God willed it, dying – so that his miserable renegade life could be saved.

My two came on again. This time, they were more subtle. The one to my left, my unarmed side, came on first, and fast, forcing me to bring my blade up to defend myself. At that, the other one rushed me, thrusting for my stomach. I pirouetted on my heel, slashing downward as I did so, and heard a yelp from one of them. But almost at once there was a cry to my left. Harris was hurt, but I could not gauge how badly. On my right, Will was wrestling with his two once more. But this time Leech had identified his man, and was moving in silently for the kill.

O'Dwyer caught my eye. He was still standing quite rigidly, and smiling. But the faintest glance to each side gave me some notion of his intent, just before he executed it. Taking my cue from him, I counterthrust ferociously toward my two assailants. The move was sufficient to distract

O'Dwyer's two guards, who turned to look upon my attack. In that moment, the Irishman suddenly stooped to reach for his cloak, lying on the table by him, and pulled from it a gleaming curved Turkish scimitar. With one sweep, he decapitated the man nearest him. The other barely had time to turn before the curved blade slashed across his stomach. As he fell, his guts began to spill onto the straw-strewn floor of the Mitre.

Even in London, the sight of a headless corpse pumping blood onto the entrails of its neighbour is sufficient to distract the most hardened killer. Leech turned from Will Berkeley to confront this unexpected assailant. The horror of the sight had worked in our favour. Despite his thigh-wound, Beau Harris now advanced like a man possessed; one of his attackers mistimed a thrust and found himself on the point of Harris's blade, which protruded obscenely from the nape of his neck. The other, sensing that the tide had turned, fled out of the back of the inn. This disheartened Will Berkeley's assailants, and sensing their indecision, Will aimed a well-chosen thrust directly into the heart of the one nearest to him.

'Stand and fight, you worthless whoresons!' cried Leech; but he was enough of a veteran to know full well that the battle had shifted against him. My own opponents looked at each other, weighed the odds, and ran. Will Berkeley moved swiftly behind Leech, cutting off his only escape route. O'Dwyer advanced upon him with the scimitar. 'Ah, fuck, so be it,' said Leech, throwing his weapons to the ground and raising his arms – only for O'Dwyer to bring the scimitar slashing down toward his skull …

Steel struck steel as my blade deflected O'Dwyer's blow, barely inches from Leech's head. The Irishman gave me a look of sheer hatred. 'He's surrendered!' I cried. 'The rules of warfare, Colonel O'Dwyer. The rules of *Christian* warfare, at any rate.'

I turned to Beau Harris, who was wrapping a large kerchief around his thigh. 'All well, Beau?' I asked.

'An entire regiment, Quinton. Or two. Remember that. I'll make damn certain they're with me, the next time I drink with you.'

Will Berkeley, who had his sword-point at Leech's throat, laughed at that.

'Well, Sergeant Leech,' I said, 'explain yourself.'

'Christ damn you to hell, Quinton.'

O'Dwyer intervened. 'Ah now, Sergeant, Captain Quinton here's a patient man. As I know full well. But Brian Doyle O'Dwyer, your humble servant, here; well, I'm not quite so patient, let's say.' He stepped in front of Leech's face and smirked. 'So the way I see it, Sergeant, is this. You have two choices. You can tell the good captain here what he wishes to know, and then we hand you over to the alderman of this ward and his constables, and you get a good honest English trial. Now who knows, you might find a jury stupid enough or corruptible enough to acquit you, but myself, I doubt that – even in England. But at least you'll get a hanging, and most of the hangmen up at Tyburn are pretty efficient these days, I'm told, so it'll be fast, and not too painful. Whereas...' He raised his scimitar, plucked a hair sharply from Leech's head and applied it to his blade, which sliced it in half almost before the hair seemed to have touched the edge. 'Fine blades, my old friends the Turks have,' O'Dwyer said quietly. 'So sharp, a man could do all kinds of intricate things to another man's privates. If he was so inclined, let's say.'

The colour drained from Leech's face, but the old sense of duty of a New Model sergeant died hard. In that moment, though, Will Berkeley applied his sword-point to the tie on the bag hanging from Leech's belt, and the bag scattered its contents to the floor. Gold coin. Large quantities of gold coin; many, many pounds worth, that was certain. Quite how many pounds would be difficult to fathom at first glance, for they were evidently foreign coins. Many were *louis d'or* and *écus*, the currency of the Most Christian Kingdom of France; an unexpectedly Catholic wage for a sometime godly Commonwealth's-man. Some were *maravedís* and *escudos* of Spain, but that was hardly unexpected, for Spanish bullion flowed out into every money market of Europe to pay that kingdom's inconceivably vast debts. But some of the coins were less familiar. I lifted one, turned it this way and that, and handed it to Will Berkeley, who raised an eyebrow, then nodded.

'Malta,' I said. 'The gold of the Knights. So, Sergeant Leech, tell me this – how does a New Model veteran, an old Puritan no doubt, come to serve that undoubted papist, Gaspard of Montnoir? And why, pray, has Montnoir sent you after Colonel O'Dwyer and myself?'

Leech was silent for a minute or so longer, as though weighing my questions and the alternatives that O'Dwyer had put to him. Perhaps he considered playing dumb, and claiming that he had never heard of any Montnoir; but O'Dwyer's scimitar was very, very close to his groin. At length his shoulders slumped, and the battle was done. 'Times are hard. Since your whoreson king disbanded the New Model, we've had to seek a wage wherever we can. And I've observed that papists are notably better supplied with gold than those of the true reformed religion. As for you, Captain Quinton – ' a sneer in my direction – 'why, you were but a sideshow,' he said. 'You were to be scared, or at best beaten until bloody. The Frenchman, Montnoir – well, he told me you had humiliated him in some way.' I thought back to the meeting on the deck of the *Wessex*, and of how pleased I had been with myself in the face of Montnoir's arrogance. The Seigneur de Montnoir evidently bore grudges, and was a man to avenge even the least slight against him. 'And as for the renegade, here,' Leech continued, but was interrupted …

'I was to be taken off to France, or to Malta, or to wherever the good *seigneur* happens to be at this moment,' said O'Dwyer. 'Montnoir wants me alive. Has always wanted me alive, since first he learned of a corsair captain of Oran who claimed to know the location of the mountain of gold.' Leech nodded at that. 'That, Quinton, is why he was in pursuit of me when you took my galley. And now Montnoir will be doubly determined to find it, through me,' O'Dwyer continued. He looked at Leech.

'Five attempts, sergeant. Five attempts you have made to seize me, each more inept than the last, as I have told the King. Methinks Montnoir could have spent his money better.'

Five attempts? As I have told the King? Of course; for what a service Montnoir had done Brian O'Dwyer! If there were still doubts about the veracity of the Irishman and his story (and God knows, Matt Quinton alone had more than a sufficiency of them!), then what could be a more efficacious way of allaying them than five attempts to kidnap him? Yes, Gaspard de Montnoir and Habakkuk Leech had done O'Dwyer's work for him, far more effectively than the man himself could ever have managed.

The constables arrived at that moment; quite probably they had been waiting outside for some time, listening to make quite sure that the fracas within had concluded. With them came the alderman for that ward, a fat, short creature who mentioned something about us all being under arrest. O'Dwyer was the first of us to react.

'Arrest, you say? I think not, Alderman. You see, before you stands your most humble servant, Lieutenant-Colonel Brian Doyle O'Dwyer of His Majesty's Irish army, shortly to set sail at the King's express behest. To sail, in fact, on the ship commanded by the tall young gentleman yonder, Captain Matthew Quinton of His Majesty's navy royal. Is the name Quinton familiar to you, alderman? Brother to the Earl of Ravensden. One of the King's closest friends.'

Although it galled me to do so, I colluded with O'Dwyer, for I did not relish the prospect of incarceration. 'Indeed so, Alderman. And please allow me to present Captains Beaudesert Harris and William Berkeley, both also of His Majesty's navy. Captain Berkeley, here, is brother to the Lord Viscount Fitzhardinge. Another of the King's closest friends.'

'So you see, Alderman,' said Beau, taking up the refrain, 'arresting us would be likely to bring down His Majesty's most severe displeasure upon you and your constables here.'

The constables looked at each other, and at the Alderman. Their common will was entirely clear, and they had their way.

A little later, after Habakkuk Leech had been taken away to the tender mercies of the Newgate Prison, the rest of us parted company outside the Mitre: Beau to have his wound tended most attentively by his sweetheart, a Miss Grainger ('demure as a nun until I get her into bed,' Beau said); Will and I to return to the palace; O'Dwyer to ride God knew where.

As he mounted, the Irishman said cheerily, 'Well then, Captain Quinton. Until the Downs, sir, when I shall join you aboard the noble *Seraph*. You'll have much business meanwhile, I don't doubt.'

Eleven

A man should go to his brother's marriage with joy in his heart and a carefree smile. Instead, I went to the nuptials of my most noble brother Charles Quinton, tenth Earl of Ravensden, with the heart and smile of a corpse. Yet it was a bright and cheery morn as the Earl and I rode out of Ravensden House. We were both attired in fine new garb, namely deep blue tunic coats with silver buttons, scarlet breeches and stockings, and fine blue silk gloves; blue, the armorial colour of Quinton. As we were finishing dressing before the mirror, a little earlier, Charles had commented laconically that we looked like a pair of somewhat disreputable French swordsmen. Otherwise, the Earl prepared himself in silence, as though for a funeral rather than a wedding, and with a mighty heaviness already upon my own heart, I knew better than to attempt the back-slapping jollity expected of a groom's supporter. Thus prepared, we left the house to the cheers of a small gaggle of retainers and tenants, brought down from Bedfordshire for the occasion. I mounted Zephyr, who seemed inclined to bolt toward the west; Musk, already mounted and in my earshot but not my brother's, murmured: 'The glory or downfall of the House of Quinton, today, by God. Take your pick, my masters.' We rode out, along the Strand and Fleet Street, across the fetid stagnation of the Fleet River by way of the Fleet Bridge, up Ludgate Hill, through the red-brick Lud Gate itself, and onward towards our destination, Saint Paul's, its mighty tower dominating the city beneath.

Our passage was slow, for our road was full of people: both those strange half-creatures who turn out to gawp at the ceremonials of any illustrious name, cheering hysterically as the great ones pass, and the far larger throng of hawkers, hucksters and the like, who cared only that their vulgar trades had been interrupted by our progress. Some shouted good wishes and all health; others, distinctly graphic advice for the bedding. Musk, riding before us in an ancient tabard bearing the Quinton arms, vigorously pummelled several who hooted abuse or attempted to touch Charles or myself. We had no other attendants. I have been to weddings where forty or more have ridden behind the groom, laughing lustily all the way to the church door, but Charles was not a man for such rowdy show (and besides, he had barely four friends in the world, let alone forty). At length, we came before the west front of the cathedral, and dismounted. As I stepped down onto the cobbles I winced with the pain imparted by my new shoes, upon which Cornelia had insisted. Here were many of our tenants and retainers – Barcocks, mostly – who had come to shower the steps of the cathedral with dried petals upon the bride's entrance. They were all joyous beyond measure, and I wondered why I alone felt as though I were processing to a grave-side. (Or perhaps, not quite alone: but as ever, Earl Charles' expression was unreadable.) We entered the cathedral by way of Inigo Jones' great new west portico, modelled upon the Roman style, its stone fresh and young alongside the dull ancient grey of the remainder of Paul's church. I looked up at the classical columns, and wondered how on earth the architect reckoned they fitted with the soaring Gothic favoured by the original builders. All architects are frauds, of course, but time can alter a man's perspective mightily. Nowadays, I would gladly favour Jones' short-lived portico over the monstrosity since inflicted upon the world by that mountebank Wren, whose demented notion of building a cathe-dral has been to deposit an enormous breast atop Ludgate Hill, for the boundless ridicule of all posterity. Then, I thought only of what was to take place within.

We passed through the west door into the long, soaring nave, known since time immemorial as Paul's Walk. Despite the rosemary and myrtle that bedecked every column, the nave still reeked a little of horse-shit. It had been employed as a stable by Noll Cromwell's cavalry, who had also smashed the windows and defaced the monuments, and the restoration of its former glories still had some way to go (indeed, a longer way to go than was left to the building itself). Ahead of us, beyond the damaged screen, we could hear a choir singing the Sixty-Seventh Psalm. On either side of us stood the lesser members of the congregation: Ravensden ten-ants and neighbours, the curious of court society, not a few creditors hoping to serve writs, all in the most resplendent finery they could mus-ter. Many wore blue bridal ribbons upon their arms and gloves upon their hands, both of which had been distributed seemingly willy-nilly by our mother. I could hear the whispers of the less discreet:

'Poor earl, looks feebler than he did – '

'Tall lad, that Matthew, but a shame his hair's going – '

'God knows how he'll get it up – '

'You mean this isn't the Kendrick wedding?'

I should have been looking cheerily from side to side, giving a smile here and a wave there, a step or two behind my brother as our ranks dictated. Even men walking to the gallows have been known to manage such levity, but I could not. Nor, if truth be told, could the earl. Charles was ever uneasy when he was the centre of attention, and he strode forward as purposefully as his ancient wounds would permit, his eyes seemingly fixed on the high altar far ahead of us. At least I managed to glance to the sides and upwards, to take in some of the sights of the building; it was as good a way as any of avoiding the eyes of any of those who stared upon me.

We passed the once-glorious Beauchamp tomb to our right, sadly shattered by those who called themselves 'the godly'; this man, Sir John de Beauchamp, had been Admiral of England in King Edward the Third's time, and I gave him a little nod of salute, as one king's sailor to another. A little further away was the simple memorial to Sir Philip Sidney, the famous poet-hero of Queen Elizabeth's time. My grandfather, who had no time for poets, knew and detested Sidney, and contended that a poet slaughtered in leading a pointless cavalry charge on behalf of the iniquitous Dutch had no right to national veneration; poor grandfather, whose own poet son died a very similar death and was accorded very similar veneration as a result. Ahead and to the left, at the entrance to the north aisle of the quire, stood the tomb of King Ethelred, named Unready in our history. I recalled something of the memorial that had so fascinated me in childhood and shuddered, for it spoke of a conspiracy against that king's elder brother by his 'infamous mother', whose sin would only be expiated by a dreadful punishment. *Does history truly repeat itself?* I wondered, as I continued my way down the nave.

So we came to the crossing, and my heart lifted not a little at the sight of the unusually long and beautiful transepts, sweeping away to either side. As we climbed twelve steps and passed through the fine carved stone doorway into the quire, I could see my close family waiting before the altar, clustered around my infamous mother like the Praetorian guard around some ancient Caesar. Rosemary, myrtle, holly berries and the like were fastened to every conceivable place, their smell finally driving out the lingering odour of horse-dung. Light streamed through the vast rose window in the east end, above the heavily defaced altar screen. Alas, the light only made it easier to see where the original stained glass had been smashed or – higher up – shot out by the musket-balls of brutal iconoclasts. All in all, it was probably an appropriate setting for the event that was about to take place: for like the building itself, this marriage would be at once glorious and desperate.

We came before the high altar, bowed, and turned to acknowledge our family. Mother, bedecked in much of the unpawned Quinton jewellery and clad in a quite astonishing scarlet jacket that might have been fashionable for half a season forty years before, was serene. Cornelia was radiant in a splendid new dress of black silk taffeta with pearl earrings, all bought specially for the occasion, and torn between her pride in being able to show herself off and her anguish over what was about to take place. Despite myself, I smiled and felt proud, for she was a sight to gladden any husband. Elizabeth pointedly wore the old yellow gown that she had worn to our wedding in Veere, and unlike the other women, she had made little effort with her hair, which resembled the nest of a discontented crow. By contrast, Sir Venner had evidently purchased a formidably expensive new green frock-coat in the French style and was the only man present wearing that highest of the season's fashions, a periwig. Tristram, who had reluctantly forsaken his magisterial gown, glowered and avoided my mother's gaze. Those of our distant cousins who had been invited, and who had been solvent or sane enough to travel to London from France, Berkshire and other such grim fastnesses, grinned inanely at Charles and myself, for they, poor innocents, had no reason to believe that this marriage would be anything other than an occasion for rejoicing and unspeakable drunkenness, as has been the case at all weddings since Christ provided the libation at Cana.

We stood, and waited. At last the trumpeters sounded a fanfare and the choir struck up a great hymn of old Tallis. I turned, and saw the Lady Louise emerge through the stone doorway into the nave, accompanied by a great wave of murmuring and clucking from the congregation beyond. For she was magnificent: clad in a gown of shimmering silver moyre, cut as low as an Anglican wedding permitted, and a delicate headdress with biliments of gold, her hair billowing out behind in the traditional symbol of chastity. Before her, she carried a bouquet of snowdrops, as demurely as the most innocent of country maids; how she obtained those blooms so late in the year was a mystery known to herself and, no doubt, the royal gardeners. Behind her came a peculiar little procession consisting of a little gaggle of blue-accoutred page boys, young Venner and Oliver Garvey among them at their grandmother's insistence, but no young lasses at all. Now, at this moment in almost every wedding I have known, the eyes of the congregation should be upon the bride alone. But this was one of the many oddities at the marriage of the tenth Earl of Ravensden, for the eyes of every man and woman were torn between looking upon the bride and upon the tall man in a plain grey coat who walked at her side; the man who would shortly give her away, and the one man within that great church whose broad black hat could remain upon his head with impunity. For the King of England to attend a subject's marriage was rare enough, but for him to play such a prominent part in proceedings was doubly unusual. Charles Stuart being the man he was, of course, he revelled in it all, nodding vigorously to right and left, smiling broadly and exuding an overpowering sense of contentment. Thus he and the lady finally came before the altar, and Louise De Vaux exchanged the most ambiguous of glances with my brother. At last, the nuptials could commence.

Barwick, the sick old Dean of Saint Paul's, began the litany of weary inevitability. 'Dearly beloved, we are gathered together here in the sight of God, and in the face of this congregation, to join together this man and this woman in holy matrimony, which is an honourable estate – ' *An honourable estate? Christ in Heaven, what was honourable about any of this?* I heard only snatches of Barwick's words thereafter, mightily troubled as I was by my own thoughts. '… not be taken in hand unadvisedly, lightly, or wantonly, to satisfy men's carnal lusts and appetites, like brute beasts that have no understanding – ' *As if this had anything to do with my brother's carnal lusts, such as they were!* '… duly considering the causes for which matrimony was ordained. First, it was ordained for the procreation of children – ' *Aye, and what guarantee was there of that, given how poor my brother's prospects of fatherhood must have been? So unlike our sovereign lord standing by, who seemed to need only to brush the skirt of a woman for her to be birthed nine months later …*

Lost in my fevered thoughts, I almost missed that most delicious and yet most dreadful moment in any marriage service. Dean Barwick looked out to the congregation and proclaimed, 'If any man can show just cause, why they may not lawfully be joined together, let him now speak, or else hereafter for ever hold his peace!'

The cathedral, the greatest enclosed space in all of London, suddenly seemed very small and very silent. I sensed the presence of Cornelia, knowing full well that she was perfectly able (and willing) to lecture the congregation for at least two or three hours on the full gamut of reasons why Charles Quinton and Louise De Vaux should not be joined together, but I had made her swear on the sanctity of our own marriage vows that she would remain silent. Instead, I glanced at Tristram. He opened his mouth, but in that moment his eyes moved from my mother at his side (whose own glare was forbidding enough) to the King, standing beside the Lady Louise. I, too, shifted to look upon our sovereign lord again, and saw that his face was now fixed in a cold, vicious mask of prohibition. His eyes and my uncle's seemed to fight a battle of wills, but in that contest, there could only be one victor. Tris covered his mouth, coughed, and the moment passed.

The dean nodded contentedly, and proceeded with the words of the marriage service. 'Wilt thou,' he asked my brother, 'have this woman to thy wedded wife, to live together after God's ordinance in the holy estate of matrimony? Wilt thou love her, comfort her, honour and keep her in sickness and in health; and forsaking all other, keep thee only unto her, so long as ye both shall live?'

Charles seemed far away. Almost inaudibly, he said, 'I will.'

Barwick turned to the Lady Louise, whose eyes were downcast and demure. 'Wilt thou have this man to thy wedded husband, to live together after God's ordinance in the holy estate of matrimony? Wilt thou obey him, and serve him, love, honour, and keep him in sickness and in health; and forsaking all other, keep thee only unto him, so long as ye both shall live?'

'I will,' said Louise De Vaux, with all apparent sincerity and meekness. I wondered if she had been equally sincere and meek on the two previous occasions when she had sworn the same oath.

'Who,' asked Barwick, 'giveth this woman to be married unto this man?'

Charles Stuart smiled broadly, and all but thrust the Lady Louise's hand into the Dean's. He, in turn, brought my brother's hand over to take hers. And so it proceeded to the peroration. Then it was my moment. Barwick beckoned for the ring, the same plain band that had adorned my grandmother's hand, and although every instinct in my body directed me to throw the cursed thing through one of the holes in the rose window, I produced it and placed it without demur into my brother's hand. The Earl, in turn, placed the ring upon the lady's fourth finger, and spoke with an unexpected confidence: 'With this ring I thee wed, with my body I thee worship, and with all my worldly goods I thee endow: In the name of the Father, and of the Son, and of the Holy Ghost. Amen.' Barwick delivered the prayer of blessing before joining the right hands of the bride and groom, proclaiming loudly, 'Those whom God hath joined together, let no man put asunder!' And then the final knife into my heart: 'Forasmuch as Charles and Louise have consented together in holy wedlock, and have witnessed the same before God and this company, and thereto have given and pledged their troth to each other, and have declared the same by giving and receiving of a ring, and by joining of hands; I pronounce that they be Man and Wife together. In the name of the Father, and of the Son, and of the Holy Ghost, Amen.'

They be Man and Wife together. In that moment, Louise Quinton, Countess of Ravensden, glanced toward me, and smiled.

It was done.

* * *

Ravensden House was too small to accommodate the veritable legion of wedding guests, and was in any case far too humble (and unsafe) to receive the Lord's Anointed. Fortunately the hall of the Worshipful Company of Thatchers stood nearby, and both the cunning negotiating skills of Phineas Musk and the promise of royal patronage had made it available for the wedding feast of the Earl and Countess of Ravensden. Resplendent in the flower-bedecked Ravensden state coach, my brother and his bride made a triumphal procession from Saint Paul's to the hall, cheered by curious passers-by. Fiddlers and pipers went before them, and the entire congregation followed behind, some now bearing torches against the cold and the gathering dusk; I suspected that not a few were already some considerable way into their cups, having come to the cathedral in that state to begin with. Cornelia and I travelled in the Garvey coach, but it was a tense journey with little of the cheery banter that families are meant to make at weddings; my wife and my sister were increasingly at odds on the matter of our new sister-in-law, and I did not relish the role of umpire. Cornelia and Lizzie did essay a few venomous remarks about the dress sense of some of the guests, but neither of them had their hearts in it. Venner Garvey and I had nothing to say to each other; my good-brother's thoughts were as inscrutable as ever, but for my part, I could simply think of nothing suitable to say to a man whom I half-suspected of ordering the destruction of Deptford Dockyard and my ship.

It was a blessedly brief journey, but as we decamped into the Thatchers' Hall, Cornelia murmured to me: 'I think I am in hell, husband. And we have worse to come, of course. The bedding of that *slet*, that *smerige heks* –'

Her tirade was thankfully drowned out by the crescendo of noise that greeted us within the hall. Musk informed me that the pipers and the fiddlers seemed to have fallen out with each other, and now seemed to be engaged in a war to see which could be the loudest and most discordant. With many of the guests already so far agitated by drink, the ribaldry that ever attends a marriage was increasingly prevalent. A wench was roughly deprived of one of her garters, which was then hawked around some of the ruder young men. A disquieting number of maidens already wore clothing rather looser than it had been in the cathedral. Even my mother was disconcertingly jolly, seated on a large oak chair at the centre of proceedings, bestowing bonhomie on all around her. Phineas Musk was imbibing ale at a prodigious rate – as he said, what are weddings for, if not a heaven-sent opportunity to eat and drink enough for a week? There was a moment's relative sobriety when the King appeared. He passed through the throng like Moses through the Red Sea, the men bowing low, the women curtsying even lower to ensure that their bosoms were fully exposed to the expert royal eye. Charles Stuart was relatively temperate himself, but he seemed to inspire – indeed, actively encouraged – the most intemperate behaviour around him, and after that briefest pause to give due reverence to Majesty, the hubbub commenced anew.

In the midst of it all stood our earl and countess, receiving the congratulations of all and sundry. My brother was as diffident as ever, but the Countess revelled in it all, dispensing her radiant smile upon one and all. As we looked upon the spectacle, Tris came to our side. 'So the deed is accomplished,' he said. 'Alas that we failed to prevent it.' His opposition to the union remained undiminished, whereas, distressing though I found the whole sorry business, my hostility had been somewhat moderated by the words that Charles had spoken in the abbey ruins. In truth, my mind was in a ferment upon the matter, clarity eclipsed by endless clouds.

In those days, one of the great delights of our English marriage custom was the bedding: the bride and groom escorted to their chamber by the entire bridal party, given possets of sack, undressed of their stockings and garters which were then gleefully thrown at the married couple, all accompanied by much mirth and lewd advice. Although ours took place in Veere, the wedding of Cornelia and myself was attended by enough English exiles to enable a passable imitation of the ritual to take place; indeed, it took some considerable time to eject from our chamber the last of the bridal party (Harcourt, this, who claimed never to have witnessed a consummation in all his days). Nowadays, of course, in these mean and prudish times under our Hanoverian masters, it is increasingly common for bride and groom to skulk off alone to their chamber once the wedding feast is done – as if their bedding should be a *private business*! Thus far is old England decayed. Back in the year sixty-three, though, such mean-spiritedness was unheard of. Consequently, there had been not a little disquiet at the news that Charles and his lady were to be bedded privately, and in an apartment of the Palace of Whitehall, no less. It was given out that this was merely for convenience: it was said that it would be physically impossible to get the entire bridal party into the earl's bedroom at Ravensden House without risking the collapse of the building. However, I also suspected that my brother's craving for solitude, and the profound embarrassment that the lewd ceremony of bedding would have caused him, might have contributed not a little to the decision, which was causing much grumbling within the Thatchers' Hall. How little I then knew.

The King came over to us. Tris and I bowed, Cornelia curtsied. Charles Stuart was in the highest of spirits: he enjoyed weddings, primarily because they guaranteed the presence in one building of a significant amount of young female flesh, yet paradoxically, of course, he took the marriage vows themselves perhaps more lightly than any other man then living. Poor Queen Catherine, who was naturally nowhere to be seen on such a day.

'Matt. Mistress Quinton. Doctor Quinton,' said the King, cheerily. 'Damnably excellent day, don't you think?'

'As Your Majesty says,' Tristram replied. 'Your very presence brings rays of sun through the winter cold to warm the House of Quinton.' In that age of dissemblers and hypocrites, Tristram Quinton could stand his own with the best of them.

'Quite, quite,' said the best of them, seemingly accepting the words at face value; but then, the King spent every waking hour listening to flattery of the most sycophantic kind. Alas, it seemed to me that he was increasingly inclined to believe it. 'The bride looks splendid, does she not? Quite splendid. And Matt – the *Seraph* is almost ready to sail, I gather?'

Women and ships in one conversation; that must have been very close to Charles the Second's idea of heaven.

'I hope in a week or so, sire. When I left her, we awaited only our guns and the remainder of the victuallers' stores.'

'Excellent, excellent. You know the importance of this voyage to me, Matt.' He turned to Cornelia. 'And Mistress Quinton – we realise, of course, that your husband's absence for so many months upon our royal service will be a sore trial to you. You must come to court. Your presence will be an ornament to it, and we are sure we can find ways to while away your time.'

My face fell, for I knew full well how King Charles preferred to while away the time of women. But as our sovereign lord passed on to a nearby gaggle of eager maidens, Cornelia kicked me on the ankle. 'Husband!' she chid, to Tristram's amusement. 'You know me so little that you think I would jump into bed with another – even with the King? Sweet Christ, I would rather bed Musk than him! Besides, Tristram and I will have business enough, these next months.' She smiled wickedly. 'After all, that injunction about no man putting asunder what God has joined together makes no mention of a woman, does it?'

My heart sank; for God alone knew what mischief my wife and uncle could make without me to restrain them.

* * *

An hour or so later, I stood in the small yard that adjoined the Thatchers' Hall, gulping in some of the cold winter air. I was desperate for relief from the increasingly noxious atmosphere within. The great room itself was filling with the smoke of sea-coal fires and many pipes of tobacco, while the assembled company was becoming ever more raucous. Drunken young men of my age were doing what they are wont to do at weddings, vomiting onto the floor or steering equally drunken maidens toward dark corners. Tristram had deserted me, deciding that this was as good a moment as any to mend his fences with my mother; as far as they could be mended, given the twenty or more years of destruction that had been wrought upon them. Cornelia, too, had removed herself, she and Elizabeth decamping together as women sometimes do. I did not wish for words with Venner Garvey, nor with any of my vapid cousins, nor with any of the increasingly inebriated bridal party. So I sought solitude and a little fresh air before returning reluctantly to the fray.

'Matthew.'

I turned – 'My Lady.'

Louise, Countess of Ravensden, stood before me. 'Not "my lady", good-brother. Please. It should be Louise, between us.'

'Louise.' The word almost choked me. But I recovered myself – 'Good-sister. I am surprised that you absent yourself from your bridal feast.'

She smiled. It was not an unpleasant smile, if truth be told. 'Ah, Matthew, that is one of the curious things about weddings, I find: no one is troubled if the bride disappears for a while.' Her voice, too, had a strangely plausible lilt and modesty to it. 'It's always assumed that she must be attending to some aspect of her dress, or her headgear, or talking with some of the other guests, out of one's sight. And as you must be thinking, I have experienced enough weddings to speak with some authority on the matter.' She was a beauty, that much was certain: a beauty of the body and the mind. Clad in that splendid wedding gown, it was easy to see why she fascinated and enslaved men in equal measure. But I recalled that the Emperor Claudius was fascinated and enslaved by Messalina, and I also recalled the bloody outcome of that marriage.

She came closer. 'I know this cannot be easy for you, Matthew,' she said. 'If – when – Charles and I have a child – '

'Throughout my voyage I will pray that there may be fruit of your union,' I heard myself say. In the flesh, the Lady Louise seemed a very different creature to the monstrous she-devil conjured up by Tristram and Cornelia.

'As I shall pray every day that your voyage comes to no mishap,' she said, her friendly expression unaltered. 'Matthew, this union is all for the good of the family of Quinton. We should be friends, you know. Charles and I hope that you will be the model and mentor for the son we hope to have – for the future earl. A brave king's captain, indeed! Who could be finer? We are even minded to give him your name, that which you share with your noble grandfather. What a legacy to pass down to a future Earl of Ravensden!' I was appalled, and yet I was a little flattered, too, at the thought of my name being passed on; although still very young, I was already half-convinced that it would never be passed on through progeny of Cornelia and myself, and that saddened me. 'One of the most pleasing things about marriage,' continued the Countess Louise, 'is that we acquire not only new husbands and wives, but new families too. A widow's life is a mighty void in so many ways. I so look forward to making dear friends of you, your sister Elizabeth and her Venner, and your beloved Cornelia, of course.'

I could easily imagine Cornelia's reaction to that suggestion if it had been made directly to her; it would probably have involved the destruction of a large amount of crockery. But perhaps the erstwhile Lady De Vaux had given me an unwitting opportunity, and the drink had made me bolder than I would, or perhaps should, have been. 'As you say, good-sister, we can be fortunate in the families we acquire through marriage. I thank God every day for Cornelia's van der Eide kin and for Elizabeth's Venner.' *That is, I thank God that all the unspeakably dull van der Eides are safely distant across the sea and that Venner Garvey is most dreadfully troubled by the stone.* 'Cornelia and I look forward to meeting your own kin, of course. Especially your daughter.'

The smile remained fixed in place, but it seemed to me that the temperature in the yard suddenly fell a little. It was impossible to tell what thoughts were racing behind those damnably still eyes. Perhaps she thought of denying it, or of demanding to know how I knew. Her answer, when it came, was measured, almost good-natured. It was the species of answer that can only be given by the most innocent or the most guilty. 'Ah, that is unlikely, dear brother. Madeleine was ever a godly child, much inclined to the church. To the Church of Rome, the faith of her father, my ever-to-be lamented Sir Bernard.' The lady lowered her eyes to the ground. 'To avoid difficulties with my second husband, whose religious opinions were, shall we say, somewhat opposite, dear Madeleine was placed with the Poor Clares at Aubigny. When she was old enough to make her own decisions, she took holy orders with them. It is a great trial knowing that one is unlikely ever to see one's child again,' said the Countess, giving a little sigh, 'but it is so pleasing that she has found her vocation among worthy people.'

The lady smiled again, and touched my arm. 'It has been so good to have had this talk with you, Matthew, even if it is only of the briefest. I am glad that we can be friends, and that there will be no misunderstandings between us. I find that very often, people hear such tales of each other before they meet that prejudices and wild suspicions grow unbidden, whereas if they do but meet and talk, friendship flowers on the most unpromising soil.' She reached over and kissed me on the cheek. 'You know, we are very alike, you and I. We both find ourselves in stations that we were not born to, you a sea-captain, me a great lady. We have had both to make our way in roles that are not natural to us, living by our wits and our good fortune. Yes, we shall be friends, I think.'

With that, she made to return to the wedding feast. I stood there, alone in the yard, and watched her pass through the door.

My head swam. Friendship? It was beyond belief – the effrontery of the woman …

My emotions did battle with each other. Her comparison of her station and mine was preposterous; and yet there was truth in it, a deeply unsettling truth coming from the lips of a woman. Her manner seemed so plausible, so sincere. She had stirred feelings in me …

No. For good or ill I was set on the other path, and by accident or design she had shown me the end of that path. For I was convinced she had now given me the means to bring her down.

$\mathcal{T}$welve

'Erith Reach be damned,' said Lieutenant Castle, blowing warmth onto his one hand as another flurry of sleet came in on the wind, 'this reminds me of a Greenland voyage.'

Seraph was proceeding to sea. True to their word, and to my considerable surprise, the ordnance office and the victuallers had sent their barges down from the Tower on the day of the wedding, or so I was informed. The guns had been hauled aboard, with Lindman in his element. I returned to the ship from London on the following day, having said my farewells. Cornelia, distraught at the prospect of my absence for many months, was still determined to find a chink in the Lady Louise's armour, and to appease my wife I was prepared to assist her to the extent of sending one letter, which was now on its way to its destination beyond the shores of England. Thus I turned my thoughts once again to the sea and the distant prospect – in all senses – of the mountain of gold.

The wind was northerly, bringing an Arctic chill which turned each breath into a little frosty cloud. This meant that we began our voyage from Greenwich under tow, up Blackwall Reach into the teeth of the wind, only hoisting sail and our ensign as we rounded the point of

Greenwich Marsh and began to fall down into Woolwich Reach, taking advantage of the ebb as it began. The flat mud-lands on either side of the Thames were crusted with frost, and sleet showers came almost with every turn of the glass. We passed the dockyard of Woolwich, crowded onto the foreshore beneath the cliff and church behind. Unsurprisingly, all work seemed to be at a stand. The carcass of a great new ship rose from the stocks; encased in frost, it resembled the bones of a mammoth lost in the northern wastes. The sole consolation of the weather was that there was but little traffic upon the river. Merchant craft were ever more timid than king's ships, so they had sought the shelter of the various anchoring-grounds, awaiting more propitious conditions before continuing their long haul up to London. A few huddled under the shore of Galleons' Reach, but there were many more in Erith Reach; the smoke pouring forth from the alehouse chimneys of Erith town told of countless Dutchmen, Lubeckers, East Country men and God knows who else entertaining themselves before a more favourable wind and tide arrived to recall them to their duties.

As we came between Erith, on the south shore, and the aptly named Cold Harbour on the north, we made a turn from south-east to just north of east. This took us toward the mouth of Dartford Creek and the beginnings of the Long Reach. I watched as our yards and courses swung, heard the ropes strain, and listened to Castle's commands to the helmsman at the whipstaff on the deck below: 'Helm a-starboard!' 'Give her more helm!' 'Steady!' The manoeuvre was easy enough: the wind was not strong, the tide was with us and we were remaining on the port tack, but I did not envy the likes of Treninnick and Tremar as they beetled about the frost-crusted rigging.

William Castle and Kit Farrell were alongside me on the quarter-deck. We were all clad in thick coats; Castle and I had the additional protection of cloaks, and the lieutenant, who had spent most of his service in warmer climes and felt the cold mightily, also wore a rough woollen scarf around his neck.

'You know Greenland, Mister Castle?' I asked.

'Went there on a whaling voyage, once,' he said. 'That decided me in favour of the Levant and the Spanish Main, that it did.'

Kit smiled. 'I think you'll find the heat on the Gambia coast more congenial, then, lieutenant!' he said. Castle nodded happily at that.

We left the mouth of Dartford Creek to starboard. Ahead of us, on the other bank, the bare and frozen low ridge of the Purfleet Hills marked the beginning of Long Reach, the great straight channel that led down to Greenhithe.

Castle sniffed the wind with his increasingly ruddy nose. 'We could lie up in the Hope and make for the Downs tomorrow, straight over the Flats,' he said. 'Tides will be right. If the wind doesn't come more easterly or strengthens, we ought to manage it well enough.'

'I'll consult with Master Negus,' I said, 'and of course with Mister Plummer too.' Our pilot, this; the Trinity House of Deptford Strand insisted that the whole of the Thames, and much else besides, was pilot water, a very convenient injunction in terms of enhancing the finances of the said Trinity House. Thus the navigation and safety of every ship had to be entrusted to a pilot, even when that ship was the *Seraph*, bearing aboard her a lieutenant, a master, a boatswain and probably at least another twenty men who were better navigators than the painfully inept Plummer. For some reason, the pilot had decided to con the ship from the forecastle – perhaps because that location removed him somewhat from the contempt and laughter of those he knew to be his superiors. Somehow I did not envisage the timid Plummer favouring Lieutenant Castle's strategy of taking the direct passage across the Kentish Flats; even I had studied the charts for this early stage of our voyage, and could now read a chart well enough to guess that in the neap tides of that season, our pilot would favour staying far out to sea, in the main channel, avoiding the lee shore of north Kent, even if it meant taking many hours more to round the North Foreland and come safe into the Downs. What I did not tell Castle was that I was perfectly prepared to adopt Plummer's cautious counsels, albeit for very different reasons. Delaying our arrival in the Downs would give me a few more blessed hours without the company of Brian Doyle O'Dwyer, who was due to join the ship at Deal after yet another secretive conference with our sovereign lord the King.

We were in the dark muddy water of Long Reach now. In the far distance, off Greenhithe, another group of anchored merchantmen waited for the weather to turn. One of their kind was bolder, and was coming up against the ebb that was carrying us toward the distant sea; presumably his cargo was particularly urgent, or else he had been chartered by a particularly demanding set of factors.

Phineas Musk came on deck in that moment. I had spoken to him little since he made his revelations at Skelthorn; he had been busy about shutting up Ravensden House, or so he claimed. Musk shivered and scowled at the gloomy clouds. As was his wont, he then marched directly onto the quarterdeck as though he were the Lord Admiral, and took up a position at what was by rights the captain's own sanctum, the starboard rail. It was always difficult to tell whether Musk remained blissfully ignorant of the conventions of the sea, or whether he knew them perfectly well but made a point of flouting them.

He looked about him at the cold, empty marsh lands that stretched away on either side of the Thames and muttered, chiefly to himself, 'Damnable place. Hasn't changed much.'

I recalled that some, like the Barcocks, believed Musk originally came from these parts. I had never tackled him directly on the subject (tackling Phineas Musk directly upon *any* subject was rarely a productive stratagem, as my recent experiences had proved), but now I made the attempt. 'You were raised hereabouts, weren't you, Musk?'

The notion of Musk having ever been a babe in arms, or even a child, was somewhat unsettling; he always seemed to me to have been hatched fully formed, for he did not seem to have aged since first I became aware of him.

Musk's eyes were fixed on the approaching merchantman. 'Aye, hereabouts,' he said, distantly, 'and thereabouts. Odd thing, that, though.'

'Odd?' I demanded.

'Seen many a ship sail up and down the Long Reach in my young days,' said Musk, offering perhaps the most profound insight into his history that he had yet shared with any Quinton. 'Never seen one flying no ensign.'

Musk, the landsman incarnate, was quite right: the oncoming ship had no colours at its stern. But – 'He's no need to fly one until he's closer to us, Musk. As long as he dips it to us, and his topsails too, in good time, then we don't seize or sink him, and the King is satisfied.'

This, after all, was the edict drummed into even the most ignorant captain of the navy from the moment he received his first commission: enforcing the marks of respect due to the king's flag in these, his own seas, was as important as defending one's own honour to the death.

'Aye,' said Musk, 'but why would a ship on this water bother to take it down? They'd have had to salute the blockhouses down at Gravesend and Tilbury, then they know damn well they're likely to meet a king's ship coming down from Deptford or Woolwich at any time, and they'd have to salute Greenwich Palace anyway – '

William Castle, who had been listening and watching with some interest, intervened. 'Probably some lazy Frieslander or Holsteiner or the like,' he said. 'I expect he's been lying off Grays or Greenhithe for a night or two after saluting the blockhouses.'

I respected Castle, but I could see Kit Farrell, too, whose keen round face was ever an open book. And now the book told a tale of mounting apprehension. 'If he's on such a leisurely voyage, Mister Castle,' said Kit, 'then why is he coming on so briskly now, with so much sail aloft? When every other ship on the river has moored to await a better day? And why so urgent a passage when he's so lightly laden?'

We all studied the approaching ship with a new intensity. She was a large flyboat, the kind of craft that was ubiquitous in every European harbour; beamy, economical and (naturally) Dutch. As Kit had noted, she was also remarkably high in the water. So she could only be bound to take on a cargo in London – but if that was so …

One of William Castle's great strengths was that he was ever open to a different way of thinking about a matter. Slowly, he said, 'Y – yes, Mister Farrell, you have a point, I think. And that's damnably precise sheeting and reefing. Almost as good as ours, in fact. No, that's no lazy northman, at all.'

Only then did my inner alarm beacon burst into flame. I tensed. All of us there on the quarterdeck had the fire at Deptford in mind; of course we did. If that had been part of a conspiracy to prevent the sailing of the *Seraph*, then surely the perpetrators would not rest at just that single attempt? But I also had my own private reasons for suspecting the oncoming flyboat. My officers might possess infinitely greater knowledge of the sea, but they did not possess the very particular knowledge – and experience – that belonged to their captain. For my officers had not just fought a brutal sword fight with Habakkuk Leech and his murderous gang. My officers were not the target of the vengeance of a deranged Knight of Malta. My officers had not listened to one of the land's most powerful politicians warn that the mission of the *Seraph* would not be permitted to succeed. The approaching ship seemed to bear the imprimatur of each or all of those dark forces, and the dread grew in me.

As calmly as I could, I said, 'Gentlemen, we will clear for battle, if you please. I would have all necessary hands aloft. My compliments to Mister Negus and Gunner Lindman; I request their immediate presence on the quarterdeck.' Then an afterthought – 'Oh, my compliments to Mister Plummer. Please tell him that his services will not be required for some little time, and that for his own safety, I suggest he goes below.'

I expect to go to my grave, and remain there, as the only captain in the history of our illustrious navy who ever ordered the decks cleared for action so far upstream between the shores of Kent and Essex that he was almost twixt Surrey and Middlesex instead. This unique event was witnessed by a huddle of curious tinkers on the footslope of Purfleet, and also evidently caused not a little surprise to the off-duty larboard watch, who emerged complainingly into the bitter cold and a particularly vicious shower of sleet. Still, the entire crew set to with a will. I heard the clatter of the wooden partitions on the main deck being taken down, the dull thuds as the gunports lifted, the grinding of the gun carriages on the decks as our new battery was run out for the first time. *Seraph* was ready for her first battle.

The grim flyboat came on, she on the starboard tack, we on the port. Of course, in the normal order of things she would give way to us, even though we had the wind – naturally, a merchant's hull should always give way to a king's, regardless of their tack or position – and salute us in her passing. But I was now entirely convinced that she had no intention of giving way to us at all. I determined to prove it.

'Gentlemen,' said I to my quarterdeck officers, 'what say you to coming to starboard by three points?'

Negus, who had joined us, was quick to respond to this most unspeakable heresy. 'Alter course at all, sir? An act unworthy of a king's ship? And alter course to *starboard*?'

'I think the King and His Royal Highness will forgive me the dishonour of giving way, Mister Negus, if it saves his ship from a head-on collision. And if you were he, what would you least expect *Seraph* to do?'

Negus and the rest saw my point, and I was mightily gratified to receive a smile and a nod from Kit Farrell, for this proposition of mine was truly stretching my infant command of seamanship to its limits. My thinking was thus. If, as I believed, the flyboat had no intention of giving way, but was determined rather upon ramming us, then he was probably gambling that we would do one of two things: either ploughing straight into him thanks to the arrogant pride, or the unvarnished ignorance, to be expected from a mere gentleman captain; or else, if the veteran navigators on the quarterdeck prevailed over their feeble chief, the *Seraph*, still on the port tack, would surely alter course to larboard to avoid collision, thus keeping the weather gauge. I prayed that the skipper of the approaching ship was no chess-playing Machiavel who might anticipate my double bluff.

If she had a skipper at all. For as the flyboat came steadily on, no man could be seen on her deck, or in her yards. She seemed as a ghost ship.

Francis Gale came on deck in that moment, looked at the approaching vessel, and raised an eyebrow.

I said, 'A prayer might be suitable, Chaplain.'

Gale improvised with considerable dexterity, as he always did. 'O Lord of hosts, fight for us, that we may glorify thee. O Lord God, preserve us from those who seek our destruction. O Lord, arise, help us, and deliver us for thy Name's sake. Amen.'

As many as were within earshot repeated the 'Amen', Musk with rare enthusiasm for such an ancient cynic. Gale said, 'Well, indeed. The esteemed Lords of Convocation didn't devise a special prayer for this situation, Captain. Let's hope the Lord is in a tolerant mood today.'

The two ships seemed to be approaching each other at an ever-increasing rate, the flyboat relentless in its course. Time for one last gesture – 'Mister Lindman!' I cried from the quarterdeck through another flurry of sleet. The gunner, down in the ship's waist, raised his hat in salute. 'A warning shot from the bow chaser if you please!' This, after all, was the nicety that we would go through to enforce the salute to the flag on any other recalcitrant merchantman.

Lindman passed on the order to the crew manning one of the two nine-pound minions, up in the forecastle, and the gun fired. The shot tore a hole in the foresail of the flyboat, but still she came on.

Musk suggested, quite mildly, that this might be a good moment to make our move. Kit shook his head. We held our course. Every man in the rigging, every man on the deck, had their eyes trained only on the flyboat.

Then, as if they were commanded at once by some invisible lever, Kit, Castle and Negus all nodded in unison.

'*Helm three points to starboard!*' I cried.

Now we would see if the King of England's confidence in the sailing qualities of the *Seraph* was well placed ...

By God, so it was! With the whipstaff brought over, our bow swung to starboard almost at once – the *Happy Restoration, Jupiter* and *Wessex* had been veritable carthorses in comparison ...

And in the same moment, the judgment of Captain Matthew Quinton, too, was redeemed. For the flyboat had made her move – made it, indeed, before I gave the order to my own helm. With a slower, broader ship and a more sluggish rudder, her invisible captain could only give his own order, anticipating the manoeuvre he felt we must make, a little while before I issued mine. Thus the flyboat, too, moved to starboard; but instead of ramming into us and causing untold damage, she passed harmlessly to larboard, barely a few feet away from our own larboard side.

'I will magnify thee, O God, my King,' murmured Francis Gale, 'and I will praise thy Name for ever and ever.' He smiled at me. 'Methinks the rest of the Hundred and Forty-Fifth psalm will be most appropriate for the next ship's prayers, Captain.'

Now, all was changed. For we were a ship of war, with fourteen primed and deadly pieces of ordnance on our larboard side. And the other was but a flyboat.

'Gunners!' I cried. 'Prepare to give fire!' Wait until the relative movement of the two hulls meant that all our broadside was able to bear – wait – '*Give fire!*'

Ours was still a raw and untrained crew, and our fire was hardly in unison. We were so close to the other that we could hear the balls striking the hull like hailstones upon a window. Many must have gone straight through, for a flyboat's scantlings are so much lighter than those of a man-of-war, but it was impossible to see until our own gunsmoke cleared – and with the wind from the north, that smoke carried back over our own deck, blinding and choking us. When at last it cleared, and we had coughed the acrid fumes from our throats, we observed that the flyboat, badly damaged and listing to larboard, was continuing her own turn to starboard, coming ever closer to the wind and to the Essex shore as she did so.

Castle saluted formally. 'Captain,' he said. 'Shall we come round, sir, take that cursed craft and arrest her murderous crew?'

Of course, that was the natural course of action for us to take; but even with as nimble a ship as *Seraph*, bringing her about, then beating back against wind and tide, would take no little time, especially in such raw conditions. We would then hardly get round into the Hope on that favourable ebb. And besides …

'She's going to run herself aground,' said Kit Farrell. 'We'd never get up to her in time.'

We held our course. We officers went to the stern rail of the poop as one man, and watched as the flyboat ran herself onto the mud of the Essex shore. The small boat that she towed behind her was hauled in, and six men climbed down into it. Six men; the skeleton crew that had sought to wreak untold damage on the *Seraph*.

But on whose behalf? My mind conjured up those same faces... Leech, Garvey, Montnoir. Whoever it was must have been mightily determined to prevent our sailing, and able to command a fair purse – for it would have cost no pittance in gold to obtain a flyboat for such a mission, and to pay a crew a sufficient wage for them to risk their lives or liberty in such a way. Discovering the answer would needs wait, for *Seraph* was sailing on majestically, downstream on the ebb, approaching the turn in the river at Greenhithe. Beyond that, it would be the Hope, the salute to Gravesend and Tilbury, the Nore, and finally the open sea at last.

Now, truly, the voyage of the *Seraph* was beginning.

PART THREE

∞

His Majesty's Ship, The Seraph

At Sea and in the Gambia River
December 1663 to April 1664

*T*hirteen

The papists have a notion called purgatory. This is neither heaven nor hell, but rather a place between, where souls wait an eternity to be judged. But one does not need to be a papist, nor indeed to die, to experience purgatory: one merely has to be aboard a ship in the Downs. On a cold, foggy December morning, with but little wind – and that contrary – there are few places that more closely resemble a bleak eternal antechamber. Once again I studied the lights and fires of distant Deal, the ghostly shape of the white cliffs to the south and the squat, menacing bulks of old Harry the Eighth's castles that lined the bay, all of them appearing and disappearing intermittently as the fog swirled about us. I looked about from my quarterdeck at the shrouded shapes of perhaps a hundred ships at anchor, the souls aboard awaiting the judgment of fair winds that would bear them toward their destinations. Norwegian timber ships bound for Spain, Frenchmen bound for London with the wines of Gascony, and dozen upon dozen of Dutch flyboats, bound for every harbour on the globe; all of them congregated in that broad anchorage. To seaward of us lay Holmes' *Jersey*, a Fourth Rate as tough and experienced as her adventurous captain, and beyond her the *Mary*, a battle-scarred Third Rate that had been called *Speaker* in Cromwell's day. Waves broke on the Goodwin Sands, the great barrier that kept ships safe between the open sea and the Kentish coast; one day, though, those sheltering sands and the waves breaking upon them would do for the same *Mary,* three other great ships and fifteen hundred blameless seamen of England, all perished in the greatest storm ever known in these isles. Even forty years before that catastrophe, I stood upon my deck and prayed that one ship, just one, would meet such a fate. She was the unkempt merchant ship of middling size that was beating down toward us from the island of Thanet.

Kit Farrell was at my side, and Kit was his accustomed cheery self, reeling off the sailing qualities and likely cargoes of ship after ship with the enthusiasm of a schoolboy. He could not know I was experiencing a kind of double purgatory that was unique to myself; for it was here, in the Downs, that Colonel Brian Doyle O'Dwyer would come aboard the *Seraph*.

Kit pointed toward the approaching ship. 'I don't envy the soldiers, cooped up aboard her all the way down to the Guinea shore,' said Kit. 'She's old and narrow. She'll pitch and yaw like a crazed thing in anything worse than a swell. And look there, sir, her owners must have cut her stern down at some point, and reshaped the bow. All to create a little more space to cram in a little more cargo and give them a little more profit. A botched job, that, right enough. Any carpenters' crew of the navy could fashion something better in a matter of a few watches, if not sooner. Aye, an ugly brute indeed is our friend, the *Prospect of Blakeney.*'

The troop ship manoeuvred clumsily through the waters of Sandwich Bay and came to an anchor between the *Jersey* and ourselves, making the private signal with the former. The longboat that she towed in her wake was pulled in to the side, and after a few minutes, a cloaked shape descended into it. O'Dwyer.

Kit sensed my mood and fell silent before he left me, for he had his part to play in this grim charade.

The boat's crew, so many unwitting Charons, came alongside *Seraph*, and O'Dwyer pulled himself onto our deck, a brown face above the deep red hue of the king's uniform. He drew his sword, saluted the king's ensign, and was in turn saluted by the whistle-note of Boatswain Farrell.

My last gesture of defiance was to remain rooted to my quarterdeck, forcing the renegade to come to me. We doffed in exchange to each other, and he looked about him with an air of a contented man.

'So, Captain,' he said in that strange accent of his, half-Irish and half-Arab, 'this is your command. A fine frigate indeed, this *Seraph*. Named for the fiery angels guarding the throne of God, as I recall. His Majesty is judicious in his choice of names.'

If not in his choice of colonels – The blackness of my mood coloured my reply. 'Indeed, sir. One day, no doubt, she will prove mightily useful for firing at the corsairs of the Straits.'

'Ah, them.' O'Dwyer remained obstinately cheery. 'You know, I had almost forgot about them?'

The innate courtesy of my kind won a close-run battle, and I said, 'You will take some refreshment, Colonel?'

I led him below to my cabin, where a glowering Musk stood over some mead and cake. The Irishman ate and drank greedily, all the while making inconsequential conversation about the weather, the *Prospect's* passage down from the Tower, and His Majesty's countenance (inscrutable, as ever) at their last interview. At length, though, the moment I had been dreading could be delayed no longer.

'Now, Colonel,' I said, in as matter-of-fact a way as I could manage, 'I have given much thought to the matter of our messing arrangements – '

O'Dwyer waved his hand airily. 'Oh, no matter, my dear captain! I am perfectly content with my humble berth aboard the *Prospect*. I know full well that honour demands you should surrender your cabin to me, as the senior personage embarked, and content yourself with one of your lesser officer's pestilential hutches. But there is no need, I assure you.'

Behind him, Musk shook his head vigorously, thereby underlining my own reaction. 'No, sir,' I replied, 'my honour would simply not hear of it.' It was not a manner of the relative status of a military colonel and a naval captain: aboard *Prospect*, among a body of soldiers who would be overawed by his rank and a crew free of the constraints of naval discipline, O'Dwyer would undoubtedly be better placed to essay the flight back to his corsair friends that we all expected him to attempt at the first opportunity. Holmes and I had discussed the matter at some length, and I concurred reluctantly with his assessment: to wit, it is an eternal truth that for all the temporary inconvenience, it is preferable to keep a mad dog in one's view and under one's control than to unleash it. 'Thus I have a compromise to propose,' I said gritting my teeth. 'A captain's cabin, even on a Fifth Rate, has ample space for two. Yet we both deserve the privacy due to our rank. Consequently I shall arrange for a partition to be erected, and a new door cut in the bulkhead yonder. You, Colonel – ' I was very nearly sick as I spoke the words – 'may even have the starboard, and the captain's quarter gallery'.

A captain and a gentleman can make no greater sacrifice than to surrender his personal place of easement, especially when it is being surrendered to a traitor of the foulest sort.

O'Dwyer seemed genuinely perplexed by the seeming generosity of my offer, but only for a moment. Then he nodded, ran his hand through his ochre hair, and spoke slowly and coldly. 'Of course, Captain Quinton. As you say. Aboard his own ship, a captain's word is as statute law.' Those cold green eyes narrowed. 'After all, who am I, a mere renegade, to dispute it, even if clad in the fine rags of a superior officer?'

The Irishman's acquiescence surprised me: both Holmes and I had expected roaring, or at least a venomous snarling, in opposition to my suggestion. On reflection, that acquiescence should have troubled me far more than it did. As it was, I summoned Carpenter Shish and his crew, and O'Dwyer resumed his assault upon the cake. The impressively efficient Shish and his men arrived within minutes, replete with deals, saws and hammers, and set to with the urgency that can only be witnessed in sailors endeavouring to impress soldiers. The din of their partition-building made impossible even the strained conversation between O'Dwyer and myself; at length, the renegade excused himself and indicated that he would return to *Prospect* to attend to the loading of his belongings and to issue orders to his second-in-command, a Captain Facey.

As we watched the longboat pull away and disappear once more into the fog that enveloped the Downs, Musk turned to me and remarked, gruffly, 'Wooden walls do not a prison make, or whatever your father's old friend Lovelace said. He'll need watching, that one.' He nodded toward the receding shape of O'Dwyer, ensconced in the stern of *Prospect*'s longboat. 'Or, better still, filleting.'

It did not take long for me to regret my honourable gesture. I was in my truncated half-cabin, attempting to rearrange my possessions around the demi-culverin that now cribbed and confined me even more than it had done before. I contemplated the chamber pot acquired for me by Musk in Dover, and shuddered. Beyond the partition, I could hear every tiny sound as O'Dwyer arranged his own possessions, which seemed to include an unsettling number of knives, swords and other blades of indeterminate size, whistling and singing all the while. To this day, I do not know whether he did so unconsciously or as a deliberate taunt to the Captain of the *Seraph*; but his musical range seemed as catholic as it was tuneless, embracing a clutch of French airs, some songs of his Irish childhood and a succession of strangely pitched Arab chants. I looked about in horror, seeking some escape from my cell. Beyond the stern window and through the fog lay Holmes' *Jersey*, but Holmes was ashore, apparently carousing with the Governor of Dover. Jordan, Captain of the *Mary*, was old, godly, and insufferably dull. I could go ashore, but Deal, that very Gomorrah of Kent, would contain an entire army of mariners, most of them whoring, drinking and brawling from dawn 'til dusk and thus on 'til dawn once more. Cornelia and my friends might as well have been an eternity away. That left only my ship, a Fifth Rate frigate of but three hundred and fifty tons burthen and ninety feet in length, and where aboard her would be free of the foul presence of O'Dwyer? Francis Gale was ashore, visiting an old friend who had a parish a little way beyond Richborough …

At last, I threw open the door newly cut in the bulkhead and made my way to the quarterdeck, thence to the poop. But here, too, no saving peace was to be found. O'Dwyer was still beneath my feet, his singing clearly audible. There were a few men on the upper deck and on the forecastle, but by chance, almost none of them were familiar faces from my old Cornish coterie. I craved solitude. I craved clear air, not the fetid fogs that still swirled around the ship, albeit now rather less densely than they had. The one reassuring sight was the stocky bulk of Kit Farrell, stepping out from the forecastle …

On impulse, I strode across the upper deck to meet him. 'Boatswain Farrell,' I said formally, 'you recall the time when you told me of the noblest experience to be found on a ship? And the best way for a captain to survey the true dimensions of his command?'

Kit looked at me quizzically. 'Indeed, sir. But – '

'I have a mind to be about it.'

'*Now*, Captain? But it's hardly – '

'Now, Boatswain.'

'Aye, aye, sir.'

Kit's expression was curious, but he was too good an officer to argue the case. It was fortunate (or, as it transpired, unfortunate) that Musk was nowhere to be seen, for he would have had no such qualms.

We went to the starboard rail, and without a second thought I took hold of a lanyard, lifted myself onto that thin palisade, and swung myself out, over the side of the ship, to obtain a footing on the lower shrouds.

Kit said, 'Gently, sir. Make sure of your grip and your footing. It's dank weather, the shrouds are sodden – '

But I took no heed. I had observed enough of veteran topmen going aloft to know the manner of it. Hand over hand, as sure of their footing as spiders ...

I climbed with the blind determination of a man fleeing a pursuing demon. At one step, the demon seemed to take the form of an Irish renegade in a red uniform; at another, a plausible, cunning bride; at another, a smiling, duplicitous monarch. Up, to the foot of the futtock shrouds that stretched out to the edge of the maintop. The true seamen went that way, scorning the lubber's hole through the top itself. Matthew Quinton, true seaman, would go that way, then.

I pulled myself outward, then up, then over, fearing nothing, and at last stood on the top, clinging with one hand to the maintopmast. I looked about me, and was amazed by the glories of what I beheld. At that height, the fog was all but gone, consigned to the parts beneath. I could see the lookout on *Mary*, staring quizzically across at me, and the masts of the myriad of ships that lay within the Downs. I could see the square mass of Dover's great keep, standing sentinel above its cliff to the south. And there, in the far distance, the matching white cliffs of France, my grandmother's homeland ...

Kit Farrell pulled himself up behind me, having maintained a respectful distance (although in truth, if he had been so minded he could have reached the top in a fraction of my time).

'Well done, Captain!' he cried. 'To be fit for the yards and tops – the mark of a true seaman, by God!'

But in that moment the breeze freshened a little, and the ship lurched. I felt the momentary terror of losing my grip on the maintop as my body followed the pitch. I clutched desperately for the maintop. As I regained my grip, I could see the fog roll away from the deck beneath, like the parting of a curtain.

The deck so very far beneath.

There were our great guns; not great now, but very small indeed, no more than little tubes. And there, some of my men. Why, even Musk, now staring aloft in some apparent dismay, was no larger than a mouse upon the floor ...

A strange picture flashed across my mind; a scene unrecalled for almost twenty years. A small excited child taken by its father to the pinnacle of a church tower, there to be shown his ancestral lands stretching all around – only to dissolve in screaming terror at the thought of such a great height, and the child's unshakeable conviction that he would inevitably throw himself from it.

'Kit,' I said, 'I fear I have been proud. Impulsive. A fool.' I swallowed very hard. 'Kit. Can't move. Can't breathe.'

The young man must have grasped my meaning at once. My face must have told its own story, for it felt strangely cold of that sudden; as cold and clammy as it feels now, here in my dotage, as I step ever nearer the graveside. My friend took hold of my free arm and forced me both to grip the maintop with both hands and to look upwards, away from that fascinating, horrifying sight beneath. With all my heart, I cursed my precipitate flight from the merely unpleasant company of Brian Doyle O'Dwyer to this far more terrible predicament.

The swell caught the hull again, and the mast lurched once more. My head throbbed, my eyes clouded and darkened. I tried to swallow, but could not, for my throat felt dry and hard. I clung ever more tightly to the maintopmast and prayed, silently but with a sudden and rare zeal, to the Anglican God of my fathers and, for good measure, to the papist God of my French grandmother.

Kit blew a short, shrill pipe on his whistle, to what end I knew not. Then he turned to me in a matter of fact way and said, 'Not proud at all, sir. The opposite, I reckon. Not many captains are willing to risk all on an ascent. And none I know who possesses a dread of heights. The men will respect you the more for it, Captain Quinton, that they will.' At that moment I cared not a jot for the respect of the men, but I was too consumed by terrors to tell Kit that. As it was, my boatswain continued his discourse as though we were whiling away a pleasant evening in an alehouse. 'Why, the first year or more that I was at sea, I feared the masthead more than Old Nick. Even fell off it once, straight into the sea. Fortunate for me, sir, it was only my uncle's ketch, so the mast was far less than half the height of this – and we were in shoal water, close off the Orford Ness, so there was but little difficulty in fishing me out. But it was a mighty fright, all the same.'

I was still very young, but Kit, of my own age, had evidently already learned a lesson that it took me many more years to master: that soothing, distracting words can diminish even the darkest of horrors. I envied him then, and not for the first time. My own age, but master of the situation. Master of the right words. Master of his captain.

A shuffling and a familiar grunt heralded the arrival of a second man on the maintop – John Treninnick, the stunted monoglot Cornishman whose dexterity upon the yards was the stuff of legend upon our lower deck. Thus the purpose of Kit Farrell's whistle revealed itself.

'Now, Captain,' said Kit, 'I'll go down beneath you, and Treninnick at your side. Through the lubber's hole this time, I think, sir.'

Reluctantly, I glanced downward, and located the edge of the lubber's hole with my foot. Kit dropped lightly through it and gripped the shrouds beneath. One force, and one force alone, impelled me to loosen my grip on the maintopmast and haul myself through the hole: my ferocious determination not to be carried down to the deck in Treninnick's arms, like some swaddling babe, thereby dishonouring at a stroke the many illustrious generations of the House of Quinton. Once I had begun the descent, a rather more practical consideration revealed itself. Treninnick, who could have been up and down the mast thrice in the time it took me to get down, was not a patient man, and clearly had to restrain himself from overtaking me. Despite his remarkable agility, he was not a markedly light man either. Thus the prospect of my fingers being crushed beneath Treninnick's calloused and pungent bare feet drove me ever downward. And all the while, as I continued to look straight ahead at the mainmast (a sight far preferable to the upward spectacle of Treninnick's feet and arse), Kit Farrell kept up his cease-less, calming banter: 'Of course, you'll find Myngs at his masthead at the slightest excuse, but that's affectation – a proud Norfolk tarpaulin, Myngs is, and he'll ever chance to prove himself better than any man of his company. Now Lawson, well, he started on the colliers, so he's not a man to climb the shrouds – '

With that, my foot struck the starboard rail, and I swung on the shroud to deposit myself upon the *Seraph*'s deck once again.

Quite a crowd of the curious had gathered upon the upper deck by now, a plainly disapproving Phineas Musk at the head of them. I con-trolled myself with some difficulty, looked about me, and said casually, 'As you say, Boatswain, the *Mary* seems to be in some danger of fouling her bower. But our deck appears in order apart from that small matter of the poor stowing of the sheet shot. Order a party to see to it, if you please.'

Kit saluted and smiled knowingly.

With that, I turned on my heel and retired to my half-cabin, where I shivered, sweated, and retched long and hard.

$\mathcal{F}$ourteen

The *Seraph* and *Jersey* were thirty-eight days out of the Downs and seven days south-west of the Lizard. This unconscionable delay in getting from one end of the English Channel to the other was caused by weather as foul as only an English winter can bring: a dirty storm, followed by dense fog, followed by a still dirtier storm before the whole process began anew. We hove to repeatedly, bringing down our yards and topmasts; this would not always have been necessary for warships, but we had to defer to the lesser sailing qualities of the *Prospect of Blakeney*. Cooped up between decks for so long, arguments and fights between Bristolians and Cornishmen broke out almost every watch, so Boatswain Farrell and his mates were kept fully occupied. The little fleet spent Christmas Day hove to and soaked to the skin in Saint Helen's Bay off the Isle of Wight, praying for the slightest glimmer of seasonal cheer and goodwill to all men. It never came. Of course, we did our best, in the true old traditions of the navy: the trumpeters came round the ship at four in the morning, playing a greeting at every officer's cabin despite being flung across the deck and into bulkheads after almost every note; Francis Gale preached on Zechariah Chapter Nine, Verse Nine, despite having to do so below decks with two men holding him relatively steady as he read from Holy Scripture; and we ate Bradbury's cremated Christmas repast of beef, plum puddings and mince pies, each man cutting his food as hastily as he could while his neighbour held his goblet steady, then each returning the favour to the other. As I stood on the quarterdeck that Christmas afternoon, watching through biting rain as the shore of Wight rose and fell crazily, I wished I was sitting with Cornelia in front of the great log fire in the library at Ravensden. Yet again, I wondered what insane urge had made me turn down my King's offer of a safe commission in the army. His Majesty's horse guards would be warm and dry in barracks. His Majesty's horse guards would not be voyaging to a land of oblivion in search of a 'mountain of gold' that did not exist. His Majesty's horse guards would …

All voyages have these moments when it seems that the weather will never alter and one will never be dry again. But alter it will, and a man's mood alters with it. Thus it was that on a January day, when England would be shivering under a blanket of frost and snow, the *Seraph* had most of her sail aloft on a truly glorious day, with sun glinting upon the waves and a steady, warming breeze from West North West.

Alas, the weather is not the only thing that can alter a man's mood. In that moment, Brian Doyle O'Dwyer came on deck.

'A very good morning to you, Captain Quinton!' he cried with unwonted good humour. 'You slept well, I trust?'

'Indeed, sir.' This was a loose translation of my rather franker private opinion: *No I did not, you foul renegade, partly because of your unearthly snoring, partly because of your very presence but a few feet from my own.* Such were but two of the unwelcome consequences of the presence of our guest aboard the *Seraph*; but there were others, not all so personal to me. The dinners of the officers of a king's ship should be occasions for boundless good cheer engendered by the fellowship of the sea. They should be times when men talk freely, delight in each others' company and raise toasts to wives, friends or kings. They should not make the guts churn with foreboding. But that is what every single meal partaken of by the officers of the *Seraph* became. It was as though a company of good fellows had invited a last guest unknown to all of them, and suddenly discovered he was the Antichrist.

Of course, O'Dwyer ignored it all, or affected to. He talked. And talked. Then he talked some more. He had experience and opinions on every matter under the sun. He advised Mister Shish on ways of remedying his problematic chain pumps. He spoke authoritatively to Lindman about the relative merits of sakers and minions, and to Negus on the tides of the Straits of Gibraltar. But above all, he talked with Francis Gale; and Francis, being Francis, at least presented an appearance of being interested in the man's words. They spoke of theology and the holy book of the Prophet, although O'Dwyer seemed to have abandoned that book's precepts as readily as he had thrown off the identity of Omar Ibrahim, judging by the way in which he consumed all the wine, sack and punch that could be placed before him. They talked of the thousands of white slaves held hostage in Algier and the other Barbary regencies – O'Dwyer admitting a little too flippantly that he had been responsible for the capture of some hundreds of them – and of the pitiful, half-hearted gestures at redeeming them made by every European nation, England included. So it went on, day after day.

Yet little by little, I started to pay more heed to what the man said: he talked well, and had knowledge and interests far beyond those of the stolid tarpaulins at the table. At first, though, he conversed very little with me when we ate, and the same was true also of Lieutenant Castle. But then, we were the two officers on the *Seraph* who had also been aboard *Wessex*, and had thus seen O'Dwyer as he was before he reinvented himself. We had witnessed his Moorish self, and his humiliation. I wondered, too, whether his distance from me was due to the fact that unlike almost all of the others, I knew that despite all his bravado, O'Dwyer was truly as a fox in a hunt, with Montnoir as relentless in his pursuit of his quarry as old Actaeon himself.

On this particular morning, O'Dwyer seemed to have no thoughts of Montnoir, nor of the mountain of gold. He looked about with interest at the work of the ship; we were making excellent time, averaging some forty to fifty leagues a day by the log, but even so, we were making ready to put up our spritsail topmast as well. Thus men were busy on the forecastle, securing ropes and blocks – garnet-tackles, they seemed to be called – to guy-ropes slung between foremast and bowsprit preparatory to the hauling out of the small mast to the very front of the ship. Such activities had been sublime mysteries to me until very recently, but now I was beginning to understand the reasoning behind placing *that* tackle at *that* point, where it could take the strain when *those* men hauled upon it.

O'Dwyer watched for some minutes, then turned to me and said, 'So much more complicated than a galley, Captain! So many moving parts. So much more that can go wrong. And, of course, of no use at all in a flat calm.'

'Well then, Colonel,' I said, 'if you're missing your galleys so much, perhaps you will seek the command of one again ere long. Or are the Barbary regents not as forgiving as our King?'

The Irishman laughed. 'Ah, Captain, now why should I seek to return to my former employers, when King Charles has been so much more mightily generous to me? Being a colonel for him suits me well enough, I think. And a ship captain's cabin is markedly more comfortable than that on a galley. Even half a cabin,' he said, mischievously.

William Castle came to my rescue, announcing that we were ready to commence the hoisting of the topmast into position. I nodded my acquiescence, though I was aware that my role in such an affair was still that of a cipher. Castle went forward to supervise the exercise, and I watched with O'Dwyer as a party containing Polzeath, Macferran, Treninnick and three of the Bristol men began to manhandle the short mast toward the bowsprit. There seemed to be some altercation among the men – Castle moved toward them, growling a warning – Upon a sudden, Macferran let go of the mast and let fly at one of the Bristolians, his young Scots fists pummelling the man about the chest and head. Two other Bristol men and a couple of Londoners joined the fray at once. Polzeath, Carvell and a couple of Cornishmen retaliated in the same instant, leaving the mast dangling forlornly. I had feared something of the sort since the early days of our voyage; some of the London and Bristol drafts were very rogues, Kit had reported much bickering in the messes, and I had already been forced to order punishments for such offences as lying and excessive drunkenness.

'What curious discipline,' said O'Dwyer, with insufferable sarcasm.

But discipline was already on its way. It came in the shape of Kit Farrell, striking men vigorously with his rattan cane, and two of his mates, who physically pulled the combatants apart. The two instigators, Macferran and the Bristol villain – a bearded creature named Russell – were manhandled away from the throng and hauled before the quarterdeck. Kit reported to me formally, saluting upon his approach, and requested to know my pleasure.

Now, this business was hardly a court-martial affair – if every brawl on every ship of war reached a court, the navy would spend its whole time doing nothing else. But in a sense, that made the matter more difficult for me. It was the sort of case that was left solely to the discretion of the captain, and that presented me with a terrible dilemma. I would order Russell flogged without a moment's hesitation; he probably deserved it for a dozen other crimes that had escaped even Kit's rigorous attention to detail. But Macferran was one of my own following, one of that heroic band who had fought alongside me in the life-or-death battle aboard the *Jupiter* off his native isle in Scotland. I liked Macferran, and although he was not Cornish himself, my Cornish coterie had adopted him as one of their own. I could hear the whispers among the Bristolians and the Londoners: 'One of Quinton's favourites. You watch. He'll get nothing, and Russell will get the lash.' Cornishmen scowled at the whisperers, but the expressions of many of them suggested that they were hoping for exactly that outcome.

I leaned upon the quarterdeck rail. 'I will not have this brawling!' I shouted. 'This is a king's ship, not some tavern, and every man on this ship is bound by the king's discipline! *Every* man!' I emphasised that, and for some reason, I glanced at O'Dwyer as I said it. 'Very well,' I continued. 'I have witnessed the incident. I do not need to hear depositions, or the justifications of the two men before me. You – Russell. Five lashes. You – Macferran. You were the original instigator. Whatever Russell said to you, no man can doubt that you were the first to use your fists. I witnessed it. So did we all. Eight lashes. Now!'

There was an audible gasp from the Cornish, and not a little muttering from the other contingents in the crew. Kit and his mates led the two reprobates forward to the capstan. Russell was the first to be stripped of his shirt and tied to the capstan spokes. His back provided clear evidence that this was not his first flogging; far from it, indeed.

Pegg, the best of the boatswain's mates, took the whip, and waited for my signal.

I nodded.

The whip lashed across Russell's back, immediately bringing up a great bloody welt. Pegg laid the next stroke across the first, making the form of a cross. The rogue made no cry. *Three – four – five*. At the last, Russell was cut loose from the capstan and given back his shirt. He donned it with apparent unconcern, shrugging off the solicitation of Surgeon Humphrey.

It was Macferran's turn. He was brave enough as they secured him to the capstan, but the first stroke from Pegg brought forth a pitiful hiss from the young Scot. His back, unused to the lash, was streaming with blood by the third stroke. Every human instinct within me demanded that I order an end to this, there and then; but on such a public stage, young Matt Quinton had to give way to Captain the Honourable Matthew Quinton, and the duty of the latter was beyond doubt.

Macferran was a brave fellow, but the lash has a way of probing to the very limits of a man's bravery. On the fifth stroke he screamed, and Kit stepped forward with a gag. The last three lashes were delivered onto a body heaving with sobs and soaked in blood. When it was done, Carvell, Polzeath and some others ran forward to hold Macferran upright, and Surgeon Humphrey stepped forward to administer salt to the wounds.

'Well done, sir,' murmured Lieutenant Castle, 'I know that was not easy.'

But I did not reply to him; instead, I addressed O'Dwyer. 'I trust you now find our discipline less curious, Colonel?'

The Irishman merely inclined his head a little, and smiled. I went below in rank bad temper.

In truth, of course, my concern to appear even-handed meant that I had been remarkably harsh by the standards of those times. Then, men rarely received more than half-a-dozen lashes; even the most brutal court-martial judging the most heinous crime never prescribed more than a few dozen strokes. Now we live in a more brutal age. The other day, for example, I heard of a court-martial imposing a sentence of five hundred lashes on a man. I have met many quite distinguished officers who opine that today's sailors are a more iniquitous crew than the saints who served in Good King Charles' golden days, and that these modern rascals can only be taught the essentials of naval discipline by imposing ever harsher punishments. Well, I am probably the only man left alive who can make a comparison on that score, and it seems to me that sailors are no better or no worse than they were sixty years ago; so if we managed our ships successfully in those not-so-golden days by ordering far fewer strokes of the lash (and having far fewer flogging lieutenants, midshipmen and the like, come to that), then what does it say for these modern times, and these modern officers?

The captaincy of a king's ship confers many burdens that a man would ordinarily seek to shirk. Flogging a good and loyal soul is one such; another is the inevitability that, sooner or later, the captain will have to give a private dinner to a passenger, especially if that passenger holds a rank superior to his own. Thus whatever the nature of Matt Quinton's private opinions on the matter, on the day following the flogging the captain of the King's ship *Seraph* found himself entertaining Lieutenant-Colonel Brian Doyle O'Dwyer in the half-cabin that remained to him. This was an uncomfortable affair on many levels. There was physical discomfort: there was no space to set out a proper table, which meant we ate on a strange contraption devised by Musk and executed by Shish that straddled the demi-culverin, providing a very nearly level surface on which to lay our pewter plates. There was discomfort of the stomach: such was the consequence of Bradbury providing prodigiously charred fare, even by his extraordinary standards. Far worse than either of these, though, was the discomfort of the mind that attended the prospect of any lengthy discourse with the Irishman.

Yet my aversion to O'Dwyer was tainted by some other emotion, although I struggled to acknowledge it. The man talked plausibly, lightly and with good humour. He described the court of the *aga* of Algier and his harem with the skill of a born story-teller. He painted the *Porte* of the Sultan in colours so vivid that I almost felt myself transported thereto. Despite myself, I listened ever more intently. The renegade had the knack of explaining even matters of great difficulty in words understandable to everyman; a knack that he shared with Uncle Tris, I thought, although the comparison was unsettling. I began to see how even our sovereign lord the King, the arch-sceptic in an age when scepticism reigned, had been convinced by O'Dwyer's tale of the mountain of gold. And yet …

The Irishman's talk of harems and wives made me essay one of my rare interventions into his flow of silken talk. 'You had a wife in Algier, Colonel?' I asked.

'Three,' said O'Dwyer. 'Well, wives of a sort. Such is the Mahometan way. Two Moorish women and a Spanish girl whom I plucked off the shore of a village in Menorca, ten years or so past. And you, Captain?'

'I have a wife,' I said reflectively. 'A Dutch woman. I love her, indeed, but three of the kind would surely test the bounds of love.' I know not why I said it; do not know to this day why I shared such a confidence with such a rogue. But the words were said, and could not be unsaid.

O'Dwyer looked at me quizzically, then smiled. 'Ah, Captain,' he said sadly in his unique brogue, 'there you have the right of it. I have seen bold young men come over to us from France or Spain – England, too – convinced that turning to the Prophet will set them on course to the beds of countless women. They learn quickly enough that the obvious advantages of the flesh are but transitory.' He took a measure of Rhenish. 'What was it that old Scot said? That women were a monstrous regiment? He knew not the real truth of his words, for unlike me, Matthew, he was not married to the regiment.'

I laughed despite myself, and raised my cup to the renegade. Thus our dinner continued in better cheer than I could ever have imagined, and despite the untrusting voice that still muttered somewhere within me. Finally, though, our conversation turned, as it was surely bound to do, to the matter of our destination; but I had not expected O'Dwyer to instigate the turn.

We had been discussing the late civil wars in England. Of course, the renegade had learned of these only at second hand, and he seemed genuinely intrigued by my child's-eye account of those tragic years. He was particularly engrossed in my description of the battle of Naseby: for any of our Cavalier breed, that battle stands as the great 'if only' of history, but perhaps it was so for the House of Quinton more than for most. Every Cavalier regretted that Prince Rupert of the Rhine, commanding the right flank of the king's cavalry, had not ordered his victorious cohorts to turn in upon Parliament's infantry, thereby winning the war at a stroke. But my family, and myself especially, regretted Prince Rupert's failure the more, as it cost my father his life.

O'Dwyer was as good a listener as he was a talker, and betrayed no surprise at such an unwonted confidence. 'Well, Matthew, that accords with my impression of His Highness, these last months. An impulsive man. A great scientist, of course – an enquiring mind, but not methodical enough. Too prone to seek the quickest and easiest solution. He attended many of my meetings with the King, and did much to convince His Majesty of the existence of the mountain of gold. As you know, the prince has long had an interest in that particular grail – an interest almost as obsessive as that of our French enemy, Montnoir.'

At once I became more guarded. 'So you persuaded the prince first, and he in turn persuaded the King?'

O'Dwyer took from his mouth a particularly dubious piece of Bradbury's handiwork that he had been chewing for some little time, looked at it curiously, and laid it upon his plate. 'Don't demean His Majesty's originality of thought, Matthew!' he said. 'The King was amenable enough to my – well, to my blandishments, shall we say? But the fact that the prince, his cousin, believes passionately in the truth of the mountain, and had sought it himself... Let us say it made my tale the more convincing.'

'To some, perhaps,' I said bitterly.

O'Dwyer smiled. 'You're not a believer, then?' he asked mischievously. Before I could reply – intemperately, no doubt – the Irishman said, 'Ah, no matter, Matthew. No matter that you and every man on this ship thinks I'm a treacherous renegade who deserves the fate of Ravaillac, or preferably worse. Fix my limbs to horses, set them off in different directions and feed the remnants to ravenous dogs and the odd demented crone – would that suffice for you, Captain Quinton?' I said nothing, taking a measure of my wine to conceal the extent to which O'Dwyer had uncovered my sentiments. 'Perhaps not for you, though, above any man. Despising a goose chase instigated by Brian Doyle O'Dwyer is cause enough for the likes of Lieutenant Castle or your friend the chaplain, simply because of who I am and what I have been. But you, Captain... ah, now, you're so much younger and yet you see so much more than them, as though you possess another eye that they lack.' He leaned forward, this unsettling, plausible man – 'For you, this is about more than me, I think, and about more than whether or not my mountain of gold truly exists – for I know no words of mine will ever convince you of that, Matthew. But you know full well that whether the mountain exists or not, ultimately this voyage is not of my making. I could have been ignored, or hanged, as you intended at the very first. Or handed over to Montnoir, come to that.' O'Dwyer appeared genuinely moved by the thought of the fates he had evaded. 'No, Captain Quinton. What you resent, I'd say, is that this entire quest stems from a prince whom you hold responsible for the death of your father and a king whom you no longer trust – '

'*Enough*, sir! This is a King's ship, I am a King's captain, and you – you – '

'– are a King's colonel. The same king, Matthew. But remember, I have come to this king, and to his England, with fresh eyes. Now, it seems to me that you, and your country, had so many expectations of this king, of how his restoration would make all things right. And yet, three years and more since his return, what did I sense in England through all of last summer and autumn? Disappointment. All those great hopes, all that excitement, all washed away by a floodtide of bitterness. The endless quarrels and petty vindictiveness of your Parliament. The hatred of Cavaliers for Commonwealth's-men, and vice-versa. The arrogance of the bishops. Above all, the whoring and vacillation of the King.' I made to protest, but could not find the words; it is not easy to protest against one's own innermost thoughts, uttered by another. O'Dwyer said coldly, 'So I should not be the target of your resentment, Matthew Quinton. Nor should my golden mountain – for that is but the easy way for a venal king and prince to abate a nation's disillusionment with them. Thus they play their pawns. You and I, Matthew, for we're nothing more than pawns in this.'

The man's words were so very plausible. I struggled with my feelings. Honour demanded that I should defend my king, but somehow, the words would not come. Charles Stuart, my brother's friend, and yet the man who had compelled that same brother and friend, a man for whom the very notion of marriage was anathema, into the worst marriage of all. Charles the Second, King of England, who had commanded me upon a voyage intended to free him of Parliament and make him an absolute monarch, just as Venner Garvey said.

So very plausible; yet as I sat there, looking upon the bronzed, worldly face of Brian Doyle O'Dwyer, I still wondered who were the pawns in this game, and who the players.

$\mathscr{F}$ifteen

A knock upon the bulkhead heralded the entry of Vincent, a scrofulous Bristolian, with an urgent request from Lieutenant Castle for Captain Quinton to come on deck at once. My head swam, but still I stood: for even if honour was laid aside, there was still the duty of a captain to be fulfilled, and with it a responsibility to some one hundred and thirty souls.

O'Dwyer followed me from the cabin.

I stepped out onto the deck, climbed to the quarterdeck, and registered that the winds were significantly lighter than they were when I went below, when we had been scudding easily across a gentle sea. But it was a warm, sun-filled day, with no cloud to be seen. No cloud in the sky, at any rate.

Castle was at the larboard rail of the poop, standing alongside Kit Farrell. It should have been Negus's watch, but he was below, being attended by the surgeon; a victim of the flux, it was said, and I hoped his sickness did not presage the coming of the Guinea fevers. As it was, my lieutenant and boatswain both had telescopes trained on the horizon to the north-east. Kit handed me his eyepiece and said, 'A sail, sir.'

I focused on the distant speck of canvas and felt annoyance and puzzlement in equal measure. We saw sails a dozen times a day, more when close to shore, and hardly any were worthy of the captain's attention, especially when they were so far distant. But I knew Kit Farrell and William Castle would not have summoned me without a purpose. 'What of it, gentlemen?' I asked.

Kit was pensive. 'There's been a ship, or ships, in that quarter for almost a couple of watches now, Captain. And another to north-west. She's in sight for a little while, then drops over the horizon, as you'd expect if she was about her trade and course. Then the same happens in the other quarter. Then we sight another sail, perhaps on a different bearing and tack, seemingly a different ship, maybe with a different rig. But – '

'They're the same ships,' said Castle decisively. 'Two of them. Trying to make us believe they're chance sightings, a different ship each time, then coming back into view just long enough to check our position and course. Dropping down beyond our sight, changing the rig, all to lull us right enough, sir. An old game. We used to play it on the Spaniard in the Caribbee, under Myngs, when we sought to follow some rich argosy out of Cartagena. There'll be a third ship, well astern, always out of sight of us but in sight of the others. And maybe a fourth, a fifth, God knows how many, out of sight astern, or on either beam or both, too.'

I glanced at O'Dwyer, and the fleeting sense that had grown upon me during our dinner – a sense that might even have been a form of liking, or at least of empathy – died with our breeze. For if we had an enemy in these waters, I felt certain that it could only be one that served the purpose of the man who had been Omar Ibrahim. But the Irishman's expression was merely curious.

'If you're right, gentlemen,' I said – a captain must always be a sceptic, even if he is less qualified than those of whom he is sceptical – 'then they'll have known for hours that we're detached from Holmes in *Jersey*, and from the *Prospect* too.' Such had been the consequence of a vicious little squall of hurry-durry weather, as the old seamen called it, on the previous day. 'If they're intent on attacking us, and assuming they out-gun us, surely they'd have struck already?'

Kit looked up at our ensign, furling ever more limply about its staff, and said, 'Not if they needed to wait for their advantage, sir. An advantage they'd gain only in light winds, or none. Which means – '

'Galleys,' said O'Dwyer without emotion. 'And in this sea, sirs, there's but one power with galleys, and the skill to try the ruse with the ships over yonder. The rovers of Sallee.'

I recalled the renegade's words before the Navy Board – *I sailed past it on a Sallee rover but the last summer.*

I turned on O'Dwyer. 'The Sallee rovers. Your late friends, then, Colonel. Come to take you back into the Mahometan fold, no doubt?'

The Irishman remained inscrutable. 'Ah, now, Captain Quinton… doesn't every man have embarrassing old friends he would rather forget?'

Part of me longed to order him chained up in the hold, as I had done to him aboard the *Wessex*. Once again the Cavalier heart of Matt Quinton did battle with the dutiful head of the captain of the *Seraph*, and as was increasingly the case, the head prevailed. There was no evidence that O'Dwyer was responsible for luring us into a trap, perhaps by means of a letter slipped aboard any of the several merchantmen with whom we had spoken on the way south. Indeed, he would hardly have needed to do so: the date of our sailing from England would have been common knowledge in every port from Archangel to Alexandria, the trade winds ensured that the approximate course of any ship bound for the Gambia would be easy enough for skilled mariners to deduce, and of course no skilled mariners knew these seas better than the notorious Sallee rovers. The very name struck more terror into Christian hearts than was even the case with their brethren, the Barbary corsairs. At least the corsairs sailed on behalf of properly constituted governments that paid lip service to the overlordship of the Ottoman Sultan. But Sallee had no government. The city was a pirate republic, nothing less. Moors and refugees from every land in Europe fetched up there, setting sail to prey on the trade of Christianity …

'The colonel's galleys,' said Castle, ambiguously. 'Three coming over the larboard horizon, two to starboard.'

I lifted Kit's telescope. There was no mistaking the low, menacing hulls. Individually they were small, and would have been easy meat for the *Seraph*'s battery; but five together was a very different case, especially as the need to supply prize crews meant that rover and corsair craft were always grossly overmanned by our standards. There might be even more men on the decoy sailing ships, and any engagement with the galleys would give them time to come up, too, even in this lightest of breezes. If this Sallee fleet caught us, and boarded, they would outnumber us at least three or four to one.

We would be dead men inside an hour.

The galleys came on. Now we could hear their dreadful cacophony: the beating of drums accompanied by the wailed ululations of the crew. That noise alone had been sufficient to make many a Christian ship surrender without a shot being fired.

Francis Gale came on deck and contemplated the sight. 'Should I recite the prayers ordained for battle, Captain?' he asked.

'Aye, Francis,' I said, 'for I think at this moment we need God's assistance.'

The chaplain of the *Seraph* stood at the quarterdeck rail and addressed his somewhat preoccupied congregation. In truth he had few immediate listeners, for most of the crew were about their duties upon the yards or at the guns. But Francis had a powerful voice, the sea was calm and it was a small ship; few of our men could not have heard his words, even above the dreadful cries of the oncoming Salleemen. The earnest clerics who had composed the Book of Common Prayer no doubt intended their sentences to bring consolation and steadfastness to seamen about to face the perils of battle; but this was the second time I had heard these prayers uttered, and I found that they only heightened the foreboding that every man on the *Seraph* (or perhaps, all except one) felt in their hearts.

'Oh God,' Francis continued, 'thou art a strong tower of defence to all that flee unto thee; O save us from the violence of the enemy...'

The efficacy of the prayer was lessened by the arrival upon the quarterdeck of Phineas Musk, whose curious features and perennially disapproving expression made him the perfect harbinger of doom. He threw a large canvas sack down about the deck. The contents clanked loudly, interrupting Francis Gale's flow.

'Breastplate,' panted Musk, 'and sword, and pistols. I'm too old for this carrying, that I am. Time you got a young servant or six, like every other bloody captain in this infernal navy has got.' He squinted at the approaching galleys. 'Damn. Always thought I'd die in a whore, not cut to pieces by some stinking heathens.'

Despite his complaints, Musk assisted me into my armour. I suspected that even if I did take on some youthful servants, they would find themselves with precious little to do; whatever his nominal rank, and however loud his grumbles, Phineas Musk would never voluntarily relinquish the proprietary rights that he seemed to believe himself to possess over the entire House of Quinton, and over Captain Matthew Quinton in particular.

Suitably accoutred for battle, I turned my attention once more to the oncoming enemy. The shrieks and ever more rapid drumbeats were louder by the minute, a hellish cacophony of approaching doom.

'Their speed, Mister Castle?' I demanded.

'Six knots, perhaps. Maybe seven.'

'And ours?'

The log-line was just being hauled in. 'Two knots!' cried a Cornish voice.

I looked at our limp sails and ensign. In desperation, I asked Francis Gale to offer up a prayer for a stronger breeze, and that generous soul obliged, although his face betrayed ample doubt in the efficacy of the gesture.

'Can we not set more sail, Mister Castle? Mister Farrell?' Their shrugs told me what I already knew. We had all sails set – even stunsails, then a new-fangled innovation frowned upon by many veteran seamen. But with such a feeble breeze, we might as well have set every inch of canvas in England, and my Lady Castlemaine's breeches with it, for all the good it would have done us.

The galleys were manoeuvring to approach from dead ahead, dead astern and from the quarters, where our formidable broadside, our one and only weapon, would be ineffective against them. Despite this, I ordered the decks cleared and the guns manned and run out on both sides; we did not need many men aloft, and perhaps some lucky shots might disable a galley or two. Yet as I gave my orders, two conflicting thoughts occurred to me. One was a memory, dim and elusive, of something that Tris had once made me read. The other was a stratagem so unlikely that it was unworthy of being spoken. Yet the prospect of being hacked to pieces by a blood-crazed horde has a way of drawing the strangest of words from a man's mouth.

So it was that I turned to Brian Doyle O'Dwyer, alias Omar Ibrahim. 'Colonel O'Dwyer,' I said. 'You have long experience of commanding such craft as those. You will know better than any of us what they can do, and what they will expect us to do. So, sir, in the name of the king and the God whom we both serve – ' Francis Gale raised an eyebrow at that – 'how would you advise us to evade them?'

The Irishman looked at me in seemingly unfeigned astonishment. He would have known that every man on that deck believed the Sallee fleet had come to rescue him. He would have seen in our eyes that we suspected him of arranging to bring it down upon us in the first place. If that was so, he would never assist us, his enemies, to evade the approaching galleys, his friends.

Yet as rapidly as the Salleemen were closing us, we still had the best part of a glass before they would be alongside. Ample time for Captain

Matthew Quinton to order the execution of an Irish renegade who lied, or said nothing.

I looked O'Dwyer directly in the eye, and smiled. *If we are to die, my friend*, I thought, *then you will most certainly die before us.*

The Irishman returned my stare. It was impossible to fathom the emotions that might have boiled behind those eyes. Finally, he said, 'Well, now. Regardless of all else, Captain, you need headway. That will buy you a little time, and perhaps time will buy you a fresh wind. At the very least, headway will allow you to manoeuvre, and it will give the rover galleys more distance to cover. And with more distance –'

Thucydides. That was the man. 'With more distance to cover,' I said, 'the more exhausted the rowers will become. They will have to lose speed to recover their strength.'

O'Dwyer bowed his head in acknowledgement. 'Just so, Captain Quinton.'

'Then how do we gain headway?'

Before O'Dwyer could respond, Kit Farrell spoke up. 'Sweeps!' he cried. 'Take the men off the guns, and put out our sweeps. They might give us an extra knot or so, probably no more at first. But as the colonel says, it will buy us time and a little manoeuvrability.'

My order to deploy sweeps was relayed down to the main deck, and no more than two or three minutes passed before the first of the long oars protruded tentatively from the sweep ports below the main deck battery. Relatively few ships in the King's Navy still carried sweeps, which could be used to aid manoeuvring in harbours and calms; they had gone out of fashion some ten years previously, and would duly come back into fashion again some ten years later, for such is the perversity of seamen. But the half-mad master shipwright who built the *Seraph* had insisted on fitting sweep ports: he was convinced our ship was ordained to bring back King Arthur from Avalon, and it would not do for his mythical Majesty to be becalmed. Thus we had fourteen sweep ports on each side. We had used them a little in the Downs: most of my Cornish lads were well accustomed to rowing craft, their vessels of choice for fishing and smuggling alike, but others in the crew were not so practised in their use. I heard not a few grumbles drift up from the deck below to the effect that they were honest English or Cornish seamen, not pestilential galley slaves. Inevitably, it took several strokes for the *Seraph*'s makeshift rowers to achieve anything like a coordinated action, with the sweeps on both sides and along the length of the hull breaking the water at roughly the same time. If our movement across the ocean was any faster, it was barely discernible. And all the while the more expert galleys came on, the shrieks of their crews and the beat of their drums growing ever louder.

William Castle pointed to the nearest craft, which was approaching fast, fine on our larboard bow. Her captain, yet another Christian renegade by the pale looks of him, had a hand raised in what might have been a gesture of defiance; or else, perhaps, a salutation to a kindred spirit that he recognised upon our deck. 'He's stretching ahead of his brethren, Captain,' said my lieutenant. 'Stretching a mite too far, I'd reckon.'

O'Dwyer nodded. 'Seeking the lion's share of the booty. My old friends favour acting in concert only until they can sniff prize money in their nostrils: then it's every man for himself.'

I whispered to Castle, for I did not wish the renegade to hear my suggestion. My lieutenant nodded and whispered an urgent reply. I then surreptitiously despatched a boy with a message for Gunner Lindman. A quiet word with Kit Farrell: he sauntered nonchalantly from the quarterdeck down to the waist, as though to attend to some urgent matter there.

Nothing seemed to change. At least, O'Dwyer noticed nothing; he was intent on the headmost galley, approaching us at a sharp angle fine on the larboard bow, safe from the arc of our guns.

Or so it thought. The *Seraph* shuddered. Slowly, painfully slowly, the bowsprit began to swing a little to starboard. Then the turn became sharper.

O'Dwyer ran to the starboard rail. His expression was unreadable, but after some moments he nodded grimly. 'Good,' he said. 'Very good. Very ingenious. Helm hard to starboard, only the forward sweeps on the starboard beam to row, full ahead on the larboard sweeps. A galley manoeuvre.'

'Not quite,' I said. 'After all, Colonel, in a galley you would still have rowers at the starboard rear sweeps. Chained to them, indeed. You would not – could not – have withdrawn them to man the larboard guns.'

O'Dwyer crossed the quarterdeck again to ascertain the truth of my words. The *Seraph*'s sudden change of direction had opened up the arc for our larboard broadside. The galley, intent on riches and careless of the risks, was too committed to its course, its rowers too exhausted to respond swiftly to any countermanding orders.

I glanced at Castle and Kit Farrell, who nodded in unison.

'Give fire!' I cried.

A nearly simultaneous roar from the eight cannon of the larboard battery on the main deck.

True to his word at my first meeting with him, Lindman had drilled our gun crews relentlessly during our voyage from the Downs. Cornishmen and Bristolians had been cajoled and cudgelled into working together until their gunnery could stand comparison with any crew afloat.

So it proved now. At Castle's suggestion, I had ordered four of the guns to be loaded with round shot and to aim low; the other four to be loaded with chainshot and grapeshot, and to aim high. The round balls smashed into the fragile bow of the galley. The range was so close, perhaps two hundred yards or less, and the scantlings of the galley's hull so light, that we could not fail to hole her fatally beneath the water line. On her upper deck, the lethal combination of chain and grape had their accustomed effect. Parts of what had so recently been men splashed into the sea or spattered the mast and deck. A few grasped hold of the crimson sockets where their limbs had been and screamed in death-agony.

The waving captain's hands now covered his eyes, attempting in vain to staunch the streams of blood that flowed down his cheeks.

The galley lost momentum. A few men on her deck – her other officers, presumably – shrieked and waved scimitars at us in defiance, but their men seemed to have little appetite for a fight. Her two fellows to larboard of us slowed, appalled by what they had witnessed, and signalled to their westerly consorts. After all, rovers and corsairs alike were used to attacking fat, near-defenceless merchantmen, overwhelming them by a combination of speed, terror and weight of manpower; but against a royal warship, even one becalmed and outnumbered five to one in hulls, those advantages were at least partly negated. Lindman's gun crews returned to their sweeps and the *Seraph* gathered speed on her new course, south and west, toward the horizon which was bound to shelter the *Jersey* – and if we assumed that, then so would the Sallee rovers and their fast-tiring crews.

As I watched the stricken galley fall astern of us, a wisp of cloth brushed my cheek. A loose strand from our ensign.

The breeze was strengthening. The king himself had assured me that the *Seraph* could outrun anything on the world's oceans; it was time to see whether that claim was yet another example of a mad shipwright's ravings and of divine-right bravado alike. As I turned to give the order for the men to abandon sweeps and man the sails, their natural environs, I caught a glimpse of O'Dwyer. He stood at the rail, looking intently upon the sinking Salleeman. It might have been the breeze, or something else entirely, but as Francis Gale intoned the prayers for the dead and dying, there appeared to be a tear in the Irishman's eye.

We were back in company with the *Jersey* and *Prospect of Blakeney*, on course once again for our rendezvous with O'Dwyer's dubious mountain. I was in my cabin, writing a report of our escape from the rover fleet for the eyes of my monarch and Lord Admiral, when I was interrupted by Shish, the carpenter, with a sombre expression upon his young face. He reported bleakly that the chain pumps were failing fast; much faster than through natural wear-and-tear. Our precipitate escape from the Salleemen, straining every sinew of the hull once the wind was properly filling our sails, must have brought the problem to a head, he said. I summoned Lieutenant Castle, and we three went below to examine the problem.

Under the main deck was the alien world of the hold, the store-rooms, and at the bottom of it all, the bilges. I have rarely been in a place so unremittingly foul. It was so low that I was bent almost double. There was little light, and the bilge-stink made me retch; on some particularly dirty ships, those rancid gases have been potent enough to kill men, and – it is said – to blow up the entire vessel. Here, beneath the waterline, the constant roar of water passing along our hull gave a real sense of the fragility of our poor craft. I knew little of the workings of our chain-pumps, but I knew all too well what the consequences would be if they failed to function: the Atlantic would seep insidiously between our planks and frames, for not even the finest caulking in the world could prevent that, and with nothing to carry it away, the water would rise within the hold. The *Seraph* would sink.

Shish led Castle and myself to the starboard of our two pumps; the other was in the same state, he said. The carpenter handed his lantern to Castle and then took away a panel that partly encased the chain-pump well. It was a simple mechanism. A chain belt fitted with plates named burrs was worked by men at winches upon the gundeck; the water then discharged from the burrs into a tube which carried it out of the hull.

Shish pointed to the links in the chain. 'Several of the esses are weak-ened, sirs. Weaker even than I suspected them to be when first I reported the defect at Deptford. It seems to me – '

'Several what?' I asked.

'Esses, Captain. The links. As I explained to you before.' I grim-aced at this exposure of both my ignorance and my forgetfulness. 'Some seem to be of old, weak metal, pewtered or otherwise concealed. Others appear to have been sawn part way through, and the cuts crudely forged over. Worse, the same is also true of the rowls on both pumps, and they are our most serious problem, by far.'

Castle shone the lantern over the very foot of the pump well, where water was lapping towards our feet. 'There's the rowl, sir,' he said. 'Down at the bottom.' I could just make out a bar, somewhat akin to a horse's bit, at the very foot of the mechanism. The chain clattered around this at the bottom of its journey, plunging each burr in turn into the water, before proceeding upward again.

'We have spare esses,' said Shish, 'though God knows if there are enough to replace all the defective ones – and who knows if the spares have not been tampered with in the same way? But we carry no spare rowls, sir. No Fifth Rate does.'

'*No spares?*' I was incredulous. 'Why not, in Jesu's name?'

Shish shrugged. 'The rowls never fail, sir. After all, there's less strain on them than on the esses, for it's the chain that does all the work.'

'Rowls never fail,' I repeated, 'except in our present case, it seems.'

'There can only be two causes, sir,' said the carpenter. 'The likeliest is those villains in Deptford yard – one of the storekeepers, most probably, selling off the good parts to merchantmen up at Blackwall or the like and passing off this poor stuff to the navy – '

Castle was dismissive. 'Not even the most venal storekeeper would take the trouble to foist a sawn-through rowl onto a king's ship, Mister Shish. Which brings us to the second cause – '

'Sabotage,' I said. 'Someone deliberately fitted defective esses and rowls to the pump, knowing they would give way during our voyage.'

Both Shish and Castle nodded, for the conclusion was inescapable. But unlike them, I also had a culprit in mind; could hear the culprit's words, still clear in my mind.

This mission will not succeed.

$\mathcal{S}$ixteen

At my request, Holmes came across from *Jersey* to consult with me and my Holy Trinity of accomplished seamen, Castle, Negus and Farrell, calling in Shish to discuss the specific issue of the pumps. The entire squadron, not just the *Seraph*, needed to take on fresh water and wine for a voyage going south of twenty-seven degrees of latitude, so there was no quibble with the principle that we should make for either Funchal or Tenerife; but the latter had rather more foundries, and with the winds as they were, we would lose less time to our voyage by making for it rather than the port of Madeira. Holmes and Negus were confident that ironfounders, coppersmiths and the like could be found on Tenerife who would be able to fashion new esses and rowls for the *Seraph* within a matter of days, if not hours, but Shish seemed less sanguine on that score. Holmes was apologetic that his *Jersey* could not assist us, but she was a much larger ship, so her chain-pumps were incompatible with ours. Otherwise, Holmes was disconcertingly jolly, abruptly dismissing the suspicions of sabotage; but then, Holmes was the kind of sea-officer who held it as gospel that every single shore official of the navy, be it the meanest storekeeper or Mister Pepys, was corrupt or incompetent or

both, and intent above all on putting obstacles in the way of old Robin
Holmes' righteous desire to be killing Dutchmen, Spaniards, or whoever
else got in the way of his sword. Tenerife it would be.

So in due course we beat up on a clear and blustery day toward
Santa Cruz de Tenerife, on the east coast of the island, a town of low
houses and campaniles nestling beneath a great grey mountain. It was
guarded by a fort on a promontory to the south, over which flew the
red-yellow-red colours of the dying, defeated Philip the Fourth, King
of Castile, Aragon, Leon, the Two Sicilies, Jerusalem, and God knows
how many other titles as meaningless as my own royal master's claim
to be the lawful King of France. Many of the men were on deck, even
those of the off-duty watch, for like their captain they were keen to
look upon this place where English arms had distinguished themselves
so recently and so decisively. Rebel arms, admittedly, but English none-
theless. For here, only a little more than six years before, General-at-Sea
Robert Blake and his men had destroyed the *flota*, Spain's supposedly
invincible treasure fleet.

I turned to Lieutenant Castle, who had been present at that battle,
and asked him to recount it to me.

'Aye, sir. Well, I was a reformado aboard General Blake's flagship,
back then. The wind was a bit less southerly than it is now – more
directly from the east, in truth.' Castle sniffed the air, as though hoping
for a trace of the gunsmoke of that great day. 'The *flota* was moored in
two lines, running north from the quay there, beneath the town – the
bigger galleons further out, making themselves a great floating battery
against us.' It was easy to conjure up the scene, for quite a number of
ships lay in the bay of Santa Cruz, roughly where the galleons must have
been. Among them was the *Jersey*; Holmes had evidently beaten us to
it, which could only mean he had found no Dutchmen to annoy. 'And
behind the galleons, Captain,' Castle continued, 'were all the batteries
ashore – see the line of emplacements, there, all the way from Fort Saint
Philip to the south of the town all the way round to the north end of

the bay? I tell you, sir, not a few of us were mighty afeared to be going up against so many guns, but Blake – well, he was already a legend by then, and most of us would happily have gone to our deaths for him.'

'You knew Blake himself?' I asked.

'Aye, sir. I knew him well enough. Like all the fleet, I respected him hugely. An honest, bluff man of few words but a powerful faith. He loved his men – fought like a lion to get them better pay and conditions. A scholar, too – they say he only took to war after failing to get a fellowship at Oxford.' Robert Blake and Tristram Quinton, exchanging quips on some high table or other; now there was a vision to conjure with. 'No great seaman, of course – none of Cromwell's generals-at-sea were. But what a soldier! What a mind, Captain Quinton! When he first put his plan to the captains, all the knowing tarpaulins born to the sea, they shouted him down. Called him a madman. Didn't speak to him for a day.' Castle chuckled, the recollection of the event still evidently fresh in his memory. 'But Blake held his nerve, that he did. He kept the Sabbath holy – wouldn't attack on that for all the gold of the world. But on the Monday, he ordered Stayner in first with a squadron to get between the two lines of Spanish galleons. Reckoned Stayner could hold his own against both the inshore line and the shore batteries while he, the general himself, brought the main fleet down the other side of the outer line of big galleons.'

I looked out toward the approaching shore, and found that I could visualise the scene easily enough. 'But,' I cried, 'surely that would mean sending Stayner's ships into the most hellish crossfire?'

'That it did. And in that east wind, it would be just as hellishly difficult for Stayner – and the rest of us, come to that – to withdraw if the plan went awry. So we watched them sail into the bay, Stayner's ships. Not a few of us thought we were waving them goodbye. Down they went, between the two lines of galleons. And then we all saw what Blake must have seen all along. By putting the inshore line of galleons where they were, the Spanish had made it impossible for their shore batteries to fire on us without hitting their own ships! But Blake made his name in siege warfare back in the war against the roya – during our land's time of troubles, sir. So he knew more than a little about the trajectory of gunfire.' I realised at that moment that a growing number of the crew had assembled on the upper deck at the foot of the quarterdeck ladders; Castle had quite a loud voice, and he now had quite an audience too. 'Anyhow, Stayner and his ships sailed in, calm as you like, all the way up to the head of the bay, and there just dropped anchor and began to blast away on both sides. And then it was our turn, Captain. Blake brought us down the other side of the big galleons, and truly, sir, the fury of God's wrath smote them mightily – ' A raised eyebrow from Francis Gale, who was listening intently, and the erstwhile Puritanical incarnation of William Castle was rapidly locked away again in that place from which it had briefly emerged – 'Well, at any rate, Captain, the Admiral and the Vice-Admiral of the *flota* both blew up, and by the middle of the afternoon, we had destroyed or taken the entire fleet – all sixteen galleons, by God!'

Francis Gale clapped Castle on the shoulder. 'A pity, then, my friend, that such a mighty victory should have been for nought. For if I remember rightly, General Blake obtained not one coin of the King of Spain's Indies treasure.'

Castle took the jibe in good part; a prouder man might have been mortified. 'Aye, well. We didn't know that the Spanish had taken all the bullion ashore and buried it long before we got there.' A good thing they had, perhaps, I thought to myself: for if Oliver Cromwell's bankrupt regime had gained the gold and silver of the Indies for itself, there might well have been no Restoration, Lord Protector Richard Cromwell would be ruling in Whitehall, and Matthew Quinton might still be scratching a living out of a Dutch garret. The parallel with the mission of the *Seraph* struck me at once, for what was I in this case if not a new and lesser Blake, pursuing an illusory dream of gold on behalf a desperate English ruler? I recalled how my grandfather in his day had chased around the Indies more than once on behalf of Great Queen Bess in search of supposedly easy pickings of Spanish bullion, and how his old rival Raleigh was executed by the less than great King James for his unsuccessful pursuit of a fabled city of gold, El Dorado, far up the Amazon river. Would kings and Lords Protector ever learn, and would poor, honour-chained fools in storm-tossed ships ever stop voyaging and dying on such lunatic quests?

I emerged from my own thoughts to hear Castle say, 'We had the devil's own task to get back out of the bay, because of course, once we'd removed all the galleons from their path, the Spanish batteries could fire on us at will. We had to warp Stayner's squadron out under constant fire. God alone knows how the *Speaker* made it out. She had not a mast left standing, as Our Lord is my judge.'

'A fine victory indeed,' I said, 'regardless of the fate of the bullion. A pity that it was General Blake's last. He would have been a mightily useful man to have on our side in the next war with the Dutch.'

Robert Blake, the greatest English seaman since Drake (although if he had been present on our quarterdeck, my grandfather would undoubtedly have disputed this assessment) – this Blake had died on the voyage home from Santa Cruz, just as his ship was entering Plymouth Sound.

Castle shrugged sadly. 'I think I knew the general well enough, sir, to say that he would never have served the king. He was too wedded to the republic and the good old cause of the godly. Which those who dug him up knew well enough, I think.' To the eternal shame of my more vengeful Cavalier brethren, the corpse of Robert Blake had been ejected from its tomb in Westminster Abbey, to which it had been committed in one of the greatest state funerals England ever witnessed, and thrown into a common grave pit. *Sic transit gloria mundi.*

We sailed on, into the bay, and came to an anchor close to the watering place of the town, slightly inshore of the *Jersey.* Holmes sent across his compliments and requested my company for dinner; pointedly, the invitation did not extend to O'Dwyer. The Irishman seemed unfazed by this, saying that he had already decided to dine with Captain Facey aboard the *Prospect of Blakeney* before taking a turn about the town. Castle went ashore at once, for his command of the Spanish tongue made him the obvious man to negotiate with the ironfounders and their brethren. So it was that a little after noon, I was rowed across to *Jersey* by Coxswain Lanherne and his boat's crew. Holmes proved to be in most excellent form. Most men shrink as the battle comes nearer; Robert Holmes was one of those who blossoms like a flower, the closer he comes to the sound of the guns. He railed against the *hogen mogens*, our derisory by-name for their High Mightinesses of the Dutch States-General, against their cunning leader Grand Pensionary De Witt, against all their cried-up seamen, and was beginning to embark on a discourse concerning the loose morality of Dutch women when he recalled that my wife was of that nation. Holmes apologised profusely and changed the subject to the weather.

Our pleasant afternoon was interrupted by the arrival of William Castle, who bore dire tidings: the ironfounders and coppersmiths of Santa Cruz de Tenerife had closed ranks to deny us new rowls and esses. The cause of this affront mightily embarrassed my lieutenant. 'It was all my fault, sir,' he said. 'I should never have gone ashore – Shish should have talked to them, with one of the English merchants for an interpreter. Somehow, they knew that I was aboard Blake's fleet in the battle here. One of them even spat in my face. They all swear that they will not raise a finger to assist the heretics who destroyed their *flota de Indias*.'

I returned to the *Seraph* in a foul humour, and called a council of my officers. There was incredulity at the perfidious actions of the founders; or as Francis Gale said, 'Great God, do they not know England is a kingdom once again? Can they not tell the difference between a royal ship of war and a rebel – begging your pardon, Mister Castle?'

The onetime rebel lieutenant nodded graciously.

This matter that had seemed so insignificant now consumed us all. We needed to sail in a day or two, and we could not do that without the parts. What, then, could convince these idle rogues of Spanish founders to make them for us? Money, of course, and we could undoubtedly obtain enough, drawn by bills of exchange upon local English merchants, to pay a king's ransom for these few pieces of metal; surely one particularly venal founder could be offered enough to break the embargo. But what guarantee did we have that the same founder, duly bribed, would not out of spite make esses and rowls as defective as those they were meant to replace? If we could not obtain reliable parts at Tenerife, we would have to send to England for them; and with capricious winter weather in easy alliance with dockyard sloth, who could say how many weeks or months it would be before we had them, if we ever did? Shish was unwilling to trust the pumps for a day longer upon the open sea, and was not even convinced that they would hold if we simply stayed at anchor. I could hardly dishonour myself and my country by grovelling to the Spanish for a dock (even if they were inclined to grant us such succour), but without one, there was a very real danger that the *Seraph* would simply sink at her moorings; *and for want of a nail, the kingdom was lost.* A part of me insinuated that an enforced stay of several months in the pleasant climate of this island, and the consequent abandonment of the goldfinding expedition, were far from unsatisfactory outcomes. Yet my honour cried out against these weasel words. This was a royally-ordained mission, and whatever my own doubts and my growing disenchantment with the royal in question, it was my duty to carry it through to the best of my ability. But above all, there was the pervasive suspicion that the planting of the defective parts aboard the *Seraph* could only have been the fulfilment of my good-brother's prophecy, and of his determination to prevent us ever reaching the Gambia river. I had thought long and hard upon his exposition of arbitrary and constitutional government, but I convinced myself that the only way of putting that to rest was to take O'Dwyer to Africa and expose his story for the great lie it had to be. If that was the outcome, both Venner and I could rest satisfied. If in a few weeks time I found myself looking across the desert at a glittering golden mountain – well, perhaps then Matthew Quinton might be forced to confront the question of whether all that wealth really should be placed in the capacious hands of Charles Stuart alone. But I wanted to confront that dreadful dilemma in my own time and on my own terms, not on those dictated by Venner Garvey and a coterie of obstreperous Spanish ironfounders.

With no obvious solution presenting itself, my officers soon became peevish. Harrington, whose knowledge of war was less sound than his grasp of a set of accounts, proposed bombarding the town into submission, but Castle and Lindman both pointed out that the Spanish could bring dozens, if not hundreds, of cannon to bear upon us; and as Castle said, it had been difficult enough even for the immortal Blake and his great fleet, let alone for one Fifth-Rate frigate. (No man there needed to ask if *Jersey* would assist us; Holmes' estimate of the odds would undoubtedly be at one with Castle's and Lindman's, and besides, he was unlikely to wait for us before sailing off to begin his own private war against the *hogen mogens*.) Kit, who knew the politics of port towns as well as any man, suggested that we should enlist the assistance of the English merchants of the place to negotiate on our behalf. That met with grudging assent from the entire council, but none of us had any faith in a measure that depended on the mediation of mean, prevaricating tradesmen.

Thus I was still in the blackest of moods when I retired to my half-cabin. Musk entered, placed a bottle of sack in front of me, and retired without a word. The day would probably have ended with the disillusioned captain of the *Seraph* slumping unconscious onto his sea bed, but the Good Lord in his mercy provided one last blessed moment of relief to lift my spirits. Perhaps half a glass had passed when I heard O'Dwyer return to the larboard side beyond the partition. He seemed to pace the deck for some moments, as though wrestling with a decision. Then he came over to my side, knocked, and did not await my reply. We exchanged what passed for pleasantries between us, he asking how the chain-pumps fared (I enlightened him but little) and I enquiring how his own day ashore had passed.

'A pleasant enough town, and it is good to plant one's feet upon land again – I'm no longer used to such long voyages, if truth be told. And Vespers were performed most beautifully at a Dominican monastery in the upper town. It is a long time since I attended a service of the old faith – it brought back memories, such memories...' O'Dwyer blinked and looked away for a moment, as though he had something in his eye. 'A strange coincidence, though, Matthew,' he said O'Dwyer. 'Everywhere I turned, I seemed to find two or three of your men! Why, now, a man of a suspicious bent might believe that they had been deliberately ordered to watch his every movement.'

I replied with as much innocence as I could muster. 'A strange coincidence indeed, Colonel O'Dwyer. But I'm sure that the presence of my men must have been a mighty reassurance to you – keeping you safe from any agents of Montnoir, let us say, or from the machinations of any Sallee Rovers in these parts.'

He smiled, but it was the inscrutable smile of the tiger. 'Yes, a mighty reassurance. You are quite right, Captain Quinton. I am most grateful to you, sir.'

With that, he left me; but before we both sank into sleep, I could have sworn that I heard him punch or kick a bulkhead.

The next morning brought the glad sight of a boat coming across from the newly arrived *Madras Merchant*, outward bound from London to the East Indies. She carried packets of mail for ourselves and the other ships, and as soon as the letters were distributed, I shut myself away in my half-cabin.

Nothing from Tristram; that was a disappointment. But there were several letters from Cornelia, and I opened them feverishly, both for what they might contain and for what they represented: the loving, witty expressions of her dear warm soul, written on papers that would have been clasped longingly to her chest before their despatch.

Cornelia's letters were ever characterised by her unique reinvention of written English. She spoke the language with fair fluency (indeed, she was mastering its more colloquial oaths with unsettling speed) but on paper she never paid much attention to such niceties as spellings, grammar and – all too often – legibility. So it was now. Even so, by assembling her letters into chronological order and setting aside all the talk of friends and the court, I was able to construct something of what had been happening in England since my departure. For instance, this was from her letter of 6 January:

Ye great hore kips away from us at Ravnsdin. This is blesing tho yr mothr thinks not. As yet miladys bellie dos not swell, wch yr brothr finds strayng. I fynde it strayngr that hee thinks hee has suf – suffy – enouff manhood to mak her so. He is moor at court thn evr he has bin, she wth him. Still we seek prooff of ye great whor's crymes. Triss wrytes to his yonge men ax ye landt – ('ax' perplexed me until I realised it was her somewhat inventive rendering of 'across') – *and travles much to seek ye trooth of her grate moneys. For my part, husband, I wayt for ye lettr frm ower frend tht will bare news of ye dauchter.*

This from her letter of 17 January:

Yr brothr and ye grate hore have com, ye court beeng gon to Hampton. She now lords it ovr us hear. Iff they ar to give ye Huis of Quinton its heir, they do so most strainglie – they mak to shair ye saim chambr at nicht, but I know they do not shair ye saim bed. You know how thin ye walls arond ye earl's chmbr are. I hear all. Ye Barkoks hear all. Yet ther is nowthing to hear, husbnd. Methnks even yr mother begginns to regrt having maid ths maridg to ths gratest of harlots, ths – The two pages that followed were wholly indecipherable.

These tidings made me mightily anxious – and as Our Saviour knows, I was already anxious enough over the fate of the infernal chain-pumps.

A little later that day, I discussed the gist of my correspondence with Francis Gale and Phineas Musk, my two confidantes aboard the *Seraph* in the matter of the Lady Louise. We could speak with some freedom, for my neighbour O'Dwyer was ashore, once again taking the air of Santa Cruz de Tenerife. And once again, he would find shifts of my men, ever present and attentive to his wellbeing.

'My wife's bitterness is to be expected,' I said. 'I can barely conceive of her and the Countess Louise existing together under the same roof. It was bad enough with her and my mother alone.'

'Quite so,' said Francis. 'But what is not to be expected, I think, is your brother's willingness to spend so much time at court. From what I have observed, he detests the institution – its vanities and its great throng of people.'

'Always has done,' said Musk. 'Just like your father, Captain. Not like *his* father, of course.'

'The Lady Louise's spell over my brother must be intoxicating indeed,' I said. 'But this suggestion that my mother is having second thoughts about the marriage – great God, I find that hard to believe. She would rather sup with the shade of Noll Cromwell than ever admit she could be wrong about anything.'

Musk and Francis both nodded, for they knew my mother well enough.

I looked at my two fellows and wondered what we could possibly achieve by our discussion of events that had taken place in England weeks before, and which we could not affect in any way. But sometimes it is good to unburden oneself. As a man of God, Francis's very presence encouraged such openness; my ancestors had confessed their sins to men like him for century after century, and it took more than a few brief generations of Protestantism to purge such sentiments entirely from an Englishman's soul (especially from that of an Englishman brought up in part by a French Catholic grandmother). As for Phineas Musk: well, his presence was of a rather different nature. But as was so often the case, it was Musk who cut to the heart of the matter.

'Fucking,' said Musk, quite suddenly. Francis and I both looked at him curiously, for Musk was not usually a coarse man. 'It all hinges on fucking. The Earl and the Countess at Ravensden – no fucking. The Earl and the Countess at Whitehall – fucking. Or so your brother suggests, if he doesn't understand why the bitch wasn't with child after their time there. So we need to know why they were fu – carnal with each other in the one place and not in the other.'

This was a simple truth, but an unanswerable one. Or was it? We simply had no direct knowledge of what had transpired at Whitehall, and Cornelia was not well placed to obtain it. Ironically, I was, despite being so many hundreds of miles away. When Musk and Francis had left, I sat and began to pen a letter to Will Berkeley, captain of His Majesty's ship the *Bristol*, requesting his intercession with his brother, Viscount Fitzhardinge, and their father, the treasurer of the king's household. If any men on earth knew the dark secrets of the court of Charles the Second, it would be the members of the noble house of Berkeley. Would that I could call on friendship and family to solve my problem with the chain-pump parts …

A storm often begins as an insignificant speck of a cloud upon the horizon, growing and darkening as it approaches. Thus it was with the idea. Once I had finished the letter to Will, I sat in my stern window, looking out over the bay of Santa Cruz de Tenerife. Small craft scurried back and forth, carrying wares to and from the Spanish, Dutch, Swedish and Hamburg ships that lay there. I watched a lofty Spanish galleon of some sixty guns come into the bay: a magnificent sight, but badly handled by her crew, who would be mostly unwilling conscripts, as Don Alonso de Villasanchez had explained to me during the Dunes campaign. Oh, how my grandfather would have looked upon that spectacle, and thought at once, *an easy prize, my lads …*

The sight of the great Spanish ship brought back memories, and the memories brought knowledge. I knew the Spanish well; better than I had remembered, if truth be told. I had lived in Spanish Flanders before my move to Veere. I had fought under the Spanish flag, albeit only because King Philip was then the only sovereign to recognise our exiled, pathetic royalist cause. I had lived very briefly in Old Spain itself, when I accompanied my brother on a mission to the Escorial. The Spanish were a people who regarded honour even more highly than we English, and respected rank above all; every peasant sought to prove himself of noble birth, only partly because nobility in Spain secured the not unattractive perquisite of lifelong tax exemption. The Spanish respected their military, too, but they were also a superstitious race, and squirmed at the memory of their terrible defeats …

The idea had grown from that tiny cloud into a mighty storm. It was unlikely and it was desperate, but ours was an unlikely and desperate cause, and what did we have to lose?

I smiled, and sent for Martin Lanherne and Julian Carvell.

The two quite different stories both began as facts. The first, told by Lanherne's men in the *tavernas* of the south part of the town, was the story of the Honourable Matthew Quinton, brother of one of the noblest earls of England and captain of yon royal warship in the bay, who had served nobly with the Spanish army under Don John of Austria at the Battle of the Dunes. Several hours' worth of Englishmen trading the story from one tavern to another meant that by the end of the night, I was supposedly a general of Spain to rank alongside Spinola and had received an honorary knighthood of Calatrava from King Philip himself.

The second story, told by Carvell's men in the northern part, needed no embellishment and no exaggeration. It was the simple truth that the young Englishman commanding the ship in the bay was the blood-heir of *el diablo blanco* himself. The natural progress of tavern communication ensured that by the night's end, most of the inhabitants of Santa Cruz de Tenerife were convinced that the ghost-ship of Earl Matthew was due on the next tide.

The net effect of the two stories combined was that by dawn, we had seven rival estimates for the new chain-pump parts. Founders competed with each other to swear upon the graves of their mothers that they would be able to fashion the esses and rowls before the sun sank again, and that the new parts would endure until the Day of Judgment.

Seventeen

The squadron duly weighed from Santa Cruz de Tenerife, *Seraph* falling in proudly alongside her consorts, and with a fair wind we set course for Cape Verde, a few hundred miles north of the mouth of the Gambia. This was an easy sail but for one curious incident. I was wakened one morning by Musk, who was in a state of rare agitation, demanding that I come on deck at once. Pausing only to buckle my sword-belt, I followed him out into the brilliant glare of another oven-hot day. Several of the men were standing at the feet of the masts, murmuring to each other and pointing upward – at sails that were blood-red.

I blinked at the sight, hoping that it was but an illusion that would evaporate as soon as my eyes became accustomed to the heat and light. But it did not. Overnight, the sails had turned red.

'There's murmuring of a curse,' said Musk. 'Sails of blood. Some are saying they presage the deaths of every last one of us upon this voyage. Poseidon was thwarted of his blood-sacrifice when the chain-pumps didn't sink us, so this is his way of announcing his revenge.'

If I knew one thing alone in that moment, it was that I needed no more doom-laden counsels from Phineas Musk. I needed heads that had been rather longer upon the sea ...

Kit Farrell came on deck, and I silently gave thanks unto my Lord. He looked at the sails, looked at me, and said, 'Well, Captain. I've never seen the like.' This was not the opinion I needed in that moment, with the muttering of the men growing ever louder. But it was sometimes too easy to forget that Kit was but a young man of my own age; although he was a hundred times the seaman I would ever be, his experience was inevitably limited. However, he had a sharp eye and even sharper wits. Looking out to larboard, he said, 'But then, I wonder if they've seen the like on the other two.'

I followed his gaze, and saw that the sails of the distant *Jersey* and *Prospect of Blakeney* were of the same blood-red hue.

'I'll summon Mister Castle and Mister Negus to the deck,' I said.

Kit shook his head. 'No need to disturb their slumbers, I think, sir. I have an idea. I suggest bringing the ship as close to the wind as she'll go, then bringing her back again – luffing and touching, in other words. We'll hardly lose ground on Captain Holmes and the *Prospect*, as we can outsail them easily enough.'

I still felt a profound dread when issuing orders independently. The memory of the wreck of my first command, the *Happy Restoration*, died hard, and with it the irrational fear that a wrong command given by Captain Matthew Quinton would end yet again in the destruction of a king's ship and a hundred or so lives. But in truth, I sensed that on this voyage I was in danger of becoming a cipher rather than a captain. Castle and Negus were so experienced and so reliable that I had been content to defer to them, deluding myself that decisions were being arrived at by a consensus of equals of whom the captain was one. I had also started to forget how much I trusted the judgment of Kit Farrell.

'Very well, Mister Farrell,' I said. 'Ahoy the helm! Luff and touch her!'

I heard the answering call from the helmsman at the whipstaff, and almost at once the responsive *Seraph* began her turn towards the wind. Closer, ever closer to the point of no return – The sails began to flap and flutter. As they did so, the 'blood' came out in clouds. Some of it settled on the deck and on those of us who stood there. Musk brushed himself furiously. I ran my hand through my hair and looked at the red stains on my fingers and palm. Laughing, I held my hand up to the crew, who were looking at each other in bewilderment. 'Sand, lads!' I cried. 'The red sand of Africa!'

The helmsman brought the ship back round onto her original course. As he did so, I turned to my boatswain. 'Well done, Mister Farrell,' I said. 'Sense defeats superstition once again.'

He shrugged modestly. 'There seemed no other rational explanation for it, sir. But if the turn hadn't shaken it out – well, I suppose I'd have favoured the notion of a curse, too.'

I noticed Carvell and Macferran standing by the main. I had quite forgotten about the punishment I had inflicted on the young Scot; the affair of the chain-pumps and the tidings from Cornelia had driven it from my mind. I liked Macferran, and hoped that my treatment of him had not caused him, and my Cornish following on the lower deck, to become resentful of me. I said something to that effect, adding haughtily that a captain had to enforce discipline aboard ship without fear or favour, but Carvell simply grinned.

'Resentful, Captain?' said the ebony Virginian, who seemed genuinely surprised at the notion. 'Far from it, sir. Macferran couldn't be happier, could you, lad?'

The young Scot gave a shy grin. 'Aye, Captain,' he said, in his soft Scottish lilt. 'Well, for one thing, you were right, sir – I started it, and I deserved it. That was obvious to every man on the ship, me amongst 'em. Being called a ginger Scots whisky-sot is no more than truth, after all,' said Macferran ruefully. 'And getting a flogging – well, it makes you a man, that it does, in the eyes of the rest of 'em. Some of the Bristol boys even share their baccy with me now. We're all Seraphim together, after all.' This, I gathered, was the by-name that my men had given themselves. It was as well that the king had decided not to christen the

ship *Cherub*. 'And the lasses over in Santa Cruz town are mightily attentive when you've got fresh welts on your back, that they are, Captain,'
said the young Scot, grinning. 'Love running their fingers over them,
they do…'

I had not previously contemplated the possibility of naval discipline
as either a mark of honour or an aphrodisiac, but Carvell's knowing
smirk at his young Scots friend suggested that I had much to learn on
both scores.

Three days later we came to Cape Verde itself, a great point of land
jutting out from the hilly coast of Africa, identifiable by the two high
hummocks that rose from it. Like every headland, it was an earthly
paradise for the legions of petrels, gannets and cormorants that wheeled
and dived around it; indeed, two high rocks were so white from their
dung that they appeared like ships under sail. We edged in between the
hummocks and the small islands to the east of the Cape, eventually
anchoring in twenty-six fathoms some three miles off a sandy bay. Here
the breeze strengthened into a gale that prevented us going immediately
round to Gorée, a small isle a mile or so to the south of the Cape, which
Holmes had a mind to reconnoitre. This was a colony of the Dutch,
who had named it after an island I knew well, on the Zeeland coast not
far from my wife's home town of Veere. When the wind backed north-
westerly, early the next morning, Holmes summoned a quite jaunty
O'Dwyer, an inscrutable Facey and myself to the *Jersey* for a council-of-
war to discuss our strategy against the island. We had barely settled into
his great cabin to examine the charts when his lookouts cried that there
was a sail in sight, coming from northward beyond the breakers of the
Cape. We strode to the quarterdeck, O'Dwyer with particular eagerness.

Holmes took up a telescope, and after a minute or so's perusal, he
passed it to me.

'Your opinion, Captain Quinton?'

'A Dutchman, undoubtedly – there are the Dutch colours, flying at her main, and she would have no reason to disguise herself in this time of peace.' *However long that time of peace has left to run, I thought.* 'Three hundred tons or so. A West Indiaman, probably. Should be a decent cargo, I conceive.'

'My opinion exactly.' Holmes did not even bother to invite the two redcoats to use the telescope, although as an Algerine galley captain O'Dwyer must have spent much longer at sea than Holmes, the long-time cavalry officer. 'Is it not shameful,' Holmes asked, 'that a Dutch ship should dare not to salute the King of England's colours in these, His Majesty's own seas?'

With that one question, Robert Holmes made to begin a war. No English captain would then have denied that our King's dominion over the seas extended as far south as Cape Finisterre and up to the high water mark of Danish, Dutch, French and Spanish shores alike. In those waters, all ships should strike their flags and topsails to acknowledge His Majesty's sovereignty over the seas; such was merely natural justice. But we were many hundreds of leagues to the south of Finisterre. Holmes was advancing a far greater, a far more deadly proposition: that the Brit-ish Seas and all the oceans of the world were one and the same.

O'Dwyer's response was immediate and enthusiastic. 'A damnable impertinence that a Dutchman should be in His Majesty's seas at all! Sink or take, my dear Holmes! Sink or take!'

Presumably the enigmatic Irishman had said the same more than once on behalf of the Emperor of Morocco or the Sultan himself. I was more wary, and said so. 'I do not recall that we were enjoined to exact the salute in these waters, Captain Holmes.'

He smiled. 'Ah, Matt, there are so many things that rulers do not explicitly enjoin their warriors to do – and yet they are done. Is that not one of the characteristics of war, Colonel O'Dwyer, Captain Facey?'

The nods of the two veterans – O'Dwyer's vigorous, the grey-visaged Facey's grudging – told their story. These three men, each of whose experience of warfare stretched for many decades beyond my own, already knew that lesson full well; and how well I have learned it since that day.

Briskly, Holmes gave the orders to his own officers, then to me. I was to proceed with *Seraph* and *Prospect of Blakeney* to the mouth of the Gambia, there to rendezvous with Holmes once he had accomplished his objective. This made perfect sense, of course, but as Lanherne's boat crew rowed me back to the *Seraph*, I could not help but note that it also conveniently left the prize and any consequent plunder solely to the mercies of Robert Holmes and the *Jersey*.

We put on sail, leaving Holmes to veer away northward. I had a perfect view of all that transpired subsequently from the poop deck of *Seraph*. We were moving away to the south-east on the wind, but still were barely two or three miles from the Dutchman and the *Jersey*, to leeward of her, when the action commenced.

'Holmes is preparing to tack,' said Kit Farrell at my side.

I nodded. *Jersey*'s sails were loosed; she came round to the new tack, closing the Dutchman relentlessly. We saw a small cloud of smoke, and moments later the sound came to us of a single shot, Holmes' warning. There was a long delay. I imagined the consternation aboard the Dutchman, the debate among her officers, the arguments for resistance, the oaths directed against the perfidious English. And as so often from such debates and arguments, the outcome was compromise. I watched as the red-white-blue of the United Provinces was hauled down from the main. But the topsails remained resolutely in place, and the Dutch ship held her course.

'Ah, my poor Dutch friend,' I murmured under my breath. 'Against any other captain, perhaps that would be sufficient…'

At that moment, Holmes began to fire his starboard battery, one gun at a time, bow to stern. The Dutchmen were brave men – held out for more guns than good sense dictated – but they were not suicides. The topsails were struck at last, then the other sails too as the Dutchman hove to; the *Jersey* had her prize.

A prize from a nation with which we were not at war. A prize taken by exacting the salute to the King of Britain's flag in seas that did not belong to Charles Stuart. She was the *Brill*, I soon discovered; forty days out of Holland, carrying brandy, lime and iron for the Isle of Gorée, and seized most unjustly within sight of her destination.

Thus are wars made.

Leaving Holmes to secure his prize, *Seraph* and *Prospect of Blakeney* made for the mouth of the Gambia, edging south along the African coast. This was *terra incognita* for us all – even Negus had never been further south than Cape Verde – and he, Castle, Kit and myself spent long hours in my cabin, poring over the charts for these waters, and out on deck, relating the charts to the reality that lay before us. Fortunately it was an easy sail in good, deep water, with no dangers from hidden currents or rocks, and never passing over a shoal with less than three fathoms beneath our keel. We passed what the charts showed as towns, but seemed to me little better than stockades filled with round, cone-roofed mud huts: Rufisco, Porto D'Ale, Juala and the like. This was a less hilly coast than at Cape Verde, lined with palms for a long way inland. We had few dealings with the Portuguese, or half-breed Portuguese, who lived in those parts, but those who were brave enough to venture out to us in shallops or like craft proved friendly enough. England's alliance with Portugal was age-old, but in more recent times it had been reinforced by our assistance to that land in its long war of independence against Spain: assistance repaid in part by Portugal's provision of a regrettably barren queen for our most potent sovereign lord King Charles.

At length, we came to a great sand bar, over a league long, covered with the fat birds that the Portuguese call *soldados,* and stinking of their musky dung. We sailed down the bar until we came to a breach, passing through into seven fathoms of water. The mouth of a great river lay before us, some two or three miles wide; beyond it, we could see clearly that the river broadened out into an even mightier stream, perhaps five or six of our English miles wide. Dozens, perhaps hundreds, of canoes thronged back and forth, along the shore, across the river, and out to two islands where it appeared salt was being mined. Three small trading vessels, a Dutchman, an Amelander and a Portugee, lay at anchor under the lee of the larger island. We followed the sailing instructions given by Holmes, who had been in this river ten years before, and made for a great tree upon what the charts showed as the Point of Bayone, on the south shore, keeping it a little off our starboard bow, tacking once the lead reported less than five fathoms. This brought us over toward the north shore, avoiding the reef that obstructed that side of the channel. Dolphins sported themselves in our bow wave as we crossed the stream. John Treninnick hooted from the main yard and jabbered excitedly in Cornish; it seemed that he had a particular liking for dolphin meat. Many hundreds of men could be spied fishing from the shore with lines, spears and nets. Fish lay drying on the beaches between them and the great palm line. Sea-birds of all sorts circled overhead, shrieking loudly and occasionally plunging onto land or water. We took our noon day observation against a brilliant, cloudless blue sky: thirteen degrees, thirty minutes north.

We lowered our topsails, hauled up our courses and anchored in the brown waters off a small islet of some three acres which the charts named as Dog Island, very close to the north shore – so close, indeed, that the channel between the island and the shore was shallow enough to be forded. A smaller neighbour, named on the charts as Pelican Island, lay a little way away. The multitude of billed pink birds thronging its low shores explained its name amply enough; but on Dog Island, not one of its namesakes could be seen. Negus ordered the lead to be slung, and the report came back that we had three fathoms, in mud and broken ground. Our landfall was a mighty relief for Captain Facey and his redcoats from the *Prospect of Blakeney*, who spilled ashore with as much delight as if they had been given tickets-of-leave to every alehouse and brothel in Westminster. Their happiness quickly translated itself into a little piece of empire-building: by the time I got ashore myself, I found that the place had been renamed Charles Island and that the redcoats were busy fortifying it. I could hardly protest, given the mission that Holmes was about, and it was no surprise that when he arrived the following morning (accompanied by his prize, the *Brill*), the expedition's commanding officer expressed his entire satisfaction with our acquisition. I was less convinced. For one thing, who would conceive of setting down a fortress in such a place, when even the most foolish army in the world needed only to wait for low tide before simply walking across to it? Even worse, it was one of the most truly awful places I have known in my life: an oven set down in the mouth of a river. The heat was like nothing I had ever experienced, even at Tangier. I made the mistake of re-reading one of Cornelia's letters on deck, in an attempt to decipher one of her more illegible passages by holding it up against the sun; by the time I finished it, the wax seal had melted away entirely, the drops joining my own sweat upon the deck. Pendeen, the swabber, dozed off shirtless on the forecastle after his breakfast ale, and before the glass had turned his body resembled a potato on a spit. Humphrey the surgeon kept him alive by God knows what means, but the man's screams kept us awake for days. By night the wind came from the land, but on many days this fell away at about ten before noon. The next few hours were truly hellish, in the literal, fiery sense of that word: complete stillness, with nothing but the most sapping heat. We soon learned to follow the custom of those parts and to retreat below decks or into the shelter of our new huts ashore, and not to emerge until well into the afternoon, when the sea wind blew and cleared the stifling furnace-air.

By the third day, we were well established in our new empire, although not contentedly so. The soldiers who had been so happy to spill ashore onto Charles Island were already complaining of its inadequacies, grumbling of its indefensibility, lack of protection from the heat and inevitable fevers to come; one soldier was already sick, and both redcoats and sailors alike were muttering that this was an evil portent indeed. We also contemplated the possibility of attack, but thus far, the land seemed benign enough. We could spy native canoes close in to both shores, but they stayed well clear of us. Further off, on the north shore of the Gambia, a few fishermen could be seen, all perfectly black in their skin, but no more organised society than that. Holmes sent a boat to the mainland; after all, he was the authority on these parts, the one man (with the debatable exception of O'Dwyer) who had been to this dreadful place before. That evening, after his boat had returned and the climate had become barely tolerable, Holmes called a meeting in his great cabin. I went across with O'Dwyer, William Castle, Kit Farrell, Valentine Negus and Francis Gale, whose sighting of natives on the shore had convinced him that here was an entire continent crying out for the true word of God, in the shape of the Church of England By Law Established and its envoy, the Rector of Ravensden. Morgan Facey, the putative governor of Charles Island, joined us. As we entered the cabin, we were all, I think, a little startled to see at Holmes' side an ancient one-legged man, propped up on crutches. How this creature had yet warded off death was a mystery: he wheezed with every breath, and a great indentation in the side of his head suggested his skull had been shattered long ago.

'Your pilot, Captain Quinton,' Holmes said. 'Despite appearances, he's the best on the river. Isn't that so, Jesus?'

Holmes pronounced the name in our English way, which unsettled me a not a little. Judging by Francis Gale's expression, it affected him even more profoundly; presumably not even the finest theological train-ing that the University of Cambridge provided could prepare a man for the revelation that the Second Coming was a crippled old Portugee eking out a living on the Gambia River.

'Hay-zuzz,' said the old man with surprising vehemence. 'Hay-zuzz, Captain Holmes, as I told you and your Prince Rupert ten years ago.' The Second Coming's English was remarkably fluent. 'Hay-zuzz Sebas-tian Belem at your service, Captain Quinton.'

I have travelled more widely since those days of my extreme and naive youth, and have long since ceased to bat an eyelid when encountering Latins called Jesus or Maria; or Frenchmen called Anne, come to that.

'Hay-zuzz, then,' said Holmes, with evident bad grace. 'He has just returned from a voyage up the coast. Before we begin our conference proper, tell Captain Quinton the intelligence you gleaned upon that voyage, Hay-zuzz.'

The old Portugee ignored the sarcasm. 'A Dutch frigate has arrived at Cape Verde. Not as large as your *Jersey*, but they say she is the precursor of a stronger force to come.'

'So,' said Holmes, 'I have no time to lose, I think.' *I*, not *we*. 'Time for us to separate, Matthew. I will sail for Cape Verde on tomorrow's tide, God and the wind permitting. I'll take Gorée and then move down the coast, taking and sinking as I go.' The glint in his eye told its own story: nothing was bound to give Robert Holmes greater delight than the prospect of waging his own private war. 'You will continue your mission up river, in quest of Colonel O'Dwyer's mountain of gold, with Belem here as your pilot and guide. This plan meets your approval, Captain?'

It mattered little if it did not, I suspected. Holmes had plainly made up his mind, his orders did not contradict the king's original instructions, and I could hardly argue with my superior officer. 'As you say, Captain Holmes.'

'So, then,' said Holmes. 'The time has come, I think, for Colonel O'Dwyer to lay before us the exact route he proposes to follow to the mountain in question.'

A chart of the Gambia river – presumably Belem's – was laid out on the table in front of Holmes and the ancient pilot. My heart sank as I followed the river upstream from our location. Place names became fewer; the detail of hills, tributaries and the like became noticeably vaguer, leaving nearly the whole of the right-hand quarter of the chart almost entirely blank. As was the custom with the charts of those days, the indigenous animals had been added here and there to enliven matters (for in truth, there is nothing duller than a bare chart). I had expected to see the crocodiles, elephants and lions that had been drawn on either side of the lower and middle reaches of the Gambia, but I was somewhat discomforted by the fact that the chart-maker had seen fit to illustrate the upper reaches with unicorns.

If O'Dwyer was alarmed at being forced to reveal his hand, he did not show it. He stepped forward to the chart table with his usual swagger, looked down upon it, frowned, and then pointed to a spot not far away from the unicorn in the top right hand corner.

'There,' he said with some vehemence. 'A month's march, I'd say, north-east from the Hill of Tinda.'

I peered down at the chart. The Hill of Tinda was almost the last name on the right hand side, before the great blankness began and well to the right of some of the other unicorns. I looked up at my officers. Castle's face was a mask; he was too much the veteran to betray his feelings. By contrast, Kit Farrell's round young face could never conceal the feelings behind it, and he was clearly excited by the prospect of this voyage of discovery into unknown, or barely known, territory. Francis Gale seemed lost in prayerful contemplation; this was always a sign that he was requesting a divine thunderbolt to strike down someone who offended him. The dour veteran Morgan Facey was shaking his head, albeit almost imperceptibly. No doubt he was calculating the effect of a month's march each way, in these conditions, on soldiers with muskets and heavy knapsacks.

But I was captain of the *Seraph*, Holmes was effectively resigning command of this part of the expedition to me (as the king had intended all along), and I knew there would be no other opportunity to nip this madness in the bud. And I thought that my means of doing so stood there before me. On crutches.

So I asked Belem the question that had burned inside me since I first encountered Brian Doyle O'Dwyer in the captain's cabin of the *Wessex*. 'Tell me, Belem. You have served as a pilot on this river for – what? – forty years or more?' The old man nodded. 'Then if you know it so well, you of all men will know if a great mountain of gold really does lie beyond it, in the lands beyond the headwaters.'

Holmes smirked, but said nothing. I caught an exchange of glances between Francis Gale and Kit Farrell. Morgan Facey's eyes narrowed. O'Dwyer looked intently at the old man. The tension in the great cabin of the *Jersey* was palpable.

The cripple looked about him, and down at the chart. At length, he said, 'Well, Captain. Myself, I've never been beyond Barraconda, there.' He pointed to a place well to the left of the Hill of Tinda, just by the first of the unicorns. 'Trading hardly ever goes on above Pompeton, here.' Almost half way across the chart in our direction, this; safely into the land of lions, elephants and place names. 'But I'm told that caravans of Moors sometimes come across the desert to those parts, from the lands far to the north. I've even encountered Arabs as far down the river as Kasang and Wolley Wolley. And there's always been much talk of gold mines, far beyond Barraconda. The natives of those parts wear even more gold than those hereabouts. It must come from somewhere.'

This was not the answer I had expected. O'Dwyer favoured me with a triumphant smirk. My officers shuffled in embarrassment for their captain. Only Holmes seemed entirely at ease with Belem's surprising speech.

'Well, then, that being so, how long do you estimate it will take to reach the location provided by Colonel O'Dwyer?'

Belem looked down at the chart and pointed his wizened finger at our location, right in the mouth of the Gambia, at the extreme left-hand side of the chart.

'From this anchorage to Tindobauge, good sailing, wide channel, so three days at most, probably less with the winds as they are and the times when you should get the flood tides. From Tindobauge, here, past Elephant Island, to Kasang, here – ten days. Beyond Kasang, the river becomes more difficult. It is tidal no more, so you are going against the current. It twists this way, then that – difficult waters for a ship this large, Captain, especially now in the dry season, when the chief wind is that which the Arabs call *Harmattan*, from the north-east. These upper reaches would be easier if you were navigating them in the deeper water and west winds of the wet months,' said Belem, 'but they will not begin until May, and of course that wet season brings the man-killing fevers, as you may find on your return. Better, perhaps, to leave your ship at Kasang, or even downstream of that, build boats there, and proceed in them. So, two weeks to build your boats, then on, beyond what you English call Arse Hill – '

I thought I must have misheard, but the glint in Holmes' eye told me I had not. 'Just what it says, Matt,' he said. 'A hill shaped like a great arse – a pair of buttocks. The custom of the river demands that crews bare their own arses at it as they pass.'

'Just so,' said Belem. 'From Kasang to Barraconda – three or four weeks. Beyond Barraconda, the stream becomes more difficult still – rapids, shoals, whirlpools and the like, as those who have been in those waters have told me. So from Barraconda to the hill of Tinda, where Colonel O'Dwyer intends to begin his march – perhaps three weeks more.'

I did the fearful arithmetic in my head. Three months or more to reach the mountain – if it truly existed, and I trusted the word of this ancient Portugee about as much as I trusted that of Brian Doyle O'Dwyer. But if it did exist – *dear God, I was becoming as fanciful as my king* – if it did, then Heaven alone knew how long at the mountain itself, mapping it, recording it, preparing the way for the Welsh and Yorkshire miners whom the king would despatch to supplement the slaves we would buy in these parts – say three months, perhaps? At least the same amount of time to cross the desert again and navigate back downstream, so another three months or so (and that made no allowance for the rainy season, its storms and its fevers). How long then to fit and victual for a voyage to England? Three months more, say… and the voyage itself, another two... thus even by a conservative estimate I could not hope to see England's shore, nor my love Cornelia, for well over a year. Our Lord alone knew how things would stand by then between my brother, my mother and the Countess Louise; or, indeed, whether Tris and his agents would have unearthed something so dreadful about the latter and her vanished daughter that the House of Quinton would shake to its very foundations. Perhaps even worse, I might miss the whole of the Dutch war that Holmes was minded to bring about – all that prize money, all that honour from playing my part in the final destruction of Holland, that nest of perfidious, avaricious butterboxes (my wife excepted). Of course, all of my calculations assumed that Captain Matthew Quinton actually managed to survive the perils of the river, the storms, the fevers, the desert, the lions, and being gored by a unicorn.

For the first time in my life, I felt a sudden urge to draw my sword, press its point to my heart, and ram it home.

Eighteen

I watched from the quarterdeck of *Seraph* the following morning as the sails were loosed aboard *Jersey* and her prize, the *Brill*. We saluted Holmes with eleven guns; he answered nine; I returned seven; he answered five; and at the last, I returned three. My crew, gathered upon the deck, gave three lusty huzzahs, though in truth, most of them were green with envy as the sails of the *Jersey* and *Brill* sank below the horizon to the west. Almost to a man, they would rather have been going to sea with Holmes, out into a fresher climate and with Dutch prizes in their sights, than heading up this fetid river on a quest of the utmost folly, born of the avarice of a king. Kit warned that some of the more refractory lads from London and Bristol were full of this talk, and that there were murmurs of them taking over the ship and sailing her as a pirate. These practical concerns brought my own thoughts out of that dismal place whither they had fled. As agreed with Holmes and the others in the latter half of the previous evening's conference aboard *Jersey*, the *Prospect of Blakeney* would be left behind at Charles Island when *Seraph* proceeded upstream. Some of the spare cannon that *Jersey* had brought with her were put into *Prospect*, thus giving her a battery of eight guns – strong enough to deal with almost anything that was likely to come that way, other than a proper ship of war – but as Holmes would need all of his own men to provide prize crews (the man's confidence was unbounded), it had been decided that the enlarged crew for *Prospect* would be drawn exclusively from *Seraph*. Kit and I went through the muster book, carefully picking out a combination of the foulest coxcombs and good, dependable men (not all from my old Cornish following; even London and Bristol can produce sound men occasionally). To command over them we sent Grimwade, the best of the master's mates, and Pegg, the boatswain's mate who had conducted the flogging of Macferran, and whom Kit regarded highly; Pegg had little trouble with recalcitrants, Kit explained, for he had been a mightily successful wrestler in his younger days. Morgan Facey divided his redcoats in like fashion. Half were to be left behind as the garrison for Charles Island, and he ensured that good men predominated in that draft. The remaining half of the soldiers, thirty in all, would take passage in *Seraph*, occupying the berths vacated by the men sent over to *Prospect*.

These moves, and the consequent transfer of victuals from ship to ship and ship to shore, took the best part of three days, primarily because such work was simply an impossibility in the middle part of the day. At last, and when I finally thought we were ready to proceed up river, Belem came back on board to inform me of a new complication.

'The King of Kombo,' he said, 'is displeased that you have come past his territory and not visited him to pay your respects. This means, of course, that he wants you to pay the dues he thinks himself entitled to from ships that pass his shore.'

This was an imposition that I would gladly have avoided, but I was mindful of the honour of my master King Charles and, more immediately, of the potential fate of the Charles Island garrison once the powerful deterrent provided by *Seraph*'s guns had moved upriver. Consequently, very early the next day a suitably impressive embassy was put ashore by the *Seraph*'s longboat. This consisted of myself, dressed in one of my better frock coats; Belem; O'Dwyer and a dozen soldiers, uniformed to impress; a dozen of my crew, including Carvell and Ali Reis, who were accustomed to such hot climes; and Lieutenant Castle, who spoke some Portuguese and could thus ensure that the pilot, whom I had mistrusted since his gesture of support for O'Dwyer, interpreted accurately.

Even so early in the morning, the sand was burning and the cracked red ground inland from it nearly roasted a man's shoes. There was almost no wind. Belem said that the village of the king was some ten of our English miles from the landing place. I was concerned that the aged, crippled pilot would struggle on such a journey, but I was soon proved wrong; the old man swung along on his crutches without an apparent concern in the world. The flocks of vultures that circled above us would have to wait some considerable time to feast on the bones of Jesus Sebastian Belem, it seemed. By contrast, the normally jovial Castle, a man more accustomed than most of us to hot climes than most of us, struggled to keep up from the very start, perspiring from every pore and gulping in great breaths of air. I suggested that he turn back, or stay where he was, but he would have none of it; he was lieutenant of the *Seraph*, he said, and honour demanded that his place be at his captain's side.

Soon afterwards, all conversation ceased. Each man was too intent on staying alive in that ferocious heat: blinking and taking breaths became tasks that required conscious effort, and I was sweating so much that I began to imagine myself a creature of water, not of flesh. Our hands came up mechanically to deter the insects that swarmed relentlessly about us. Familiar birds (egrets, terns, lone eagles, the ubiquitous vultures) shared the air with strange species of every colour: blue, red, yellow, green, a veritable rainbow in flight. We sighted the occasional monkey or antelope, and many oxen and cows – which were allowed to roam free, the natives having but little idea of how to farm them to good effect – but alas, my mind was too set on resisting the heat and staying alive to take much interest in such fauna. About an hour into the journey, I was lost in thoughts of Cornelia, and a pleasant vision of making love with her in the Ravensden ice-house, when ...

An almighty explosion rent the air, close to my right ear. Birds scattered in every direction, animals visible and invisible cried their fright or defiance. I knew it at once for what it was; had heard enough muskets roar in my time. Like every other man in the company I flung myself onto the hard, roasting red ground, fearing that we were under attack ...

Like every other man in the company *but one*. I looked around, saw there was no other evidence of an attack, and got to my feet. The whole company gathered around the one soldier who remained standing, a young Londoner named Baynes, and examined his musket. We took turns to touch the barrel, and to look at the cock stand, which was half bent.

The gun had been fired spontaneously by the heat.

After a march of perhaps four hours, ever deeper into the palm trees that fringed this whole coast, we came in sight of the village where the King of Kombo held court. This was a circular enclosure surrounded by a stockade of wooden hurdles; whitewashed round houses, perhaps two or three hundred in all, lay within. Goats were everywhere, seemingly taking the place of sheep in these parts. They seemed smaller and coarser than our English goats, although one kind had a shiny black skin that matched its owners' in a manner pleasing to the eye. The people themselves took not the slightest notice of us, for as Belem explained, they were well used to seeing white men coming to pay tribute to their king. The men of this Mandingo nation were tall and jet-black, wearing only cloths around their loins or, in a few cases, long white cotton shirts that reminded me of the surplices of our clergy. All wore a profusion of leather amulets, or gris-gris as Belem called them, on every available piece of flesh – about their foreheads, around their necks, on their

arms and ankles. These were somewhat akin to the relics of the Popish church, the papist Belem explained: this amulet to protect against
flood, that against fire, and so forth. Some men carried spears or bows,
but most were merely sitting about on the ground in groups, playing a
game which seemed to require the rapid movement of pebbles between
holes cut into a wooden board. The women eyed us rather more curiously. Some bore their babies upon their backs. All were naked to the
waist, wearing only a garment of cotton upon their lower parts; all had
fantastical decorations worked into the skin of their backs. I wished my
Cornelia with me, to witness this scene, but then I thought better of
it; if she saw such skin-decoration, she would undoubtedly want some
for herself.

The king's palace – little better than a larger version of the huts of his
people – lay at the centre of the village. A guarded gate led into a yard,
where two men, clad identically to the others in the village, bowed to us
and led us toward the large royal hut.

'Tetees,' the Portugee said. 'The heralds. They will lead us to His Majesty's presence.' He nodded toward the other men who milled around
the yard, eyeing us more curiously than those outside. 'Braffoes and
cabasheers,' murmured Belem. 'Captains and officials of the King of
Kombo.'

So very like a court of Europe, I thought, were it not for the searing
heat, the profusion of naked flesh and the strangeness of the setting.
The tetees led us up to the entrance of the hut. The flap was pulled back,
and we were led inside. Blessedly, it was a little cooler within; but only
a very little.

The interior of the great hut was matted, and contained no furniture
at all. Seven women sat around the wall at the sides, seemingly entirely
uninterested in the proceedings; I later learned from Belem that these
were the king's wives. Various braffoes and cabasheers also stood by the
wall. Two men were playing a stringed instrument not unlike our lute;

another played a raised, organ-like instrument (a balafon, Belem called it) with seventeen keys, which were played by striking them with a soft round ball at the end of a stick. As for the king himself, he sat in the very centre of the hut. He had no throne, and I wondered how in the name of heaven he ever managed to lower himself onto the mat, or rose from it thereafter. For the King of Kombo was the hugest man I ever saw. This vast creature was clad plainly, in the same manner as his subjects, in a simple cotton shirt and breeches. The only symbol of his royal authority was a pointed cap not unlike an episcopal mitre. Apart from his great size, the most remarkable thing about him was the gris-gris adorning his body. For unlike those worn by his subjects, the king's gris-gris were chiefly of gold.

O'Dwyer, Castle and I followed Belem's lead, for he had informed us of the etiquette of this court during the first, and more talkative, part of our march. The old Portugee made towards the throne, bowing as low as his infirmities would permit. We placed our hands upon our breasts, which His Majesty reciprocated. The king then extended his vast hand. Each of us in turn stepped forward, gripped the upper part of the royal hand, then the lower, then joined palms and shook hands. Finally, we sat down before the enormous presence of His Majesty the King of Kombo.

O'Dwyer took the lead, as the senior officer among us, his rank of colonel giving him sufficient authority to deal with all such local chieftains and potentates. This, after all, was the sole reason why this so-unworthy renegade had been granted his otherwise unjustified rank, or so the Earl of Clarendon, Lord Chancellor of England, had informed my brother. The Irishman apologised profusely for our tardiness in paying our respects to His Majesty, but indicated the bags of money and bottles of brandy that we had brought in tribute, trusting that these would be sufficient compensation for our inexcusable disrespect. Whatever my opinion of O'Dwyer, it was impossible to deny that he managed this saccharine speech with far greater aplomb than Matthew Quinton could ever have brought to it. The king's fearsome expression mellowed more than a little.

The king spoke no English, as was to be expected, but had the pidgin-Portuguese of the coast and relied upon Belem's interpretation. He expressed gratitude for our tribute, proclaimed his undying esteem for the King of England, but then focused entirely on O'Dwyer. 'I have seen many Englishmen, Colonel,' said the king through Belem, 'but I have never before seen one that could pass so readily for an Arab.'

'Why, Majesty,' I said mischievously, 'Colonel O'Dwyer, here, is not an Englishman but an Irishman, which is something quite different. What is more, he has spent many years living as a Moor. He tells us he has been in these parts before – or at least, somewhere beyond the upper reaches of this river.'

O'Dwyer's glance at me could have been taken for a gracious acknowledgment by those who did not know him better. However, the king was delighted by the revelation, and ordered refreshment brought forth. Attendants came out with bottles and cups, and poured a light, almost clear liquid.

'Palm wine,' whispered Belem. 'Pray it is fresh, for after half a day or so, it will turn sour. Good for a man's health, though – cleans out the kidneys and makes him piss.'

We raised our cups to salute the king, he raised his to us, and we drank. I was more than a little relieved to find that the bitter-sweet palm wine was perfectly tolerable to my English palate; indeed, it was not unlike a young white wine when first brought into England. The wine was accompanied by bowls of rice, the great staple of those parts, and by the meat of a bird not unlike to pheasant. All in all, the entire affair was proceeding in a most satisfactory way, and once we had concluded the meal, O'Dwyer formally asked the king's permission to return to our ship and proceed through the waters of his realm to the upper reaches of the river.

The vast king shrugged, which in his case meant a slight quivering of his mighty mound of flesh. 'Ah, my friends,' he said through Belem. 'Of course I wish to aid my royal equal King Charles. But it is difficult. I hear other counsels.' He was evidently uncomfortable now, searching for the words. I exchanged a glance with O'Dwyer, who was as perplexed as myself. 'I hear the counsels that told me to invite you here in order to detain you,' the king said, 'and not to allow you to proceed up the river. The counsels put forward by the other envoy who has come to us.'

Before I had time to digest this news, the king raised his hand. One of the guards pulled upon the curtain and signalled to some man or men beyond. The King of Kombo said, 'It is so difficult to weigh the relative merits of different lands, and the arguments that their envoys present. Thus it is with you, representing your mighty King Charles – and the ambassador, here, representing the most illustrious King Louis.'

The name 'Louis' did not require Belem's translation. The French ambassador stepped into the royal presence. As he did so, I felt that powerful shock which usually comes only with the death of a loved one or a severe wound.

The French ambassador was the Seigneur de Montnoir.

Montnoir was dressed exactly as at our first meeting aboard the *Wessex*. The silver-starred black cloak of a Knight of Malta enveloped him like a shroud. As in our previous encounter, he seemed entirely oblivious to the ferocious heat. His face was the same blank skeletal mask.

I looked upon him in a dream of shock and bewilderment as he bowed to the king.

'Your Majesty is most gracious,' Montnoir said in surprisingly fluent Portuguese, translated back to us by Belem. 'It is pleasing to renew my acquaintance with Captain Quinton.' His nod in my direction certainly betokened no pleasure. 'And I have desired to meet this other gentleman for a very long time. He goes by many names, but I believe I should now salute him as Colonel Brian Doyle O'Dwyer.'

O'Dwyer smiled and bowed in acknowledgment. If he felt dread at the appearance of his would-be interrogator – and perhaps executioner – he did not show it.

The King of Kombo's expression, so benevolent but a few minutes earlier, was now harsh and hostile. 'The French envoy, here, offers me gold. A great deal of gold, in fact, on condition that I prevent the English expedition sailing up the Gambia, wipe out your fort on the Island of Dogs, and hand over to him the person of Colonel O'Dwyer, here present. Would that be the state of it, My Lord Montnoir?'

'As Your Majesty says,' Montnoir said silkily, sensing that his triumph was near.

'Whereas the English seize an island of my kingdom, and then do nothing but offer me cheap trinkets and a vague promise of the future friendship of King Charles. Now, I understand from the many traders upon this coast that King Charles is set but uncertainly upon his throne, and has little money.' Instinct demanded that I protest, but how could I protest against the simple truth? And dear God, if even this mere local potentate knew of our monarchy's dire weakness, then what hope did my cause stand? The king continued, 'Whereas these same traders tell me that the France of King Louis is mightier by the day, as the gold brought by the Lord Montnoir amply proves, and has also made alliance with my old friends, the Dutch. And why should I, the King of Kombo, care if one white man is handed from the custody of another white man to yet another?' Even the confident O'Dwyer grimaced at that. 'So. This seems to be the heart of this case. The king will think upon it.'

And with that, the vast mound of flesh closed its eyes and nestled down upon the mat as though asleep. The rest of us merely stood there. The heat was intolerable. Sweat ran down me; I dared not glance down, for I could have sworn I was forming a puddle upon the floor. William Castle was suffering greatly, his face growing ever redder. Montnoir was serene, that awful smile fixed upon his face. Flies and God knows what other forms of insects circled us like courtiers in search of a free banquet. There could be no talk without His Majesty's permission, so we all merely stood like dumb folk.

The wives and courtiers of the king looked upon us with greater curiosity. Some whispered to each other knowingly in their own tongue. No doubt they knew how the decision would go. The king's own summary of the situation had been succinct enough. Montnoir had might upon his side; might and gold, and those two are ever an irresistible combination.

I glanced at O'Dwyer, who was looking about at the fittings of the hut, and perhaps at the royal wives too, with a curiously detached air. Did it really matter if this devious renegade was turned over to Montnoir, who would doubtless soon expose his story for the worthless pack of lies it was? I chided myself for such an unworthy thought. Regardless of my own opinion of O'Dwyer, for him to be given over into the custody of the French by a mere native – and for myself to be detained for however long, perhaps for ever, by that same native – would be a perpetual stain upon the honour of Matthew Quinton and of England. And then what of Cornelia, and the fate of the House of Quinton?

My thoughts ran to increasingly desperate ways of remedying the situation. If a message could be got to the *Seraph* – but how? If Captain Facey and his men could march here – to do what, exactly, as a mere sixty men against the hundreds or thousands of savages that the King of Kombo could muster (and God knew how many Frenchmen at Montnoir's back)?

We were all nearly fainting in the heat. Even O'Dwyer, who had spent many years in such temperatures, was beginning to close his eyes sleepily and then blinking them open with a start. Only Montnoir seemed immune to it all, as cold as a visitor to a mausoleum. Perhaps I could draw my sword and take him hostage, forcing the king to release us …

His Majesty stirred in that moment. 'The king has judged,' he said. I stiffened. Montnoir smiled. There was a pause. The pause lengthened.

At last, the king continued, 'And his judgment is… His judgment is for England. Colonel – Captain – you may resume your voyage.'

I felt myself in a dream, from which I would surely awake to learn that my true fate was to be imprisoned for ever in this African hell-hole. The one thing that made me realise we had triumphed so unexpectedly was the face of the Seigneur de Montnoir. His smile had been transformed by the king's judgment into a scowl as ferocious as that seen on any church gargoyle. 'You favour England? You deny my gold, and my right, and the power of my king?'

The King of Kombo shrugged and spoke at some length through Belem. 'Yourself apart, My Lord, the power of the King of France seems very far away. And I do not know your king, nor any of your princes of France. Whereas ten years ago, I was visited by a great prince of England. Rupert, his name was, the cousin of King Charles himself. A mighty warrior.' The king bowed his head; evidently he fancied himself a great warrior too, or had been one in his younger days until the fat folded his belly. 'Prince Rupert did me great honour and paid me much respect, and in turn, I respect and honour the name of the prince. He had with him a lieutenant – one Holmes, as I recall. An ingenious and active man. Now, it seems to me that if England possesses such men as Prince Rupert and Holmes, and the two gentlemen before me now, it does not need the gold of France. What is more, the ships of every land in the world have sailed past my feeble Dog Island, yet only the English dare to seize it and raise their flag upon it. The English are evidently a bold and fearsome people, and I would have friendship with such a race.' The king shifted upon the mat and swatted away a huge fly. 'Besides, I am told that the same Holmes is upon this very coast, and could be here within a matter of days. I have seen this Holmes fight. One of my regiments fought him on the shore, and with only a dozen men at his back, he cut them to pieces. The King of Kombo fears no man, but I do not relish Holmes coming here to avenge his friends. No. England has the right of it.'

The king raised his great hand to indicate that the audience was at an end, and the tetees stepped forward to the same purpose. O'Dwyer and I bowed in unison. Before we left the tent, I stared hard into the gargoyle-face of Gaspard de Montnoir. As we passed, he hissed in French, 'This does not end here, Quinton.'

I bowed, as one should to an ambassador of the Most Christian King, but I could not restrain a grin of triumph as I did so. Yet as I left the hut, stepping out into the even warmer furnace outside, my thoughts turned to the bitter irony of our survival. My freedom, and perhaps my life, had been bought solely by the reputation of that old villain Robert Holmes, and by the name and memory of Prince Rupert of the Rhine. For nearly twenty years, my family had looked upon Rupert as the man responsible for the death of my father, Earl James, at the battle of Naseby; yet now, in some way, Rupert had saved me. Such are the tricks that history, or God, plays upon us.

Nineteen

The march back to the ship was ten times worse than that to the village. We were past the worst time of all, that between ten and noon, but the sea wind was weak that day, and the palms barely moved, the vultures circling them like sentries. I felt like a man walking through hell-fire. The soldiers, commendably smart and military on their march to the royal enclosure, were all stripped to their shirts or the skin, thus emulating my seamen, who from the outset had no uniforms to concern them. Even Ali Reis and Carvell seemed uncomfortable. We stopped every few minutes to gulp greedily at our leathern bottles of water. O'Dwyer told me of his alleged journey beyond the great desert that had taken him to the mountain of gold, and of other overland journeys that he made, south from Algier. They had been hotter than this, he contended, and he explained how one could find water even amidst the oceans of sand, but I barely listened to him. My concern was with Castle, who was turning redder by the minute; I seemed to be watching the man fry before my eyes. He was still cheerful, dismissing my concerns with a wave of his solitary hand, but each answer seemed to take a few more breaths, and shorter ones at that. I was minded to rest until the evening and resume the march then, and discussed this strategy with Captain Facey. He argued plausibly that darkness might increase the risk of ambush by Montnoir and whatever Frenchmen he had with him. Besides, there might be lions in these parts (Belem nodded at that), and God alone knew what other sorts of beasts that roamed only by night. So we went on.

We were almost on to the beach itself, with Charles Island and the masts of the *Seraph* in sight, when Castle simply sat down on the ground, opened his mouth wide, and dropped down dead.

I ran to him and felt for a pulse, as Tristram had taught me to do, but the man was gone. I looked upon his face in stupefaction and with a mounting sense of horror. William Castle, this valiant old tarpaulin who had sailed with Myngs and fought with Blake, lay dead at my feet. He had been a good friend to me in two commissions, a steadying influence and a trustworthy mentor. Such a man should have died with honour in battle, or else full of years and surrounded by his family. Instead, Castle had perished in this damnable place and upon a contemptible fool's errand of a mission. I choked back tears and swore that I would see justice done to his widow in Bristol and their four sons.

It fell to me to say a prayer over the body of this good and honest man, but I could manage nothing better than 'In the name of the Father, and of the Son, and of the Holy Ghost, Amen.' I sent a man to the *Seraph*, and he returned with fresh men who were better able to carry the lieutenant's corpse than the exhausted party who had made the march. Our arrival back at the ship was greeted by solemn faces upon the deck. The men had respected William Castle, and I wondered how his own Bristol followers would respond to his loss. His natural authority and good humour had held in check many of the tensions between the factions in the crew, and I feared what might now happen as we made our way upstream.

With Castle dead, the *Seraph* needed a new Lieutenant. I was silently thankful that Holmes was away; no doubt he would have used his seniority to foist one of his creatures upon me. As it was, no man raised any objection when I immediately appointed Valentine Negus to Castle's post. Then I summoned Kit Farrell and appointed him Master in Negus's place. Grimwade, the senior of the master's mates, might have felt aggrieved, but I learned that he was more than content to be left aboard the *Prospect of Blakeney* at the river's mouth, believing that his chances of returning to England alive would be considerably enhanced by that choice. There was also no demur when I elevated Martin Lanherne to the rank of Boatswain, vacated by Kit. Some of the Bristol men would grumble, I reckoned, but then, many of them would have grumbled if Saint Francis of Assisi had been set over them, especially if they believed Assisi to be in Cornwall. As I handed him the whistle and cane of his office, Lanherne was entirely lost for words – for the first and, as it proved, the only time in my acquaintance with him.

We held the funeral rites for the late Lieutenant of the *Seraph* that evening; keeping a body for any time at all in that climate was simply inconceivable. There was some talk of burying him ashore on Charles Island, but the unanimous opinion of my ship's officers was that an old seaman like William Castle was entitled to the age-old ritual of farewell for dead mariners. At dusk, we placed his corpse, shrouded in a hammock, upon the starboard rail. Cannonballs were fastened at the head and the feet. Francis Gale, clad in full canonicals, intoned the words of the funeral service; and at their conclusion, a file of Facey's redcoats fired off a volley. O'Dwyer, Facey, Negus and I raised our swords in salute. The body was pushed over the side, and plunged into the dark waters of the Gambia. Lindman fired a funereal salute of muffled guns which must have impressed the warriors of the King of Kombo if they were watching from the shore, as I suspected they were. Perhaps it even impressed the Seigneur de Montnoir, if he was still nearby. At the end, we had done well by William Castle after all.

As the congregation dispersed, Francis turned to me and said, 'You know what they'll say on the lower deck. A burial before our voyage upriver has truly started, and the burial of such a vital man at that – a bad omen, Matthew. There'll be more talk of the ship being cursed.'

I shrugged. 'That's but the way of seamen, Francis.'

'True,' he said. 'But ally that to the return of your friend Montnoir and even I could start believing in it.'

The next afternoon, and with awnings rigged over all of the upper decks, the *Seraph* got under way. This, Belem advised, was the way to make passage up the estuary of the Gambia and avoid the excesses of the climate: make as much progress as possible with the sea breeze and cooler weather from the late afternoon through into the first part of the night, the lower river being free of the rocks, shoals and sunken trees that made night navigation impossible further upstream, then proceed again from dawn until about ten or eleven in the morning while the *Harmattan* blows cool, finally dropping anchor and sleeping through the worst of the heat until three. We adhered to this regime even if the helpful flood tide coincided with the hottest part of the day. Thus we partially abandoned the immutable system of watch-keeping, turn and turn again every four hours, that has sustained England's navy since time immemorial. We drew lots for those who were to keep the watch at anchor in the middle of the day, officers and men alike. There was much argument in the messes over who gained most from this arrangement. The midday-men, as they became known, were denounced as idlers who did not have to climb the masts or work the ropes by night; but not a few of the others were secretly pleased that they did not have to face the most terrible heat of the day.

The first stage of our journey was but a short one, for I had seen from the chart that the first of the river's formidable obstacles lay barely ten miles from our anchorage. We swung out beyond the cape that sheltered Charles Island, tacked into the main stream, and at once could see ahead of us the feature that had so animated the mind of Sir William Penn during the meeting at the Navy Office.

'Well, Captain,' said Belem, 'there it is, dead ahead. San Andreas, as we Portuguese call it. Jakob's Island, as the present occupants prefer.'

Unlike Charles Island, the fort-isle of San Andreas lay more centrally within the Gambia river. The channel to the north was narrower than that to the south, but even so, it was easily a mile wide, and Belem stated that a large ship, rather larger than *Seraph*, could traverse it with ease. A town, named by Belem as the port of Jilifri (and which my men soon rechristened Julyfree), stood upon the north shore, opposite the fort. The island itself was small, less than a mile in length or breadth, and rose but a very few feet above the water. Herons, kingfishers and the sacred bird of the Egyptians, the ibis, waded upon its shore and in its shallows. Most of the area of the island was taken up by the fort, but from a distance this struck me as but a feeble affair, a square curtain wall with a rudimentary bastion at each corner. Of course, in my later years I visited most of the mighty works erected by Marshal Vauban across France and Flanders, but even so by then I had seen the formidable defences of Dunkirk and Breda, and a score of the other great fortifications of Europe. Thus I looked upon the low sandstone ramparts of Jakob's Island with a certain degree of contempt; taking this, even with the tiny force available to me, would surely be an easy task, and why should Holmes have all the glory? But as we came nearer on the evening sea-breeze, I saw that the fort was more formidable than it first appeared. I counted thirty, perhaps forty iron guns on the ramparts, and they were not of small calibres; at least some of them were larger than anything that *Seraph* bore.

I considered clearing for action. After all, the Dutch flag flew above the fort, and following Holmes' capture of the *Brill*, who knew what intelligence might have been sent to this distant outpost of the United Provinces, and who knew how the garrison might have reacted? Moreover, we had received no word of what Holmes might have done at Gorée; what if the fort had?

* * *

I kept my telescope trained on the ramparts, but it was clear that a warlike reception was the last thing on the garrison's mind. A couple of sentries wandered forlornly along the wall-walk, presumably wishing that they were down below, where chimney-smoke suggested the preparation of the garrison's evening meal. Every few minutes, an officer came up to look out at us with his own telescope. Presumably his thoughts were similar to mine, and his reaction must have been the same. *If you show no sign of fighting, my friend, then neither shall we.*

We drew parallel with the south shore of the fort-island, and I ordered the dropping of our best bower anchor. An hour's courtesy call on the garrison would not go amiss, I decided, as a personal relationship with its commander might be of use to me at some future time. Purser Harrington quickly assembled a suitable offering of Madeira wine, Hull ale and salt beef. A boat's crew was mustered in proper order by Julian Carvell, the new Coxswain of the *Seraph* following Lanherne's promotion to Boatswain, and I was rowed ashore in some state. O'Dwyer opted to remain on board. This surprised me, as I thought he would have shared the opinion of Morgan Facey, who did accompany me; a soldier should never neglect an opportunity to examine a position he might one day have to attack. The Irishman's decision to do precisely that should have concerned me more than it did.

A slovenly, ancient guard upon the foreshore greeted Facey and myself with a torrent of gutter-Dutch and led us up into the fort. My first impression of it was confirmed. The feeble rampart surrounded a rough parade ground. Most of the low wood and thatch buildings clustered under the east rampart; thus they would be sheltered a little from the morning heat, but open to the west wind from the sea in the afternoon and evening.

A squat, strongly-built man of perhaps fifty years, clad in a rough shirt, baldric and large hat after the Spanish fashion, stepped out and lifted his hat in salute.

'Otto Stiel, My Lords,' he said in good English, 'late captain and governor of this fort in the service of that most excellent and mighty prince, Jakob, Duke of Courland. Now the same for the Dutch West India Company.'

Captain Stiel's explanation of his status left little doubt where his true loyalties still lay. Belem had told me but the day before that there was some doubt whether the transfer of the island from Courland to the United Provinces had ever been completed in law, partly because Duke Jakob had been reluctant to admit that his small province on the east shore of the Baltic was perhaps not the best suited of all the lands of Europe to building a mighty colonial empire in Africa and the Caribbee.

I introduced Facey and myself, and Stiel led us into his quarters. Now as I have said, my intention had been that we would exchange courtesies for an hour, and then get under way for our intended night passage. I did not anticipate that I would finally by rowed out to the *Seraph* as the sun came up, with the formidable dawn chorus of the river birds nearly splitting my skull. Nor did I anticipate being manhandled ignominiously onto my own deck by my boat's crew, to be greeted by the quizzical reproof of Brian Doyle O'Dwyer and by the disapproving scowls of Valentine Negus and Kit Farrell. This was not entirely the fault of my own weak will, or so I told myself. I had previously considered Morgan Facey to be a paragon of sobriety, a veteran of the old Cavalier army and a stout man. But as is so often the way, it all turned on one sentence.

'You have a good command of our tongue, sir,' said Facey to Stiel as we exchanged gifts.

'I am glad you say so, after all these years,' said Stiel. 'I had many excellent times in your civil wars, in Sir Ralph Hopton's western army.'

That was enough. Within moments, the Madeira and the Hull ale were being uncorked, and Stiel was producing bottles of some unutterably fiery drink of his own land. Foreign mercenaries had been common enough on both sides during the civil war – after all, what other appellation could be given to Rupert, Prince Palatine of the Rhine, to name but the greatest of them? – but to come to this arse-end of the known world and find a man who had fought in the noblest and most successful of all the king's armies was surely worthy of raising a cup or two, was it not? And when he realised that I was the son of the Earl of Ravensden, the report of whose death at Naseby had made Stiel weep – well, was that not also worthy of a cup or two? Stiel reminded us that his Duke Jakob was a godson of our late sovereign King James, a connection clearly deserving of two cups. Or three. By the time Facey and Stiel discovered that they had fought in several of the same battles and had three or four mutual friends, our fates were sealed.

It was only when I woke late the following afternoon, barely in time to order the weighing of our anchor for the passage I had intended for the previous evening, that I recollected that the gifts loaded onto Facey and myself by the generous Stiel at our unsteady departure included a package of letters for our ship, delivered by a Bristol vessel that had taken a cargo of wax, hides and slaves from Jilifri a few days before. Sadly, there was but one letter addressed to Captain Quinton of the King of England's ship the *Seraph* upon the River of Gambo in Africa. That was not the actual inscription upon it, however; for the actual inscription was in French, and the grandiose wax seal was one I knew well.

I tore open Roger's letter with unseemly impatience, annoyed at myself for sleeping away almost an entire day.

My dearest, noblest friend and gallant warrior! it began; and so it continued for no little while, this reply to the letter I had sent him just before the *Seraph* sailed from England. At length, though, I came to an utterly shocking sentence, written almost as an aside: *Ah, my friend, I envy you in your voyage in mysterious parts – the Gambo river, no less, in pursuit of the legendary mountain of gold …*

Sweet Jesus! Good-brother Venner had the rights of it after all. If Roger knew of our mission, then presumably so did the entire court of the Most Christian King. And if that vast and notoriously verbose establishment knew of it, then so did the whole of the world. Strangely, after the first moment of shock had subsided I felt very little concern at this revelation. Whether the world knew of it or not mattered nought: indeed, whether the mountain really existed or not mattered nought. For good or ill, I would continue up this endless river to whatever fate awaited me. But I prayed that Roger's letter contained the solution to another, perhaps darker, secret, the question to which I had craved his answer for so long.

Now, Matthew, let us turn to the matter of the alleged daughter of the Comtesse Louise, upon which you wrote to me before your sailing. I decided to entrust the mission to Aubigny to no man other than myself, for I have observed that Mothers Superior, who consider themselves very mighty ladies indeed, are inclined to send mere messenger boys packing, whereas they are considerably more circumspect when dealing with noblemen of France. So it proved when dealing with the Mother Superior of the Poor Clares, a most formidable lady. Aubigny is almost an outpost of your own land, Matthew – the castles there belong to your king's cousin, the Duke of Richmond – and the convent is full of the flower of English virginity. Unfortunately, none of the virgins bear the name of Madeleine De Vaux, and never have. None of them could even be that child under another name. I concluded this after most extensive and, I may say, exhaustive enquiries among the sisters. I knew you would not want me to rest following this disappointment, dear friend, so on my journey back to my own territories I took the pains (and pains they were, I assure you) to call at the English convents of the Benedictines, Augustinians and Blue Nuns in Paris, and of the Benedictines again in Pontoise. Alas, my enquiries on your behalf at all the other English convents of France and Flanders had to be conducted by letter, but that has probably been in the best interests of my health. The conclusions of my researches are one and the same, whatever the means of carrying them out: a Madeleine De Vaux is not, and never has been, cloistered within one of the English convents.

Your beloved Cornelia and I have already corresponded upon this matter, as no doubt she will inform you in her own hand. It occurs to us both that

there are other enquiries that we should now pursue, calling once more upon
the assistance of your esteemed uncle, the learned Doctor Quinton, and by
the time you receive this, that stratagem should be well advanced.

   I remain, my dear comrade-in-arms, your most humble, loyal, grateful,
affectionate and undying friend,

   d'Andelys

I put down the letter and stood in my stern window – or rather,
the starboard half of my stern window – staring out at the receding
fort-island and the brilliant red sunset taking place behind it. A flock of
strange great birds flew by, across the face of the sun. I felt a powerful
conflict tearing my heart: the conflict between duty to my family and
to my king.

   From that conflict stemmed a succession of questions, each more
difficult to confront than the last. What might Roger, Tris and Cornelia
have discovered in the weeks since this letter was sent from France? What
if the Countess was with child by now? And, at the very last, the oldest
question of them all, the one that had intruded into my nightmares and
my waking thoughts for as much of my life as I could remember. What
if Charles was dead – perhaps killed by the exertions of mounting his
wife, or if the suspicions of Tris and Cornelia were justified, slaughtered
by that same wife's malevolent hand? What if, in that dusk upon the
Gambia river, I was already the Earl of Ravensden?

   I heard O'Dwyer come into his half of the cabin – *my cabin, damn*
him – and put such foolish thoughts aside. Nothing I could do in this
fastness would remedy the matter of the Countess Louise. Even if I
had the ship brought about at that moment, and ordered all sail set for
England, it would be many weeks before I could be home – there to face
a certain court-martial for deserting my mission, and even more certain
dishonour.

   No. The die was cast. For good or ill, the fate of Matthew Quinton
rode with that of Brian Doyle O'Dwyer and the quest for the mountain
of gold.

$\mathcal{T}$wenty

Early the next morning, I stood under the awning on the quarterdeck of *Seraph*, and looked out upon the astonishing scene around me. The great blue-brown river stretched away for miles on either side of us, and although we were going only under courses, we easily had enough sea-room to have spread topsails, even when the tide was low. We were sounding every two glasses, but each time we had at least five fathoms beneath our keel. The banks were lined with impenetrable groves of trees that rose directly from the salt waters of the river: mangroves, Belem called them. Every few miles, clearings had been made in the swamp and landing places set up. Many of these were little more than rudimentary jetties, but some, especially on the south bank, were quite large wharves that could accommodate European ships. We sighted several Portuguese and Dutch vessels, most of which, Belem asserted, would be taking on cargoes of salt to carry further upstream, where that commodity was very rare. Most of the trade of those parts, though, was carried on by the Mandingo natives in their canoes. The profusion of these craft upon the river reminded me of the Thames, for like their northern brethren, the canoes darted this way and that, some going north-south from one bank to another, others travelling up or down stream, yet seemingly never colliding with each other. Even under our awning and so early in the day, the damp heat was already sapping. Those of us on the quarterdeck – Belem, Negus, Kit Farrell and myself – all ran with sweat. Taking Belem's advice, we all carried makeshift fans of wood and sailcloth with which to cool ourselves and to ward off the ever-present insects, especially the mosquitoes and the flies whose bite brings the sleeping sickness.

Musk came on deck, grumbling in his unique way. 'Never going to complain of an English winter again,' he said. 'Give me cold, I say. This heat is unnatural. Satan's breath, I reckon. If God had meant Phineas Musk to live in such a clime, he'd have made certain I was born – *sweet Jesus and all the angels, what in the name of Hell's fire is that?*'

He pointed at what seemed to be a red-brown rock, a few yards from our starboard quarter. But then the rock rose a little further out of the water, and two great eyes returned the stares of the quarterdeck officers of the *Seraph*.

Belem smiled. 'Behold the river-horse, gentlemen,' he said. '*Hippopotamus*, as the ancients called it.'

Thus for the first time in my life I looked upon this massive beast, so much larger than the ox; a creature so awesome that the Egyptians worshipped it as a god. I recalled reading about it in the works of Pliny, but to see it alive, barely a few yards from myself – !

Musk evidently did not regard the river-horse as a fit object for curiosity. 'Vicious looking beast,' he said. 'Is it likely to attack us?'

'They,' said Kit, pointing at other 'rocks' nearby, and at beasts lying in the mud at the shoreline. 'If they were minded to attack us, Mister Musk, I think they would comfortably outnumber us.'

'It will sometimes overturn a canoe or attack men ashore,' said Belem, 'but ships upon the river are safe from it. The river-horse is an evil-tempered beast, but by day, when it soaks itself to avoid the heat, it is also very lazy.'

'Bald, evil-tempered and lazy,' I said mischievously. 'Why, Musk, does it not resemble you more than a little?'

Musk, to his credit, took it in good part; by nightfall, indeed, he had taken to referring to *hippopotamus* as his good-cousin.

A little further upstream Belem had us steer closer to the south shore, saying that the channel ran deeper on that side for a few miles. This took us close to a landing place where a Dutch flyboat lay at anchor. A long line of black men, all chained together, was shuffling down towards the wharf, overseen by a gaggle of other blacks and a small group of white men.

I asked him the extent of this trade in these parts.

'It grows year on year,' he said. 'Not as great on this river as it is down on the Gold Coast, it's true, and not as great as the shipping of ivory, but still a mighty trade. I'm told that over in the Barbadoes and suchlike places, they find the men from these parts too lazy. Doesn't surprise me, that. Still, the kings on the south shore especially, Kombo and Kiang and the like, grow rich on the trade. They're always fighting with their neighbours, so there are many prisoners of war to sell, and criminals from their own people. Sometimes more criminals than there are crimes, depending on how many mouths have to be fed, or so they tell me.'

We watched as the line of chained man was led down to the wharf, where a boat awaited to take them out to the flyboat, at anchor a half mile or so offshore. One man stumbled, or collapsed in the heat, and dragged the two on either side down with him; all three were whipped to their feet.

They were innocent days, the 1660s, when set against the boundless evils of our present time, and I could not have envisaged the heights to which this slave-business would rise. What I was witnessing was but the early beginnings of it. Indeed, to my shame Holmes and I were partly and inadvertently responsible for its rise; one of the stated ambitions of the Company of Royal Adventurers, whose cause we were meant to serve, was to seize the trade in slaves from the Dutch and to develop it for the enrichment of England. But that day, upon the river of Gambia, my private opinions on the matter were formed. I recall being at a reception in Kensington Palace a few years ago when a mean north country viscount was holding forth upon slavery, contending that the Romans had favoured it, and the Romans were clearly more civilised than ourselves, *ergo* slavery must be a mark of a civilised society. Ah yes, I remarked, these being the same Romans who crucified Our Lord and fed his adherents to the lions?

The next day, we approached a town on the south shore that Belem named as Taukorovalle. The river was narrowing a little now, and the swamps on the north shore had formed themselves into an impenetrable mangrove wall. On the south, herds of elephants and smaller groups of *hippopotamus* cooled themselves in the mud flats. Taukorovalle itself was a mean place, barely worthy to be called a town, with the same types of huts that had filled the King of Kombo's village. But Belem advised that the town sustained a lively trade in most commodities, and so it proved: barter (with salt as our chief asset) brought us an impressive stock of goats, hens, milk, butter and oranges, as well as quantities of palm wine and the local beer, which Belem named as *dullo* (and which, compared to good strong English ale, was as good as its name). Purser Harrington and Steward Musk were mightily pleased with these additions to our victuals, but our most unusual acquisition was less of a success: Francis Gale and I both had a mind to try elephant meat, and although it was easy enough to obtain, Bradbury's cooking reduced it almost to cinders. Thus, months later, when Tristram asked me whether I had tasted this great delicacy, I could reply only with an honest 'yes and no'.

Taukorovalle was the seat of another local king, to whom respects (and 'customs duties', that familiar euphemism for bribes) had to be paid. I half-expected Montnoir to have reached the place before us and to have suborned this potentate rather more successfully than he had the King of Kombo, but my fears seemed groundless. The king was quite a young, languid man, and an altogether more straightforward creature than his equal downstream. Straightforward and considerably more avaricious: not for him the presents in kind that had satisfied the King of Kombo. He was satisfied only with gold coin, a significant quantity of it, and was reluctant to accept King Charles' sovereigns instead of the Dutch florins that were evidently more to his liking. I had little doubt that this monarch would not be as swift to reject Montnoir's gold as his colleague at Kombo had been.

A ship lay at anchor in the stream off Taukorovalle; not a flyboat but an older and narrower type of vessel with a high stern. It seemed strangely out of place in these waters, and it flew colours that I did not recognise: blue, with a white cross upon dark red in the canton. We hailed it, and the man who came aboard us proved to be a countryman of Captain Stiel. Unlike the amiable Stiel, he spoke no English, but both his Dutch and my own were tolerable enough for us to understand each other. He named himself as Valdis Vestermans, chief mate of the *Krokodil*, originally intended to establish a trading post for the Duke of Courland further up the river, at Kasang, our own destination. Vestermans was one of only eleven men remaining to her, a quarter of her original crew; the rest, including the master, had died of the fevers during the last wet season. The ship had run onto a nearby shoal during a storm, and although this surviving remnant of her crew managed to refloat her, they were struggling to repair her and make her ready to return down river, where they hoped (with little optimism) to recruit enough men to form a crew that could carry her back to the eastern end of the Baltic. Vestermans was an old seaman, and as such enough of a pragmatist not even to think of asking an English man-of-war if she could delay her voyage, or lend a few dozen men, so that his crew could complete their work. I wished him well, and so we parted; but the formality of taking him to the larboard rail brought me a troubling sight. Tide and flow meant that larboard faced the shore, and as I said my farewell to Vestermans, I noticed two men in earnest conversation upon the strand of Taukorovalle. They were Brian Doyle O'Dwyer and Jesus Sebastian Belem.

From Taukorovalle, the river ran a little north of east towards Tindobauge, the next important town. The channel was narrowing now, and I estimated that the tidal mud flats would soon become an increasing obstacle to our proceeding under sail, at least by night. Belem said that the river ahead was also full of rocks and submerged trees, which inclined Negus, Kit Farrell and myself toward the same conclusion. But we were also experiencing longer calms – we were almost upon the cusp of the dry and wet seasons – and with the tides weakening with every mile we took away from the sea, the river current flowing downstream against us became a steadily more formidable foe. Consequently, I ordered an extra two glasses of rest in the middle of the day, for I knew that the men would soon have the back-breaking work of towing ahead of them. I spent much of that brief holiday lying on my sea-bed, unable to sleep in the stifling heat, praying that I did not become fodder for a mosquito, and debating with myself on whether to tackle Belem about his meeting ashore with O'Dwyer. There was little sound beyond the ceaseless song of the birds, the occasional call of a baboon or some other beast, and the casting or drawing in of lines by those men who braved the heat of the upper deck in order to fish.

Then I heard O'Dwyer's familiar, unwelcome voice from behind the partition.

'Well, Captain – you've had a mind as to how you'll spend your riches from this expedition?'

I sighed. I wanted conversation with no man, and especially not with this one; I wanted only sleep.

'No, Colonel,' I said tersely. 'I have not thought upon it.' *Because there will be no riches to think upon.*

'Ah well… I should. The mountain of gold is… well, it could be many things to many people. But for you, Captain, it could prove very lucrative. Very lucrative indeed.'

I was tired, I was hot, and despite myself, I said that which had been in my thoughts since my very first meeting with the Irishman on the deck of the *Wessex*. 'There is no mountain, O'Dwyer. It was a lie that you invented to save your neck. God forgive England for having a king who can be gulled so easily by the likes of you.'

I heard the renegade's low chuckle. 'Ah now, my poor Captain, you're still only staring at the obvious, that you are. After all, what brought our friend Montnoir chasing after me all across the Mediterranean, and now down in this place as well? What brought Prince Rupert himself here?' A pause – 'But it seems to me that you're having a poor return for all your exertions thus far. I've seen you laying out your own credit for victuals at Tenerife and Taukorovalle, and no doubt the king won't pay you a penny until well beyond the end of this voyage. Is that not always the way of it?' I kept my peace. I would not allow my mouth to agree with O'Dwyer, though my head and heart knew the truth of his words all too well. It always was the way of it; captains of Charles the Second's navy invariably had to employ their own credit on expeditions abroad, hoping thereafter that arrears of pay, if and when they were eventually settled, made good the shortfall, and that bills of exchange were not rejected by some clerk upon the slightest of pretexts.

'So what I was thinking was this, Captain,' the renegade continued. 'Supposing I was to go ashore at one of the towns upstream – Mangegar, say, or Kasang – and make contact with some of the Arab factors who come down to those parts. Well, I know those sorts of men, you see. It would be an easy matter to arrange an advance against your share of the mountain.' *Dear God* – 'But they're discreet sorts of men, the Arabs. They'd be scared off, I reckon, by the sight of too many of your rude tarpaulins – '

Damn the man! He thought so little of me that he thought I could be bribed as easily as some cheap mercenary! Bribed to allow him to escape back to his Barbary friends, no doubt.

Of course, a man of no honour might have considered it thus: if there was no mountain of gold, then what was lost if the Irishman simply vanished? Nothing; for that was what this same man of no honour would have expected of another man of no honour. Who would know the truth? No man; for we were very, very far from England. But what would be gained? A goodly purse of gold, and no accounting for it to the Lord Treasurer or Lord Admiral. Gold in hand, and not the vague hope of the accumulated arrears of my eight pounds and eight shillings a month, paid many months hence. Gold that might prove useful insurance against the prospect of yet another change of rule in England, if yet another Stuart king lost his throne through his own duplicity and weakness.

Fortunate, then, that Matthew Quinton was not a man of no honour. That knowledge suddenly weighed heavily upon my dutiful heart.

I lay there for some time, saying nothing. I heard a soft 'Captain?' from O'Dwyer, and a little later, a whispered 'Quinton?' Then there was nothing, and after a while longer, I heard the man's intolerable snoring begin. He must have assumed that I, too, had fallen asleep.

Instead, I reached into my sea-chest and produced the document that had been handed to me by the king himself upon Newmarket Heath.

Secret and Additional Instructions to be Observed by Captain Matthew Quinton, read the legend upon it. By royal command, it had remained unopened all this time; was only to be opened, indeed, in a very specific set of circumstances. These circumstances had been described to me by a discreet royal whisper in my ear just before Pepys and I were dismissed from the royal presence on that late summer's day at Newmarket, now so long ago and so very far away.

I made my decision and ran my finger under the wax seal. I unfolded the document slowly and silently so as not to awaken O'Dwyer.

I read. And I smiled.

Twenty-One

Above Tindobauge, the next large town upstream, the river narrowed to less than a mile wide. We usually rowed and towed for the best part of the day, and also for much of the night. Thus we but barely resembled a man-of-war. Our two boats and our sweeps pulled us forward as well as they could, but this was hot and sore work even by the relative cool of the night, so I ordered the men relieved at every turn of the glass. With no work to do aloft, the rest of the men waited their turn upon oars, snatching some sleep upon the deck (cooler than the messes below decks, but more prone to mosquitoes) or fishing from the rail. We became accustomed to the sounds: the splash of the oars into the water, the constant heaving of the lead and calling of our soundings, the endless buzzing and clicking of the insects, the occasional bellowing of an elephant or roar of a lion. Above us, great storks and tiny, colourful parrots soared or plunged; and, ever present, the vultures awaited their moment.

All in pursuit of the chimera at the end of the river, the mountain of gold. *If old Bosch could be brought back to life in our own times,* I thought, *he need look no further for his Ship of Fools.*

So it went on. The nimble *Seraph*, which under full sail and with a favourable wind could cover a full ten miles each hour, was now lucky to manage five in a day. There were fresh reports of peevishness in the messes, of strong words, and petty thefts and over-eager fists, the sure signs of a fractious and increasingly unhappy crew. Deprived of William Castle's firm, fair leadership, the Bristol hands were particularly forward in voicing their discontent: I received more than one delegation intent on denouncing Bradbury's cooking, or the state of the wine, or the allocation to quarters, but it was obvious that behind each respectful request, each deferential grumble, lay an unspoken plea to abandon this benighted voyage and rejoin Holmes, who was rumoured to be sweeping up untold Dutch riches all along the Guinea coast. Although he could say nothing, the captain of the *Seraph* had not a little sympathy with such arguments.

And on either side of us lay mysterious, threatening shores, often empty, sometimes swarming with beasts, sometimes peopled by natives who eyed us with who knew what emotions. Once, the sun was so strong and my mind so addled from too long on deck that I could have sworn I glimpsed an impossible sight on a clear patch of ground beyond the mangroves: two riders, one in a dragoon's uniform and bearing in his hand the white fleur-de-lis banner of the Bourbons, the other an unmistakeable figure in the cloak of a Knight of Malta. I blinked and the apparition was gone, but it unsettled me mightily.

Worst of all, sickness was increasing, an ominous sign indeed so many weeks before the beginning of the wet season, when the fevers would be at their height. Since losing Castle, we had committed to the river one of the better Bristol men and one of Facey's soldiers. Humphrey, the surgeon, had four more under treatment, two of whom had come to him in the last day alone. He suspected the marsh ague, malaria, in three of the cases, though the fourth, young Penhallow, my companion in severing the cable during the fire at Deptford, had a fearful case of the bloody flux. There was little point in prescribing the eternal surgeon's remedy of bleeding to him; a pity, for Lanherne reckoned he had the makings of a good seaman. I sorrowed as I agreed that Penhallow should be given up for dead and laid upon a platform in the hold to await his end.

Early one morning, with the dawn just breaking, we were nearing the landmark shown on Belem's charts as Elephant Island. The river flowed around it in two remarkably deep channels, with twenty fathoms' water or more. Rupert and Holmes had reconnoitred this as a possible site for a fort, it seemed, but were soon dissuaded; and in truth, I have never seen a less military isle. It was nothing more than a tangle of high mangroves, some three leagues in circuit. I sent a boat's party to examine it, but they reported that the ground consisted of a clay-like slime, and that the high tides lapped over it to a depth of a foot or more.

With my curiosity about the island satisfied, I went below to visit the dying Penhallow. To this day, I do not know quite why I did so. I think I felt guilt that this good and honest fellow, one who had followed me so loyally and assisted me so notably at Deptford, would die on my account on such a desperate fool's errand, and I was mindful of the dire impact his death would have on his ancient widowed mother. Both Kit Farrell and Musk chided me for this womanish concern for just one rude tarpaulin's death, but somehow I felt that young Penhallow deserved his captain's company as he took his final journey. Thus I went down into the very bowels of the ship, to the hold itself. That dark space was blessedly cool, although the climate made the bilges stink even more prodigiously than usual. The platform on which Penhallow had been placed was concealed behind a pile of victuallers' barrels. The young man, his flesh grey and damp, was wholly unaware of my presence. I sat and prayed silently as his breaths got shallower and further apart.

I do not know how long I sat there – perhaps one turn of the glass, maybe two. My thoughts soon wandered from prayer, and meandered through my own dark concerns: O'Dwyer, Montnoir, the Lady Louise. I was not even aware that Penhallow had stopped breathing; I was so wrapped up in my thoughts that I did not notice the moment of his death.

I prepared to rise, but then stayed, and held my breath. Another was in the hold with me. Beyond the barrels, I could hear what sounded like a timber being levered from the deck. I stood and stepped out from behind the barrels.

In the dim light of that low place, illuminated by just one lantern, I must have presented a spectral sight to the man. He was standing, a crowbar in his hand, above a hole in the deck. He had evidently pulled away the board that had covered it, which now lay to one side.

He stared at me in blind incomprehension, and then a moment later in utter terror.

'Captain – '

'Mister Shish?'

The carpenter of the *Seraph* still stood there, staring at me. My first thought upon seeing him had been that he must have been about some business naturally connected with his office; the removal of a timber board from the deck fell naturally within the carpenter's remit. But his horrified reaction at the sight of me and the way in which he kept the crowbar raised told a very different story. And why would the carpenter concern himself with the removal of one board in the hold? Surely he would have despatched one of his crew to attend to such a trivial matter?

What matter, though? I had no idea. I also had no weapon, and Shish still brandished the crowbar like a cutlass.

'What are you about, Mister Shish?' I asked.

'Captain – Captain, oh Jesus – it must be God's judgment upon me –' With that, the young man dropped the crowbar onto the deck and began to sob uncontrollably.

I needed assistance, and above all, I needed expert advice. 'Ho, there! Ho, anyone!' I cried. But there was surely nobody within earshot …

Phineas Musk stepped into the light. Likely he had come below to see where the foolish young heir to Ravensden had got to. 'Aye, Captain?' he said.

'Musk, fetch me Mister Negus and Mister Farrell. Discreetly. Do not mention why I wish to see them, and do not mention this to any other.'

'Aye, sir.'

Musk went, leaving me alone once again with the carpenter, who seemed to have lost all control of himself: he merely stood there, shaking and sobbing, reciting psalms and Puritanical prayers to himself.

At length, the lieutenant and master of the *Seraph* came into the hold, accompanied by Musk. Negus stepped over to the space in the deck where the board had been levered off, looked down into the dark place beneath, and nodded grimly to Kit Farrell.

Negus looked directly at Shish and said abruptly, 'And what business did you have with the garboard strake, Mister Shish?'

The young man shuddered and shook his head. 'Narrow channel,' he sobbed. 'Easy to get men off, and to shore – '

'Aye, after you'd sunk the ship,' said Kit. 'The garboard strake, sir,' he said, turning to me. 'The only outside plank reachable from inside the hull. Lifting the limber board, here, would allow him to get at it. Then he could jam the crow against a floor timber, lever it up, and make a leak that we would not be able to stop in time before the ship sank.'

'Damnable,' said Negus. 'Mightily damnable. And the chain pumps – your doing as well, Shish?'

Still the carpenter said nothing.

'Sabotage, then,' said Musk. 'Sounds much like treason to me. And we know what's done to traitors ashore, that we do. Hang 'em until nearly dead, draw the steaming entrails while they still live, then chop the bastards into quarters. But I expect the navy does things differently.'

'Not so very differently, Mister Musk,' said Negus in his broad Yorkshire burr. 'The sixteenth Article of War is the pertinent one, I think. "All sea captains, officers and seamen that shall betray their trust… shall be punished with death." A court-martial offence – a capital offence, indeed. Mister Shish, sir – if God so wills it, then you will hang.'

The young man could hardly have looked more devastated if the Lord Chief Justice of England himself had pronounced sentence, the black cap atop his wig. Of course, the dour Negus was quite right. It was difficult to imagine a case that fell more exactly within the terms of the sixteenth Article of War, for which the sentence was rightly unambiguous. But Shish was not a natural traitor, that much was certain. He was certainly not an obvious agent of my adversary, the Knight of Malta. Which meant …

'What did he offer you, Tom?' I asked, as kindly as I could. 'What was the price?'

The young carpenter must have had few tears left to shed. 'I – I cannot say – '

'Your loyalty to my good-brother is commendable,' I said.

Kit and Valentine Negus both looked upon me in utter astonishment. Musk merely raised his eyes and nodded, for unlike the other two, he knew Venner Garvey.

Shish was taken aback by my insight. His reply, when it came, was hushed and halting. 'I was to find a way of stopping the ship, or else delaying it, without endangering the lives of the crew – your life above all, Captain – and if possible without betraying myself,' he said. 'Not easy to reconcile, those goals, that they're not.'

'Indeed not,' I said. 'Besides, I presume you were only to come into play if his other schemes against us failed – the fire at Deptford and the flyboat in Long Reach?'

Shish shook his head. 'Only the flyboat, Captain. She was intended to ram us in the bow. That would be unlikely to kill or maim many, or any, but it would create enough damage to force us into dock for repair. Perhaps many months of repair. And no ship could be fitted out to replace *Seraph* before the spring.' Aye, that had the hallmark of Venner: delay, play for time, wait for the king to change his mind or have it changed for him. 'The fire at Deptford – well, that truly was an accident. Fires in the dockyards happen all the time…'

Musk scoffed, but I sensed that the miserable Shish spoke true. Risking the destruction of Deptford dockyard, several king's ships and perhaps many lives too was not what Venner Garvey was about. I had lost count of the number of times I had heard my good-brother advocate a great expansion of the navy, but only if that navy was controlled by the great men of Parliament, to wit, himself, and not by those dangerous adherents to arbitrary government and popish sympathisers, Charles and James Stuart.

'Well, Shish,' I said, 'my good-brother's concern for the wellbeing of myself and every man on this ship is gratifying. But you have still to answer my question. Why, man?'

'He – he convinced me that it was for the cause of Parliament,' the carpenter said miserably. 'The cause for which my father fell at Edgehill, when I was but five.'

The same age I was when my own father fell at Naseby.

My answer was grim. 'Aye, no doubt. Sir Venner Garvey can be mightily plausible. But you're no fanatic, Shish. I can't see you risking your life just for the Good Old Cause. What did he offer you?'

The carpenter looked down to the deck and whispered, 'One hundred and fifty pounds. A third of it, I received before we sailed from Deptford. The remainder was to come to me upon my return to England.'

Negus whistled, and Kit said, 'Great God, sir, that's six year's wages for a ship-carpenter on a Fifth Rate!'

'Aye,' I said grimly, 'quite a mountain of gold.'

'And if I was found out,' Shish said, 'or died in the execution of my task, then my widow was to receive a pension of fifty pounds a year for life – ample to provide for our little Joseph – ' At that, he broke down. 'Oh Susan – Susan, my love! How I have disgraced you – '

As Shish sobbed, I thought much upon the sixteenth Article of War. It gave a captain no discretion in such a case; why should it? What discretion was needed in a case of a man heinously encompassing the destruction of his own ship? What clearer betrayal of a sea-officer's trust could there be?

And yet…

I looked at Negus; I knew his opinion, right enough, although there was also something else in his eyes that I could not quite identify. I looked at Kit, and for all his sympathy with Shish's circumstances, he was too good an officer to question the Articles of War. I looked at Musk, and strangely, I knew exactly what he was thinking, too: it was along the lines of *Sweet mother of Christ, the young master is going to make an almighty fool of himself once again.*

'Well, then,' I said, 'it seems that I must fly in the face of my officers and the law of the land.' Musk groaned, Negus frowned, Kit looked at me curiously, and Shish continued sobbing. 'By the terms of the sixteenth Article, the course of action is beyond doubt. However, the matter is complicated, of course, because a capital case such as this must be judged by a court-martial under the terms of the thirty-fourth Article, as I recall, and by that same article, we cannot convene a court-martial without a quorum of at least five captains. And, gentlemen, we stand no chance of assembling such a quorum until we meet again with Holmes or some other squadron of English ships.' Negus shrugged; this, at least, was an undeniable truth. The waters continued to lap around our hull, and in that dark and stinking place below the waterline, a court-martial seemed a very distant prospect indeed. 'Moreover,' I said, obfuscating and legalising after the fashion of my teacher in such affairs, Tristram Quinton, 'the matter is complicated further by my close relationship to the instigator of this entire business, Sir Venner Garvey. Therefore, I could not possibly sit on any such court due to conflict of interest – and by the same token, I cannot pass down even interim judgment upon Mister Shish in the meantime. By all the ancient laws and traditions of the sea, a captain cannot merely resign his powers temporarily to his lieutenant or any other officer in such a grave case – ' Negus and Kit both looked perplexed, as well they might, for that particular 'ancient law and tradition of the sea' had been invented in that very moment by Captain Matthew Quinton – 'and besides,' I said, 'we are several hundred miles up the Gambia river, gentlemen, and I certainly do not intend to proceed any further in such dangerous waters, nor to go back downstream again, without a competent carpenter aboard this ship.'

'Sir,' said Negus, gravely but urgently, 'surely you cannot intend to release this traitor – '

I knew I risked bringing down the wrath of a court-martial upon myself – perhaps even a capital sentence with it – but the more I thought upon it, the simple truth of my final pronouncement grew upon me. We needed a carpenter. We certainly needed a carpenter more urgently than we needed a point of law. *And what if – ?*

Oh, yes, I would not put that past him, by God! I recalled the way Venner Garvey played chess, and the most unlikely and ruthless sacrifices he was prepared to make to achieve his ends. Perhaps he had gambled all along that if his agent failed and was discovered, the captain and officers of the *Seraph* would abide exactly by the letter of the Articles of War that Venner himself had played a part in steering through Parliament – imprisoning or executing young Shish, thereby imperilling the mission through the absence of a capable carpenter.

This mission will not succeed.

Perhaps not, Venner; but if it does not, it will not be because of you.

'Mister Negus, Mister Farrell,' I said, 'I take full responsibility for this upon myself. I will at once write a letter to the King and the Lord Admiral, absolving all of you of blame in this matter, the letter to be sent to them if the need arises.' I had not ignored the possibility that my Lieutenant and Master would see this incident as proof of my incapacity, and relieve me of command under the terms of the self-same sixteenth Article of War, for betraying my trust; but I believed I knew them both better than that. 'Meanwhile,' I continued, 'I ask this of you. We five men, here in this place are the only ones who know what has happened in this case. All I ask is that none of you speaks a word of it to any other soul, at least until we are back at the river mouth. Mister Shish is a free man. He remains the carpenter of the *Seraph*. In public, we will treat him, and he will treat us, as if nothing has happened. Are we agreed?'

Kit spoke first. 'Sir, think what you might bring down upon yourself if you do this – '

'I have thought upon it,' I said emphatically. 'Are we agreed?'

Kit nodded. Negus shrugged and said, 'If you write the letters you talked of, then aye, agreed.' Yet there was still something in his eyes: an evasiveness that I had never witnessed in him before.

'Fucking mad,' said Musk, 'like all of the bloody Quintons.' I took that as agreement.

Finally I looked upon Tom Shish. 'Well, Mister Shish,' I said, 'you have your life, and your freedom. For the time being, at any rate. Perhaps you will yet have an opportunity to redeem yourself upon this voyage.'

The young man's gratitude took the form of another flood of the most pitiful tears.

Twenty-Two

Elephant Island and the incident with Shish were well behind us, both literally and metaphorically. The carpenter had retired to his cabin, pleading a touch of fever, and no man queried that. Valentine Negus was colder toward me; we both knew that he now held my life in his hands, for if he betrayed our agreement, he could make himself captain of the *Seraph* in the blink of an eye, condemning Matthew Quinton to the gallows (or, if the king was feeling particularly merciful, the block). Even Kit was more reserved than was his wont, but he had good cause to be. He had already perjured himself on my behalf at one court-martial, and I think both he and I knew instinctively that he would not be able to bring me off if I faced a second one. Kit Farrell, not a man to truant and ever the most faithful friend, had even excused himself from one of my regular lessons in navigation and two of his own in writing; a case of his spying the writing on my wall and fearing for himself if his patron fell, I concluded grimly. Thus it was a curiously subdued group of men who stood on the quarterdeck of the *Seraph* as we continued our course upstream.

The land was changing now. The mangroves were thinning, and in their stead came red cliffs, sometimes high enough to dwarf the *Seraph*, and rough scrubland on either side of the river. An entire army could hide in such terrain, and I had the discomforting feeling that many hidden pairs of eyes were watching our ship's passage. The water was green here, not the mud-brown of the estuary. The channel began to ravel into great loops and was often obstructed by low islands of silt; even Belem admitted that the navigation of these parts was little better than guesswork, for the channels shifted with each new season. We sounded constantly, Kit and his mates sometimes running anxiously to the forecastle rail to inspect a possible sandbank ahead. A few stretches of the river were still wide enough and deep enough for us to hoist courses, usually in the late afternoon, and to make a little progress under sail until darkness came; but for the most part, we rowed and towed. We were beyond the limited cooling effect of the sea winds, so I felt mounting pity for my men as I observed them, watch upon watch, straining their backs for this most futile and desperate of causes. But I knew even worse was to come. At Kasang, our next intended port-of-call, we would have to abandon the *Seraph* entirely, leaving her in the care of a skeleton party while the reminder of us proceeded ever further upstream in shallops or like craft, which we intended to build at that place. I dreaded the prospect: I was already enough of a man-of-war's captain to feel deeply uncomfortable at the thought of losing the firmness of her deck beneath my feet, the reassurance provided by her thirty-two pieces of ordnance, and the relative comfort of even a half-cabin. But there was one other cause for my reluctance to commit our mission to much smaller and flimsier craft. For we had new company upon this higher stretch of the river. There remained a steady traffic in canoes, albeit lighter than downstream. We still encountered *hippopotami;* there were elephants galore, parading like regiments along the bank or cooling themselves at the water's edge; and we had a legion of new friends in the air, among them delightful grey-orange-black birds that truly belonged in Egypt, or so Belem said. But increasingly, our most frequent companions were the mighty and malevolent beasts that slid silently in and out of the stream on all sides of us: crocodiles.

We were but a few miles from Kasang by Belem's reckoning when the disaster befell us. It was late in the evening, but still light, and we were about to change the boats' crews. The long boat had been pulled in to the larboard side, and her exhausted crew were starting to climb the ladder. I was watching from the quarterdeck with Kit, Negus, Belem and O'Dwyer. There was a jolt – *Seraph* must have glanced a shoal. But the longboat ran full onto it, and reared upward as it rode over the sandbank. The twin shocks of the boat and the ship striking did for the two men then on the ladder, a Londoner named Gibson and a Hayle man called Treharne. I can see their faces still, etched upon my ancient memory. They fell back, beyond the stern of the boat, into the dark waters of the Gambia.

There was a moment of silence and stillness.

Then the two men broke surface, calling out for help, in the name of God, all help! Kit ran to the upper deck rail and barked orders to the men still in the boat to push off and rescue their colleagues ...

Too late. I saw the two great scaly shapes upon the water, swimming toward the men with terrifying speed. Belem and O'Dwyer crossed themselves.

Treharne was taken first. The crocodile must have bitten him in the middle, for as the man screamed and the blood gushed, I saw his legs and groin float free for a moment before they, too, were consumed. Gibson, who could swim, tried to put up a fight, but in a sense, that made it worse for him. He struck out with his right hand, and the beast took it off with one snap. Gibson howled in agony, but in the next instant, the crocodile took off the rest of his arm.

Facey had some of his men in position now, and their muskets cracked as they opened fire on the beasts. It was a futile gesture. I saw the second beast rear up, its deadly jaws opened wide. It took Gibson's head in its mouth and snapped the jaws shut.

I strode to the starboard rail and leaned hard upon it, desperately gulping air into my lungs and trying to keep the vomit down. Even now, far beyond sixty years afterwards, I shudder when I recall that incident. I pull my blanket tighter around me, and take a sip of port wine to steady myself. For I have witnessed death in many forms – indeed, have caused it in many forms – but I have surely never seen anything to equal the raw and savage devouring of Gibson and Treharne, God rest their souls.

The ship's company was still subdued when, next morning, we finally came to an anchor off Kasang, another base native town of whitewashed round houses, surrounded by a ditch and a timber stockade. This port sheltered below a red hill, fifty yards or so in height, with small trees on its slopes. Two small Portugee vessels and a Dutchman lay at anchor before it. The two former seemed deserted, their crews either ashore or dead of the last season's fevers, but the Dutchman was making ready for a voyage with some urgency, no doubt prompted in part by the unexpected appearance of an English, and thus potentially hostile, warship; her skipper seemed unconscionably grateful that my only demand upon him was to carry our outgoing mails to sea with him. Unlike most of the so-called 'ports' that we had passed, where men had to wade ashore through swamps or mud flats, this Kasang at least had a decent sand beach, on which canoes were being built or caulked. Women came down to the water's edge in numbers, ready to trade with us: they offered rice, eggs, fruit, *cuscus* (a kind of gruel of those parts), hens, and in several cases, themselves, a fact that did not go unremarked by my increasingly excited crewmen.

I granted leave readily enough. The men deserved some respite after all their exertions, and it would take their minds off the horror that had befallen their shipmates. Moreover, the next weeks would be harder still: my crew would have to turn shipwrights to fashion the new craft that we needed to carry all our company further up river, and moving most of our supplies out of *Seraph* into our new flotilla would be back-breaking work in this climate. Tom Shish would need to repay my pardoning of him many times over, for overseeing the construction of the boats would be his task. Then, if Belem was correct, the voyage itself would be harder than anything we had encountered thus far, struggling against rapids, whirlpools and God knows what else as we ventured further and further into the land of unicorns.

I was preparing to go ashore myself when O'Dwyer addressed me. He had been more subdued than usual during the latter stages of our voyage; as well he might, I reckoned, for if his story was truly false then every mile brought him nearer to exposure and retribution. O'Dwyer must have had much to contemplate, and now he stared at me with a curious expression.

'Well, Captain,' he said, 'did you give any more thought to the proposition I broached to you?'

'Proposition, Colonel?' I asked innocently. 'I recall no proposition, sir.'

His eyes narrowed and he tilted his head a little, as though searching for something within the recesses of my skull. 'Ah. No. I conceive myself in error, Captain Quinton. My apologies.'

With that, he and I went ashore. We parted without a word, I to go my way in company with Belem and Francis Gale, O'Dwyer to go his; only his would be attended, discreetly as ever, by relays of my most trusted men.

This Kasang was but a small place, but it was evidently a hive of trade. Great stocks of cotton, wax, ivory and hides lay under awnings, awaiting a ship to come up the river or an Arab caravan to come down from the north or east. Indeed, I spied two or three Arab factors, unmistakeable in their robes and headdress, but they steered well clear of this young infidel sea-captain. In turn, I trusted that O'Dwyer would steer well clear of them, a trust born of the orders I had issued to my men to ensure he did precisely that. Craftsmen vied with each other to offer us the prized possessions of those parts: scabbards for swords or daggers and round shields, all covered with leather and painted in any design that we chose. I took a conceit to have one with the armorial crest of Ravensden, and Belem's translation of my description enabled a cheerful near-naked savage to produce one in less than an hour. He seemed delighted with his payment – a flask of brandywine – and I was equally delighted with my acquisition, which adorns my wall to this day.

My perambulation was intended to have a purpose. I needed to ensure that we could build our craft without interference, and for that, it would be important to establish good relations with the natives of this place. I planned to visit the local king either that same evening or early on the following day; his 'palace' was some two leagues inland, Belem said. I prayed that this petty potentate would be more immediately tractable than the King of Kombo, and that I would not be surprised again by the unexpected arrival of the Seigneur de Montnoir. In the meantime, I complied with the orders that I had issued to my men: smile, be polite, distribute largesse (such additional commandments as 'thou shalt not get fighting drunk' and 'thou shalt not rape' had been spoken discreetly by my officers to those thought most inclined to break them). Yet as I looked upon the seemingly friendly bare-breasted girls and women of the place, the smile upon my face was akin to that of the local terror, the crocodile. Behind it, I feared how exhausted seamen and soldiers, cooped up for too long aboard ship in this sickly and ferocious country, might behave in such a haven of earthly temptation.

With the sun approaching its zenith, we sought a place that could provide us with two or three hours' of shelter. Belem led us to the hut of a half-breed of his acquaintance, a river trader named Moreno, and there we partook of palm wine and a little rice. That consumed, we settled ourselves upon the mats and let the heat and the wine take their course. A persistent fly annoyed me, but seemed of no concern to Belem or Moreno, who were already asleep. The hubbub of the town beyond the hut gradually subsided as its inhabitants sought their own shelter. I slipped into that curious place where one is half asleep, and aware of it, and half awake, and aware of it …

The hubbub was increasing. Francis Gale shook my arm.

'Those are English voices, Matt,' he said. 'Raised English voices.'

We got to our feet and ran in the direction of the beach. Despite the searing heat, a large circle had formed upon it: sailors, soldiers, natives alike. Men were screaming derision or encouragement. I pushed my way through the throng, into the heart of the circle …

John Treninnick was wrestling with the hugest of the soldiers, one Hallett. My men were urging on Treninnick, who in truth needed little encouragement for such combat. He was in a rage, screaming the foulest Cornish oaths, and trying at every thrust to gouge the eyes out of the much taller redcoat. But Hallett was nothing loth. He was using his greater height to advantage, howling defiance at his opponent and try-ing for a grip on Treninnick's unnaturally short neck, hoping no doubt to throttle the life out of him.

The audience seemed crazed with bloodlust, like spectators at a bear-biting. In truth, I had feared something of the sort – if not sol-dier against sailor, then mess against mess or watch against watch. Petty resentments can fester for weeks in the confined space of a ship, where they are restrained by the Articles of War and the boatswain's cane, but putting a crew down upon a welcoming shore can be akin to opening a Pandora's box of violence. Already a few complementary scuffles were breaking out in the crowd.

'Stop this!' I cried. 'I will not have this brawling and rioting! You represent the honour of England – '

In truth, I was effective as old Canute; I was unarmed, the crowd's blood was up, Treninnick did not understand English, and as a sol-dier, Hallett was unlikely to obey a mere sea-captain. I could hardly demean myself by physically pulling them apart, and my boatswain was aboard the *Seraph* – I could see Lanherne looking on in horror from the quarterdeck …

Fortunately, Francis Gale had no such concerns. He strode forward, gave Hallett a mighty punch in the stomach that winded him, then struck Treninnick a fearsome blow on the jaw that drove back even that formidably strong creature. In the brief moment before the two combatants could come to grips with each other again, or turn their combined rage against him, Francis raised his hands in the eternal gesture of supplication and cried, 'Let us pray!'

The circle of spectators fell sheepishly to their knees. Hallett and Treninnick looked about them and fell reluctantly to the beach in their turn; even if Treninnick did not understand the words, he knew the gestures well enough, and he also knew better than the soldier that thanks to our land's civil wars, Francis Gale was as accomplished and unconventional a fighter as he was a man of God. The chaplain of the *Seraph* hastily embarked on a recitation of the Fifty-First psalm, enunciating the words slowly and weightily: 'Have mercy upon me, O God, after thy great goodness; according to the multitude of thy mercies do away mine offences. Wash me thoroughly from my wickedness, and cleanse me from my sin...'

All around me, tempers and enthusiasms calmed, as Francis knew they would (for the *Miserere Mei* is a distinctly lengthy psalm, especially when delivered at a funereal pace). A mob that had been braying with blood-lust but moments earlier was slowly transformed into as respectable a congregation as one could hope to find.

Morgan Facey arrived just then, flustered, red of face and out of breath; he had been reconnoitring the approaches to the town, considering its defensibility in the event of an attack by a rival native kingdom or Montnoir's French troops. I acquainted him with the situation. He shook his head sadly, for we both had the same thought: so much for our intent to impress the natives with the sobriety and restraint of our English race.

When the psalm finally concluded, we ordered all soldiers and sailors back to the ship. Then Facey and I confronted the two miscreants, Martin Lanherne coming across from *Seraph* to interpret for Treninnick.

'He thieved my new dagger-scabbard,' said Hallett. 'Just bought it, that I had. Put my head down to sleep through the noon-day, and when I was wakened, it had gone.'

Once the charge had been translated to him, Treninnick launched into an impassioned stream of vitriolic Cornish. 'He denies it,' said Lanherne. 'Says he's never seen the scabbard. Says he's no thief.'

This struck home with me; I knew Treninnick well, and although he would readily crack a man's skull if provoked, he was at least an honest brute.

Facey interrogated Hallett anew. 'If you were asleep and did not see this man take the scabbard,' he asked, 'then why did you accuse him of stealing it?'

Hallett shrugged. 'He was seen taking it. By the colonel. He woke me and told me.'

Facey and I exchanged a horrified glance. 'Colonel O'Dwyer?' I gasped.

'Aye, sir,' said Hallett, who (as Facey told me later) was an impressionable creature of little intelligence. To such, the word of such a grand officer as a colonel would be unimpeachable.

'Then where,' I asked with mounting dread, 'is Colonel O'Dwyer now?'

Lanherne's face fell, and he hastened in search of Polzeath and Tremar, who were meant to be watching the renegade during that hour. He returned with two mortified Cornishman. The colonel had found a native woman, they said, and had retired to a hut with her. They had watched the hut, and he had not seemed to emerge from it. But now, when they and Lanherne had entered it, they found the hut empty. Colonel Brian Doyle O'Dwyer had disappeared.

The renegade's defection had been expected for so very long, yet now it had happened, a palpable sense of shock pervaded the crew of the *Seraph*. Some of it was tinged with shame; my trusted Cornish followers who had kept watch over the Irishman at Santa Cruz de Tenerife had come to look on it as a cheerful private game in which they colluded with their captain, regarding the surveillance of the renegade as a matter of personal pride. Polzeath and Tremar were especially mortified, but their shame was reflected in every quarter of the ship, for men knew full well that they had been duped into spectating and scuffling upon the beach. O'Dwyer had done his work well. To create a diversion by pitting a soldier against a sailor was ingenious enough (such contests being certain to attract an ample audience of both breeds), but to set Hallett and Treninnick at odds was cunning indeed; Treninnick, virtually the mascot of my Cornish following, was bound to attract sympathy and support in large measure, but his strength and Hallett's size would guarantee a lengthy fight.

With a heavy heart, I ordered a council-of-war to meet in the steerage of the *Seraph*. We would have to make at least a token search for O'Dwyer, even though I knew full well that it was likely to be little more than a forlorn gesture. Before I ordered the despatch of this futile expedition, I decided that it was time for a reckoning with the man who seemed to have done more than most to bring us to this pass. Thus I summoned the pilot, Jesus Sebastian Belem, to my cabin.

'Well, old man,' I said bitterly, 'you might be a cripple, but you have led us all a merry dance these last weeks, I think.'

'Captain?'

'You and O'Dwyer. I've seen the two of you in secret conclave – aye, no doubt plotting the means by which he would be able to escape!'

The old man was impassive; more impassive than I would have been if faced with such a serious charge. 'You are mistaken, Captain,' he said. 'Colonel O'Dwyer wished only to learn from me something of these parts. Of the temper of the King of Kasang and his neighbours, and of the nature of the country round about. Nothing beyond matters of fact.'

A calmer, older Matthew Quinton would have asked what those 'matters of fact' were, but at that time I still had too much youthful impatience, exacerbated by the heat and my anger at the Irishman's flight.

'Damnation, Belem,' I cried, 'you as good as supported the traitor in his story! Before Holmes and myself, aboard the *Jersey*, you actually encouraged the idea that there was a mountain of gold. Why in God's name did you do that, man, unless you were some sort of confederate of his? Why give credence to this foul lie from the blackest of liars?'

Belem looked at me curiously. 'Captain,' he said, 'with respect, I had never encountered Colonel O'Dwyer before that day, and I never said that there was such a mountain. I said there were tales of gold mines beyond Barraconda, which is true. Has always been true, since first I came upon this river. But tales do not mean that those mines really exist. I said that Moorish caravans came across the desert from the very north of Africa and traded in gold, which is also true, and that the chiefs of these parts wear much gold – as for that, Captain, use the evidence of your own eyes.' *So O'Dwyer's tale of the great journey across the desert might well have been truth – omitting only the mountain at the end of it.* 'Now, if men wish to construct a legend of an entire mountain of gold from these half-truths and rumours, well, that it is their affair.' I was dimly aware of some noise upon the deck above, but thought nothing of it. 'It seems to me, Captain,' Belem continued, 'that this is just what your Prince Rupert has done, since first I knew him in these parts ten years ago. A great warrior, but a – what is the word you English use? – ah yes, a romantic. That is it. And if the romantic prince has convinced your king that ten years of wishful thinking has transformed the stories he heard on this river into a real mountain – and if your king is fool enough to believe him, and this man O'Dwyer too – well, that is their affair, and do not blame Jesus Sebastian Belem for it. Besides,' said the ancient Belem, smiling at last, 'consider my position, Captain Quinton. I am an old man. A very old man, and a cripple. My only income comes from the pilotage of this river, for I am fit for no task ashore. Now, I have observed that those who come seeking the mountain of gold are prepared to pay much higher fees for pilotage. Your Prince Rupert, for one. He paid me a true prince's ransom. So, Captain, consider this.' The old man looked at me levelly. 'If men come here wishing to find a mountain of gold, do you really believe I would tell them it does not exist?'

The door of my cabin opened, and an impossible apparition stood framed within it.

'And why should you, when in truth it does so?' said Brian Doyle O'Dwyer.

Twenty-Three

I had convinced myself that I would never see the renegade's face again, or hear his silken words. I was shaken to my core. For his part, O'Dwyer simply dismissed Belem – aboard *my* ship! – and smiled that insufferable, charming smile that I had seen and resented so often since our first meeting.

'My apologies, Captain,' he said, 'I should have sent you word. I should have expected you to be concerned for my safety, and to wish to know my whereabouts.' He said it with an apparent absence of irony. 'An appalling breach of military etiquette on my part. But I encountered this Arab factor, you see, and thought he might be a useful man to furnish provisions for our expedition to come. And in truth, it was good to be able to speak the Arabic again, if only for an hour or two.'

I struggled with my emotions. There was relief, certainly; but along with it came anger and doubt. Above all, doubt. The man could have slipped away, that much was certain. He had escaped the sentinels I appointed to watch him, and had he so wished, he could have been far away from Kasang. Yet there he was, as confident and arrogant as ever, lording it in my half of the captain's cabin of the *Seraph*. His presence raised the most potent of questions. For all these months, had I been wrong about Brian Doyle O'Dwyer? And if I had been wrong about him, had I also been wrong about the mountain of gold itself?

Somehow, I managed to say, 'We were indeed concerned for you, Colonel. We were on the point of sending out parties to search for you.'

I should have tackled the man over the blatant lie he had told to the soldier, Hallett, but such rational thoughts were driven away by the shock of the Irishman's reappearance. As, perhaps, he had intended.

'How touching,' said O'Dwyer, pleasantly. 'But you need have no more concerns about me, Captain Quinton, for I am quite safe, as you can see. Never safer, I think. Now, the ship is at a mooring after a long and arduous voyage, and days of hard work lie ahead for soldiers and sailors alike – building the canoes to take us upstream, and so forth. And your crew has had its shore leave curtailed, entirely because of my inconsiderate behaviour. Thus, might not an evening of festivity at my personal expense be appropriate, Captain?'

I was still not thinking clearly, and I could see no objection to what the renegade was proposing. There had been not a few grumbles when O'Dwyer's disappearance put paid to any prospect of extended leave among the manifold attractions of Kasang, especially the more nubile ones, and the Irishman was undoubtedly correct in his assessment of what lay both behind and ahead of my crew. Moreover, there were still tensions aplenty between mariners and redcoats, Bristolians and Cornishmen, so an evening of holiday aboard the *Seraph* seemed amply justified. As O'Dwyer departed to his own half of the cabin, I sent for Lanherne and gave the necessary orders. A little later, I heard cheering all along the main deck as the news was relayed to the messes. It's said that a captain should not seek too much popularity; but I thought of those who had already died upon this voyage, and of the unknown number who would certainly die of fevers, ravenous beasts or God alone knew what else in the weeks and months to come, and judged that this was one night when a little popularity for Matthew Quinton – and even, God help us, for Brian Doyle O'Dwyer – could not go amiss. I sent for Martin Lanherne to give the necessary orders.

But something troubled me: something I could not quite name or measure. Half an hour later I stood upon the forecastle, almost in the very beakhead itself, and shared my thoughts with Francis Gale, Valentine Negus and Kit Farrell.

I was in a deep sleep, the deepest I had known in our whole time upon the River of Gambia. Not even the carousing from the messes, continuing long after the night watch would have been set at sea, served to disturb me. It must have been the very middle of the night, when all should have been quiet upon the ship – yet there seemed to be a voice …

'Alarm, boy!'

The door of my cabin was open. Beyond it, I could hear the ship's bell begin to ring out from its belfry on the forecastle. There was no light, but I was aware of a presence standing above me. A blade glinted in the moonlight that glimmered through the stern window. In that instant, I knew the man about to kill me was Brian Doyle O'Dwyer.

The blade came down, straight for my eyes, but I just had time to throw my head to the right. I felt something nick my ear, and knew it was the traitor's knife.

'Not so fast, fuckhead!' cried a familiar voice behind the Irishman. Phineas Musk leaped across the cabin with unexpected agility, thrusting his own short-bladed knife at the traitor.

O'Dwyer turned. Still barely awake, I kicked out and caught him on the thigh. He lunged at me again with his blade, embedding it in my mattress. As I reached for my sword, O'Dwyer ran the few strides to the stern window and flung it open. I saw him, framed for an instant against the moonlight, before he flung himself into the abyss beyond. As I reached the open window, I heard a loud splash as he entered the water.

I stared into the blackness, my eyes adjusting slowly to the night. As

Musk came up beside me, I saw O'Dwyer pull himself out of the water into a low, silent shape that could only be a native canoe. He turned, looked at me, and seemed to shrug. Then he touched his forelock before making a Moorish hand-salute.

As his canoe pulled away, I became aware of others. Many others, surrounding the *Seraph*. I heard the first clashes of metal against metal on the deck above, the first shrieks of death-agony.

'Ship's under attack,' said Musk unnecessarily.

'To the quarterdeck, then, Musk!' I cried, reaching for my pistol and tucking it into my belt. My ear stung, and I was aware of a warm trickle oozing down my neck. 'And Musk,' I said, 'thank you.'

'Bloody drunken sailors, keeping me awake,' he said, as we began to run forward. 'Lucky for you I wasn't dead to the world.'

The upper deck of the *Seraph* was a battlefield. A small band of my men held the quarterdeck and the forecastle, but the waist was filled with shrieking natives armed with the short spears, knives and decorated shields that we had seen on sale in the streets of Kasang that same morning. More and more of them streamed over the ship's rails on both sides.

I fought my way to the quarterdeck rail, where Kit Farrell was wielding two cutlasses to deadly effect. As he swung with the right, cleaving a native at the shoulder, he lunged with his left, impaling another on the blade.

'Mister Farrell!' I cried. 'How stands the fight?'

'Nearly took us by surprise, sir,' he said, gasping for breath. 'Thankfully we had keen-eyed, sober men on lookout. As you ordered.'

I saw Francis Gale drive his blade straight through the ribs of a man who was attempting to clamber onto the poop rail. The bloodied iron protruded like a skewer from the dying man's back before Francis pulled his sword free and turned in search of his next opponent.

I looked about me and saw my lieutenant. The sight was very brief: he levelled two pistols at tribesmen clambering over the starboard rail and fired, clouding both of us momentarily in smoke. When it cleared, the men on the rail were gone and Negus was already reloading. 'Any of our men in the waist, Mister Negus?' I cried.

'I think not, sir! We fell back on both ends of the ship. Captain Facey's men are holding the forecastle, but with so many of the enemy in the waist, we can't get the rest of our men up quickly enough from the main deck.'

'Time to make some space, then!'

One of the quartergunners had already brought one of the swivel guns across from the larboard rail and fixed it to the quarterdeck rail instead. Following his lead, other of our men brought up another two. I took the nearest myself and found myself standing next to Lindman, who manned the next gun. A man whose face I could not make out thrust a lighted match into my hand.

'Loaded and primed, Master Gunner?'

'Of course, Captain,' the Swede replied grimly. 'Canister shot.'

'Very well, then. Give fire!'

I put the match to the linstock. The gun went off with a tremendous recoil and a great cloud of acrid smoke. I heard a strange whistling sound, then the dull noise of bodies and body parts falling upon the deck. A wailing went up.

'Seraphim, with me!' I cried.

I ignored the quarterdeck ladder, jumping directly onto the upper deck. In another time and place, I might have felt sympathy for those before me: at such close quarters, the effects of canister shot are a sight drawn straight from the picture gallery of Hell. Round balls take men apart or tear off limbs, often killing swiftly, but canister spreads a deadly cloud of small iron balls. The bodies closest to the quarterdeck swivel-guns lay upon the deck, peppered like so many bleeding sieves. Some of those further away lived, but had lost eyes, noses or mouths. Blood oozed upon the deck.

Yet the natives seemed undaunted. More of them poured over the rails, so that even as my party advanced from the stern and Facey's from the bow, joined now by more of our men coming up from the deck beneath, we were pressed ever more tightly inboard. I struck out with my sword, deflecting spear thrusts and stabbing into naked flesh. At my side, Musk and Francis Gale fought like the veterans they were. This was not the fighting found in genteel fencing manuals; this was evil, kill-or-be-killed viciousness, and we had our casualties too. I saw Russell, the Bristolian who had quarrelled with Macferran early in our voyage, take a dagger thrust into his neck. His blood spurted like a fountain over those nearest to him.

Other men were coming into the fray from below. I caught a glimpse of Tom Shish, fighting with the fury that only the redeemed can find, wielding a half-pike as though he was born to it. Harrington, the purser, waved a cutlass above his head, roaring defiance as he brought it down to cleave the skull of a naked savage. Even Bradbury, the maimed cook, had a blade in his one good hand, sticking men as though he was making the juices run free from a roasting ox.

The moonlight glinted on a spear-point, coming at me from the right – I swung my sword up, deflected the thrust and at once swept my blade into the side of my assailant's head, opening his skull and spilling his brains. We were almost meeting Facey's men now, the soldiers advancing grimly in two ranks as though they were upon the practice ground. As I watched, one of the redcoats reacted too slowly to a spear thrust which struck hard into his groin. The soldier fell to his knees, cupping his manhood in his hands so it would not spill onto the deck, before falling forward and going to his God.

It was discipline and modern weapons against sheer weight of numbers now, and the issue was still in the balance. Then I saw that one of the natives was dressed differently to the others. His arms were decorated in the gris-gris that had adorned the King of Kombo, and he wore a similar mitre-like headpiece. He was a tall, striking figure, whose skin seemed lighter than that of the warriors alongside him. As he fought, he uttered a word that I recognised all too well: *'Stront!'*. It frequently escaped the lips of my wife, the Dutch being more delicate in my mother's hearing than the English equivalent or even its French alternative, *merde*. I gestured to Musk and Gale, and we began to cut our way towards the richly clad man. The natives around him fought even more ferociously than those we had battled through already, but at last I had what I sought – a space, a few precious feet of open space – I reached to my belt with my free hand and lifted the flintlock pistol.

'*Overgave, uwe majesteit!*' I cried in Dutch – surrender, your majesty.

The man looked me up and down, took in my bloodied sword and my pistol, and nodded. His knife and spear fell to the deck.

I sat the King of Kasang down in my half-cabin and offered him some wine, which he drank lustily. He did not seem bitter and vengeful at the deaths of so many of his men; evidently his culture valued the warrior, and respected a victorious enemy. His surviving tribesmen had retired to their canoes, but we could hear the swish of paddles as these circled the ship, waiting for some sign as to the fate of their chief. I had no doubt that this was no victory, but a mere truce, and all depended on the discourse between the King and I in the next few minutes. I sent for Belem to translate, but it was swiftly clear that he was not needed; the King spoke almost flawless Dutch.

'My mother was a Dutchwoman,' he said, 'wife to a factor who resided at Kasang. When he died, my father took a fancy to the notion of a white wife.'

'Then tell me, Majesty,' I said, paying this potentate all due respect, 'how did you come to fight for our traitor, the man called O'Dwyer or Omar Ibrahim?'

'The latter, in his dealings with me,' said the King. 'He came to my court this afternoon, dressed in the Arab fashion.' I nodded; so that was why O'Dwyer had disappeared for some hours. 'He knew of my war with the King of Niani, beyond the ridge, and swore that he could provide me with the weapons to win that war. The weapons aboard this ship, which serves the enemy of my mother's country.'

Belem was rueful. 'I told O'Dwyer of it,' he said. 'During my description of these parts, I mentioned that the King, here, was half-Dutch and much inclined to their cause. And I told him of his war with Niani.'

It was not difficult to see how O'Dwyer's fertile mind had worked. Belem had inadvertently told him of a ruler who favoured the Dutch, and who wanted something that the renegade offered to provide. All O'Dwyer had to do was escape the attention of my men for a few hours in order to make his suit directly to the King. At first, I had been mystified by O'Dwyer's return to the *Seraph*, and almost convinced myself that I had misjudged the man. But during my conversation upon the forecastle with Valentine Negus, Kit Farrell and Francis Gale, the four of us pieced together a far more sinister explanation for the Irishman's actions. True, he could have escaped during the afternoon, but then we would have been in close pursuit, with a fair chance of running him down. Far better for his cause if no-one at all from the *Seraph* was left alive to pursue him; an end to be achieved by lulling the captain and crew with his unexpected reappearance, then ensuring their guard was lowered even further by proposing a night of abandon and debauch, making them incapable of resisting the attack by his new ally, the King of Kasang. And if, at some time in the future, it became convenient for Omar Ibrahim to don the guise of Brian Doyle O'Dwyer once more: well, who would be able to dispute the word of the sole survivor of the tragic expedition to locate the mountain of gold?

I almost felt a new respect for the enigmatic O'Dwyer. Yet there were more immediate matters to be settled, and they hinged upon the disposition of the man sitting before me, the King of Kasang.

'Now, Your Majesty,' I said, 'it seems that we have much in common, you and I. You have a Dutch mother, I have a Dutch wife. So let us talk truthfully of the present state of the world beyond this river, and of the ways in which I might be able to assist you in your dealings with the King of Niani.'

Twenty-Four

Most of the officers of the *Seraph* were gathered in its steerage, looking down upon the chart that Belem had placed upon the table. It was just after dawn, barely a few hours after the attack by the Kasang tribesmen, and we were all mightily tired, stinking of sweat and gunsmoke, yet grimly determined about our business.

'If he's making directly for Algier, he'll go due north,' said Facey in the gruff way of the old soldier. His arm, pierced by a tribesman's spear, was bandaged and held in a sling.

The ancient pilot shook his head. 'A difficult route – just one man, crossing all of that great desert – unless he has the good fortune to fall in with a caravan of Arab traders travelling back from these parts toward Timbuctoo or the like. In which case, he's more likely to go north-east, as most of the traders will be coming to and from Barraconda and the lands above there. We can discount south, I think – away from his destination, and he will find no friends among the peoples to the south of the river.'

I looked at the men around the table. We, the officers of the *Seraph*, almost certainly all had the same thought: we would never catch the renegade now. In one sense, his stratagem had worked perfectly. Fleeing during the night rather than the day, and using his allies' onslaught to delay us, gave him a greater head start on us. As he would have known, too, we were also inevitably exhausted from the fight. O'Dwyer seemed to have stacked the cards overwhelmingly in his favour.

But the attempt had to be made. The honour of the King of England and, more importantly, of Captain Matthew Quinton, demanded it; but so, too, did something much more tangible, a cause more personal and palpable. Eleven of our men had died in the night attack, seven Seraphim and four of Facey's soldiers. Most of these had been good men. I thought most of poor Summercourt, a stout man, and the eleven children now fatherless in their cottage upon Bodmin Moor; and Trevanion, the friend of my loyal followers Polzeath and Tremar, strong men who had lifted his body delicately from the deck with tears streaming down their faces. Morgan Facey seemed particularly affected by the death of one Tysoe, who had fought for the king all the way from Powick Bridge to Worcester fight, the first and last battles of England's civil war, three miles and nine years apart, only to perish in this miserable place in an obscure fight that would soon be lost to history. From beyond the bulkhead came the unmistakeable sound of sailors scrubbing their blood, and that of the natives, from the deck. *Ergo,* Brian Doyle O'Dwyer had caused the deaths of eleven good and true Englishmen, bringing misery to eleven families who would not learn of their loss for many months to come, and of scores of loyal subjects of the misled King of Kasang. Dead men, their widows and their orphans screamed out to us for revenge.

Thus I studied the chart with almost ferocious concentration. I thought hard upon what I knew of Brian Doyle O'Dwyer, and of all my dealings with him. *No*, I thought, *I will not make a fool of myself in front of these veterans – it is an insane proposition …*

And yet somehow I blurted it out. 'Is it not possible, gentlemen, that O'Dwyer will attempt to go north-*west*? Toward Cape Verde? The shortest route to the sea, after all.'

Negus seemed on the point of laughing at his captain's youthful folly. 'Aye, Captain, and toward Montnoir as well, and the rest of the French at Fort Saint Louis. He will hardly escape from the lion's mouth to put himself into that of the tiger.'

I persisted; somehow I sensed Cornelia's invisible presence, and she would have persisted until doomsday. 'Quite so,' I said, 'but remember, he sailed with the Sallee Rovers – the very gentlemen who essayed to attack us, no doubt in hopes of liberating their friend. Sallee is not too far north, gentlemen. And I think the Rovers often come down to Cape Verde or beyond – do they not, Belem?' The old pilot nodded. 'Well, then. What if O'Dwyer aims to rendezvous with some of his old ship-mates on the Senegal shore?'

None of them could fault the logic of this. Thus we resolved upon three search parties. The smallest, under Negus, would set out along the least likely route, that due north toward the desert. Facey would take half of his redcoats to the north-east, leaving the remainder as a guard for *Seraph*. Not that we feared another attack from the King of Kasang; he had been assuaged by his conversation with me, and even more so by our generous provision of swords and muskets for his war against Niani, and wine with which to celebrate his inevitable victory. Thus Kit Farrell and I could set off confidently for the north-west with a party of seamen, leaving Gunner Lindman in command of the ship – for in truth, his skills were unlikely to be required during a manhunt, whereas Kit's ability to navigate by sun and stars would be invaluable. Boatswain Lanherne and Coxswain Carvell were devastated that they would not be required – the latter had a mighty urge to see a lion or two – but I had a dark, unspoken thought at the back of my mind. If Negus, Castle, Kit and I were all devoured by wild beasts, or slaughtered by a cannibal tribe, or simply died of heatstroke and thirst, like poor Castle, then the *Seraph* would require a sufficient body of sea-officers capable of taking her back to England. Otherwise, we were unanimous that two days would be suf-ficient for the pursuit. Our desire to avenge our fallen shipmates, and to uphold the honour of our country, had to be tempered by two rather more pressing considerations. The first was the need to get back down river before the wet season and its deadly fevers struck the Gambia. The second was the ever-present thought that somewhere downstream waited the Seigneur de Montnoir, for I was certain that the Knight of Malta was not done with us yet.

An hour or so later, the three search parties took leave of each other outside Kasang town. Kit and I set off for the north-west at the head of an eclectic little army. A dozen men of the *Seraph*'s crew came along with us, all volunteers: my old comrades-in-arms Polzeath and Tremar, desperate to redeem themselves for O'Dwyer's escape; Treninnick, who also felt guilt for his part in it, albeit needlessly; Macferran, four other Cornishmen, two Londoners and even two of the formerly obstreperous Bristol draft, Ayres and Brownjohn. The two last had the makings of good men, and evidently recognised the hard truth that with Castle dead, their futures in the navy depending on ingratiating themselves with a new patron. Despite all my imprecations, Francis Gale and Phineas Musk also insisted on accompanying me. I could understand Francis's sentiment: it was a heaven-sent opportunity to see something of the country, and as he had said, before him stretched only long years of preaching sermons to the unresponsive congregation of Ravensden. Musk, who favoured comfort so mightily, should have been expected to be averse to some nights of sleeping under the stars, but as ever Phineas Musk was a law unto himself. He would grumble ceaselessly about the discomforts of the expedition, yet would never consider not being a part of it. We had with us a native guide, a young savage recommended by the King of Kasang and named by Belem after the Portuguese fashion as Joao Paz, although he also answered to a name in the local tongue that might have been Mamadou. Communication between us was not easy, but he understood a little Dutch thanks to all the butterbox crews that traded upon the river, and we were just able to make ourselves intelligible to each other.

We moved away from the river into broad grassland interspersed by huge trees that seemed to grow upside-down, their branches resembling roots thrusting out into the air: *baobab*, said Mamadou. It was now the late afternoon, but the hot breeze from the north-east made our progress uncomfortable. This was an alien land. We scanned every bush for signs of threat; jumped at each new noise. My discomfort was increased by the knowledge that when darkness fell, the beasts of those parts would come into their own. We had not gone far when we saw a lion far off, lying languidly in the shade of a *baobab*, but fortunately it seemed unconcerned by our presence. Mamadou gestured for us to continue. We white men looked at each other uncertainly, but our guide's assessment of the lion seemed accurate enough. Whether he and his kin remained so uninterested in the cool of the night was, by contrast, of interest to us all.

'The Irishman had time to thieve a horse, that he did,' said Musk. 'Five hours' start he's had, maybe six. If he's on a horse, on firm ground like this he could be thirty or forty miles ahead of us now, maybe even more. Getting further ahead by the minute. And all we're doing is bidding fair to be a lion's supper.'

'Musk has a point,' said Francis. 'Even on foot, and even in this heat, O'Dwyer could be – what? – ten miles ahead of us by now. After all, he is more accustomed to this climate than we.'

'I know it,' I said. 'In truth, it will take a miracle to rank with the loaves and fishes for us to find the renegade. But honour demands that the effort be made.'

'Ah, honour,' said Musk wearily. '"What is honour? A word. What is that word, honour? Air. A trim reckoning. Who hath it? He who died o' Wednesday." The First Part of King Henry the Fourth, as I recall, not that I can abide that over-rated scribbler from Stratford. 'And what's today? Wednesday. Methinks yonder lion has a Musk-eating look about him.'

'Well, Musk,' I said with as much jollity as I could muster, 'you are, in truth, the most fleshy of all of us. I think yonder lion would gladly feast on you before any of the rest.'

My jest fell on stony ground. In truth, I was probably the only man in our party who conceived of honour as our chief reason for pursuing O'Dwyer. All the rest, even the normally amiable Kit Farrell, were set upon revenge: Francis Gale explained animatedly to Horning, a Londoner who was one of the more godly in the crew, how Our Lord's words in Matthew and Saint Paul's in Romans did not preclude the wreaking of our rightful vengeance upon the treacherous renegade O'Dwyer.

At dusk, we lit a fire, cooked and devoured some guinea-fowls that Mamadou had downed, and made our arrangements for the night. O'Dwyer would probably not press on through the darkness on his own; that, at least, gave us an advantage. We would take two hours sleep, with three men standing guard, then press on a few hours more before sleeping another two hours just before dawn, when the guards from the first shift could have their slumber. By taking another two hours' sleep in the middle of the next day, and then repeating the process anew, we could both march for eighteen hours in every twenty-four, a rate that I doubted O'Dwyer alone could sustain, and also distribute the watch-keeping duties fairly among all. And I truly meant 'all'; this was no time for officers to stand upon the privilege of their rank. As a signal of my intent, I moved that Francis, Kit and I should have the first watch. This caused some astonishment and protest among the men, who held that it was not right for the captain or a Reverend to do such menial work, and stand guard over rough tarpaulins such as themselves. But I held my ground, although in truth I was tired enough after the previous night's exertions.

Thus I stood my watch, musket in hand, upon that desolate plain, listening to the myriad sounds of the night from the clicking of insects to the distant roar of lions. It was a bright night, and I tried to identify stars that Kit had once taught me. Was that Aldebaran or Os Baleni? And that – the Horn of Aries, surely? But looking too long into the night sky brought on an overwhelming urge to sleep, and I turned my thoughts elsewhere; I had already fallen foul of enough of the Articles of War without adding a breach of the twenty-seventh by sleeping on watch. But when it came to my turn to sleep, just before dawn and after a few hours of night marching, I never knew a more comfortable pillow than the earth of Africa, nor experienced a deeper slumber than during those two blessed hours when I slept beneath the stars.

We pressed on at dawn. Privately, I was convinced that we had no hope of overhauling O'Dwyer, even if he had come in this direction to begin with: the entire plain was a highway, many miles broad, so the chances of finding one man within it beggared belief. But out of honour, a thirst for vengeance or sheer cussedness, we went on. Musk talked with Francis Gale of the folly of the doctrine of predestination, of the relative merits of port wine and sack, and of God knows what else. I talked with Kit of the prospects for a Dutch war, and of how to handle a ship in the shoal waters of a lee shore. I talked for an hour or more with Ayres and Brownjohn; it occurred to me that knowing good men in Bristol might be to my advantage when the new Dutch war that all expected eventually began. They were wary at first, unused to conversing with any captain, let alone an earl's brother, but in time they lowered their guards and talked freely of their hopes and fears, of the prospects of war, of the king's poor treatment of his sailors by way of bad pay and victuals. Brownjohn in particular impressed me: he was a young man of twenty or so, but he knew his business, hoping to prosper in it to provide for his young wife, and I marked him down for promotion to a petty officer when a vacancy permitted.

All the while, the heat sapped our strength, the beasts of the plain roamed about us and the birds circled above us, taking no notice of us at all. At last, when the noonday sun demanded that we halt and rest, Mamadou recommended that we shelter by bushes that would provide shade and a good stock of edible berries. There we settled, with Musk as one of the duty watch. Before settling onto the scorched ground, I went into the bushes to piss, and coming into the clearing beyond ...

Disturbed by my sudden appearance barely four yards in front of it, a great lion raised its head and looked me full in the eyes.

I stood stock still and stared back at the beast. I felt my heart pound furiously within my chest. The beast still stared. The rest of its body, from its neck to its tail, was perfectly still. As was I; for somewhere in the depths of my memory, perhaps in my reading of the tales of the Christian martyrs or in Uncle Tristram's explanations when we had gone to see the great cats in the Tower menagerie, I recalled that a man confronted by a lion should endeavour not to move at all, and should show the beast no fear.

I can state with some authority that this is not easy advice to follow when faced by *leo magnus*. Every sinew in my body seemed to be pulling me into the posture of turning and running. I barely breathed. I thought of my friends, but a few yards away and yet ignorant of my plight: of Francis Gale, who would have to say a prayer over my stripped bones; of Musk, who would declaim that it served me right for ordering this foolish pursuit; of Kit Farrell, who had saved me from death by drowning only to attend my death by devouring. I thought of Cornelia, and her tears when she learned of my end. I thought of my place in the history of the Quintons: not a great warrior, like my grandfather, nor even a poet-martyr, like my father, but the only one of the name to be eaten alive by a wild beast. Tristram might even laugh.

Still my heart pounded. The creature seemed to be studying me, serenely contemplating my smell, my strength and my will. It would surely pounce – its jaws opened …

Keep your eyes open, boy, face it down …

There was a noise to my left. I saw Brownjohn, his hands at his breeches, coming into the bush for the same purpose as myself. But he blundered into the vegetation too loudly, and when he saw the beast he cried, 'Lion! Oh sweet Jesu, save me!' before turning and running. The lion's stare turned in a moment from me to the Bristolian. The creature that had seemed so still, so somnolent, sprang up and moved with astonishing speed. Barely half-a-dozen great strides …

The lion's mouth bit into Brownjohn's leg, severing it. Blood spurted onto the soil of Africa. The young man's scream was unearthly. He turned as though to fight off the beast, but the move only sealed his fate. A great paw came up, claws ripping eyes and face from the skull as the teeth sank into the Bristolian's side.

I stood like a statue, seemingly unable to move, unable to do anything but watch the horror unfolding before me. Only the familiar roar of a flintlock musket stirred me into action. I turned and saw Phineas Musk, already recovered from the recoil and preparing to reload with a suspiciously practised manner that I would never have credited to him. Behind him, Kit and some of the men were also loading and aiming. But although the beast had not been hit by Musk's shot, it had taken fright from the noise and was already bounding majestically across the plain at inconceivable speed. To this day, that lion remains the fastest object that I have ever seen move upon the surface of God's earth.

We ran to Brownjohn. Even then, so early in my life, I had seen many men dreadfully torn and maimed in battle, but I had never seen a human being in such a sickening state as the poor man before me. His face and half his body were gone, yet somehow, he still breathed. One eye, hanging in the bloodied remnants of a socket, still blinked at me. He tried to speak, but that last effort was too much, and poor Matthew Brownjohn went to his maker. He and I shared the same name, and but for him, I might have been the corpse upon the baked soil of Africa.

We buried Brownjohn in the shade of a baobab, digging deep down in the hope that the corpse would not be dug up by a ravenous beast of the field. Francis Gale stood at the head of the grave and from memory intoned the order of service for the dead. The rest of us made the responses and the amens: a curiously correct manifestation of the Anglican faith in such an unlikely and terrible place.

Brownjohn's terrible death shook every man in the party, their captain included, but at first it did not weaken the resolve to press on after the treacherous O'Dwyer. However, another afternoon and night in the wild proved sufficient to test that resolve to its very limit. My body was sore and cried out for proper sleep, yet still the sun beat down. Still there was no sign of Brian Doyle O'Dwyer. Still beasts roared nearby and far away, and inwardly I began to dread the thought that they would devour us one by one, emulating the fate of poor Brownjohn. Still the vultures circled. Awakening from an inadequate slumber to find insects crawling over one's flesh proved almost as great a terror as confronting the lion. Worse, my men were starting to grow testy; even the best and most loyal, Polzeath and Tremar, began to murmur that they no longer looked on our journey as a quest for revenge and redemption, but as an almighty fool's errand. I assured my party that we would turn back at noon, as agreed with the other two parties, and they seemed content with that. Thus we pressed on for a last few hours.

It was perhaps an hour before noon when we emerged from the scrub into a great clearing, wherein stood a vast stone circle not unlike our Stonehenge, at the edge of a great cliff looking out over an expanse of country beyond; we had been climbing almost since leaving Kasang, though so slowly as to be barely noticeable. In his broken Dutch, Mamadou told me that this had been a sacred place of the old nations of those parts. The sight revived some of my Cornish lads, who said there were also many such places in their own county, and we walked among the stones with wonder. Finally, we all went to the edge of the cliff and looked out.

'Perhaps Eden looked very much like this,' said Francis Gale, nodding in appreciation of the biblical spectacle before us.

Certainly, the vast expanse could have populated many Arks: herds of elephants roamed within our sight, and antelopes, leopards, and God knows how many more beasts, marching or racing across the great grassland that stretched to the furthest horizon and the great blue curtain of Heaven itself. What it apparently did not contain was humanity, and least of all one cursed Irish renegade.

I contemplated that glorious, deadly sight one last time, then turned to face my loyal party. 'Well, men,' I said, 'we have done our duties to our king, to our slaughtered shipmates and to ourselves, I think. If O'Dwyer came this way, then he has his freedom. Perhaps he may yet encounter a lion with a hunger and meet the same fate as poor Brownjohn. Or if it truly is Eden, then perhaps he, too, will encounter a serpent that will do for him.' There was a thin laugh at that. 'Whereas we, my friends, can now return with honour to our ship, and to old England.'

'Amen to that,' said Phineas Musk.

And with that, we turned and began to retrace our steps back to the river. There was time, now, for reflection.

I talked with Francis of the mountain of gold, and how the king might react to the news that he had been duped by O'Dwyer. My old friend was sanguine; Charles Stuart was unreadable, he said, and would either dismiss it with a jest or clap us all in the Tower, depending on how well he had bedded his latest whore that morning. I talked with Kit of our coming voyage downstream, of the hazards to be expected and of what obstacles My Lord Montnoir might attempt to throw in our way. Although O'Dwyer and the chimera of the mountain of gold were as lost to him as they were to us, I had little doubt that the Knight of Malta would not see it that way, and would look for any opportunity to humble Matthew Quinton. And then, as I stood my watch at night upon the African plain, looking up at the moon and listening to the innumerable strange noises of the place, my good-brother Venner Garvey's words came back to me, just as he had spoken them to me that day in the undercroft of Ravensden Abbey.

This mission will not succeed.

Well, Venner, you have had your way. God damn you to Hell for it.

Our return took us less time than our going out; barely a day and a half. Although already exhausted and burned, we were all more willing to forsake rest and sleep in order to get back to our little wooden world than we had been to pursue a long-gone traitor. However, our unexpectedly early return meant that when we arrived in Kasang at dusk on the following evening, the night watch aboard *Seraph* had already been set, and no boat waited at the water side to take us out. By the time the ship responded to our hail, Mamadou had already found a large canoe and a party of his kinsmen willing to row us out, and it was in that condition that I approached my command once again. As we neared the ship, I looked up, and by the dusk-light I saw a peculiar sight upon the deck of the *Seraph*: two Arabs and a near-naked black slave were standing there, watching our approach. I was hot, exhausted, and not thinking clearly. My first reaction was that in my absence, Lindman and my other officers had sold the ship to the Arabs. By the time I hauled my sore body onto the deck to be greeted by the pipe of Lanherne's whistle, I was in thoroughly peevish mood. It took me a moment to realise that every man on the upper deck of the *Seraph* was grinning broadly. Every man but one.

It is a peculiarity of the human senses that we can sometimes look directly at another man that we know well enough, and because we do not expect to see them in some such place, or some such garb, we look straight through them as though they are perfect strangers. Thus it was that evening on the deck of the *Seraph*. It still took me a moment more to recognise the slave as Julian Carvell, Coxswain of the *Seraph*, and the two Arabs as Ali Reis and Brian Doyle O'Dwyer. The latter was manacled.

'What in the name of Heaven – ' I spluttered.

'All their idea, sir,' said Lanherne. 'Carvell and Ali Reis, between them.'

Even by his standards, the Coxswain's grin was particularly broad. 'Well, sir, we reckoned there was nothing to be lost by trying our luck to the south, to see if the Colonel, here, had gone that way.' The erstwhile officer in question kept his eyes fixed on the deck, and said nothing.

'Ah, it was more than luck, Captain,' said Ali Reis. 'I reckoned that if this Omar Ibrahim was seeking to rejoin the Arab race, then he would think as an Arab once again. And an Arab would not make the obvious move expected by infidels – ' He bowed his head to me and my fellow officers – 'with due respect, of course. After all, sirs,' smiled Ali Reis, 'it was we Arabs who introduced chess to Europe.'

'Besides,' said Carvell, 'Ali here spoke with some of the men of the town, after you'd left. He's picked up enough of their tongues in our time upon this river. They pointed him to an old man who had supplied the renegade with Arab garb, and had seen him going off across the river to the southward.'

'So I studied the pilot's charts, Captain,' said Ali Reis, 'and concluded that our friend here would make his way south and east, then work back up the river to the vicinity of Barraconda, where he was like to meet with a caravan bound for Timbuctoo. He was unlikely to go far from the river, not knowing the land. But the Coxswain, here, perfected the trap.'

Carvell was uncharacteristically bashful. 'Well, Captain, all I reckoned was that this far upstream, an Arab factor and his slave would be less conspicuous than a couple of seamen in old English slop clothes. But it worked better than ever I imagined. He didn't recognise us, y'see, sir. We'd got ahead of him – '

'And he approached us,' said Ali Reis triumphantly, 'crying *As-Salamu Alaykam*!'

'That he did,' Carvell laughed, 'until he saw a naked Mandingo level a matchlock pistol at his brow.'

'Well, gentlemen!' I cried. 'I commend you both for your initiative, by God! The king shall hear of this, have no fear.' I shook the hands of both Carvell and Ali Reis. Then I stepped in front of O'Dwyer, and at last, the renegade raised his eyes to meet mine. 'So, Colonel O'Dwyer,' I said, 'or I think Omar Ibrahim is more appropriate again, perhaps? Fleeing back to the corsairs, I see, as I always knew you would – as you would have done when the Rovers came upon us at sea, or else at Tenerife, but for my men – '

Even now, the bravado of the foul rogue was breathtaking. 'Not at all, Captain – I was merely seeking guides to take us to the mountain more directly, and the factors who could provide an advance upon its profits, *as you and I discussed –* '

I raised my hand. 'No, Irishman. Enough. Your silken words won't save you from the noose this time – not with the blood of eleven Englishmen added to all the lies you've told.' The renegade shrugged; eleven deaths were evidently only a little matter in the weighing of Brian Doyle O'Dwyer's conscience. But I had the measure of him now. 'Captain Matthew Quinton will finally execute upon you the justice you should have receive the moment you set foot on the deck of the *Wessex*,' I said. 'And if you think you'll get a chance to mislead my king once again, O'Dwyer, then you're more mistaken than you can possibly conceive.'

I was almost twenty-four years old at that time, and had left childhood behind me long before; civil war and exile are powerful enough aids to maturity, but following the deaths of my father and grandfather, and in the absence of my brother and Uncle Tris, I had effectively become the senior male in the household of Ravensden at the age of five. Even so, I could not restrain a childish glee as I gave two orders in quick succession: one, to chain the traitor O'Dwyer in the hold; two, for the carpenter's crew to demolish the partition in my cabin and return the whole to me.

Twenty-Five

When I addressed a council of the officers of the *Seraph* later the next morning (after a particularly blissful sleep in my sea-bed, whose comforts I had never appreciated so much), I looked out upon the faces of changed men. It was not only the welcome fact that my cabin now reached the entire breadth of the ship, giving all of us ample room to stretch ourselves. It was as though a mighty chain had been cut from all our ankles; even Tom Shish was smiling, for the first time since the discovery of his intended sabotage. It was also one of the briefest and most unanimous councils of that sort I ever experienced. When I put forward the proposition that O'Dwyer's mountain of gold had been exposed as a monstrous fraud, and that I saw our duty as being to return downstream as fast as we could to pursue the other part of our orders, the harrying of the Dutch, every man smiled, cried 'aye!' and pounded his hands upon the table.

Thus it was that four nights after the arrest of O'Dwyer, the *Seraph* dropped anchor once more off Taukorovalle, close to the Courlander *Krokodil*. She was now more nearly shipshape, but God alone knew how good a fist her tiny crew would make of it on the river, let alone out in an Atlantic gale. I proposed to hold another council shortly, for we faced a pressing dilemma under the terms of our orders. There was now nothing to stop us attacking Jakob's Fort on San Andreas in the name of King Charles and old England, but I was reluctant to shed the blood of that good fellow Captain Stiel and his garrison; moreover, Captain Facey and I had seen for ourselves the formidable battery of the fort, and there was no guarantee that we could capture – or even sail past – such an arsenal. Thus I needed to know Stiel's temper and intentions, and crucially, I also needed intelligence of Holmes' actions, for we had received no word of his war-making mission since proceeding upstream.

Consequently, Belem went ashore to glean what he could from the Portugee and half-breed factors of the town. When he returned aboard and presented himself in my cabin, where I was discussing the almost forgotten matter of the Countess Louise with Francis Gale and Phineas Musk, he had a bleak expression upon his ancient face. 'It is as you feared,' he said. 'Word has come of Holmes' capture of Gorée. The garrison on San Andreas has been sent orders to fight you if you attempt to come down river. I am told that your friend Stiel was unwilling to do so – vowed to surrender to you as soon as you came into sight.' The old man frowned. 'But he has been persuaded otherwise, it seems. Persuaded, along with all the rest of his garrison, by a large bribe in gold, provided by – '

'Montnoir,' I said. Belem nodded. 'The gold that the King of Kombo refused has found a home after all, then. So Montnoir now commands the fort, and will turn its guns against us if we attempt to force a passage.'

'A Frenchman commanding Dutch?' cried Musk. 'Well, not Dutch. Those Russians.'

'Courlanders, Musk,' I said. 'Courlanders, not Russians.'

'Same thing. But how's that happen? I mean, since when are the Dutch, or the Russians – Cour – them, friends of the French?'

Francis Gale smiled. 'Since the treaty of mutual defence and alliance between King Louis and their High Mightinesses of the States General was concluded a year or two back, Musk. Now, you and I might fairly say that an alliance between the Most Christian King and a heretical republic is hardly a marriage made in Heaven, and is certain to end in blood one day. But that, Musk my friend, is what the great men of every nation call "diplomacy"'.

'And as he took such delight in telling us,' I said, 'My Lord Montnoir is, after all, an accredited ambassador of King Louis. So put yourself in Captain Stiel's position, Musk. I think that if such a mighty personage, with such impeccable credentials, offered you a very large purse of gold, then even you would fight against your own mother, would you not?'

'Did that *gratis* enough times,' said Musk, 'but I see the justice of the case.'

I summoned the council of my officers in the great cabin of *Seraph*. The assessments of the senior men present, Negus and Facey, were equally bleak. Yes, we could attempt to force a passage past the fort, but its battery was stronger than our own – much stronger, if the garrison moved guns across from the north rampart to the south or vice-versa, depending on whether we chose the south or north channel. They would have ample time to do so, given the uninterrupted view up river that Stiel and his new commanding officer possessed. We could attempt to slip past by night, but the moon was bright, we would of necessity be moving slowly and carefully, with less sail aloft than by day, and there was thus a danger that we would make an even easier target for the fort's gunners. Of course, we could try to take the fort; both Facey and I were confident that it could be captured easily enough, if only we could get close enough to make a breach in its ramparts and get enough men ashore. But that was an almighty *if only*, given the power of the battery ranged against us. We discussed the possibility of getting word to our men aboard *Prospect of Blakeney* and at Charles Island. If they could come upstream to reinforce us, and we could mount an attack on the fort from both sides – This was an attractive proposition, but it was

Belem, of all people, who demolished it. It would probably take at least two days to get a message to the mouth of the river, rather longer for the other force to make its way upstream. The pilot's intelligence established that Montnoir already had a score or more of his own Frenchmen in the fort, others were downstream toward the mouth of the river, and could we be certain that the Knight of Malta did not have other reinforcements on their way to him, perhaps overland from Fort Saint Louis in the Senegal? Moreover, by ordering our entire force upstream we would be effectively abandoning the mouth of the river, and nothing was more certain than that Dutch ships would appear at some point to avenge Holmes' depredations. Could we really risk a two-pronged assault on Jakob's Island, only to find the mouth of the Gambia sealed against us by overwhelming force thereafter?

As often happens in such cases, we were soon going in circles, revisiting schemes we had rejected but half a glass earlier. Negus and Facey began to argue, albeit politely, if on no better grounds than that a sailor and a soldier must argue sooner or later. My mind began to wander. I looked out of the stern windows. Beyond the *Krokodil*, a lone elephant cooled itself at the river's edge. I thought of Hannibal taking an army of those beasts over the Alps; I needed such ingenuity now, by God! I searched my memories for stories that I might have read, or heard. As so often, such thoughts resolved themselves into one question: *what might my grandfather have done in such a case?* After all, his legend had been sufficient to get us clear of Tenerife …

I was a child of ten or eleven again, listening to Tris tell the tale of what Earl Matthew had done in command of the *Ark Ravensden* off the Azores in the year ninety-two.

'My father detested Francis Drake, young Matt, as I often told you before. The world was too small for both of them. But he acknowledged Drake as a mightily skilled seaman. So, when faced with that great Spanish galleon off the isle of Graciosa, he recalled how Drake had captured the Concepcion *on his voyage round the globe…'*

I leaned over to Kit Farrell and whispered to him, for I recalled something that he, too, had once said to me, during this very voyage. Kit, whose good humour toward me had seemingly been restored by our recent land-voyage, seemed puzzled at first, then smiled broadly and nodded vigorously in approbation.

I looked up. I raised my hand, and Negus and Facey fell silent. 'Gentlemen,' I said, 'I have a proposition to put to you. Musk – please ask Mister Shish to join this council.'

Those in the fort – Montnoir, Stiel, all of them – would have seen the two ships coming down to them on the strong south-easterly breeze off the land, avoiding the native canoes that thronged the river, out of the very first glimmers of the dawn. There was *Seraph* in the main channel to the south of the island, trying to force that passage: the wider channel and so the obvious one for her to take, as it afforded the greater sea-room for manoeuvring. Every inch a royal warship of England, her sails were sheeted home with precision, the lion figurehead cut through the waves at her bow, and the great red-and-white ensign spilled from the staff at her stern. In the north channel, and some way astern, was the ungainly *Krokodil* under her Courland colours, finally making her way back to the open sea after so many months stranded in the upper reaches of the Gambia. Her much-decimated crew struggled to control her as she slewed to and fro across the channel under loose, slovenly sails.

As they aimed their guns at the magnificent sight of the oncoming *Seraph*, Montnoir's men must have been filled with grim anticipation; for they knew full well that their weight of shot would tear apart the beautiful, fragile frigate.

I stood with my officers on the quarterdeck of my *Seraph*. Nerves, fear and determination struggled to gain the upper hand in my emotions.

The fort opened fire. For the hundredth time, I wondered if I had chosen the correct strategy. About that many men had died aboard my ill-fated first command, the *Happy Restoration*. Would history repeat itself here? Would Matthew Quinton's inglorious naval career end with him being cut in two by a Courlander cannonball?

Montnoir's gunners did not yet have their aim. Shot was falling just short of the *Seraph* in the south channel, but it would be only a matter of time before the Dutch, French and Courlander men on the ramparts found their range and bearing. Naturally they had massed most of their battery on the south rampart, seeing *Seraph* heading on that course. My crew were nervous and whispering among themselves, for they all knew the monstrous risk their raw young captain was taking with their lives. Still the *Seraph* bore down the south channel, straight into the withering fire that would fall upon her at any moment. I held my breath. The first shot struck just behind the head. A second went through the foresail. The enemy were gaining confidence now, truly getting their bearings, and still *Seraph* did not return fire. The fort's south rampart battery opened up with ever more vigour. As it did so, its own gunsmoke drifted back over it. The wind was ideal for Montnoir's gunners, whose view of the ship in the south channel would not be obscured.

But their view of the *Krokodil,* slewing drunkenly all over the north channel – a view already made dim enough by the darkness of the dawn – ah, now that view was obscured even more by the smoke that drifted back over the lightly armed north rampart, whose defenders were in any case looking south, to see how their more favoured brethren did. And after all, most of the men in the fort were Courlanders themselves. They had seen the *Krokodil* go up river. They knew that ship, and they knew her crew. She was one of their own, and nothing to concern them on a morning where they had hotter business to transact.

A succession of shots slammed into the *Seraph*'s hull. Soon the beautiful frigate, still pressing on under full sail, would be smashed to pieces …

Now or never, boy, cried a familiar voice in my head.

'Mister Negus! Mister Shish!' I shouted. 'Time to end the charade!'

'Aye aye, sir!'

With that, an unexpectedly large crew raced up the shrouds of the *Krokodil,* sheeted home her courses and let fall a profusion of topsails. The tipsy Courlander suddenly assumed an immaculate appearance, running in directly for the north shore and rampart of San Andreas. Axes in hand, the carpenter's crew ran to cut away some of the false bulwarks that had been erected around the rail and head. As the deals fell away, the lion figurehead of a king's warship emerged, roaring in proud defiance. The painted canvas hiding the quarter-galleries was torn off. Gunports, painted over to conceal them, opened to reveal a formidable battery of demi-culverins and sakers, their barrels now hauled through the hull by a crew ten times the size of that left to the *Krokodil.* Finally, the Courland flag came down, and the red-and-white of old England went aloft in her place.

The *Seraph* – the true *Seraph* – was ready for battle.

'Mister Lindman!' I cried.

'Sir!' replied the bluff Swede.

'Command the guns, sir, if you please – as we discussed!'

'Aye, aye, Captain!'

The hoisting of our true colours had also been the signal for two dozen or so of the native canoes to change course abruptly and make for the island. The near-naked 'natives' aboard them drew up muskets and swords from the depths of their craft. Captain Facey waved from the leading canoe. The remainder of his men were already making their way up to the main deck of the *Seraph* to form the landing party with my starboard watch.

I turned to Francis Gale. 'Let us pray, Francis, that Kit and his crew on *Krokodil* do not suffer too terribly in our stead.'

The chaplain nodded, and extemporised a prayer for our friends.

The sun was rising now, and before we ran in directly under the shore of the island it was just possible to see the false *Seraph,* taking the punishment designed for us. Daylight made it easier to see the limitations of the two disguises conjured out of nothing, and in so few hours, by Shish and his men; *Krokodil* had been cut down at the stern to masquerade as *Seraph,* and no amount of painted gunports, false gun barrels, and wood-and-canvas quarter galleries and stern windows, rounded off by an especially impressive false figurehead, could turn her into a plausible man-of-war for very long.

But it had not needed to be for very long.

'Give fire!' roared Lindman, and as one, the larboard battery of the *Seraph* bombarded the north rampart of the fort.

Montnoir and his men must have looked behind them at that moment, for at once there was movement on the south rampart. Guns were being pulled back and swivelled round, either to be moved to the north side or – because any man would realise there was no time to take enough of the guns across – being elevated so that they could fire over the north rampart from where they were, albeit at the cost of accuracy.

Seraph fired again. Negus judged that we were now in our best position without over-running the island, and I gave the order to drop anchor. On our starboard side, Facey's canoes were coming alongside to take on the rest of the landing party. A third broadside. As the smoke cleared, I saw three breaches, if not four, in the north rampart. With that, I left the quarterdeck and made my way down into a canoe that also contained Francis Gale, Musk, Lanherne, Macferran, Ali Reis, Treninnick and Carvell, along with three or four of the Bristol men and a half-dozen soldiers. We paddled out under the bow of the *Seraph* and made directly for the narrow beach beneath the north rampart. The defenders now had a few more men on the north rampart, trying vainly to lower the elevation of the guns to fire grapeshot upon the invaders or else firing sporadically with muskets. But *Seraph,* too, was firing grape now, and the effect of our broadside on that rampart was truly dreadful.

My canoe struck the sand of the island and I leapt out into the shallow water, raising my sword to beckon the men forward. But men need no commands at such times. What needed to be done was obvious: reach the rampart, get over or through it, kill whoever stood in the way. For my part, I ran up the beach with Francis Gale at my side, a man who had experienced enough sieges to know the truth of that dictum better than most. We reached one of the breaches to find it clear. Some of the enemy's soldiers were standing in the middle of the parade ground, pointing muskets or pikes vaguely in our direction, but they were but a disordered rabble. As Facey's red-coats and my seamen charged them, they turned and fled to the south rampart. *Good*, I thought – I had a mind to avoid shedding the blood of Stiel's Courlanders if I could avoid it ...

There was a sudden cry from our left – '*Saint Denis! Jeanne d'Arc!*' – and a party of two dozen or so rushed out at us from the cover of the carts under the west rampart. Some of Montnoir's Frenchmen, then: diehards, like their leader, armed with swords and half-pikes, driven by religious fervour and centuries of resentment against the English.

Francis Gale smiled. 'Ah, now this is more like it! Thank you, Lord!' – and with that he set off on a one-man countercharge.

I waved my sword above my head to rally the Seraphim nearest to me. With one voice, we charged Montnoir's forlorn hope.

'Frenchmen,' grunted Musk, smashing his musket-butt into the gut of an oncoming enemy. 'Good. Can't make head or tail of this diplomacy business,' – musket-butt crashed down onto skull – 'but you know where you are, killing Frenchmen.'

A bearded brute rushed me with a half-pike. I ducked to my left, deflected the blow with my sword, and cut the man hard in the thigh. I glanced to my right and saw Carvell and Macferran wrestling with two Frenchmen. John Treninnick was surrounded by three of them; the enemy must have thought that the strange, stunted Cornishman would be easy prey, only to be disabused as he charged them single-handed, cutlasses flailing in both hands.

Another one came at me. A decent swordsman, this one, and evidently an officer, trained in best use of a blade. He slashed at my shoulder: steel struck steel as I blocked his attack. I lunged for the heart, but he was good enough to parry and counterthrust. Once more he came on, but now he faced three, for Francis and Musk were at my side. Still the valiant Frenchman attacked, but as my blade struck his once again, Francis feinted to his left and ran him through the shoulder. Simultaneously Musk applied the coup-de-grace: musket-butt smashed into knee-cap, shattering it. Our assailant fell to the ground, screaming in agony, and we turned to address our other enemies. But the Seraphim and the redcoats, coming up from the beach in greater and greater numbers, had made short work of the other Frenchmen on the parade ground.

I looked up and could see Montnoir upon the rampart, poised and unmoving in his black cloak, not deigning to join the fray himself. He seemed to be ordering another party of his troops to depress some guns to fire grape or canister into the yard, even into his own men. But the hopelessness of his cause must already have been apparent even to the grim Knight of Malta. Not a few of the Courlanders were already surrendering, seeing the utter futility of dying for two countries – France and the Netherlands – that were not their own. Stiel had already distanced himself from Montnoir and seemed to be gesturing to his men to disengage. The fort itself was built only to withstand assault by native tribes, and as the dream of the Courland empire passed into dust, it was no longer maintained even to that standard. Any modern ship of war that could run in close enough under its guns, and put a body of trained men ashore, would have been able to take it ...

Especially if it was attacked from two sides at once.

As we approached the south rampart from the parade ground, we heard the eruption of gunfire beyond the fort, and the unmistakeable sound of shot striking the wall on that side. Kit Farrell, acting captain of the *Krokodil* – the false *Seraph* – must have brought at least some of that vessel's ten guns to bear.

It was the final straw. As Facey's troops trained their muskets on them, the men on the south rampart raised their hands in surrender. Gaspard de Montnoir and Otto Stiel came down the steps and approached me.

Both presented their swords in the age-old gesture of defeat: Montnoir with a squint of hatred, Stiel with a cheerful grin of relief.

'You will live to regret this, Captain Quinton,' said Montnoir. 'A gentleman, a true man of honour, does not gain victory by ruse and trickery.'

'Really, My Lord Montnoir?' I said. 'Then how, pray, should a true man of honour obtain his victories? By bribing native chiefs and Eastland mercenaries to do his work for him, perchance?'

In that moment, Facey and two of his men lowered the Dutch and Courland flags flying above the fort and hoisted the Union Flag in its place. A ragged cheer went up from the men. Imperial England had its newest outpost, and I took some pleasure in renaming it James Fort: James, the name shared by the Duke of York, brother and heir to my king, and by my father, who had fallen in a far mightier battle.

So, with victory secured, there remained the matter of my reckonings with the Seigneur de Montnoir and the Irish traitor O'Dwyer.

Twenty-Six

It was a blessedly cool evening. The sun was starting to sink far in the west, beyond the mouth of the Gambia where, we were assured, the Union Flag still flew over Charles Island, and our friends were safe aboard the *Prospect of Blakeney*. We would soon join them there, but one matter remained to be disposed of, there in His Britannic Majesty's proud new fastness of James Fort. We officers of the *Seraph* had taken a little refreshment in the garrison room vacated by Stiel and his people: some bush rat, a turtle dove or two, and the inevitable palm wine, which I was finding increasingly to my taste. I have observed many times since that it is always important to eat and drink heartily before an execution; it is so much better for the digestion than attempting to do so afterwards.

The others went out, and only Valentine Negus and I were left, for we had somewhat more elaborate preparations to make for the parts we were about to play. I was buckling on my sword belt when the acting lieutenant of *Seraph* stepped over to me very quietly and said, 'Sir, that matter of Mister Shish, and his capital offence against the ship. You wrote the letter to the king and the Duke of York, I presume?

Intending to send it when we reached the mouth of Gambia, or if any of us requested it?'

I bridled at this seeming insult to my integrity. 'Of course I did, Mister Negus.'

'Yes, sir. Of course. My apologies.' Negus seemed to be struggling for words. 'Well, Captain, the thing is this – Let us say – Well, it just seems to me that after his exertions to disguise the two ships, would it not be a fitting thing if that letter was – lost, shall we say?'

I smiled. 'My sentiments precisely, Mister Negus. A fitting thing indeed, as you say. Thank you.'

The Yorkshireman still seemed troubled. 'But – but there is one thing more, Captain Quinton. I have thought much upon the will of God in this matter, for it has troubled me greatly.'

'Mister Negus?'

'I did not know you were Sir Venner Garvey's good-brother. Not until that day with Shish, down in the hold.' He would not now look me in the eye. 'I was uncertain, sir. I was so new to commissioned rank, and you had placed upon me such a great responsibility by confiding in me your leniency to Shish. I believed I had to cover myself against the possibility that I was colluding in something illegal, so I wrote a full account of the circumstances and sent it in the mail we put on that Dutchman leaving Kasang. I sent it to my cousin, sir, and he is the chief factor for Sir Venner in the alum trade at Whitby. I now bitterly regret sending it, Captain. I pray it does not place you in difficulties.'

My heart suddenly felt hollow. Yet Negus's apology had been so humble, his justification of his own actions so entirely meritorious, that I could not condemn him. And I knew at once that any reckoning with Venner Garvey would be many months, if not years, away, if it ever came at all; Venner was inscrutable enough to keep such a document close until the day when it might be of use to him, as he did with every other piece of information he possessed.

Mastering my emotions with difficulty, I smiled at Negus. 'You did right, Mister Negus. And you need have no concerns for me. My relations with my good-brother are – complicated, shall we say? But he will not seek to bring me to the block, if only for my sister's sake.'

Even as I spoke the words, I prayed that they were indeed true.

With that, we went out into the courtyard. Both Negus and I looked the part of commissioned officers of the King of England: we were attired in breastplates, tunics, cloaks and hats, our swords hanging from our baldrics. It was the first time that Negus had ever worn the full regalia of a commissioned officer, all of it purloined from the dead William Castle's sea-chest, and he looked remarkably uncomfortable in it. Even I, who was more accustomed to the garb, found it uncomfortably hot attire, even in the relative cool of the African evening; but it was the only costume fitting for what was about to unfold.

What lay before us was a grand spectacle. After all, we were in the august presence of an ambassador of the Most Christian King – a Knight of Malta too, no less – and I was determined that My Lord Montnoir would be suitably impressed by the power and dignity of the way in which the subjects of His Britannic Majesty conducted such proceedings.

Thus Facey had his redcoats arrayed in their tunics in four ranks, their muskets held smartly at attention in front of them. On the opposite side of the parade ground, Boatswain Lanherne had provided an equal number of seamen from the *Seraph*, assembled in as close an approximation to uniform clothing, and as close to a passable imitation of attention, as any naval crew could manage. The ship's officers, headed by Master Farrell, were arrayed in front of the men.

Our prisoners formed the third side of the square, discreetly watched from the rampart above by Facey's remaining musketeers and two of Lindman's crews manning swivel-guns loaded with grapeshot. In front of the former garrison stood Otto Stiel, perhaps the happiest surrendered captive I ever saw, and the Seigneur de Montnoir, who most certainly was not.

In the very centre of the parade ground, a gallows had been erected. The redeemed Tom Shish and his crew had relished this task; as he said, naval executions are usually such basic affairs, merely dangling a man from a yardarm, so an opportunity to produce a killing machine of true workmanship was rare indeed. He had even installed a trapdoor to outdo anything seen at Tyburn.

Once Negus and I were in position on the fourth side of the yard, O'Dwyer was led out of the cells by two of the redcoats whom he had so recently and so nominally commanded. The renegade looked about him as though he commanded the proceedings, and as he regarded the gallows, he laughed. Francis Gale, standing upon the contraption in full canonicals and flanked by the two hangmen, was reading in his strong, clear voice from the First Epistle to the Thessalonians: 'The Lord himself shall descend from heaven with a shout, with the voice of the archangel, and with the trump of God: and the dead in Christ shall rise first…'

O'Dwyer was brought before me. I had been certain of the necessity of the act I was about to commit; I had almost convinced myself of the rightness of it. But face to face with the Irishman, my certainties receded. Despite myself, I could not but recall the rogue who had at times proved to be strangely diverting company. I could not but feel a twinge of guilt that I was about to kill the man who had effectively saved my life when he acted so swiftly against Habakkuk Leech's gang.

O'Dwyer's initial calmness unsettled me further. 'Well, Matthew,' he said in a quiet, friendly manner, 'so we come to the noose at last. Where you would have sent me all those months ago, eh? But perhaps it's still not time for Brian Doyle O'Dwyer to feel the rope on his throat.' Then the consummate actor assumed another role, one intended for a wider audience. He sneered, and shouted so that all could hear, 'You can't hang me, Quinton! You don't have the authority – you're but the captain of one miserable little frigate! Besides, there's no law that permits the navy to judge the army! I can only be tried by a court-martial – a *military* court-martial – and where will you find a quorum of officers with sufficient rank to judge me, a Lieutenant-Colonel?' He looked around him in triumphant contempt. I noted not a few nods of agreement among Facey's redcoats. 'Among your miserable warrant-men and rough tarpaulins? Even if Holmes returned, the two of you would still have no right to do it. I demand a proper trial, Quinton. A fair trial. No law of England allows you to be judge, jury and executioner over me, man! I demand to be taken back to England. It is my right, I say!'

Montnoir took a step forward. With a confidence quite remarkable in a surrendered man, he said, 'I know little of your English law, Quinton, but I presume from the expressions of your men that this Irishman is quite correct.' He was right, in one sense; like most Englishmen, my crew were so imbued with notions of fair trials before twelve good men and true that they would be uncomfortable with the apparently arbitrary proceedings they had been called to witness. As, indeed, was their captain. 'Thus you have only one course open to you that allows you to emerge from this affair with honour,' continued the plausible Montnoir. 'You must surrender him to me, as a fully accredited ambassador of the Most Christian King and the Grand Master of Malta.' Montnoir's eyes, black and unfeeling, drilled their coldness into me. 'My own men are downstream with a shallop. We will carry him away with us. There will be no lasting damage to relations between France and England. This – this travesty will not even need to be drawn to the attention of your King, Quinton.'

I was as impassive as I could be, with the eyes of my crew and the surrendered garrison upon me. But inside, my stomach churned. 'What possible use can you have for him, My Lord?' I said. 'This man is a murderer and a liar. He was directly responsible for the attack on the *Seraph* that led to the deaths of eleven men, and in any country on earth – yes, even in France – that alone would be enough to justify his death. And we know that the mountain of gold does not exist. The prize that would buy you the Grand Master's throne and the right hand of King Louis – ' Montnoir was startled by Roger d'Andelys's intelligence; but Montnoir startled meant merely a slight furrowing of his brow. 'This man can give you nothing, Montnoir. You should be happy to see a noose around his neck.'

'Perhaps his tale is a lie as you say. Perhaps it is not.' This was ever Gaspard de Montnoir's greatest strength and his greatest weakness, in one: an entire and stubborn refusal to accept defeat, or that he could ever have been wrong in any matter. The man should have met my mother, for in that, they were peas from the pod. 'And the deaths of eleven men of no rank are of little consequence to me,' said Montnoir, coldly. There was a growl of anger from the Seraphim. 'In any event, Captain, you will please surrender him to me. Now. Immediately. My authority in this place is beyond doubt, unlike your own, and I think your King will not dispute it – especially as your actions here have already threatened to provoke a breach between our two kingdoms. Do you really think that King Charles will weigh the life of this renegade equally with the prospect of a war against France and the Dutch combined?'

I looked about me. My men were confused. O'Dwyer grinned. Stiel and the Courlanders were perplexed. Montnoir's own French were sneering, sensing their imminent victory.

I let the silence last a few moments more; then I turned to Phineas Musk.

'Mister Musk,' I said. 'Please read the document that you have upon you.'

The captain's clerk of the *Seraph* licked his lips, stepped forward, and took out the parchment that I had first opened in my half-cabin after O'Dwyer had put to me his insidious proposal that I should collude in his escape.

'*Secret and Additional Instructions to be Observed by Captain Matthew Quinton,*' he read from the cover before opening the document itself. '*We, Charles*' – Musk swallowed hard, for even he was daunted by the knowledge that he was reading the words of a king, written in His

Majesty's own hand – *'We, Charles, by the grace of God King of England, Scotland, Ireland and France – '* Upon the word 'France', I glanced at Montnoir – *'Supreme Governor of the Church of England, Defender of the Faith, do hereby make known our royal will, to wit: that in the event of manifest treason being committed against ourselves and our realms by the man known as Brian Doyle O'Dwyer, awarded by us the commission of Lieutenant-Colonel in our Irish army; and in particular, that the existence of the mountain of gold, much cried up by the said O'Dwyer, is proved to be a fiction of his creation; then our trusty and well beloved subject Matthew Quinton, captain of our ship the* Seraph, *is hereby granted all powers secular and ecclesiastical above any person or court within any of our realms and territories, and also granted our own royal authority earthly and spiritual, with all powers attendant upon the same; and after exercising these powers upon the said Brian Doyle O'Dwyer, the said Matthew Quinton is granted full and free pardon for any actions committed in our name.*

Given under our hand, the court at Newmarket, the twenty-third day of September, 1663.

Charles R

Musk held up the king's signature and the unmistakeable wax impression of the Privy Seal in front of the renegade's nose. The Irishman blanched, and suddenly seemed much older. Musk then carried the document over to Montnoir, who stared at it as though it was the Holy Grail.

'There is, of course, a copy in the possession of His Majesty's Secretary of State,' I said, praying that there was. I was no longer as confident in the promises of princes as once I had been; the voyage of the *Seraph* had buried the trusting young Cavalier that had been Matthew Quinton. 'So you see, Omar Ibrahim of Oran, at this moment, and in this place, I am much more than judge, jury and executioner. I am the King of England and the Lord God, all in one.' I turned to Montnoir. 'And My Lord, I think even you will concede that such authority outdoes that of an ambassador of France.' The Knight of Malta flashed me a look of pure hatred, but he followed it with a slight, yet reluctantly deferential, nod of the head.

At last I straightened. Despite my doubts, I somehow felt the presence of my feudal forebears, who would have delivered many such sentences in their own times: stringing up outlaws from hanging oaks, or in my grandfather's case, ordering mutineers flung from yardarms.

Coldly, I said, 'Omar Ibrahim – Brian Doyle O'Dwyer – whatever your name, you are a traitor, you are a murderer, and you are a dead man.'

In truth, my guts were churning within me, and I struggled to subdue the nerves that threatened to convulse me. *Dare I do this? Dare I send any man, even this man, to his death in this way? Can one piece of paper truly hold at bay Gaspard de Montnoir and all the laws of England?*

I nodded, and O'Dwyer's escorts dragged him toward the steps of the gallows. His confident swagger had gone now, and he struggled against his confinement. Ahead of him, Francis continued his litany by reciting the One Hundred and Twenty-First Psalm: 'I will lift up mine eyes unto the hills: from whence cometh my help...'

Up the steps, onto the stage assembled lovingly by Shish and his crew, where the soldiers handed their charge over to the hangmen, Phineas Musk and Ali Reis. Both had volunteered for the task: Ali Reis to avenge O'Dwyer's treachery against his adopted Arab people and the faith of Mahomet, Musk simply because he had always possessed a conceit to hang a man. As they took hold of him, I raised my sword, ready to deliver the signal to send the Irishman to whichever of his makers would receive him.

Francis concluded the psalm: 'The Lord shall preserve thy going out, and thy coming in; from this time forth, for evermore.' He began the private prayers, and O'Dwyer finally stopped his struggling. Then he did the strangest thing. This renegade, this faithless turncoat, began praying audibly in the Latin of his first faith, the faith of his Irish childhood. *'In manus tuas, Domine, commendo spiritum meum. Domine Jesu Christe, accipe spiritum meum. Sancta Maria, ora pro me…'* Despite myself, I began mouthing with him the words that my Catholic grandmother had taught me: '*Sancta Maria, Mater gratiae, Mater misericordiae, tu me defendas ab hoste –* ' Too late, I saw Montnoir's gaze upon me, and the curious expression in his eyes.

Musk stepped forward and tightened the noose round O'Dwyer's neck. As he did so, the renegade laughed.

'Oh, the beauty of it!' he cried. 'To be hanged for a metaphor, indeed!'

Musk stepped away, but I kept my sword raised. Even now, at the end, I wished to hear more words from the mouth of this too-plausible Irishman; and after all, even our late sovereign, King Charles the Martyr, was permitted a last speech from the scaffold by the inveterate enemies who had brought him to it. 'Aye, I talked too much of a mountain of gold, that I did,' said O'Dwyer. 'The poetry of my race, Captain; a figure of speech if you prefer, and it's brought me to this. I wished for more than the mere command of a corsair galley, you see, and I wished to be away from Algier – from the enemies I had made there, my regiment of wives at their head.' Despite myself, I felt an unwelcome surge of sympathy towards the renegade. 'So I bragged of this knowledge I possessed, knowing how many great men believed in the existence of such a mountain and wished to find it. I thought I could ingratiate myself into the service of one of them – and if the mountain was never found, well, I reckoned I could satisfy my employer with the other riches of Africa. But I had forgotten how such a tale grows in the retelling, and how mighty it would be by the time it reached Malta.' He sighed. 'I had not reckoned on a man so twisted and deluded that he would follow me to the ends of the earth for my pretended knowledge – ' Montnoir seemed to bite his lip at that, but perhaps after all these years I am attributing too strong an outburst of emotion to that dark figure – 'or on a king so desperate for gold that he would swallow any farrago I placed before him. So be it. Your Montnoirs and King Charleses, the so-mighty rulers of this world, all they wish to know of are *literal* mountains of gold, immediate

339

answers to their prayers for glory and power.' Montnoir scowled. 'Aye, I die for a metaphor, all right.' O'Dwyer looked out through the greatest of the gaps blasted through the north rampart of the fort that very morning. There, on the northern shore near Jilifri, another long line of forlorn, chained men was being prodded toward a slave ship. O'Dwyer laughed then, at the last. 'Of course there is a mountain of gold, Matthew Quinton. *You are looking upon it.*'

With that, I dropped my sword and Musk pulled the trapdoor lever.

Thus perished Omar Ibrahim, alias Brian Doyle O'Dwyer, once a slave taken from Baltimore in the County of Cork.

EPILOGUE

∞

His Majesty's Ship, The Seraph

The Chops of the Channel
July 1664

I was torn between fear and admiration for the great man-of-war bearing down on us. Admiration had come readily, at the first proper sight of her, for the French have ever built beautiful ships. High sided, graceful lines, narrow and speedy, not overgunned like so many of our English slugs. And this one was a true beauty: sixty-four guns, no more, in a hull the size of one of our biggest Second Rates. *Seraph* was fast, but this great ship, approaching rapidly from the east upon the starboard tack, would be able to keep up with us if we turned and fled. For flight was the first thought in my mind. My first duty as a king's captain should have been to make this impertinent Frenchmen strike to our monarch's flag, regardless of the disparity in size. But far from steering away and avoiding an unpleasant confrontation, as he could have done easily, this magnificent leviathan had deliberately turned toward the *Seraph*. Far from preparing to strike his topsails and ensign, he had put on more sail and raised at his staff by far the largest and most flamboyant white fleur-de-lis standard of the Bourbons that I had ever seen. This Frenchman sought an encounter with us. There had been no word of a war from any of the myriad merchantmen we had encountered as we edged into the mouth of the Channel, but then, as Holmes and I had demonstrated so recently, wars were no longer commenced by the niceties of heralds in tabards reading out proclamations. Yet there was one thought more terrible than the possibility of being destroyed by this grim greyhound of the sea: the thought that induced the fear.

Francis Gale, at my left side, gave voice to it by asking, 'Is it him, do you think?'

Kit Farrell, at my right, said, 'I'd reckon there are fair odds on it, Reverend. Who else would have cause to seek us out so deliberately?'

Valentine Negus, at the starboard rail of the quarterdeck, had kept his telescope on the Frenchman for at least half a glass. '*Le Téméraire*,' he said at length. 'I'd stake my life on it. Saw her being built at Brest when I was on a trading voyage there a couple of years back. They said she'd be the finest ship on earth. Dutch design, French grace. That's what they said.'

Phineas Musk, standing close to Negus, said, 'How did he know where we'd be? He's a bloody warlock, that Montnoir.'

I sighed. 'We've encountered enough French craft, Musk, all the way up from Madeira. And when we made our landfall at Ushant, you can be sure the report would have been on its way back to Brest and Paris as soon as it was written down. Ample notice for our friend, there – and he's had cursedly good weather to keep station on the course we'd be bound to run from Ushant homeward.'

Negus took one last observation through the glass. Then he turned to me. 'Your orders, Captain?'

Francis, Kit, Musk and every man within earshot fixed expectant stares upon me. Of course, my duty was clear: I should compel Montnoir and his cursed *Téméraire* to strike to King Charles' flag, or sink in the attempt. Given the disparity in force, the latter outcome was considerably more probable than the former. But a king's captain, a man of honour, had no option.

'Gentlemen,' I said, attempting to affect a confidence I did not feel, 'we will clear for action.'

On my command, the familiar ritual commenced. Our drummers began their relentless beat, summoning the men to their stations. Down came the bulkheads and the cabins. Up went the yardmen and the topmen. Sails unfurled and were sheeted home. The trumpeters took up their positions at the stern and began their discordant shriek at our oncoming foe. Musk produced my sword and breastplate, insisting on buckling the latter across my body, grumbling endlessly about damned cheating Frenchies. Francis Gale disappeared below and re-emerged moments later in canonicals before commencing the Church of England's designated prayers before a battle at sea. Finally, our entire starboard battery ran out in one almost simultaneous movement, for Gunner Lindman had truly transformed my men into a crack gun crew during our lengthy passage back from Africa ...

But even the finest gun crew on a thirty-two gun frigate would have been daunted by the sight they then beheld. The gunports of *Le Téméraire* snapped open with a precision that would have stunned Blake and Drake alike, and they snapped open simultaneously *on both sides of the ship*. Sixty-four guns, no less, all manned and primed. Our challenge had been taken up even before it could be delivered; taken up, and contemptuously dismissed.

I looked about. The eyes of every man on the ship seemed to be upon me. I looked at the faces of my friends: Kit Farrell, determined and ready; Francis, preparing himself and everyone else for their imminent passage to eternity; Julian Carvell, cheerfully preparing to take as many Frenchmen as possible with him to Hell; Phineas Musk, complaining bitterly that he still had unfinished business to attend to ashore. The Cornish lads, and the London and Bristol boys, were to be united in death as they had not been united in life.

No. I would not be responsible for a slaughter that was truly pointless. One man, and one man alone, should and would face his maker this day. I turned to my officers and said, 'Mister Negus, Mister Farrell, we will heave to. Mister Carvell, you will prepare a boat's crew, if you please, to take me to the French ship. As soon as I am aboard, you will take command, Mister Negus, and make all sail away from her.'

There were protests at this, none louder than from Kit and Musk. I quieted them. 'He wants me, I think. Me alone. Not you, not this ship. If I am right, all of you will have your lives and your honour, for only your captain will have been dishonoured by surrendering. If I am wrong – well, you are in no worse a state than you all expect to be in but shortly.'

The protests became more muted; after all, they were not the sort of men to disobey a direct order from their captain, and most of them knew in their hearts that I was right.

A few minutes later, I said my farewells to my officers. These were brief, but a shake of the hand, for I had no inclination for tears, to which we English are ever too inclined. I made light of it all, saying that I would merely sample My Lord Montnoir's wine and return before the change of the watch. But when I looked into the eyes of each man of them, I knew I beheld the stares of men who are looking upon a dying friend for the last time. Kit gripped my hand tightly and promised we should meet again. Negus nodded grimly, for he, of all of them, was the most convinced that I was doing the right thing. Francis Gale said a quiet prayer over me. Musk simply said, 'And just what the hell do I tell your wife?'

Only this last, the bluntest farewell of all, almost broke through the emotionless mask that I had donned. With that, I stepped off the *Seraph*, in my mind for the last time. Trying to avoid the eyes of my men, who lined the rail, I climbed down into the boat.

Carvell's crew contained other old friends, all normally happy to chatter to their captain for hours upon end. Now they rowed silently, Polzeath, Tremar, Macferran and the others, though all kept their stares intently upon me. I swore I saw a tear in Macferran's eye, though it might have been the spray.

The only talk came as we were almost in the shadow of the towering hull of *Le Téméraire*. Tremar pointed back toward *Seraph* and said, 'That's odd, Captain. Old Treninnick, up there on the main top. He's jumping up and down, and pointing at the Frenchie. I – I'd swear he was laughing, sir.'

Polzeath grunted. 'Touched in the 'ead. Always said his days down the mines would take their toll on him one day.'

'Silence, there!' snapped Carvell, relishing the authority that came with a petty officer's rank.

We came alongside the mighty French ship. She had a proper entrance port, elaborately gilded all around, and I was greeted at this by a junior officer who bowed stiffly in salute. He led me through the main deck, past ranks of gun crews at their weapons, all gazing blankly at this English officer as if I was the Man in the Moon. I was surprised by the lack of stench; the French sailor was notorious for his habit of relieving himself between decks. The captain of *Le Téméraire* evidently enforced a higher standard, but then, I should have expected that from the fastidious Seigneur de Montnoir.

Up a ladder, onto the main deck, every step taking me closer to my fate, back into the sunlight – where I was greeted at once by one of the most almighty cacophonies I have ever heard. The ship's trumpeters – seemingly a dozen of them, as against *Seraph*'s two – blared out a tune that seemed to provide the treble line to the bass of the ship's batteries on both sides as they began a terrible simultaneous double broadside. I feared for my ship …

Feared for it in that brief moment before the entire ship's company of *Le Téméraire* burst into song. '*Te deum laudamus!*' they sang. '*Te dominum confitemur!*'

The captain of *Le Téméraire* stepped forward and doffed his elaborate broad-brimmed hat in salute. 'Well, Captain Quinton,' he said, 'we meet again.'

'You bastard,' I hissed. 'You utter bastard, Roger.'

The captain's cabin aboard *Le Téméraire* bore more than a passing resemblance to the public salon in the Chateau d'Andelys, where the seventeenth Comte of that name held court. The deck was even adorned with an Indian rug. Amid these splendours, my old friend and I took wine, laughed (in due course) about the jest that he had played upon me, and looked out of his vast stern windows toward the *Seraph*. Relays of men were going between the two ships to exchange respects, officer to officer or mess to mess; John Treninnick was being feted with particular vigour for spotting that the proud captain strutting the quarterdeck of *Le Téméraire* was none other than the former messmate he had known as Roger Le Blanc. The proud captain himself was evidently relishing the opportunity to entertain his old friend aboard the great ship that he had commanded for some three months; but once the initial sense of shock subsided, I was consumed by an overwhelming feeling of jealousy.

'You have this great ship,' I said, 'one of the greatest in the world. I have but a Fifth Rate frigate. And yet even you, *mon ami*, must confess that my experience at sea is rather greater than yours.'

'True, *mon ami*,' replied the comte, quite equably. 'But then, France has far fewer candidates for command than England, and with respect, you had less time at sea than I when you were given your first ship.'

'But *Le Téméraire* is rather greater than my first ship, Roger!'

My friend smiled. 'I do possess a certain influence, Matthew. And they have given me veteran officers beneath me, to ensure that I do not endanger our Most Christian King's investment. The sailing master, for one – a surly Huguenot of Dieppe, but most useful at keeping us off – what is the term, a lee shore? Now, let us take a turn about the deck. I have much to show you. And much to tell you.'

I trod the decks of *Le Téméraire* as though in a waking dream. Roger pointed out his batteries of gleaming twenty-four and eighteen pounder guns; much lighter than the weapons that would be found on English ships of similar size, but the French cherished speed and grace above all. Speed and grace would be of precious little use in a broadside-to-broadside battle with the *Sovereign*, I thought, but I did not share this insight with my friend.

As we walked, we talked. Roger had news of the man I had expected to encounter there, on the quarterdeck of this mighty French man-of-war. 'Alas, Matthew, Montnoir seems to be more than ever in the favour of my king. He scuttles between Malta and our court, and I do not doubt that whatever business he is about, it is not to the benefit of England or of yourself. I fear you have made a great enemy who will stop at nothing to be avenged upon you, *mon ami.*'

I shuddered, for I judged that I had already encountered the Seigneur de Montnoir enough for one lifetime.

At length we came to the poop deck of *Le Téméraire*, over which the fleur-de-lis standard fluttered splendidly in the breeze, and looked along the whole upper deck of Roger's magnificent command.

We exchanged some more conversation about the qualities of the ship, then her captain turned to me and said, 'You have had no mail, these last weeks?'

I shook my head. 'None since Funchal. Afterwards, we were battered relentlessly by the storms of Biscay – driven far to the west, and had to beat back up toward Ushant again.'

'I thought not. It is why I – well, diverted my ship, let us say. I wished to intercept you. That you could hear the tidings from a friend rather from a letter at Falmouth or Plymouth.'

Tidings? My first thought was for Cornelia, but Roger had attached no sense of foreboding to her name – Then that other bottomless dread, the one that had consumed me since our departure from the mouth of the Gambia, overtook me. 'She has had a son,' I said, resignedly.

Roger looked at me sadly, looked away over his ship's rail, and then returned my gaze. 'No,' he said.

This answer was so unexpected that I had to grip the rail for support. '*No?* Then what tidings –? You found her daughter, or the evidence of her true origins? Her murders have been exposed?'

'None of these things, alas, though not for want of trying on all our parts. For instance, your uncle still seeks the missing page of the parish register – it is said that the priest who conducted the marriage went into the Americas when your king returned, so even if he still lives, it will take many months to find him. Even then, of course, it might all be the pursuit of the goose, as you English say. Or perhaps he might choose not to reveal anything to agents of a king he regards as the Antichrist.' Roger shrugged, for the ways of our dissenting sects, and their very existence, were an oddity to him. 'And we have had no more good fortune with finding the lost daughter, although I undertook further rigorous inspections in the convents of Flanders.' I raised an eyebrow at that. 'But as to the most immediate and important matter – no, the Countess of Ravensden has no child. Those are the tidings, Matthew. The most unlikely tidings.'

On the horizon, two great Dutch Indiamen were sailing warily, no doubt glad to be well away from the French and English warships in their sights. I turned from them and gazed blankly at Roger. 'Why unlikely? It never seemed so likely to any of us that my brother could father a child.'

The comte d'Andelys sighed. He nibbled his lip, seeking the words with which to deliver the blow. '*Mon ami*, he was not the one intended to father it.'

My thoughts struggled to digest what I was hearing. I clutched the rail even more tightly. 'Then – '

'It is easy to see what your mother and brother thought,' said Roger. 'To whom do you turn if you seek a son to continue a dynasty? If you wish to guarantee the birth of an heir? Why, to the most fertile man in Europe. Who else?'

'*The King.*'

'Your king, yes. Though God knows, my own runs him close in fecundity.'

'But – Roger, in the name of God, why would the king do such a thing?'

The Frenchman smiled bitterly. 'It is hardly a burden, in his case. But your Uncle Tristram, who stayed with me some weeks ago while journeying to a disputation at the Sorbonne, tells me that there are bonds of mutual obligation between King Charles and your brother that no man understands but those two alone.' This I knew well enough, but even so, to carry it to this – 'The king seems to regard himself as repaying a debt to your brother. And the Lady Louise offered herself as the vehicle,' Roger continued. 'Strangely, she was one of the seemingly few women at court – no, in England – that your monarch apparently had no interest in bedding. But she became aware of the fact that a Countess of Ravensden was sought, and selflessly put herself forward for the position.'

'To wheedle her way into the king's bed, and into his affections!' I cried. But as I already sensed, she would not be the first, nor by any means the last, woman to exploit Charles Stuart's notorious weakness for a comely ankle or a well-scrubbed bosom.

'That is what is assumed.'

'But Tris cannot have known that – '

'Oh, her function was common knowledge at Fontainebleau,' Roger said, airily. 'We possessed certain intelligence that not even your esteemed uncle could ever hope to learn. Remember, Matthew, that France is a nation much richer than your England. Consequently, our king and his ministers are in a position to – shall we say, to pay judiciously for information and loyalty.'

'Bribes! Pensions!' I protested.

'I would prefer to call them retainers, I think, or expenses. *Mais oui*, we supply money to many in England. Courtiers, ministers, mistresses, members of that bizarre institution you call Parliament – it is just what we French do, *mon ami*.' He shrugged. 'We have an interest in ensuring that our neighbours think and act in – well, in as French a way as possible. So it is in this case.'

The truth, when it came, was like a hammer upon my heart. 'You are paying her,' I said angrily. 'She is a French agent.'

The sumptuous costumes that the Lady Louise always wore; the grand style that she always maintained; and yet, the apparent fiction of the great wealth from the estates inherited from two husbands. The paradox was all too clear, now I thought upon it.

Roger was uncomfortable, for he knew how much pain these revelations would cause me. 'She, and many others in your country, are happy to accept the gold that our treasury can offer them. That much is true, certainly.' He lowered his voice conspiratorially, so that his subordinates on the quarterdeck could not hear. 'Matthew, you and I, we are but puppets of the greater ones above us. So you were, in your recent foolish quest for that illusory mountain of gold. Above all, we are the pawns of two mighty and capricious men, Charles Stuart and Louis de Bourbon.' I recalled with a shudder that Brian Doyle O'Dwyer had once said something similar to me. 'Your king decides to father a child on behalf of one of his closest friends – so be it. Our king decides that the mother of that child should be one of his agents, who will thus gain a potentially useful degree of intimacy with your king – so be it.' He placed his hand on my shoulder. 'So you see, *mon cher ami,* to continue a campaign against the lady would be the height of folly, flying against the express wishes of the kings of England and France. For good or ill, old friend, you cannot bring down the Countess of Ravensden. Neither you, nor Tristram, nor Cornelia, should even attempt it.' He stared deeply into my eyes. 'But there are consolations in all this, of course.'

I could find no consolation in that moment. My brother, mother and two monarchs had connived in a conspiracy to foist a bastard heir on Ravensden, *and I could raise not a finger against it.* All I had, all I aspired to be, derived from my loyalty, and that of my family, to King Charles the Second; and no matter how shaken my loyalty had been by the voyage in quest of the mountain of gold, the simple truth remained that everything I held dear in life depended upon the whim of that crowned enigma. How could I reject a policy that was favoured not only by him but also by the cousin that he idolised, King Louis the Fourteenth? Nevertheless – 'Aye, consolation,' I said with difficulty. 'The consolation that she has not bred.'

'Despite not inconsiderable efforts on the part of your king, or so our sources within the palace of Whitehall suggest. Oh, and yours, too – your friend Captain Berkeley wrote to you to similar effect, but I presume that letter miscarried with the others.' Roger smiled tentatively. 'As well, then, that our agents read it first.' He waved a hand as if to suggest that such blatant interference in the private correspondence of English-men was but second nature to the French. 'Now as experience tells us, Matthew, King Charles does not usually need to make any effort at all. His passing within a few inches of any woman is normally sufficient for her to produce a large, ugly black-haired child some nine months later. The failure in this instance is a mystery to all, especially the king, and a disappointment to some, especially your mother. So savour your moment, Matthew Quinton. You remain the heir to Ravensden, how-ever ambivalent you may feel about that position. And there is your other consolation, of course.'

'Another – ?'

He clapped me on the shoulder, and was at once the cheerful, care-free soul that I had once known as Roger Le Blanc. 'Your country will soon be at war with the Dutch, *mon ami*! Why, I believe that you have played a not insignificant part in ensuring that this will come to pass – capturing a fort of theirs in the River Gambo, I hear? Their High Mightinesses at The Hague are greatly displeased.' He pointed out to sea. 'So should not a captain of the King of England be making all sail to enforce the salute to the flag upon those two Dutch Indiamen on the horizon? And even if they do give you the salute, might not that same captain find an excuse to seize them regardless, and seek to have them condemned as lawful prize?' Roger grinned broadly. 'Might not such a glorious windfall of prize money be ample compensation for Captain Matthew Quinton?'

I thought upon it, and at last, I smiled. 'Ample compensation indeed, My Lord d'Andelys. A veritable mountain of gold, in fact.'

HISTORICAL NOTE

The Mountain of Gold is based loosely on a true story. In 1651 the tiny royalist navy-in-exile was operating on the coast of West Africa, and its commander, Prince Rupert of the Rhine, heard rumours of the existence of such a mountain, far up the Gambia river. Rupert proceeded some way upstream with a force that included Robert Holmes, who was granted his first command during this expedition. After the Restoration, Rupert persuaded the king to back two expeditions to West Africa. These were both commanded by Holmes and were nominally under the auspices of the newly formed Company of Royal Adventurers, later renamed the Royal African Company. The first expedition, in 1661, was aimed at the Gambia and was explicitly an attempt to find the 'mountain of gold'; the second, in 1663-4, was a much more ambitious attempt to drive the Dutch from the Guinea coast. As Matthew recounts, these expeditions, and the creation of the Royal African Company, have been seen by some as the beginnings of properly organised British involvement in the slave trade, but in practice, the development of that trade formed a relatively small part of both the objectives and immediate outcomes of the two Holmes expeditions. On the other hand, the two expeditions – especially that of 1663-4 – were certainly among the most important catalysts leading to the outbreak of the second Anglo-Dutch war, although contrary to the accounts in some older histories, Holmes did not sail on to New Amsterdam, force its surrender, and name it New York; that was accomplished by a separate expedition commanded by Richard Nicholls. For the purposes of this book, I have combined various elements of the two Holmes expeditions. For example, the fort on St Andreas island was captured and named James Fort during the 1661 expedition; I have greatly exaggerated the strength of the fort, which actually put up almost no resistance (Holmes' assessment of the size of the garrison provides one of the first recorded uses of the phrase 'two men and a boy'), but the circumstances of its debatable transfer from Courland to Dutch rule were as described here. However, the capture of the *Brill* and Holmes' assault on the Dutch trading posts took place during the 1663-4 expedition, again very much as described. I have taken several incidents directly from the manuscript journals of Holmes' expeditions, now held in the Pepys Library at Magdalene College, Cambridge: these include the 'red sails' off Cape Verde and the spontaneous firing of the musket during the march to the court of the King of Kombo. (There was such a potentate, although I have invented his gargantuan proportions.)

The character of Robert Holmes is based closely on the written record, notably Pepys' *Diary* and Richard Ollard's judicious biography, *Man of War: Sir Robert Holmes and the Restoration Navy.* As in this book, he tended to be known interchangeably by his military rank of major and naval rank of captain until he ultimately received a knighthood in 1666. Pepys' unjustified suspicion that Holmes had seduced his wife, their clash over the appointment of the Master of the *Reserve* and Pepys' mystified ignorance of buggery can all be located in the diary. I have also based the characters of Pepys' colleagues on the Navy Board closely on the accounts of them that he provides. Other real-life characters to appear in this book are the Earl of Teviot, Captain William Berkeley, John Shish and John Cox. Morgan Facey and Otto Stiel were also real people, and served in the capacities described in this book; but I have invented personal histories for them. Both William Castle's description of the Battle of Santa Cruz and Matthew's of the 'Great Storm' of 1703 are based closely on the historical record, while my accounts of both Old St Paul's and Deptford Dockyard are based closely on a number of contemporary or near-contemporary descriptions. 'Chips' remained a problem for the naval administration until the beginning of the nineteenth century. The Battle of Deptford Bridge took place in 1497 in the manner described by Martin Lanherne and John Tremar; to this day, it remains a source of great pride and regret in Cornwall. However, I took some liberties by instituting a pope-burning procession in Wapping in 1663. These outbursts of anti-Catholic sentiment really only began on such a scale some fifteen years later.

My account of Tangier as a British colony is based on many sources, notably EMG Routh's venerable *Tangier: England's Lost Atlantic Outpost*. Fortunately, the seventeenth century River Gambia, along with its flora, fauna, social system and rumoured existence of gold mines or mountains, was described in great detail by several contemporary travellers: I relied especially on the accounts provided by Jean Barbot and Richard Jobson, published by the Hakluyt Society, together with the original manuscript journal of Holmes' first expedition and Zook's *The Company of Royal Adventurers Trading into Africa*. The character of Brian Doyle O'Dwyer is fictitious, but it is not inconceivable that someone very much like him could have existed. Charles the Second's leniency toward plausible rogues was a byword – hence his treatment of Colonel Blood following the theft of his crown jewels, to which Matthew refers, and his decision to award the command of a royal warship to Bartholomew Sharpe, a genuine 'pirate of the Caribbean'. Many European renegades (about 15,000 at any one time, in fact) served in the corsair fleets of the Barbary regencies of North Africa, and both the adventurous spirit and ferocious fighting qualities of the corsairs were legendary. The attack on Baltimore in 1631, by no means the furthest flung of their attacks, happened very much in the way that O'Dwyer describes it, and is still remembered in that corner of County Cork; it has recently been the subject of a book, *The Stolen Village* by Des Ekins. Whether the corsairs were unscrupulous pirates preying on Christian shipping, or were merely responding to constant Christian duplicity and treaty violations, remains a matter for the verdict of history. The corsairs, and the British response to them, are covered in my non-fiction book, *Pepys'*

Navy: Ships, Men and Warfare 1649-89, and in Adrian Tinniswood's *The Pirates of Barbary* (2010).

The Seigneur de Montnoir is a fictional character, but I have based my account of the Knights of Malta closely on the record; for example, during the latter part of the seventeenth century French knights certainly dominated the galley fleet of the Order, with many of them later going on to high commands in the French navy. Further afield, French bribes were very much a feature of political life, and of the royal court, during Charles the Second's reign; several of the king's mistresses were in receipt of them. The king's treatment of the Earl and Countess of Ravensden was inspired very loosely by the story of his principal mistress, Lady Castlemaine (later the Duchess of Cleveland), her cuckolded husband and their son, later the first Duke of Grafton, whose paternity was debated for the first seven years of his life until the king belatedly acknowledged him and changed his surname from Palmer to Fitzroy. It would not have been unlikely for a nobleman like Roger d'Andelys to be given command of such a great French warship as *Le Téméraire* in the 1660s, but the French navy actually had no ship of that name until 1671. How the name (*sans* accents) came to be borne by one of Nelson's ships at Trafalgar, later becoming the subject of 'Britain's favourite painting', is another story.* The *Masque of Alfred*, which culminates in 'Rule, Britannia', was not written by James Thompson and set to music by Thomas Arne, who was indeed the son of an upholsterer of Covent Garden, until 1740; but I could not resist the modest anachronism of bringing the song's composition forward by a few years.

Mariners might object that my account of the near collision between the *Seraph* and the 'mystery ship' in the Thames flies in the face of the time-honoured 'rules of the road' for sailing vessels. In fact, there is little certainty over when those rules first became 'rules' at all, and it was certainly the case that in the seventeenth century, British royal

---

* Impressively told by Sam Willis in his *The Fighting Temeraire* (2009).

warships expected merchant ships to give way to them, and to 'salute the flag', within the broadly defined 'British seas'. There were also many collisions in confined waters, and this element of the plot was inspired by the fact that one of the frigates on the first Holmes expedition, the *Kinsale*, was badly damaged in a collision with a merchantman in very much the same waters while putting to sea. Finally, the poignant epitaph on the grave of Henrietta Quinton actually exists: it can be found on a memorial in the parish church of Clare, Suffolk.

ACKNOWLEDGEMENTS

In writing *The Mountain of Gold*, I have been fortunate once again to be able to call upon the assistance of the other leading authorities on the Restoration navy. In particular, Richard Endsor and Frank Fox provided detailed information on the nature and capabilities of seventeenth century warships and were always willing to provide advice; our discussion about the best way to sabotage a Fifth Rate frigate proved particularly memorable! Peter Le Fevre assisted with other aspects of the book, and once again, David Jenkins ensured that my descriptions of the sailing qualities of square-rigged ships remained within the bounds of possibility. I am grateful to Chris Mazeika of the Master Shipwright's House at Deptford for providing me with a detailed insight into the layout and surviving structures of the dockyard. Servee Palmans introduced me to some particularly interesting recesses of the Dutch language, while my former colleague Andrew Wilson of www.classicspage.com followed up his translation of Harry Potter into ancient Greek by providing me with the Latin translation for Phineas Musk's introduction of Tristram Quinton.

Particular thanks are due to Peter and Rosie Buckman of the Ampersand Agency for keeping me 'on task', to my editor Henry Howard for his constructive and invariably helpful input, to Tom Bouman of my American publishers Houghton Mifflin Harcourt for rigorous suggestions that undoubtedly improved the book, and to Ben Yarde-Buller of Old Street Publishing for his continuing confidence in 'The Journals of Matthew Quinton'. Finally, once again my greatest debt is to Wendy, my partner, both for her steadfast moral support and for her detailed advice on many aspects of the story. The female characters in particular owe much to her insight!

J. D. Davies
Bedfordshire, March 2011